FIND ME AGAIN

To Jerry, always

FIND ME AGAIN

A Rebecca Temple Mystery

Sylvia Maultash Warsh

A Castle Street Mystery

THE DUNDURN GROUP
TORONTO

Editor: Barry Jowett
Copy-editor: Andrea Pruss
Design: Jennifer Scott
Printer: Transcontinental

Canadian Cataloguing in Publication Data

Warsh, Sylvia Maultash
Find me again / Sylvia Maultash Warsh.

Sequel to: To die in spring.
ISBN 1-55002-474-4

I. Title.

PS8595.A7855F55 2003   C813'.6   C2003-904051-8

    2   3   4   5   07   06   05   04

Conseil des Arts du Canada   Canada Council for the Arts   Canadä   ONTARIO ARTS COUNCIL CONSEIL DES ARTS DE L'ONTARIO

We acknowledge the support of the **Canada Council for the Arts** and the **Ontario Arts Council** for our publishing program. We also acknowledge the financial support of the **Government of Canada** through the **Book Publishing Industry Development Program** and **The Association for the Export of Canadian Books**, and the **Government of Ontario** through the **Ontario Book Publishers Tax Credit** program.

Care has been taken to trace the ownership of copyright material used in this book. The author and the publisher welcome any information enabling them to rectify any references or credit in subsequent editions.

J. Kirk Howard, President

Printed and bound in Canada.⊛
Printed on recycled paper.

www.dundurn.com

Dundurn Press
8 Market Street
Suite 200
Toronto, Ontario, Canada
M5E 1M6

Gazelle Book Services Limited
White Cross Mills
Hightown, Lancaster, England
LA1 4X5

Dundurn Press
2250 Military Road
Tonawanda NY
U.S.A. 14150

FIND ME AGAIN

Europe around 1740

chapter one

Rebecca

August 1979

She was there, but she wasn't there. Rebecca wavered before the cloth-covered headstone. She felt numb, an absence of sensation that, as a physician, she knew was a bad sign. Knew objectively, but could do nothing about. *Let yourself go, baby*, David would have said. But David was dead.

The rabbi began: "A thousand years, in the sight of our eternal and merciful Father, are but a day; the years of our life but a passing hour. He grants us life and life He has taken away; praised be His name."

The birds cheeped in the maple and chestnut trees that grew at the edges of the vast cemetery. A gentle wind fluttered the leaves while Rebecca stood resolutely on the narrow walkway between the graves, her father on one side, her mother on the other. She seemed to be hovering in a narrow corridor, her peripheral vision gone, eclipsing the familiar faces of friends, relatives, colleagues that floated around her as if behind glass, like spectators to her grief. She had struggled to put off this day, this unveiling of the monument, which could have been scheduled months ago. Up to a year after was traditional, but the High Holidays were next month and then it would be too late.

Her mother-in-law had not pressed her. Sarah had not been in a hurry, herself, to finalize the death of her only child. Earlier in the summer they had set off with misgivings for the little shop on Bathurst Street to choose the monument. That experience had been surreal — the tiny old man in shirt sleeves and yarmulke, leading her and her mother-in-law out the back to show them samples. How many different shapes and colours were there to signify death? How was one to choose? How did the little proprietor manage stones that weighed literally tons? His son was larger, greeted them with perfunctory politeness in the yard while hosing down a finished piece of granite.

Poor Sarah had already been down that road when her husband died five years earlier. Rebecca let her take the lead in the arrangements, though she knew Sarah's pain matched her own. They rarely spoke of their mutual loss, indeed Rebecca realized that she steered clear of Sarah whenever possible, simply to evade the subject. She felt particularly helpless in light of Sarah's past, a life filled with loss — most of her family had been killed in the Holocaust. Only her sister had survived. What did one say to someone who had lost everything once, and then lost everything again?

The rabbi continued: "David Adler has been taken from our midst. We are pained by the hole in our lives. Yet love is strong as death; the bonds created by love last forever. We have the blessing of memory, through which the lives of our departed continue to be with us."

Rebecca had driven to the cemetery with her parents, who let her sit quietly in the back while they talked about how nice the salads, cheeses, smoked fish, and herring looked, all ordered from a local restaurant. Would they survive, crammed in the fridge waiting for the guests who were invited after the service? Her sister, Susan, in from Montreal with her husband, how tired she looked, and no wonder, did you see how tall and rambunctious the three boys were? Wonderful boys, so smart. Her parents went quiet then. Rebecca understood the silence. Her younger sister had a husband and children while Rebecca's husband was lying beneath the stone that was about to be unveiled. She had put off having children until her medical practice was established. But then David was diagnosed with diabetes and one complication followed another. Before her disbelieving eyes, he went blind, developed kidney failure, and died. Her beautiful, beloved David with the red hair and mischievous eyes and irreverent humour.

He would have scoffed at the traditional unveiling. Wasn't it enough to just erect the stone? Why did Jews have to make such a production out of everything? The man at the funeral home had said something about emotional healing through the expression of grief. As a physician she understood that. But as a mourner, she dreaded it. She desperately evaded her grief, hoping that if she didn't acknowledge it, it might just lie there beneath the skin and leave her alone. She could go through the motions of her life, tend to her patients, deliver babies, read medical journals during dinner, and not remember, for a few hours at a time, that she had lost the love of her life.

Rebecca was pulled out of her reflections by her mother's tightening grip on her arm. She tried to focus, but all she could see was David lying lifeless in the hospital, his skin grey, his mouth open.

Sooner than she expected, the rabbi leaned over the stone, pulled the strings that held the cloth covering in place. It fell off to reveal the lettering. Rebecca's breath caught in her throat. "David Adler" was chiselled in the black granite. "Born December 27, 1945, Died October 5, 1978." David Adler. No longer a person, now only a name on a stone. Until that moment, her life had seemed suspended, as if time had stood still since David had taken his last breath. Now it was over. He was really dead and death was final. She would never see him again.

"In the name of the family of David Adler, and in the presence of his family and friends, we consecrate this monument to his memory, as a token of our love and respect. May his soul be bound up in the bond of life eternal. Amen. Let us recite the memorial prayer, *Eil Malei Rachamim.*

"*Eil malei rachamim sho-khein bamromim hammtzei m'nukhah* ... God all compassionate, grant perfect peace in Your sheltering presence, among the holy and the pure ... Now the mourner's kaddish: *Yis-gadal V'yis-kadash sh'mey rabo* ... Glorified and sanctified be God's great name throughout the world which He has created to His will. May He establish His kingdom in your lifetime and during your days, and within the life of the entire House of Israel speedily and soon; and say Amen."

Grief was like sex, Rebecca thought, balancing a plate of food on her knees at her parents' house. It went on in private behind closed doors. Everyone knew it was happening, but no one talked about it. No one really wanted to know the details. Not even those closest to you.

Rebecca, picking at the egg salad on her dish, sat between Iris, her office assistant, and Susan, both of them agreeing that Montreal's restaurants were more interesting than Toronto's, but would lose customers since the Anglos were leaving in the wake of the separatist surge. Iris and Susan exchanged the names of favourite restaurants. Rebecca didn't blame them. It felt good to be distracted. They all understood that this was their job here. They didn't want to know the pain in her heart any more than she wanted to know about their sex lives.

Most of the guests had eaten lunch, expressed their condolences, and left. Rebecca was helping her mother and sister clear the dishes from the living room when Sarah approached her. She looked tired. Her mother-in-law was an elegant woman of five-foot-two in a black linen skirt and matching jacket. She always wore heels higher than Rebecca, who insisted on sensible shoes. Apart from lipstick, Sarah wore no makeup, but she coloured her chin-length wavy hair auburn. She had been quietly pretty once, still was, really, with her small nose and delicate mouth. She would have looked young if not for her eyes: careful, self-protective, dark with the memory of pain.

"Could I speak to you a moment?" she asked, with her trace of Polish accent.

Rebecca led her to a corner of the living room.

"I hate to ask you today — we're all upset — but I've been putting it off." She glanced at Rebecca for direction.

Rebecca nodded for her to continue.

"I used to know a woman in Poland, she was connected to my family. She's coming here in September, bringing her daughter for medical treatment — I think she has leukemia. Anyway, she asked if I could find a doctor for her. And I remembered you worked with a professor who specialized in blood. Am I right? Is it a blood specialist she needs for leukemia?"

Rebecca was confused. She had always understood that Sarah had no one left in Poland. After the Holocaust, Sarah and her sister were the only survivors of her family. "Did you say someone connected to your family?" Rebecca asked.

"It's a long story." Sarah stopped there, watched Rebecca.

"I thought people couldn't leave Poland. The Communist government and all that."

"She has special permission. Because of her daughter's illness. I told her I would ask you about the doctor."

Rebecca could see Sarah was not going to give her any more details. Not that it was her business. She was not about to pry into a past that was laden with heartache. Yet for as long as she had known Sarah, and as long as she had been married to her son, Sarah had never mentioned anyone left behind in Poland.

"I'll see what I can do."

chapter two

Sarah

September 1979

Sarah felt old as the world. The buoyancy of the airport crowd dismayed her. All those expectant faces fixed in one direction: the glass door through which would spill those they loved. There was no door on earth like that for her. No people like that for her. Certainly not Halina. Sarah had never thought she would see her again. Or at least she had hoped. So how had she ended up here, in the centre of the mob, the dizzying excitement, the impatience of the young men shifting foot to foot, the brown family sharing pizza out of Tupperware?

Through the plate glass partition she watched the passengers mill about, collecting luggage from the rotating carousel. Waiting for Halina was like staring down a tunnel into her former life. The tunnel had always lain in ambush, but so far she had managed to avoid falling in. Now Halina beckoned to her from a darkness that had been waiting there for forty years.

Halina had not asked to be met at the airport, had given no other information in her letter than the date of her arrival. It had taken only a phone call to the Polish airline for Sarah to learn the flight time. There was only one flight a day from Warsaw.

Halina would be sixty-four now. Odd the way she had stopped aging in Sarah's mind. All she could remember was the way Halina had looked just before the war. Tall and shapely at twenty, she stood behind the sparkling glass counter of the jewellery shop in Kraków, her straw-coloured hair in a sleek pageboy. On the wall behind her hung an elaborate clock in a carved gilt frame darkened with age. The clock's hands had stopped at two. *A broken clock will not inspire confidence in our customers*, Sarah's father had said, coming into work one morning. Sixteen-year-old Sarah had gawked at Halina, awed by her beauty. *The clock isn't broken*, Halina said to her. *It's waiting for us.* And she began to laugh, her coral red lips baring white teeth.

The memory was so elusive after all these years, Sarah wasn't sure it was real. She only knew that four years later the Germans had attacked Poland and she desperately needed to get out of the city. She turned to Halina, who had worked for Sarah's parents for six years in the store. She was the only Gentile Sarah could trust. So she had saved herself, her husband. But at what cost? She came back to Kraków when the calamity was over. Only there had been one more calamity to befall her. At Halina's door.

Six years of war had taken the freshness out of Halina's complexion. Her large bones kept her from looking hungry, but the shop was gone. Everything was gone.

Everyone. Her precious one. Halina stood at the door saying something she couldn't comprehend. She heard the words, but they made no sense to her. They did not penetrate. She finally heard Halina say, *You mustn't blame me*. Yusek stood beside her, patting Sarah's head as though she were a dog punished by mistake. *It wasn't my fault*, Halina had said. *There was nothing I could do*.

Sarah flinched. A small Indian girl bumped into her arm, and the airport materialized around her.

She moved her head from side to side to loosen the knotted muscles in her neck. Deep breath from the bottom of her diaphragm, the way she taught her students. Not that she was going to burst into song, but it felt good to gain a modicum of control over something. People kept moving in front of her, blocking her view.

What would Halina look like, at sixty-four? Sarah was pleased at how well she had aged. She dyed the grey in her hair, had gained only fifteen pounds after forty years. Still, would they recognize each other?

Passengers stepped out through the automatic doors at a slow but steady pace. Sarah spotted two blonde women heading for the glass doors, one pushing a luggage cart brimming with suitcases. A shock of recognition when she looked more closely at the taller one struggling with the cart. In a grey business suit: Halina. Her hair thinner, a whiter blonde, her waist thickened but her legs still shapely in pumps. She carried herself like a queen, head held high, her eyebrows arched critically. Her companion was much younger, though her hair was a startling white, lifted off her neck and pinned into a roll. Her pale face was unhindered by makeup. Sarah felt a sudden pang through the heart. It was the daughter. Yes, she was sick, but at least Halina *had* a daughter. She had had a daughter for all those years.

Sarah stepped around the crowd, keeping them in sight. Mother and daughter advancing in her direction. The arriving passengers were separated from the waiting crowd by ropes that framed a corridor of escape. Halina, looking haggard after the long flight from Poland, examined the faces of the crowd and suddenly settled on Sarah. Sarah had forgotten that she'd be unexpected. Had just assumed that Halina didn't know anyone in Toronto and had taken it upon herself to pick them up.

The cautious look on Halina's face kept Sarah in her spot. Thirty-five years separated them. That, and events neither could control. The hands of the clock waited as Sarah searched Halina's face for the young woman she used to know. Halina hurriedly peered around, as if someone else might be waiting for her, then handed her daughter the large black leather handbag she was clutching. She headed straight for Sarah.

She placed her hands on Sarah's arms and kissed her on both cheeks, stopping short of an embrace. "I didn't want to trouble you," she said in Polish, using the familiar "you" as if it weren't a lifetime ago since they'd last met.

"It was very kind of you," she continued. "I would've recognized you anywhere. You haven't changed at all. You look so young."

"You, also, have not changed. Still beautiful." She replied in Polish, though the language felt strange in her mouth, like someone else's tongue forming the words. She rarely spoke her native language, lately only in times of distress, like when David had died.

"This must be your daughter," she said in Polish, looking at the younger woman who had approached and was leaning on the cart.

"This is Natalka," said Halina.

The daughter came away from the cart and held out her hand. "How do you do?"

Accented English. Her long elegant neck, the high cheekbones, gave her the look of a gazelle.

"You speak English?" Sarah asked her.

"I studied a little."

Natalka's green eyes illuminated her pale face, the wisps of white hair that had escaped the pins to curl around her cheeks. The skin beneath her eyes was dark. She was striking in an olive green cape. When Halina had written about her daughter's leukemia, Sarah had felt an abstract kind of sympathy. Too bad, so young to be that ill. Now with Natalka beside her, the horror of the thing became real. Halina was going through the same thing with Natalka that Sarah had experienced with David. But she didn't feel sorry for the mother, only the daughter. Halina had had her for all those years. She should be grateful.

"Was it a long flight?" Sarah asked.

Natalka looked at her watch. "We left early this morning on the train to Warsaw. Then the plane left shortly after noon." She twisted her arm around so that Sarah could look at her watch. "This is the hour for us." It was fifteen minutes past midnight. Barely dinnertime in Toronto.

"You must be exhausted," Sarah said.

She turned to Halina, with sympathy, only to find her attention elsewhere. She appeared to be communicating with someone at a distance. Very slightly shaking her head, giving a short jerk of her hand near her waist where it might go unnoticed. Sarah kept smiling at Natalka but searched the crowd for the target of Halina's signals. Sarah was impatient with the intrigue: if Halina knew people here, why didn't she say so?

"Was someone picking you up?" Sarah asked.

Halina flushed and abruptly began to move the luggage cart toward the exit. "No, no, we were going to take a taxi."

Sarah took a last look at the people still waiting for passengers: no one appeared particularly interested in them.

"Where are you staying?" she asked them.

Halina took a piece of paper from her jacket pocket and handed it to Sarah. In a large, bold hand the name and address of an apartment hotel on Yonge Street in midtown Toronto.

It was five-thirty and rush hour when they hit the 401 highway.

"I can't believe all the cars!" Halina cried. "Are we far from the hotel?"

"About half an hour," Sarah said.

Halina was watching out the side mirror as they drove. Was she expecting someone to follow them? Sarah began to check her rearview mirror but didn't know what she was looking for.

One time she checked in the mirror and found Natalka watching out the window with cool, intelligent eyes. She really was lovely with good skin, though pale, and a high forehead. Had her hair turned white during her illness? Natalka met her eyes in the mirror and Sarah looked away.

Halina had settled into her seat and seemed to doze off as they travelled east along the highway. Sarah drove her Camaro at barely the speed limit in the right lane, letting cars pass. She used the highway out of necessity, but she didn't like it. The speed frightened her. Several cars stayed behind her in the slow lane. The one immediately behind was a blue compact. At one point it passed her, leaving a black sedan in its wake. She didn't recognize the makes of cars the way David had. David could've named every car driving past her. He'd loved cars since he was a little boy. The Camaro had been his until he fell in love with the sporty red Jaguar. He told her the Camaro would make her younger, so she took it off his hands to please him. Her darling David.

It was nearly a year now since he'd been gone. She couldn't bring herself to say "die," to even think "die." Children were not supposed to die before their parents. She didn't know how she had survived it; she had simply gone on. Her heart had not stopped as she thought it would. Her lungs kept breathing, though every now and then she gasped for air. The room would become close and suddenly there was no air and she prayed for death. In that moment she would think, *What would I regret? My sister, Malka, and her husband. Rebecca, who suffered when David died and still cannot bear my presence because my face reminds her of his. My music...* Then she would begin to breathe again and the moment would pass.

The car radio flickered into her consciousness. "U.S. President Jimmy Carter met Egyptian President Anwar Sadat at his Camp David retreat to discuss plans for peace in the Middle East. Mr. Sadat denied rumours that he has received death threats at home from factions opposed to his conciliatory position on Israel."

Sarah switched the channel to some classical music. She exited the highway at Yonge Street and drove south about a mile to the hotel. It turned out to be an elegant four-storey building in an art deco style.

"Let's see if they can help with the luggage," Sarah said, leading the way to the entrance. Halina carried the large leather purse on her arm.

Behind a polished wooden desk sat a muscular middle-aged man with a moustache, his dark hair thin at the front. He surveyed them without expression.

"This is Mrs. Nytkowa and her daughter," Sarah said, taking charge as the English speaker. "You have a room reserved for them."

His brows furrowed as he glanced at some papers out of their sight. "Mrs.—?"

"Nytkowa."

His thick lips pursed, he flipped some pages, shook his head. "You sure you have the right place?" Slight accent, east European.

Sarah was surprised when Halina began in accented English. "Sir, this is Natalka Czarnowa, famous concert pianist. Pan Baranowski bring us ..."

"Pan Baranowski?" he exclaimed, sitting up very straight. "He don't say nothing to me."

"You call him!" Halina said.

The man picked up the phone wordlessly and dialed.

Sarah took another look at Natalka. A scrap of memory tried to surface. Natalka Czarnowa. Fifteen or twenty years back there'd been a pianist who had caused a stir with her idiosyncratic rendition of a waltz in the Chopin competition in Warsaw She developed a reputation in Poland, then performed in the Eastern bloc — Moscow, Kiev, Budapest. Every now and then Sarah had come across a notice about her but had never connected it to Halina's daughter, since she didn't know her married name.

The concierge waited through several rings, then put the phone down. He shrugged. "I got no instructions."

Sarah had not scheduled any students that evening, knowing she'd be busy with her guests. She hadn't counted on putting them up for the night, though.

"I'll take you to my place," she said finally. She turned to the man. "Here's my phone number." She handed him one of the cards she kept in her purse in case she came upon someone who wanted singing lessons. "This is where they'll be."

The man curled his lip, then studied the card as if it would be useful for killing cockroaches.

Sarah's house in Forest Hill was not the large, expensive kind the area was noted for. It was a compact two-storey building, the last on a dead-end street filled with idiosyncratic one-of-a-kind houses, none of which was particularly stylish. Sarah's front lawn had been taken over by a large elm tree, eliminating any need for a gardener. Beside her drying patch of grass, the street ended abruptly at the foot of a grey-painted garage. Its door displayed a "No Parking" sign so weathered that it seemed the owner of the large estate stretching back from Sarah's upstairs window had forgotten it years ago. Down the street, a triplex and a few semi-detached homes sat waiting to surprise anyone who had taken a wrong turn off the swanky end of Spadina Road.

Halina clucked her tongue when they pulled into the driveway. "Such a magnificent house!" she said.

She had written in her letters that though she held an important job in Orbis, the state tourist board, life in Poland was hard. She lived with her daughter and young granddaughter in a five-room apartment, much larger than the usual, and shopped in the special stores reserved for foreigners and Communist party members, of which she was one. This meant she didn't have to line up for her groceries like most people and could buy western delicacies like ketchup and corn flakes. Yet sometimes she ran out of butter or eggs and was forced to line up like ordinary people. She considered it an insult for someone of her stature in the party.

As Sarah inserted her key into the lock of the front door, she turned to glance back down the street. A black sedan, like the one she had seen behind her on the highway, was pulling into a driveway to turn around and head back out to the main road. Halina's behaviour was making her paranoid.

Sarah led her guests into the living room, where a baby grand piano took up half the parquet floor.

"Of course!" Halina exclaimed in Polish. "I should've known." She touched the satiny finish of the wood with worshipful fingers. "I told Natalka how talented you were, even when you were young. If it hadn't been for the war ... Natalka, she sang like a bird! A wonderful bird!"

Halina's eyes shone at her with such admiration that Sarah became embarrassed at her ungenerous feelings.

"Do you still sing?" Natalka asked.

Sarah nodded. "My voice has changed over the years with age." She turned to Halina. "I can't reach the high notes like I used to."

She suddenly felt shy and distracted them by taking them on a tour of the rest of the house: the kitchen, the small den with its sofa and TV on the first floor, the two bedrooms and study upstairs. The two guests took everything in, commenting on the wonderful broadloom, the well-equipped kitchen, the miraculous bathroom with the whirlpool, the stupendous number of telephones (three).

Sarah made some tea and served them bagels with cream cheese and smoked salmon, then the coffee cake she'd made earlier in the day.

"You shouldn't have gone to so much trouble," Halina said. "This cake is delicious. Like the ones I remember your mother used to make."

Sarah felt her heart sink. She rarely thought about her mother anymore. She didn't want to be reminded of her death, and the war. There were a lot of people she didn't want to be reminded of, for the same reason. It seemed that when someone died a tragic death, it became their one defining feature, the happy times forgotten.

They ate in the dining room in full view of the piano. The guests could barely keep their eyes off it.

They seemed to be getting a second wind when Halina said to her daughter, "Play something for us, Natalka."

The younger woman's face clouded over. "No, please. I am tired. I will play badly."

"It's just for us, darling," Halina said, the endearment sounding cold in her mouth. "Try out the piano."

"Mama wants to show me off," Natalka said, not looking at her mother. "But you are a musician, Mrs. Adler. Tell her one must be prepared to give a good performance. I do not want to make a bad impression."

Halina looked away in disgust.

"Well, of course, I'd love to hear you play," Sarah said, "but you must be very tired from your journey. I can wait until you've had —"

Suddenly the doorbell rang.

Halina sat bolt upright. "Are you expecting someone?"

"No," said Sarah, rising from the living room chair.

"Don't answer it!" Halina said. She picked up her leather handbag and jumped to her feet, looking ready to flee.

"Don't be alarmed!" Sarah said. "No one will harm you here."

She stepped down the stairs to the front entrance. Through the small pane of glass in the door she could see a handsome middle-aged man. She opened the door.

He gave a courtly bow of his head and smiled. "I'm so sorry to disturb you, but is there a Mrs. Nytkowa here?"

His English was impeccable with a trace of Polish accent.

"Are you a friend?"

"Yes, an old friend from Poland." He glanced behind her to where she knew he would see nothing but a wall leading to the basement.

"How did you find her?" Sarah asked, keeping her voice pleasant.

He held up his hand to show her the card with her address on it that she'd left at the hotel. She was torn. He seemed to be perfectly harmless and straightforward. Yet Halina was dreading the meeting. She was spared the decision.

Halina appeared at the top of the stairs. "Michael! You found me!"

Sarah stood aside so that the man could enter. He quickly climbed the stairs.

"Hela!" he said. Embracing her carefully, he kissed her on both cheeks. Then he held her at arm's length to look her over.

"You look marvellous," he said in Polish. "Still beautiful as ever."

He was a tall, lanky man in a navy blazer with brass buttons. Wavy light brown hair touched the collar of his champagne white shirt. His face was tanned and closely shaven, his skin giving off a hint of some expensive scent.

"I beg your pardon, Sarah," Halina said in Polish. "This is Count Michael Oginski. We knew each other during the war."

She began to put her hand out to take the one he was offering. Instead of shaking her hand, he lifted it delicately to his lips.

"Delighted," he said. Then, beaming at Halina, he said, "This lady saved my life."

At first Sarah was surprised, then confused. She hadn't been the only one to go to Halina for help in those desperate times. And a count, yet. But then why was Halina so nervous about seeing him? What was she afraid of?

Sarah remembered the handbag Halina was so protective of. She searched the room: it had been tossed carelessly beside the couch as if it were no longer important.

"Michael," said Halina, bringing him into the living room, "here is Natalka."

His eyes shone as he stepped toward her. He took both her hands in his, then brought one of them up to his lips. "I remember you when you were a little baby. A beautiful little baby. My father and mother were your godparents. At your christening. How you cried and cried. We had to carry you around in our arms like a little princess."

"Was I so bad?" Natalka asked, smiling mischievously. "Mama never told me."

"You were a sweet child," Halina said, suddenly wistful. "He was a young boy who never saw a baby before. Still wet behind the ears, himself. Of course babies cry."

Sarah made more tea. Once they were all seated around the dining table, she asked in Polish, "So how did you two meet?"

Halina began. "Michael's parents managed a large estate owned by a nobleman. They, themselves, were aristocrats —"

"— but had no money," Michael interjected. "As you know this was common in Poland, where gentry were penniless and had to hire themselves out to the nobility."

Sarah remembered the strict class structure in Poland, where peasants made up the majority. Jews were a different category altogether and stood quite outside Polish society.

Halina continued, "My parents dealt with the peasants directly. They farmed, themselves, but they were overseers, answerable to Michael's parents. I usually visited my family in the summers, but during the war, when it got too dangerous to stay in Kraków with a child, I ran to their place in the country. That's when I met Michael. He saw me pushing the baby carriage one day, obviously from the city, and we became friends."

"Natalka was born during the war?" Sarah asked, her heart pounding. "What year was that?"

Halina took a sudden breath, glanced at Natalka. "1940," she said.

Sarah felt her arms and legs go numb. "That can't be right. You were pregnant that time ... when I saw you? It was February." She stared across the table at the elderly woman but saw the young, beautiful Halina she had sought out that day in 1940.

"It was winter. I used to wear large sweaters. You probably couldn't tell."

"But you didn't say anything ..."

"I wasn't telling people." She glanced nervously at Natalka.

"You should've told me. Maybe I would've done things differently."

Halina stared vacantly behind Sarah, not looking her in the eye. "It wouldn't have made any difference," she said, "believe me."

Why should I believe her about anything, thought Sarah.

Michael and Natalka watched them in puzzled silence. Halina recovered first. She was adept at landing on her feet.

"You remind me very much of your father, Michael," she said.

His face went flat, but Halina didn't seem to notice. "Michael's father was a very handsome man. Tall and blond, always with a joke." She studied his face. "You have his eyes."

Michael looked down at his hands. "He found you very beautiful."

A tension grew between them. Sarah wondered what other skeletons were mouldering in Halina's closet.

Finally Halina said, "In those days, you were a pimply-faced fifteen-year-old, skinny like this." She lifted a finger into the air.

So he is older than he looks, thought Sarah.

"Well, go on," Halina said.

Michael took a deep breath, preparing to continue his story. "Things kept getting worse," he said. "By the time I was seventeen, I had to leave the estate. The Nazis were always rounding up young men — they shipped them out for slave labour. Some they just shot at the edge of the woods if they felt like it. I ran away. I found a group of partisans deep in the forest. Neipolomice, you may know it, some kilometres east of Kraków."

Another little shock went off inside Sarah. Yes, she knew Niepolomice. It wasn't that important by itself, only as the first step of her journey all those years ago. Time had buried the memories, but they were resting in shallow graves.

Michael continued. "The partisans became my family, a bunch of ragged boys and a few older men. We attacked German soldiers whenever we could. This was how we got weapons. Some of us were killed. New men joined us.

"We were always hungry. We knew which farmers we could trust and went to them to beg for food. But they had little themselves, and they were always afraid the Germans would find out. They would be shot if the Germans knew they were giving food to the partisans. We were starving. It was winter and there was nothing to eat. We decided that everyone would go out and try to find their own food and those who survived would return in three weeks. I took the chance and came back to the estate but I didn't go to my parents. They were not young, I didn't want to put them in danger. I went to

Halina. I was nearly dead. She hid me and gave me food. In three weeks I went back to find my group. Only a handful of them returned. The rest were probably dead."

"Your father would've taken you in," Halina said.

He looked at her with surprise. "I didn't want to go to him."

"He was angry later, when he found out. He was your father."

Michael's face went pale, but he said nothing.

"Sarah knows what it was like then," Halina said. "She was in a camp during the war."

Michael's eyes turned toward her. "Which one?"

Sarah never talked about the camp. She didn't need to. It crept into her dreams regularly and seemed to live right behind her eyes.

"It was a labour camp," she said finally. "Not far from Kraków."

Michael nodded but left it alone. Sarah silently thanked him for his sensitivity.

Natalka began to rub one of her eyes.

"I'm sorry," he said. "You must be very tired after your journey. I'll take you back to the hotel whenever you're ready."

Halina blanched. "Oh, Michael. Do you mind terribly? We're so tired. Our bags are upstairs already. We will stay here tonight and come to the hotel tomorrow."

Sarah had anticipated as much.

Michael tried to hide his surprise. "Janek is expecting you ..."

"I'm going right to sleep." She threw an apologetic look at Sarah. "Look at Natalka. She can't keep her eyes open. I'll speak to Janek tomorrow. He'll understand."

"Do you really think so?" Michael said, giving her a sidelong glance.

"No," she said. "But he'll have to wait."

That night, while Sarah tossed in her bed, Ulica Stradomska shimmered behind her eyes, Weinstein's Jewellery Store, where her father and mother took turns tending to customers. When Halina was young, right up to the time she married, she worked in the store as a clerk. Then, after her marriage, she left to work in the clock shop on Florianska for her husband's family. The Weinsteins had the best prices in the city for diamonds and gold, but some Poles would not buy from Jews. They were, however, willing to plunk their *zloty* down into the soft, white hands of a Christian girl behind the same counter. Sarah saw her father sitting at the table in the room behind the store, a jeweller's loupe pressed to his eye as he squinted at some gem. She heard later that he had survived life in the ghetto in Kraków, unlike her mother, who had succumbed to the deliberate campaign of starvation and terror devised by the occupying Nazis. He had then been sent to Mauthausen, where he'd been forced into a crew lifting large rocks for some make-work project. He was a wiry man of fifty-six with long, slender fingers that knew how to fix the clasp of the most delicate necklace. He was unused to hard labour. According to a witness who managed to find her after the war, he collapsed after a week of hauling the rocks. He was in great pain with the hernia. Then when infection set in, they knew it was over for him.

Sarah hadn't thought of that for a long time, and she didn't thank Halina for releasing the memory.

She rolled over in bed, struggling against the inevitable. She could fight it while she was awake, with her piano, her music, her books around her. But once she fell asleep, she dropped headlong down, down the tunnel of years and landed in her old life. The familiar ancient buildings of Ulica Miodowa lean toward her, throwing long, steep shadows that swallow up the cobblestones. *Where have you been?* they whisper. *You loved us once, why did you run away?* The voices grow into reproachful shapes in darkened windows, silhouettes behind curtains with hands stretched out to her; footsteps approach, recede. Which is her house? Is her mother still waiting for her? Where are her sisters? She floats toward Ulica Stradomska, the stars of the night sky barely clearing her head. Rayzele is weeping softly in her arms. How do children *know? Hush, little sweetheart. They mustn't hear.* Her strawberry curls glint in the heart of the darkness, tiny scythes that flick at Sarah's throat, bringing sobs. The wind blows her into Ulica Grodzka, she can't stop the wind. She can't stop. *Hush, little sweetheart. They won't find you. I won't let them find you.*

Suddenly the weeping stops, darkness fills the void, and her arms ... her arms are empty. Does she still have arms? Rayzele — where is Rayzele? She looks and looks, but darkness flows around her like ink, she is drowning in night. Then, in a street ahead, a light wavers above a door. A soft weeping behind it. She floats toward it as if her feet know the way, have been there before. A murmur of weeping. The door flickers as she approaches; waxes and wanes in the sprinkled light. She must reach it before it dissolves in a puff. It is her only hope.

Only the closer she comes, the further the door recedes. Smaller. Smaller. Don't let it disappear. Go faster! She pushes herself through the shadows of the street. Her heart knocks against her chest. Faster! But the door shrinks, contracts into the distance. The weeping grows louder. Sarah stops. She is losing her.

Rayzele! she cries out.

In an instant the door towers above her, so high the top wavers into the night. She puts her hand out to touch it: the wood is familiar under her fingers, thick and cold. A little push. It yields. The vast door creaks open. Her heart pounds, pounds in its cage. A sliver of light slants into the black street. Her pulse beats against her temples.

She gasps and is pulled toward a different light. She turns over and wakes up.

chapter three

Rebecca stood at the patio door in the kitchen watching the sun set on David's garden. Stillness hung in the rosy air, a purity of light in the long moment before light dissolved. At the beginning of the summer, she had knelt in the two long flower beds on either side of the backyard and pulled the weeds. They had grown in abundance among the snapdragons and poppies and black-eyed Susans, the euonymus and rhododendrons that David had spent years planting. But she missed a few weekends, and before she turned around, the weeds had spread their tendrils and thorns among the flowers. Guilt brought her back to the flower beds a few more times, but she knew she could not tend David's garden the way he had. Now, in the middle of a hot September, the weeds had won. A neighbourhood boy cut her lawn regularly, but David's handiwork, like David, was gone. She could've gotten the kid to pull the weeds, she supposed. But it rankled that the garden had survived the man who'd created it, the man who'd loved her. It rankled that the world went on without him, as if he didn't matter.

The first anniversary of his death loomed before her like the memorial stone they had raised on his grave in August. She could hardly believe it would soon be a whole year. The fourth day of the Hebrew month of Tishrei, a few days after the start of the High Holidays. Rosh Hashanah, the Jewish New Year, would never be the same again, always the association of his death. It was supposed to be a time of celebration. Friends and relatives would present each other with honey cakes, sweet things for a sweet year. David would slice up an apple, arranging it on a dish, and they would dip the slices into a pot of honey. Now, she watched out the patio door, where she could still see him bending over the snapdragons, working the earth with his little trowel, his orange-red hair echoing the colours of the garden.

The phone rang on the counter and she was pulled back unwillingly to the present.

"Hi sweetie, what's doing?" her mother asked.

Rebecca flicked on the kitchen light and took a deep breath of relief. "I was just going to make myself something to eat before going to Sarah's. I'm going to meet her guests."

"It's very sweet of you to get involved." Her mother's voice rasped on the phone. Rebecca wished she could persuade her to stop smoking.

"It would've been hard for Sarah to make arrangements otherwise," Flo continued.

"It's the least I can do. She never asks me for anything."

"You don't have to feel guilty. Why don't you bring her over here tomorrow for dinner? She can bring her friends. I'll throw in some extra chicken and soup. It'll be a nice Friday meal for them."

"They aren't Jewish."

"It'll still be a nice meal. And Daddy can try out his old jokes on them."

Her father had been a pharmacist who in his retirement had discovered Neil Simon's plays and had decided his own jokes were just as good. Hence he had started writing some comedy and using his family as a sounding board.

"They probably don't speak English."

"So he'll use sign language. Nothing stops your father from communicating. He's already starting to wave his arms at me. I think he's trying to tell me something. Here —"

"Hi, doll face. How's my daughter-the-doctor? Did you see any interesting diseases today?"

"Just the usual — boils, warts. Then a guy came in with his foot stuck in his mouth."

"That's not interesting. Happens to me all the time. Give me his number. I'll let him in on the cure."

"There's a cure?"

"Yeah. You have to light up a cigarette every time you feel the urge to say something stupid."

"The cure sounds worse than the disease."

"If you're going to be critical, I won't let you in on my secrets anymore. By the way, how many surgeons does it take to replace a light bulb?"

"I give up."

"Three. One for the consult, one to take out the bulb, and one to tell you that you should take out the socket too, now that you're not using it anymore."

She giggled into the phone.

"Uh-oh, your mother's signalling to me. Here."

"What are you having for dinner, dear?"

"I was just going to make myself some eggs."

"Well, never mind. Just as well on such a hot night. You'll have a good dinner tomorrow night. Give my regards to Sarah."

Voices droned on the CBC as she drove her little red Jaguar south through the side streets west of Avenue Road and around the campus of Upper Canada College. A discussion between pundits.

"What about the American political scene, Craig? There's speculation that Ronald Reagan will seek the Republican nomination for next year's election. A lot of people think being governor of California is good practice for the White House."

"It's hard for some people to take him seriously, Peter. They run those westerns on late-night television, and he looks awfully good in a cowboy hat. That probably got him elected in California, but we're talking about the presidential race here."

"Well come on, Craig, let's be fair …"

After a five-minute drive, she pulled into Sarah's driveway on that strange little side road in the heart of Forest Hill. She stopped beside the Camaro, which used to belong to David, and stared at the familiar beige leather seats. This was why she avoided Sarah. Too many reminders. The woman, herself, because she was David's mother. Not her fault. A tactful, cultured woman who would never knowingly hurt Rebecca. David had been Sarah's only child, and the loss had devastated her. Yet she somehow managed to cope better than Rebecca, who couldn't look at her without seeing David.

She forced herself toward the front door. Maybe it was the looming anniversary that was bringing down this melancholy upon her. She had kept the sadness at bay since the unveiling, but now her body responded, demanding attention. Her heart felt like it had shrunk in her chest; an emptiness expanded in her and threatened to take her over. She would stay for a polite hour or so, then make her apologies and go home. She pressed the doorbell.

Sarah did not rush to get the door. Rebecca wondered if she had the wrong night. Finally Sarah stood in the doorway, her eyes large with anxiety. She wore a pastel blue blouse tucked into a matching cotton skirt that showed off her trim waist.

"I'm so glad you're here, Rebecca. Something's happened."

Her usually creamy complexion had gone sallow. Without explaining, she led Rebecca up the stairs to the living room slowly, as if she were too tired to go faster. Books lay strewn on the floor, thrown down from their shelves, along with framed photos and knick-knacks and sheet music. Drawers in the dining room buffet sat agape, their contents jumbled. Rebecca stuck her head in the doorway of the kitchen: the cupboards and drawers stood open, some gadgets on the floor.

"We were out all day," Sarah said. "I took them for supper, then when we came back …" She lifted her palm in the air. It began to shake, and she clasped her two hands together in front of her waist.

"Did you call the police?" Rebecca asked.

Sarah stared at the chaos on the floor. "I don't think they took anything."

"You won't be able to tell, in all this mess. Did you check the silver? Or any jewellery upstairs?"

Sarah stared into space, her eyes empty.

"Sarah?"

Sarah shook her head. "I can't think. I'm sorry."

A pang of guilt shot through Rebecca. She'd always thought of her mother-in-law as strong and independent, but Sarah looked suddenly very small and vulnerable.

She took Sarah's arm and led her to the sofa. "You've had a shock. Just sit down and take it easy."

Sarah still stared into space.

"How about if I call the police?"

Sarah's gaze drifted to the stairs that led to the second floor. "Halina is very suspicious of authority. She was very nervous when I mentioned police. You can understand how it must be for her, coming from a Communist country. I didn't have the heart …"

"They may've done some damage. You may want to call your insurance company. By the way, how'd they get in?"

Sarah looked toward the living room windows. "I don't know."

"Was the front door locked when you came in?"

"Yes."

"What other door could they get in?"

"Only the patio door at the back."

Rebecca got up and went through the dining room into the den. She pulled open the curtains drawn across the glass patio door. Everything was intact. They hadn't gotten in this way.

Because of the structure of the house, all the windows on the first floor were too high off the ground for easy access. Rebecca checked each one in any case. Leaving Sarah resting in the living room, she went down the stairs to the entrance landing, then further down the open staircase to the basement.

She was nearly at the bottom when she heard it. A sudden stirring sound, a rustling emanated from the darkness in front of her. She stopped, frozen. Someone was there.

She fought the urge to run back up. Felt along the wall for a light switch. When the light came on, she found herself looking into the startled brown eyes of a large raccoon. It had halted partway through the broken window above the washer and dryer. Shards of glass sparkled on the enamelled tops of the appliances.

"Shoo!" Rebecca said.

The raccoon sat back on its hind legs and peered at her, unconvinced.

This time she waved her arms around and raised her voice. "Shoo!"

The raccoon wearily turned its rotund furry body around and crawled back out the empty window pane.

She looked around for something to cover the opening with. An old furnace filter leaned against the wall. She moved a wooden chair beside the washing machine and stood on it, lifting the filter to press it across the window. An uneven fit, but it would have to do.

She found a cardboard box nearby and gingerly placed the large pieces of glass inside. Using a sponge from the sink, she cleaned up the smaller bits.

In the living room Sarah was kneeling on the floor gathering books into piles.

"He broke one of your basement windows," Rebecca said. "I covered it over for now, but you'll have to get it replaced."

Sarah stood up, anxiety tensing her lips. "Thank you, dear." She absently handed Rebecca the books she had picked from the floor. "I'll go upstairs and get my guests."

Rebecca glanced at the books in her hand: *The War Against the Jews, Medical Bunker: Buchenwald, The Siege of Stalingrad*. The books on the floor were a mixture of history and music. She lifted them in stacks and lined them up on the coffee table.

She picked up a framed wedding photo of David and her from the floor. She in her white satin gown, cheek to cheek with him in his brand new tuxedo. This was why she avoided coming here. She didn't want to be reminded of what she'd lost.

By the time Sarah returned with her guests, Rebecca had cleared a path on the floor to the couch.

"This is Halina," said Sarah, "and this is Natalka."

"Pleased to meet you," Halina said, her handshake sweaty. Her grey eyes were puffy with fatigue.

Natalka squeezed Rebecca's hand firmly. "I want to thank you for your trouble on my behalf," she said in surprisingly good, if formal, English.

"It's my pleasure. I'm glad I can be of help."

Sarah had said she was in her late thirties, though she looked older. Maybe it was the premature white hair, thought Rebecca, or maybe it was the struggle against the cancer that had begun its treacherous course in her body. The woman's complexion was bluish pale, the skin beneath her eyes thin and transparent. Yet there was a beauty in the curve of her neck, the perceptive green eyes.

"This is terrible!" Natalka said, raising her hand toward the disorder. "Who would do such a thing?" She said something further in Polish to Halina, who shifted her eyes placidly over the room as if she'd seen many a break-in.

"Sarah, if you don't mind," Rebecca said, "I'm going into the kitchen to call the police. I'll be back in a few minutes."

She had just stepped out of the room when Halina began a tirade in Polish. Rebecca heard *policja!* and *milicja!* among the supplicant phrases. Everyone followed her into the kitchen. When she picked up the phone, Halina threw her hands up to her head and began to wail. There must've been a universal language of begging that relied on body language rather than specific words, thought Rebecca, watching Halina's face turn pink from effort, her eyes moistening with tears, hands gesticulating, stretched palms out, to her.

Natalka turned away in embarrassment, her long neck arched as if she'd just seen something interesting on the ceiling, but they all seemed to be waiting for Rebecca's decision. Halina could barely look at her, her eyes darting around the room with anxiety.

"Things are different here," Rebecca said. "We live in a free country ..."

Natalka placed a hand on her mother's arm, but she was not calmed; instead crossed her arms tight over her chest and shook her head vigorously.

Recognizing defeat, Rebecca replaced the receiver.

Halina deflated, sighing.

Sarah gazed toward the kitchen counter. "I'm going to make tea."

Halina nodded at Rebecca. "Thank you, *Pany* Doctor."

Rebecca and Natalka returned to the living room, leaving the two older women to their preparations in the kitchen.

"I must apologize for my mother's behaviour. She is very nervous on this trip."

Natalka wore a loose navy blue shift that showed off her shapely legs, but not her waist. Bending over the coffee table, she retrieved Rebecca's wedding picture.

"He was very handsome," she said. "Sarah told me what happened. It's so unjust when young person dies." They both gazed at the framed photo, but Rebecca felt the poignancy of Natalka's illness.

"How long you were married?"

"Seven years."

"What kind of man he was?"

Rebecca was surprised by the question. "He was very handsome, very warm. When he walked into a room, all the women turned to look at him. Tall, thin. He moved like ..." She closed her eyes. She didn't want to remember.

Natalka picked up a small framed watercolour he had done for Sarah of a child sitting at a piano. "Is this ...?"

Rebecca nodded.

"He was fine artist."

She leaned over Rebecca until the loose wisps of her white hair nearly touched Rebecca's face. "Did you ever understand?" she said slowly. "I mean, why he was ill. Why he died."

Rebecca knew she didn't mean the diabetes.

In a low voice Natalka went on, "I never talked to anyone about this ... I struggle to understand why I am ill and not someone else. I have done something evil? God is punishing me? First He give me my talent, my gift of music. Everyone always say it was gift from God. I did not use it wisely and now I'm punished? Or maybe it's *because* He gave me talent so my life is cut short, like burst of flame that must die. I cannot understand it, I cannot." Her sea green eyes questioned Rebecca as if she might have an answer.

"You can't blame yourself," Rebecca said, struggling to respond with something helpful. "We can't know why some of us have less time than others. But it would be wrong to think it was something you'd done. Good people, people who've never harmed anyone, die too soon. There are no explanations. The only answer is to live life as if every day counts."

Tears filled the green eyes. Her head bowed on the long, graceful neck. "I am not ready to die."

Rebecca's heart contracted in her chest. Instinctively she put her arms around Natalka's shoulders and held her as her body heaved soundlessly.

Sarah and Halina could be heard chattering in Polish in the kitchen. Rebecca found a tissue for Natalka, who composed herself, dabbing at red-rimmed eyes.

"You know, I do not feel sick. I do not believe doctor when he tells me I am so sick. I think I am just tired."

According to Sarah, Natalka's Polish doctor had told her she had leukemia. Her skin was white pale. Rebecca noticed some blue-yellow stains on her forearm.

"Do you bruise easily?" she asked.

Natalka shrugged. "Maybe."

"I'll do a complete blood work-up when you come in."

Natalka stood up and began automatically to pick things up from the floor and arrange them on the shelves and tables in the room. She found all the sheet music that lay scattered around and gathered it in a bundle.

Sarah and Halina carried the tea things to the dining room table, which the intruders had left undisturbed. Sarah cut each of them a square of coffee cake as they sat around the oak table.

If Halina noticed her daughter's swollen eyes, she seemed to make no reference to them. Instead, she said something to Sarah in Polish, pointing to the cake. Sarah responded in Polish. Prickles went up Rebecca's back. She had never heard her mother-in-law speak her native language before, and it made her uneasy. She seemed very different with Polish in her mouth. Animated in a more primitive way. Suddenly she seemed a stranger. Maybe Rebecca didn't know her mother-in-law at all.

Natalka was watching Rebecca. She said, "My mother asks about the cake. It's very good and she wants to know how to do it." She lowered her voice. "It is pointless question — ingredients to make such a cake are too costly at home. Now if she had recipe for turnip cake — then I would write this down."

When Rebecca gave her a puzzled look, she said, "We have many turnips in Poland."

"Are things so bad there?" Rebecca asked.

Without changing expression, she said, "We are more privileged because of Mama's position. We get as many turnips as we want."

Rebecca smiled and took a sip of her tea. "I've heard it's hard to get out of a Communist country. Did they let you go on compassionate grounds?"

Natalka's mouth pursed. "'Communists are not interested in compassion. They do not care if people are ill. We have more advantage because my mother works for Orbis. The state travel. She arranges for Polish workers to have vacation. Whole factory will go to the seaside or Carpathians, and she arranges this." She gazed off in a mocking way. "In my mind I can see five hundred workers from a factory that make tractor parts lying like sardines on beach. Each one has thermos bottle filled with vodka, the main recreation in Poland."

Her eyes turned back to Rebecca with a sly look. "So, in her position we can get visas. You see, she is also in the Party." She seemed to cut herself off, perhaps thinking that Communists were not a proper topic of conversation in the west.

But Rebecca was curious. "What's it like in Poland under the Communists?"

She considered the question for a moment. "I never know anything else, so I can't say."

She turned to Halina. "Did you hear the question, Mama? How is in Poland under Communists?"

Without a moment's hesitation Halina responded. "It is much better than before," she said. "Everything more fair."

"She doesn't have tape recorder under the table," Natalka said, her eyes smiling.

Halina ignored this remark and began a conversation with Sarah in Polish that did not include the younger women.

"I must be fair to Mama," Natalka said to Rebecca, "she is not good Party member. She joined in order to survive. Of all countries, Poland suffered the most in the war. Nothing was left after. The Germans set fire to everything when they retreat. I believe, in English you call it, 'scorched earth.' Nothing left but ashes. And then, before smoke could settle, Soviets arrived and told us the ashes were theirs.

"She was alone with me. Her husband left. She didn't want to go to countryside with her parents. So she joined Party. Better to live with the victors than starve, even if your own people hate you."

"The Poles resent people who joined the Party?"

"Only three million Poles belong out of thirty-five million people. Why do you think I'm musician? When I was child, nobody would play with me. I had lots of time to practise."

Rebecca grinned.

"Now of course, everything is changing. You have heard of Solidarity Party?"

"A little," Rebecca said.

"They are very popular in Poland. Big trade union. They protest against the Party. Mama is starting to be a little scared."

"Does your husband belong to the party too?"

She shook her head. "We are divorced. He is engineer. He has new wife and young son. My daughter stays with them while I come here."

The other two women had stopped talking. Halina turned to Rebecca and said, "What will happen to my daughter now? Natalka has appointment with you tomorrow?"

She watched Rebecca with somber anticipation.

"I will examine Natalka in my office." She smiled to show her it was all routine, no reason to worry. "I'll get a complete history and order blood work. Then in a week or so, she will go see a very good hematologist — a blood specialist — at the hospital. He will also examine her and look at the results of the blood tests. He's the one who will decide what to do. She'll be in good hands."

"Please tell doctor we do anything to save her life. Money no object."

Natalka went white.

Rebecca said, "He will do everything he can."

"I'm sorry," Halina said. "But I am so afraid for her." She took one of Natalka's hands in her own and kissed it. Natalka averted her eyes and said nothing, her dry sense of humour silent for the moment.

Rebecca felt a wave of grief roll over her and needed some air. She looked at her watch. "It's late. You're probably still tired from your journey. I'll let you get some rest."

After saying their goodbyes, Sarah led the way down the entrance stairs to see Rebecca out. The older woman opened the door and jumped, nearly falling back into Rebecca a few steps behind. Two men hovered outside the door in the diffuse glow of the street lamp. With the light coming from behind, their faces were in shadow.

chapter four

The men did not make any move toward the door.

"Do you know them?" Rebecca whispered.

Sarah seemed frozen.

"Turn on the outside light," Rebecca said quietly.

Sarah flicked the switch. The two men developed faces and became human.

"I'm not sure," she said. Then, "Oh, it's Halina's friend." She opened the screen door with hesitation.

Rebecca pulled back up the stairs. She didn't have the heart to leave Sarah with a house full of strangers.

The first man stepped in. "I am so sorry to disturb you when you have a guest, but Janek is very anxious to see Halina."

Sarah moved aside so he could pass. A tall middle-aged man with an attractive tan bowed his head graciously. A strand of sandy-coloured hair fell across his forehead.

"Rebecca, this is Count Michael Oginski," said Sarah. "This is my daughter-in-law."

Rebecca smiled a greeting from the second step. She had never met a count before.

She reached out for a polite handshake, but to her surprise, he lifted her hand and bent over it in the pantomime of a kiss. "Please, call me Michael." He held her eyes, studying her, until she looked away self-consciously.

Behind him followed an older, much shorter man shaped like a bulldog, squat with jowls. He wore dark, horn-rimmed glasses. The man looked familiar. Rebecca had seen his picture in the paper.

"I'd like you to meet John Baron," the tall man said. "This is Sarah and … Rebecca."

That was it, thought Rebecca: Baron Mines. He owned a uranium mine that had been in the news lately. Some problem with the workers.

"Very good biblical names," said the older man with a thick accent, squinting at them with a critical eye. He wore an expensively tailored charcoal grey suit despite the heat. His small blue eyes flashed with impatience to the top of the entrance stairs.

"Where is she?" he asked.

Sarah started up the stairs. "This way."

Both women stood waiting at the edge of the living room, Halina with her head high, arms loose at her sides, Natalka a few steps behind, her chin at an expectant angle.

John Baron stopped at the top of the stairs. When he spotted Halina, a crooked grin spread across his jowly face. He tilted his head in a show of examining her. She gave a small, nervous smile. Finally he spread out his arms and stepped forward to kiss her on both cheeks, then held her at arms' length.

"Hela, Hela!" the man exclaimed.

He jabbered some comments in Polish that Rebecca took for compliments because Halina blushed and pushed the white-blond hair back from her face.

She put her arm out for Natalka and brought her forward. Baron kissed her politely on both cheeks, then pulled back in another show of observation. From the rising intonation of his voice and the exclamation at the end, Rebecca guessed he had offered up some more superlatives. Natalka smiled graciously and blushed.

Halina must have countered with some kind of suggestion because Baron tilted his head and wagged his finger at her. Sarah nodded and smiled politely, murmuring a phrase in Polish. Then she translated for Rebecca.

"Halina has invited them to hear Natalka play."

Natalka stiffened. "But I'm not prepared. I'm sorry but ..."

Halina whispered in her ear while Natalka stared straight ahead, setting her jaw.

"Of course, Mama."

Halina nodded happily to Sarah who gestured everyone into the living room.

"Please stay, too," Sarah said to Rebecca.

Rebecca wished she had made good her escape a few minutes before the men arrived. Except that Michael was still watching her, and Michael was interesting.

Halina led Baron to the sofa, while Sarah removed two chairs from the dining room table and brought them to face the piano. She sat down in one. Rebecca hesitated until Michael gestured toward the loveseat. When she was seated, he sat down beside her.

Natalka marched to the piano bench, her back straight in that practised way of performers, haughty, controlled. Rebecca saw her glancing sideways at Baron. She sat down on the bench and took a deep breath. She opened and closed her fingers a few times, then sat with her hands poised above the keys, concentrating.

Finally her fingers pounced onto the keyboard with an expressive chord that announced a Chopin waltz. Her elbows moved in and out with the grace of a cat, her long-fingered hands stroking, pounding, stroking the notes.

Baron sat back in the sofa, looking ill at ease, his arms folded across his chest. His head bobbed up and down with the beat of the music. Michael sat on the edge of his seat, engrossed.

Rebecca didn't know much about music, but she knew she had never heard anyone play like this. They all clapped enthusiastically when Natalka finished.

"Bravo!" Baron cried. "Bravo!" He murmured something to Halina, who averted her eyes.

"Magnificent!" Michael said.

Baron stood up suddenly and held his hand out for Halina. She questioned her daughter with her eyes, then took the proffered hand and stood up. Natalka had an expectant look on her face.

Baron took three steps to stand in front of Michael. He spat out a few words in Polish and stuck out his hand. Michael stood up. He glanced at Halina, puzzled, but after some prodding from Baron, he reached into the pocket of his blazer and fished out his car keys.

Baron grabbed the keys, turned and gave a curt bow of his head to the company. He kissed Natalka on both cheeks, then, taking Halina's arm, he propelled her toward the front door.

Rebecca had a fleeting impulse to try to stop him, but the look on Halina's face was not fear. She was not resisting. She was embarrassed.

Baron marched her down the stairs and out the front door without a look back. Sarah stepped down to close the door he had left open.

"I apologize," Michael said in a hesitant voice. "You must excuse him. He has not seen his wife for thirty-five years."

Rebecca glanced at Sarah to see whether she knew.

Sarah stared in the direction of the door, looking shell-shocked. "She got married just before the war," Sarah muttered. "I never knew her husband's name."

Rebecca glanced at Natalka. The woman's eyes were closed and she had gone pale. Michael was the first to reach her as she clung to the piano. He spoke to her softly in Polish, then gently took her elbow and guided her to the sofa as if she were made of glass.

Rebecca and Sarah stood awkwardly at the edge of the room.

"I beg your pardon," Natalka said, looking up at the two women. "I don't remember my father. But I was hoping ... I thought he would be interested to ..." She turned away.

Michael sat next to her, his arm extended behind her on the back of the sofa. "When the war broke out," he said, motioning them to sit down, "Janek joined the *Armia Krajowa*. The Home Army, in exile in Britain. He fought in many battles and distinguished himself as a soldier. When the war ended, the Communists took over Poland. He came home to see his wife, but he couldn't live in a Communist country. That's when he immigrated here."

So Natalka hadn't seen her father in thirty-five years, and now that she was here, he hadn't spent more than fifteen minutes with her before bolting out the door. Rebecca could understand why she was upset.

Natalka brushed her hand over her eyes. "What he is like?" she said, facing Michael. "Tell me about him."

Michael leaned back into the sofa. "Janek is a very strong, determined man. He knows what he wants, and he'll do anything to get it. That's a recipe for success in business, and he has been very successful."

"Those men with the pickets downtown," Sarah said. "Is that his company?"

Michael winced. "They've come down from the mines to demonstrate here. The situation is serious."

"Excuse me," Natalka said, "but I must ask: Why he didn't take us with him when he left?"

The room went quiet. Michael blinked several times as if thinking. "I can't tell you that. I don't know." He seemed embarrassed, as if he did know but wouldn't say. "But at the end of the war nothing was simple. Everyone was in a state of shock. Maybe he wanted to go and your mother wanted to stay. All I know is ... that he has always loved you. He's very proud of you."

Natalka turned belligerently to face him. "How you know that?"

He paused a moment, looking at her. "He told me. I've known him for years. You're his only daughter. He has a son with his second wife."

"Then ... why he never wrote to me, or tried contact me? He only answered when Mama wrote."

Michael smiled tiredly and turned to examine the empty bookshelves. "Janek is a talker, not a writer."

Picking up some of the books piled on the coffee table, he veered in a different conversational direction. "When we were here yesterday," he said to Sarah, "your shelves were full of books."

"I'm rearranging things," she said.

Michael put down the book he was holding, glanced at Rebecca, then stood up. He strolled past the small table on which the sheet music had been deposited. Bending over it, he flipped through some of the pages.

"Mrs. Adler, do you sing? Your card said you teach vocal students."

Sarah nodded.

"I'd love to hear both of you together. You and Natalka."

The two women looked at each other. Finally Natalka said, "My mother told me you had a beautiful voice." Discreetly, she wiped away a tear.

Suddenly Michael gasped, lifting out a sheet.

"The 'Skye Boat Song'!" he exclaimed. "I've come across this in my research but I've never heard it. Can you do this one?"

He handed the page to Natalka, who perused it briefly.

Sarah blinked, glancing self-consciously at Rebecca. "It's an old folk song for choirs."

Michael watched her expectantly. When she didn't move, he said, "Oh, humour me, ladies. This song is dear to my heart. I'm longing to hear the melody. Do you know the history behind it?"

Sarah and Natalka exchanged glances, thereby admitting their ignorance.

"The doctor must know about Bonnie Prince Charlie?" He turned his dark blue eyes toward Rebecca, who shrugged her shoulders.

"Well, then, if you sing it for me, I'll tell you what it means."

He stepped toward the two musicians, a handsome figure in his navy blazer, his sandy hair falling over his ears. He held out a long, graceful hand first to Natalka, then to Sarah, leading them to their places.

Sarah stood in the curve of the baby grand piano. She squared her shoulders and tilted her head back. Loosely clasping her hands in front of her, she stared straight ahead, concentrating.

Rebecca noticed her diaphragm working up and down in preparation. She knew Sarah made some extra money giving vocal lessons, but she herself hadn't actually heard her sing since the wedding eight years earlier. One of those tearjerkers from *Fiddler on the Roof*. Rebecca had been too preoccupied at the time to take much notice.

Natalka began to play a simple melody in chords. Sarah began with a soft, clear soprano that grew stronger until it filled the room.

> Speed bonnie boat like a bird on the wing,
> Onward the sailors cry,
> Carry the lad that's born to be king,
> Over the sea to Skye.

Rebecca was stunned by the richness of her voice. The slight Polish accent she always spoke with disappeared in the song, and the words flowed out of her throat with a poignant clarity.

> Loud the winds howl loud the waves roar,
> Thunderclaps rend the air,
> Baffled our foes stand on the shore,
> Follow they will not dare.

> Many's the lad fought on that day,
> Well the claymore did wield,
> When the night came silently lay,
> Dead on Culloden field.

The song was a haunting melody rendered in Sarah's liquid voice. Rebecca sat bathed in the sound. She didn't want to move. She looked up at Michael, who also appeared spellbound. He was the first to speak.

"I can't tell you how glorious that was. You have such a beautiful voice. You should've been on the stage."

Sarah smiled and blushed with pleasure.

"You took me right into Scotland. A glorious song for a glorious time."

Rebecca waited for the two women to sit down. "Tell us about the Prince," she said.

"I'm writing a historical novel that takes place around 1750. It's hard to avoid the Young Pretender — Bonnie Prince Charlie — if you're interested in the eighteenth century. His father was the Catholic James III of Scotland — the Old Pretender — but the interesting connection was that Prince Charles Edward Stuart, his real name, had a Polish mother."

Sarah raised a skeptical eyebrow. Rebecca, however, was impressed with an artistic project as large as a novel and wondered what his connection was to the crude John Baron.

"Yes," he nodded with emphasis. "His mother was a Polish princess. Maria Clementina Sobieska, the granddaughter of the seventeenth-century Polish king, Jan Sobieski. I've even read that the Prince spoke English with a Polish accent, though he was raised in Italy. His mother called him *Carluśu*.

"What I found fascinating was the interconnectedness of everything. My main interest is the last king of Poland, Stanislaw Poniatowski, who ruled in the eighteenth century. You have, no doubt, heard of *him*." He playfully directed this at Sarah, who bowed her head in acknowledgement.

"Well, here was a significant portion of British society ready to fight for the succession of a 'real' British king, a descendant of King James, the Bonnie Prince Charles Edward Stuart. Only one of his many given names was Casimir, and he wasn't really any more British than the German King George."

Rebecca vaguely recalled the Stuart pretenders to the throne from her high school history and was amused by this revisionist slant.

"Part of my story is set in England and so I kept bumping into information about the Bonnie Prince and Culloden in Scotland, where a ferocious battle was fought in his name. Many Scots fought and died for the Prince. They were massacred by the King's soldiers, and then their families were massacred. The Prince had to be whisked away in a boat to the Isle of Skye. He'd been supported by the French king, who hoped to put a Catholic prince in his control on the throne of England. The Prince roamed Europe for a while, then lived the rest of his life in Italy, disappointed and drunk."

Rebecca glanced at Sarah, whose face was pale with fatigue. "Thank you for the history lesson," she said. "I look forward to reading your book when it's finished."

She stood up. "It's late, and I have an early day tomorrow."

"Before you go," Michael said, "I wanted to invite all of you to my house on Saturday. I have a beautiful pool in the back. It'll still be hot and we can all go swimming. Those too lazy to swim can sit around the pool and sip wine. What do you say?"

Rebecca and Sarah exchanged questioning glances.

Natalka folded her arms across her stomach. "I have no clothes for this."

"What you're wearing is fine," he said. "You can sit in one of the lounge chairs and sip wine in the sun."

She smiled.

Michael jumped to his feet. "Good. Then it's settled. Come over after lunch. I'm a bachelor and I don't cook, but I serve lots of wine." He took a business card out of his wallet and wrote an address on the back. "It's on Baby Point Road just off Jane Street north of Bloor." He handed the card to Rebecca.

"By the way," he said sheepishly, "do you think you could drop me somewhere? Janek took my car."

"Of course," she said, a surprising excitement rising in her throat. She glanced at Sarah with some guilt.

"Rebecca just lives around the corner," Sarah said. "Maybe I can call you a taxi."

Rebecca avoided eye contact with her mother-in-law. She wasn't sure she wanted Sarah to know what she was thinking.

Michael looked from one woman to the other. "Of course. It was thoughtless of me. It's not far to the subway. I can get Janek's car at the office."

When they were heading to the door, Rebecca took heart and said, "I can drop you at the subway. I'm going in that direction." She gave Sarah a reassuring look.

She led him outside to the driveway.

"This is a beautiful car," he said, easing himself into the passenger side of her Jaguar XKE.

It had been David's before he'd gone blind. He'd been so attached to it that she hadn't had the heart to sell it, even after he died. She'd sold her own car, an Oldsmobile, and kept his. It still felt odd having a strange man in the car.

Sarah waved from the door as they pulled away.

Rebecca felt Michael watching her. "How long have you been working on your novel?" she asked as she drove down Spadina Road.

He hesitated. "A long time. I don't usually talk about it, but I felt very comfortable in the company." He looked sideways at her.

"How far along are you?"

"I've got twelve chapters, almost two hundred pages."

"You've done a lot of research?"

"Years," he said. "The eighteenth century was very exciting. It was really the beginning of the modern era — the Enlightenment, the intrigues between the major powers in Europe. And the revolutions: the birth of the United States and the rebirth of France. I've buried myself quite completely in the period and I'm enjoying myself immensely."

Rebecca drove along St. Clair Avenue toward Yonge Street. She pulled over, in sight of the subway stop at the corner. During the day the volume of traffic at this intersection would have prevented her from sitting at the side of the road for more than a minute. But at this hour on a weeknight only a few cars passed by. Across the road, red lights spelled out "Fran's" over the twenty-four-hour restaurant. The large, simple letters glowed red in a cursive script underlined in hot neon.

"Where does the king of Poland come in?" she asked.

"He's one of my main characters," Michael said. "A handsome, charming fellow with the best of intentions who managed, by an inevitable series of circumstances, to wipe Poland off the face of the map. It took one hundred and twenty-six years and World War One to restore it. But my story is more personal. I'm interested in the king as a man."

He looked out to where the lights of Fran's marquee blinked amid the surfeit of neon. "We can talk about it over coffee," he said, pointing his chin at the restaurant.

"I can't, tonight," she said.

"I'm sorry," he said. "I'm so excited about my book I become a bore. Is your husband waiting for you at home?"

"I'm a widow," she said.

"I'm so sorry." He paused a moment watching her. "How about tomorrow night?" he said.

Her eyes travelled over his face, the long patrician nose, the lines creasing the skin around his clear blue eyes. He was older than she was, but cut a dashing figure. He had managed to impress her and put her at ease at the same time. She had never had coffee with a count before.

She was having dinner at her parents' house tomorrow night. "I'll meet you in there at nine-thirty," she said.

chapter five

Michael

Michael gazed out the windows of his office on the twentieth floor of the Baron Mines Building. Ropes of cars snaked along the Gardiner Expressway within view of Lake Ontario. One of the perks of the job, this loft high up in the financial heart of Toronto, looking south over the lake. The iron blue water usually soothed him the way only water can. But it had been a fitful day, impossible to concentrate with the lawyers scrambling in and out, holding their briefcases in front of them like shields. Janek scowled more than usual, charging through the hallowed carpeted halls of their Bay Street offices as if the devil were behind him. He raised his voice at the lawyers but he screamed at the secretaries. They stopped telling him when a reporter called for an interview. There would be no interviews. Michael would have been willing to speak to the press — he had always handled Janek's public relations, such as they were — but the lawyers forbade any contact with the media. Michael had questioned this at first, then retreated.

Into his leather chair watching the lake: the white-crested waves rolled over the blue surface for miles; mute seagulls rose and fell, so small from there that all he could see was the movement. That was what had happened to the miners up north. They'd become so small and far away that they had all but disappeared in Janek's mind. Their problems were of no concern to him. Was it his fault they were dying? They worked for him, he paid them good wages, what more could they ask? The lawyers knew what more. That was why they forbade interviews. The company was guilty.

Michael was a figurehead on the board of directors, held no sway over Janek or the chief engineers. He was there to smooth feathers that inevitably got ruffled by Janek's brusqueness, but in the end Michael's effect was cosmetic because Janek always did what he wanted. If people called him a sonofabitch, Janek didn't mind, as long as they continued to do business with him.

Michael had a desk full of work but he'd had enough today. He picked up his briefcase and came out of his office. His secretary looked up from her typing, surprised.

"I'm going home," he said. "Take messages."

He was heading down the hall when the door to Janek's office flew open in front of him.

"Not today, Professor!" Janek barked, pushing a large man in a tweed jacket out the door into Michael's path.

Janek rolled his eyes at Michael before slamming the door shut. Michael knew that look. It did not bode well for Professor Hauer.

He blinked at Michael, his skin blotchy with effort.

"I'm very sorry, Professor," Michael said. "You were lucky to escape. This has been a bad day for him."

Hauer shook his head with some force, the thick brown hair falling straight over his ears. "I must discuss the details of the project with him. Time is of the essence, he doesn't understand. We must work out some of the finer points so I can assure the university that plans are going ahead. That finances are in place."

Michael knew that Hauer was fishing for some reassurance from him about the money he'd asked Janek for.

Michael gestured that they should walk together to the elevator. He had no news for him and hoped the professor would not delay him talking about the infernal business. Hauer had his heart set on a Chair in Polish Studies and had taken advantage of Michael's scholarly debt to him to gain access to the great man himself. Michael didn't blame him. When he'd gotten bogged down in the details of eighteenth-century Poland, he had come to the Slavic Studies Department at the University of Toronto looking for help. He had been directed to Hauer, who'd given him a list of books, lent him some out of his personal library, and acquiesced to Michael picking his very knowledgeable brain.

Michael avoided his eyes in the elevator, pretended to study the floor numbers flashing over the door. After meeting for several months, Hauer had come to understand who Michael worked for, or at least, the reputed extent of his fortune, and without any warning, he had approached Janek with the idea of the Chair. Michael's estimation of the man had rearranged itself. He had knocked himself off Michael's pedestal, but still, the scholarly achievement, the respect and honour of such a profession! These were the things Michael would have wished for himself if things had been different. He escaped when Professor Hauer walked out of the elevator on the first floor of the Baron Building. Michael quietly hung back, and when the professor turned and realized his companion was continuing to a lower floor, it was too late. The surprised look on Hauer's face was precious. The door slid shut and Michael was free. He felt a twinge of guilt, allayed by the memory of the ridiculously servile letters the man kept sending to Janek, which Janek threw at Michael without opening.

At first Janek was intrigued by the idea that the university would name a Chair after him. The John Baron Chair in Polish Studies. He agreed to a lump sum that Michael thought was very generous but that he knew Janek could well afford. Then the project hit a snag. Some bureaucracy at the university, the professor said. But Michael speculated that perhaps Hauer was overreaching; maybe his tiny office in a shabby building reflected his position in the pecking order and the university had no intention of supporting his proposal. In any case, Hauer relentlessly found opportunities to prostrate himself before Janek, either in person or by mail, to ensure the benefactor would not change his mind when the university authorities finally came through.

Michael was walking through the underground garage to his car when Janek's limousine drove past him toward the exit. The day's events flooded back on him, the miners, the lawyers, the shouting, and he felt his blood pressure rise. Janek had always been a ruthless man, but Michael had accepted that cold-bloodedness as a requisite for his success. Business was hard, only the strong survived. He wondered if Hauer would care how the money had been made. Michael had been supported in style by the company for years. It would be hypocritical to complain now.

He drove his Olds out the exit of the underground garage. To his surprise, Janek's limo stood on the exit ramp like a beached whale. It was surrounded by angry men hoisting homemade signs into the air. The chauffeur was leaning on the horn, which was emitting a monotone wail. The demonstrators in their work clothes — plaid shirts and jeans and work boots — looked out of place in the core of Toronto's financial district. The usual denizens of Bay Street, business men and women in new fall suits and stylish leather shoes, stared at them as they passed by.

The strikers looked angry but intimidated at the same time, hanging back a polite distance from the car. Instead of hurling abuse at the man in the back seat, they enclosed the car in a shy, awkward circle, murmuring among themselves. Michael knew Janek would be shrieking at the chauffeur to get him out of there.

The driver's side window floated down. Official cap on, the chauffeur stuck out his head. "Get away from the damn car, or I'll run you down!"

That was a mistake. Anger overcame shyness and arms reached in to pull the driver out of the window. The men became a mob and crushed around the car. Michael's back stiffened and beads of sweat erupted at his temples. Everything began moving in slow motion; the shouts flattened into a noise that hovered above his head and he was in the gulag again, in Siberia, where prisoners were shadows of men the world had forsaken. The ground was grey dust where grey barracks squatted beneath a grey sky. It was always bone-rattling cold. The prisoners covered themselves with whatever rags they could find to keep warm. The lucky ones still had old handkerchiefs and shirts they could wrap around their faces to cut the biting wind. But one didn't want to appear too lucky, or come to the attention of the guards. Once a guard noticed you, you were in trouble. But they didn't have to do their own dirty work. A guard just had to mutter a name into the ears of a few starving prisoners and offer them an extra helping of soup in an exchange that benefitted them both. Then the guards stood by and watched the prisoners pound the transgressors with their fists. Michael had seen his father pounced on by exhausted, ragged men with filthy beards who had been promised another helping of mush. His father had lived only a few weeks after that.

"You goddamn bastards ... let go of me!"

The shouted words brought Michael back to the car, the strikers, the struggling driver: a sudden tableau before him. *Calm down*, he thought, *calm down*.

In spite of the limbs flying and bodies lurching at sudden angles, everything was surprisingly quiet; only a periodic expletive reached his ears.

The driver's torso was halfway out the window when one of the strikers yelled for them to stop. Everyone stopped. The leader was a wiry man with dignified posture, his shoulders erect. "Stay calm, boys," he said. "This won't help us. This man is a worker, like us."

The driver was released and struggled back into his seat. The men retreated back to their previous polite distance, but their faces had changed. The anger had won out and solidified in the grim eyes, the hard set of their jaws. After a minute of pulling himself together, the driver shot the limo out of the exit ramp. Michael followed slowly behind.

His eyes darted from man to man as he passed through them. They formed a gauntlet on two sides, half-heartedly lifting their signs at his car, but no one recognized him. Janek was the only one who got his picture in the paper, but if anyone were really interested they'd find Michael's name listed under the Board of Directors of Baron Mines as Secretary-Treasurer. Or with less digging, they'd find him in an annual report, a prospectus for one of Janek's schemes, even the block of executive names in the foyer of the building.

Was that how the letter writer had found him? Simard or something. No, he knew more about Michael than his position in the company. He'd said in one of his letters that he'd been in the mine for twenty years. He said that John Baron was a heartless bastard but that Michael was different and would understand how a man might work in an airless shaft for twenty years because he needed the money. And anyway he was told he was lucky to have the work, only now he couldn't work anymore because he couldn't breathe. Maybe they'd met during Michael's early days when he'd gone up north to act as Janek's agent checking out prospectors and claims traders.

He could've seen Michael's name in the *Globe* or the *Toronto Star* since he was the one in charge of relaying information to the press. Usually that meant offering reporters expensive liquor and the company spiel about how grateful John Baron was to Canada for giving him the opportunity to become filthy rich. Not in those words. "Giving back something to my adopted country," or some crap like that.

Michael had always been in the background of the company, trying to balance Janek's blunt style and bad temper, smooth any feathers ruffled after business meetings where Janek carried on with his usual acrimony. But hadn't Michael been just as guilty? All those times people from Bear Lake had called raising questions about the safety of the mine, the poison dust they had to breathe in, the radioactivity released by the uranium. What had he ever done about it? Had he even mentioned it to Janek, to show he was concerned there was a problem? He had left it to Janek and his engineers to manage the mine and its structural defects. He was just a personal assistant, a pretty face with no real power. They were the ones who were supposed to know what they were doing. Well, maybe they did and they didn't care. They knew there was a price to pay for success and they were only glad they weren't the ones paying it. Maybe Janek didn't set out deliberately to kill people, but he also didn't care if they died along the way to making him rich.

Friday afternoon traffic along the Gardiner Expressway was always mad. Leaving an hour earlier didn't help much either, but taking Bloor Street was not an alternative. It was a long way to his home in the west end of the city.

Mrs. Woronska was just locking up the side door of his house as he pulled into the driveway. She stopped when she saw him, a mountain of a woman in a homemade flowered apron, her wavy grey hair pinned back in a bun.

"I just put your dinner in fridge, Count. A delicious salmon. I didn't expect you so early. I go back and heat up for you." She turned to put the key back in the lock.

"Mrs. Woronska — it's all right. Go home to your family. They're probably hungrier than I am." He shooed her away with a wave of his hand. "I'll warm it up when I'm ready. Thank you."

"*Smacznego*," she said. Then she smiled guiltily and said, "Gut appetite."

He had asked her to speak English to him because he found that she became embarrassingly obsequious in Polish, addressing him as if he were royalty. She would fall into the ancient serf/noble pattern as if she had just come from planting potatoes on his estate. It amused him that he had been labouring for years to link his family to royalty, but when faced with someone grovelling at his feet, it distressed him.

He watched her cross the quiet street to her own house where her grown daughter and son-in-law and grandchildren were probably waiting for their supper. He paid her to prepare dinner for him during the week, good home-cooked meals that let him avoid the rich restaurant food that usually gave him heartburn.

Tonight he needed a drink. He went into the dining room where he kept his liquor and poured himself a gin and tonic. Mrs. Woronska's salmon would wait. Usually after being in the office all day, it was a luxury to come home to spend the evening alone with a good meal, some wine, and his work. His real work. That would comfort him, but he needed something stronger tonight.

He sat down at his desk in the den. When he had first started writing, his purpose was to solve the mystery of his family. Shortly before Aunt Klara died in 1967, she had sent him a packet of very old letters she'd managed to hang onto even during the war. Buried them in a box in a distant corner of the yard. When she survived the war, she dug them up and hid them under a floorboard. To get past the censors, she'd given them to a German visitor who'd taken them out of Poland and mailed them to Michael.

Those old letters were what had got him started. His curiosity instantly aroused, he'd never looked back. Most of the letters were written by his father's grandmother, a delightful old bat who had died at the turn of the century at the respectable age of eighty-three. They were dated from the mid-nineteenth centruy, most of them on the occasion of a birth or death. One especially detailed letter about the family from his paternal grandmother filled in the blanks of his father's sketchy version. With that letter in hand, he'd begun digging into archives and public collections in Paris and London — and had made some startling discoveries. If he were right, his family did indeed stem from some very royal blood. There was only one problem: in order to accommodate his theory, history would have to be rewritten. No big deal. It would be a novel. A very small royal someone who had died in all the history books would have to be resurrected. Both Polish and Russian scholars would have to rewrite texts. A whole new area of scholarship would be born. He was willing, rather eager, to start that little revolution. He had almost all the proof he needed. Only Halina's contribution, that was what was left, and everything would fall into place.

In order to reach a wider audience, he had decided to write the book as a novel. With the understanding that characters and events were historical. Let the scholars come after him. It would only sell more books.

Apart from the satisfaction of his discoveries, a startling thing had happened to him somewhere along the way to writing his book. In his headlong plummet into the eighteenth century, he had grown to love the characters he had plucked out of history while they were still young enough for him to understand, before they grew into legends. He hoped he had done them justice.

It enthralled him to find lives that formed a complete arc. He could look back on them and know how they lived, loved, thought, from the mounds of letters and biographies they had left in their wake. He knew them a lot better than he would ever know his own father, a man who gambled and drank too much and neglected his family, a ghost during Michael's boyhood. Except for his affair with Halina. That episode in his father's life was concrete for Michael, too real. The war changed everything. People's real natures crystallized and became set in stone. Some became heroes. Some became killers. All of them struggled to survive. Then after the war, the gulag began a new life of suffering for Michael's family. With his entertainments withdrawn and their lives in danger every day, his father turned into a real father and became a man who cared perhaps too much. One day when starvation pulled at his stomach, Michael stole some potatoes. When the guards came after him, his father confessed to the theft. Three prisoners were awarded a piece of potato in their soup that day for punishing the thief. Michael's father survived the beating but in his weakened condition developed pneumonia and died. During the dozen years Michael had been working on his book, he felt his father peering over his shoulder as his pen skidded across paper.

He opened the drawer of the desk and pulled out an envelope. His heart skipped a beat every time he read the letter inside.

Dear Count Oginski,

We're all very excited here about *The Stolen Princess* and have chosen to publish it as our Polish history book this year. It will appear as part of a short list, which includes a book on the history of the Ukrainian Catholic church, a volume on Russian icons, and a biography of Peter the Great. As a small press publishing books of Slavic interest, we are able to issue only one book on Poland every few years and have chosen *The Stolen Princess* from among several worthy submissions.

We only require the documentation of which we spoke, regarding the validity of your connection to the historical principals in the manuscript. Once we are assured of your family connection, we will go ahead with publication.

Sincerely,
Vladimir Golovin, Slavic House Press

Michael gazed out the window that looked over the back, the bright blue pool, the end of the yard falling away toward the ravine of the Humber River. *The validity of your connection to the historical principals.* That all depended on Halina, who had the proof in her hands. She had to honour her part of the agreement or.Janek would not just blithely open his wallet. Michael would have to remind her of her promise.

chapter six

Sarah lingered inside the screen door watching through the glass as Michael stooped over to get into the little sports car. Rebecca slid in behind the wheel. After a minute the car pulled out of the driveway, its windshield glittering beneath the streetlamp. Sarah felt uncomfortable letting her go off with a stranger, though he seemed a decent fellow. In her lifetime she had seen people who seemed decent turn into monsters in an instant.

When she returned to the dining room Natalka was clearing off the dishes.

"You don't have to do that," she said, picking up the last cup and saucer.

"I want to help," Natalka said.

Her pale face was beautiful, the round smooth forehead, her neck a graceful arch beneath the white hair pinned into a roll. When she moved, her stomach bulged beneath her loose shift. Halina had explained about the enlarged spleen, said her daughter was very self-conscious about it.

Sarah avoided looking down. "You must be tired. Why don't you go upstairs and lie down?"

Natalka followed her into the kitchen. "I don't want be alone."

The odd thing was that that was exactly what Sarah wanted. She felt awkward with Natalka, partly because she was a well-known musician, partly because she was Polish. And Polish anti-Semitism was legion. She wondered if it was still thus, considering there were no Jews left in the country. Though she had never thought of Halina as anti-Semitic, so she was unlikely to have passed it on to her daughter. Halina's attitude to people was non-denominational: if they could help her she didn't care which God they prayed to.

She gave Natalka a wan smile and turned on the tap in the sink to begin washing the dishes. Natalka picked up the dishtowel and took each plate out of the drainer as it was deposited.

"These are so pretty," Natalka said. "What kind flowers they are?"

"They're wildflowers. I like them too. There's a daisy; there's clover. A poppy."

Natalka smiled shyly. "Mama talk about Janek and Michael," she said. "Not much about you. She only tell me about you when we are coming. She said your parents were good to her." She placed a dry dish on the counter. "How she knew them?"

Sarah rinsed the soap off a cup and placed it in the drainer. "She worked in their store."

Natalka was in the middle of lifting a plate when she stopped, holding it in midair. "Worked in their store?"

Her eyes waited also. Sarah hoped she wasn't spoiling some revision of history Halina had devised for herself.

"It was a jewellery store on Ulica Stradomska."

Natalka nodded with recognition. The well-known street led to the hill where Wawel castle towered over the city. Sarah still remembered it from her childhood.

"Your mother was very beautiful. I think people came into the store sometimes just to look at her standing behind the counter. She was a few years older than me and I looked up to her. Then we both got married and we didn't see each other much after that. She went to work for one of her husband's relatives. When the war broke out my husband and I fled Kraków."

"What about rest of your family?"

Sarah stared at the dish she was soaping up. The sponge in her hand. It all began dissolving like picture trouble on a television, sound trouble, all she could hear was the rhythm of her own heart. And how could that still be going when she had lost everything? When she had lost Rayzele?

A noise brought her back. Natalka placing a dry dish on the counter.

"I'm sorry," Natalka said, concern clouding her eyes. "My mother was lucky," she said. "She had parents in the country, so she went there. Where you went?"

Sarah rinsed off the dish and automatically picked up another, swallowing the lump in her throat.

"We just got on a train and went. Anywhere. The city was filled with Nazis. We were desperate to get away. Together with my sister and her husband, we headed to Neipolomica, not far from Kraków."

"Yes, I know it. There's a large park there."

"But we were young and stupid and we wore our city coats and fashionable hats. You know what the peasants look like with their babushkas. We stood out like sore thumbs. Everyone on the train knew we were Jews. So when we got off, someone had already denounced us. The police were waiting for us. They took us to their jail."

Sarah glanced sideways to find Natalka engrossed in her story.

"Lucky for us the commandant there knew my father. They'd been in the first war together, in the same outfit. My father always sold him jewellery wholesale. The commandant came to us in the middle of the night. He said he was letting us go as a favour to our father, on condition that we disappear and never come back. He told us to take the ferry that went up the river, that was our best bet. So before dawn we rode up the Vistula to a place my brother had run to. But he and his wife were being hidden by a farmer, there was no room, so we only stayed there a few days. Then we walked to a town where they had a spring. You know, a kind of resort where people go for the water. But it was empty because of the war, so they let us stay in these small rooms with wood stoves. We worked there picking potatoes. They paid us in potatoes."

She felt like her feet were straddling forty years and would collapse beneath her any moment. She rinsed the last saucer and turned off the water. "I haven't thought about this for a long time. These aren't happy stories."

"Please go on," Natalka said. "I like to listen."

Sarah picked up another tea towel and took a dish out of the drainer. "It was always cold at night, so we needed wood for the stoves. When we could, we went to the forest near there to pick up the dry branches from the ground. One day, two men came riding through the forest on horses toward us, my sister and me. You could see one was the master and one the servant. The lord was on a huge horse, and dressed in a beautiful flowing sheepskin jacket and high boots, like from another century. The other horse was smaller and the steward carried everything — bags, rifles. They must've been hunting.

The lord said 'Don't they know they aren't allowed to be here.' Something like that. Then the servant repeated it, as if we hadn't heard. I said to the master, 'We're just picking up the dead wood.' The servant very sternly said, 'You don't speak to Jasny Pan like this. You speak to me.' Jasny Pan. I always remembered that. 'His Excellency,' I guess you would translate it. We were too insignificant to even speak to him directly.

"The master said, 'This is a private estate. They can't just come and take what they want.' I still had nerve then, it was before we went to the camps, and besides, I found the situation ridiculous. I said, 'We're cleaning your forest by removing the dead brush — we're not *taking* anything.' The servant said to the man that we must be the Jews working on his estate. Then a strange thing happened. The lord suddenly said, 'Ah, *Zydy*. They can go.' And they turned their horses around and rode away, the large horse leading the smaller one. The servant turned around with a nasty look, like he wanted to make sure we weren't going to throw something at them."

"You were afraid?"

"Not of them. What could they do to us? We'd already lost everything. This was before the Germans overran the smaller towns."

"What happen then?"

Sarah began putting the clean dishes away into the cupboards. "We walked from town to town, always one step in front of the Germans. In Stopnica we heard that some wealthy Jews in town had offered the Germans money if they took the younger Jews to work in a labour camp. Instead of a death camp, you understand. So we volunteered. My sister didn't want to go. But when she saw us heading for the truck at six in the morning, she followed with her husband."

"Your sister survived?" Natalka asked.

Sarah smiled. "Against all odds. I still remember when a year later we were transferred from the labour camp to Buchenwald. She somehow got her hands on two coats, though it was August. She wore one and carried the other on her arm. As soon as I saw that we were going on a train, I knew there was no point taking anything. She wore extra clothes beneath to have for later. I just went with what I had on my back. When she saw I wasn't taking a coat she was angry. She said, 'Don't ask me to give you anything later because I won't. I'm not going to wear myself out carrying this, then give it to *you*.'"

Sarah shook her head slowly, hating the memory. "They separated the men and women then when we got to the railroad siding. The men went on a different train. I didn't see my husband again until after the war. We were in cattle cars for three days. No food, no water. No toilets. You can't imagine the smell. We were packed like sardines, standing up, with no room to sit down. Women died around us. When we got to Buchenwald, the first thing the Germans did was to take everything away from us. Everything. The clothes on our backs, the combs in our hair, our photos, even our wedding bands. Then they put us in the showers. We were afraid it was gas, but then real water came out and we all just laughed with relief, like crazy people. Malka wouldn't talk to me after that for a long time, as if it was my fault she lost her coats."

A dish slipped out of Natalka's hand while she was depositing it on the counter and made a loud clatter. "I'm sorry," she said. "I'm so sorry."

What was it about Natalka that drew out those memories stored almost out of reach? She had never talked to Rebecca so openly. Yet there was one thing she had never told anyone. Only Yusek had known and Yusek was gone.

Much later that night, when Sarah was finally asleep, she left the safety of her bed, her adopted country, the continent that had shielded her for thirty years, and floated like a wraith into Kraków again. She drifted down through the charged night past the rooftops of Ulica Miodowa, past the fourth-floor window where she used to stand watching the people stroll down the narrow street. Black now. Empty. Where is everyone? *Is dinner ready, Mama?* A gust of wind blows her up the street. *Can no one hear me?* They must still be at the store. With only her will, not her feet, which she seems to have forgotten somewhere, she makes her way across Ulica Dietla to Stradomska. A street she'd trod upon daily for nearly twenty years. Yet she doesn't recognize it. The road and sidewalks have been torn up, revealing substrates of earth buried for centuries. Chunks of concrete swim amid sand and brick in a frenzied jumble that might be the entranceway to hell.

The storefronts hang back in deep shadow. *Mama? You can go home now, I'm here.* She is sure this is the one, but where are the rings set with amber, the necklaces sparkling against velvet in the window, the gold bracelet she coveted? Closer. Get closer. She gazes into the black, searching the vacuum. *Where's Rayzele?* her mother's voice echoes from inside. Suddenly a sweet weight fills her arms and Rayzele blinks up at her, eyes large with fear. Sarah hugs her to her chest, memorizing the pressure of her body, determined not to lose her this time. When Sarah looks up, shadows have swallowed up the shop and are coming for her. The void opens like a yawn and begins to suck her in. She is not ready.

She yanks herself away, lurches toward the limestone hill at the top of the street where Wawel perches, its towers lost in the black sky. *Look at the pretty castle*, she says to Rayzele, but when she looks down her arms are empty. *I will not lose you again*, she screams into the void. She knows where Rayzele is and she heaves herself along the foot of the hill with all the speed she can muster, but the liquid air slows her down. She is swimming in slow motion toward the sound of her baby's breathing. But the wind howls to drown it out, makes her look up at the castle, where the ghosts of Polish kings stare down at her severely from the battlements, muttering judgment beneath their beards, their crowns sharp with portent. Beside them hovers a wondrous woman Sarah recognizes, though she's never seen her before. She is Esterka, the Jewish love of King Kazimierz the Great of six hundred years ago, masses of black curls framing her mournful face as she wrings her hands. She wrings them for Sarah. *There!* She points away toward the old town. *Hurry, before it is too late.*

Sarah glides along Ulica Grodzka. She knows the old town lies ahead, but the darkness deepens the further she drifts. The buildings lean toward her, she can smell their breath as she passes: the sourness of greed, musty treachery. *So you're back*, they murmur in her ear. *What did you think you'd find? You don't belong here.* Her hands push them away in waves like a swimmer. Her feet kick and propel her through the soupy black night. She will not give up until she finds her.

The dark disorients her, she could be staring into her own heart, when, without warning — a light. A sharp splinter of light cuts into the black distance. She sails toward it as if it is the harbour. The light becomes a crack between the jamb and a door. Becomes soft weeping. She touches the thick wood of the door, but it will not budge.

Rayzele! she cries.

Her fists pound at the door, her pulse pounds at her temple, her heart pounds in her chest, *Rayzele! Rayzele! Rayzele*! until the door creaks open another fraction and it becomes hard to look into the light. Her eyes cannot bear it, but she must struggle to keep them open. The light becomes crystalline, diamonds aimed at her eyes.

Rayzele! she cries. *I'm coming!*

When Sarah opens her eyes again, she is tangled in her sheets and a Toronto dawn is setting her bedroom alight.

chapter seven

Rebecca pulled her Jaguar coupe out of the staff parking garage behind Mount Sinai Hospital. She could do this route with her eyes closed. The night-like chill from the covered garage gave way to the sudden warmth of day on Murray Street. The patients she had just visited that morning were doing fine. Two had had troublesome organs removed (one gall bladder, one appendix), one was recovering from a mild stroke, and one had delivered a baby. Everything was fine.

Natalka would be her first appointment of the day. She had scheduled forty-five minutes for her so she could do a thorough examination. Rebecca wasn't looking forward to it. She had seen her share of terminal illness and preferred treatable diseases. Something she could prescribe a drug for: high blood pressure, bronchitis, an overactive thyroid. She was grateful that the rest of her day would be taken up with sore throats and stomach upsets and scripts for birth control pills. That would do nicely. Iris would have everything organized for her, bless her. Only first she had to examine Natalka and hope that her condition was still in the early stages. Thank heavens a specialist would take over her treatment.

She drove south down University Avenue, the showcase of Toronto, its six lanes of traffic divided by sculpted stone monuments planted with impatiens and marigold. She turned right onto Dundas. On the outer edge of Chinatown people were already threading their way through stalls of fruit and vegetables and souvenir T-shirts that spilled onto sidewalks. The crowds and the splash of primary colours always cheered her.

A traffic report came on the radio: "Avoid Bay Street at Wellington if you can. Motorists are slowing down to take a look at the strikers carrying signs ..."

She switched stations. A man's voice shouted over the din. "For the first time in history a wildcat strike has shut down the uranium mine at Bear Lake. These men have come down in their work clothes — some are at the Legislature hoping to get the attention of Premier Bill Davis, and some are here, in front of the offices of Baron Mines. The strikers are slowly marching around in a circle, carrying handmade signs. Here's one that says, 'We want fresh air.' Another one: 'Baron Mines Death Trap.' I'm going to wade in and speak to this fellow. What is your name, sir?"

"Bill Roberts."

"Mr. Roberts, you're the union rep, could you tell our listeners, what does this sign mean, 'We want fresh air'?"

Some static crackled. "We work in Baron's uranium mines in conditions you wouldn't want for your dog. The ore's filled with silica dust and gives off these radioactive gases. It's poison. Our men are dying of lung cancer and what they call silicosis. We think it's the conditions in the mines, but the company won't talk to us.

We want some straight answers. We've got the right to know if our work is killing us."

"Why do you think they won't meet with you?"

"John Baron's only interested in his profits. We dynamite the ore down there — that gives off tons of poison silica dust — and we do it in the same shaft we breathe in. Other companies build hard rock mines with two shafts, one for bringing up the ore, the other for ventilation so people can breathe. John Baron only built one shaft 'cause he didn't give a damn if we could breathe or not." The man's voice cracked with emotion. "He didn't want to spend the bucks, and what with the radiation down there, we're dying of cancer at four times the average."

"What do you want Baron Mines to do?" asked the interviewer.

"They got to dig down that other shaft, give us proper air while we're down there working — we're bringing up the ore that's making them rich."

Rebecca drove up Beverley Street then turned left on D'Arcy. In spite of the morning sun warming her through the window, she shivered as she pulled into the small lot behind the medical building. John Baron had appeared only crude and selfish during their brief meeting; now it seemed he was also avaricious and cruel.

Iris sat at her desk behind the counter in the waiting room, checking over lab and x-ray reports that had come that morning. She looked up at Rebecca over her spectacles. "Good morning, love."

Iris was elegant, as usual, in a grey silk suit despite the large curves of size-twenty breasts and hips. Her short hair swept up from her neck in blond wings. What a comfort she was. Rebecca would be lost without her.

The phone rang. Iris answered, "Dr. Temple's office."

Rebecca took up her usual position behind the counter, in a chair off to the side where she could look at reports.

"No, that's all right, Mrs. Mullins," Iris said into the phone while handing Rebecca some lab results. "I know you're concerned for the baby. Come in at one o'clock."

After Iris had hung up, Rebecca raised an eyebrow at her.

"She's got a sore throat," Iris said, "but she doesn't want to take antibiotics because of the baby."

"I'll wait for a culture before putting her on anything," Rebecca said. "But she's in her third trimester. She can take some penicillin if she needs to."

They worked quietly for a few minutes.

"Is Nesha coming for Rosh Hoshanah?" Iris asked.

Rebecca didn't look up from the report she was reading. "No," she said. "His son has a new girlfriend and they're invited to her parents."

Rebecca continued to check over the blood tests and consult reports in front of her. Nesha had been flying in from his home in San Francisco once a month since they had met in the spring. Though she looked forward to Nesha's visits, this month would be different. This month she would light a *yahrzeit* candle to mark the first anniversary of David's death.

Nesha knew all about death, having witnessed the destruction of most of his family in the war. But she couldn't share this with him. She couldn't share it with anyone, not even Sarah, her mother-in-law, who yearned to share it with her, who would have to mourn alone. She loved Sarah in her own way and felt guilty for neglecting her, but it was all Rebecca could do to force herself to call on Sundays and pretend she'd like to talk to her more often but had no time.

The phone rang and Iris began a dialogue with a drug rep. She wheeled her chair off to the side cabinet where they stored the little boxes and tubes of medication samples the salesmen dropped off. She unlocked the cabinet door. Which samples did they want this month? More sulpha? More diuretics? More birth control pills? Yes, yes, and yes.

With Iris's attention engaged elsewhere, Rebecca opened the drawer of the desk and felt deep inside with her hand. She had given Iris instructions to remove all photos of David from the office. His artwork had gone first. All his paintings and sketches had been replaced by reproductions of Van Gogh, Monet, and Pisarro. But Rebecca still kept the small, framed photo of them taken by a stranger in the Tuilleries garden. It was 1976 and they were in Paris on a pilgrimage for David's art. Three years ago. Rebecca prodded the picture to the edge of the drawer and sneaked a look.

It had been taken shortly before they'd discovered the diabetes, before her world had fallen apart. They'd been married for five years then; were thinking of having children. Their arms were wound around each other's shoulders as they grinned into the camera. They looked so young then, so happy. She hardly recognized herself. Not that she had changed so much, physically. Still the same dark bushy hair, the prominent cheekbones. But the expression of joy on her face — that was something she could only recognize from the distance.

"Try around lunchtime," Iris said to the drug rep on the phone. "She may have a few minutes then."

Rebecca quietly closed the drawer. She didn't mind talking to the men who came round with their oversized cases filled with sample goodies. It was an easy way to find out about new drugs. And her patients benefitted from the free medication supplied by the supposed largesse of the drug companies. A working symbiosis.

Iris stepped over to the wall of colour-coded files and began to retrieve the folders of patients who had appointments that morning.

"My kids have put in their order for Rosh Hashanah," she said, continuing to work. "They're tired of turkey, so I'm going to make a brisket. Oh, and you won't believe this: Martha's bringing a friend. A man. It must be serious if she's bringing him for the holiday."

"You must be pleased," Rebecca said.

"I'm terrified. What if he hates my cooking? What if he hates my house? I could be starting off on the wrong foot with my future son-in-law."

Rebecca smiled.

"You're lucky with Sarah," Iris said. "She's a good mother-in-law. She doesn't push herself on you, and she's an exceptional woman."

Iris and Sarah had gotten to know each other during David's illness. Each spoke glowingly of the other.

"Still, it's nice you're doing her this favour."

Rebecca winced with guilt. She could hardly have refused. Yet now that she had met Natalka, she was eager to help in any way she could. Halina had called Sarah out of the blue after a very spare correspondence of not more than four letters over thirty-five years. She was desperate to get treatment for her daughter's illness and hoped Sarah could help her. She knew Sarah's daughter-in-law was a physician and had asked her whether Rebecca could examine Natalka and recommend a specialist to see her. Natalka seemed to have chronic leukemia, better than the acute kind, but not by much. In both cases the bone marrow produced too many white blood cells, a process that devastated the body rather quickly in the acute disease, but took a bit more time to wreak its havoc in the chronic version. With standard medical treatment she might survive three years. Her Polish doctor had told her he could do nothing more for her, but her chances would be better if she could get to the West, where they were experimenting with new drugs and treatment.

Rebecca remembered Janek's disinterest in Natalka. Perhaps it wasn't disinterest. Perhaps it was anger. Her illness was going to cost him a fortune. Rebecca, herself, was happy to examine Natalka without payment. And under the circumstances, the surgeon might waive his usual fee for services. But the lion's share of the cost was hospital-related. Operating room expenses, including anaesthetic and the specialist who would administer it, lab tests, radiation, chemotherapy, hospital stay, nurses, and on and on. None of it would be covered under the province's socialized medical insurance since they were foreign visitors.

Footsteps sounded on the stairs leading to the second floor office. Rebecca heard low voices on the landing. Sarah stepped through the doorway first, followed by Natalka and Halina.

Iris immediately came around the counter into the waiting room and warmly embraced Sarah. Rebecca followed two steps behind, noting the outlandish difference in the size of the two women: Iris, tall and broad in her grey suit, Sarah just five feet two and slender, a blue-patterned blouse tucked into a matching skirt.

"It's so nice to see you again!" Iris said, beaming at Sarah.

Rebecca pressed her cheek to Sarah's in greeting. She looked tired, Rebecca thought. Probably still agitated about the break-in.

Sarah introduced the other two women to Iris. After inquiring about their stay in Toronto, Iris engaged Halina and Sarah in conversation. Meanwhile, Rebecca detached Natalka from the group and ushered her into an examining room. Natalka wore a loose mauve shift dress that barely disguised the protrusion of her abdomen when she moved.

Rebecca spent twenty minutes asking her questions to get a complete medical history. She had been in good health until four months earlier, when she had begun to feel excessively tired. The only time she had ever been hospitalized was when she had delivered her daughter, Anya, fifteen years before. Rebecca underlined "fifteen," glad that the daughter was old enough to be a candidate for a tissue match if Natalka needed a bone marrow transplant.

Rebecca was listening to Natalka's answers, writing short notes in her file, when the woman's voice shifted from matter-of-fact to personal.

"I am very embarrassed, I must tell you something. Mama did not tell even Sarah." She paused, swallowed, then continued. "Doctor in Poland — he was not sure about the leukemia. Blood tests not clear. He said it could be, but it could be something else. He does not know what. He only knows I can die from it. He wrote letter that I have leukemia so I can leave Poland for treatment. Mama helped one from his relatives with visa."

Rebecca was taken aback at first, but realized that nothing much would change in the way of her examination or the tests she ordered. Their methods were questionable, this mother and daughter, but what would she have done in the same circumstances?

Rebecca continued her questions. There was no cancer, kidney disease, or lung disease in her family. Halina's father had died of heart disease, her mother, old age. Rebecca found nothing in her patient's background that connected her to leukemia, no exposure to radiation or to the chemical benzol. Her only symptoms, apart from the extreme fatigue, were anemia and a dull ache on her left side that wouldn't go away. And nosebleeds. Spontaneous nosebleeds that were hard to stop.

Rebecca took her temperature and looked into her eyes to see if there were any hemorrhages in the retina. Both were normal. An encouraging sign. She had Natalka sit on a chair while she stood behind and gently moved her fingertips over her entire throat, checking the lymph nodes.

"Tilt your head to the right, please," she said. She felt for the cervical nodes beneath the relaxed neck muscle. "Now to the left."

She pressed her fingers delicately around the lymph nodes, feeling whether they moved freely or were fixed to one spot.

"Is it tender here?" she asked.

"No."

The nodes were firm and slightly enlarged, but discrete. They weren't fused together like they would be in Hodgkin's disease. Rebecca knew enlargement was slow to develop in leukemia.

She patted the examining table. "Please lift up your dress and lie down. I'm going to check your abdomen."

Natalka lifted the mauve cotton fabric, draped it across her chest, and lay down, her head on a small pillow.

As Rebecca had already noted, the left side of the woman's abdomen was swollen.

"Put your arms at your sides" Rebecca said, "and bend your knees up. It relaxes your stomach muscles."

Rebecca rubbed her hands together briskly. "I don't want to touch you with cold hands."

At first, Rebecca moved one hand very lightly over the area to get a general picture of her abdomen.

"Now breathe deeply."

She slid her hand an inch at a time from one quadrant to another. Natalka lay without a sound until Rebecca moved her fingers to the bloated left side below her ribcage. Then she winced.

"It's tender there?" Rebecca asked.

The patient nodded.

There were many reasons why her spleen might be enlarged, ranging from infection to metabolic disorders. And then there was leukemia. The out-of-whack bone marrow filled the spleen with white blood cells, making the area ache, a common complaint of leukemia patients. The Polish doctor had given Natalka the opportunity of knowledge. Western doctors could get to the bottom of her illness. Whether the prognosis would change depended entirely on the nature of her affliction.

Rebecca continued her examination. To palpate the liver and kidneys she tilted her hand slightly with her fingers depressing the abdominal wall further to the right so that she could feel the edges of the organs. Both were the right shape and size and where they were supposed to be. It was a little tricky feeling the liver around the spleen, but at least Natalka was slender. Rebecca had several obese patients whose liver and kidneys were well hidden beneath a layer of fat and refused to reveal themselves under her hand.

Unlike the liver and kidneys, the spleen could not be outlined unless it was diseased or abnormally enlarged.

"Could you please place your left arm under your lower back?" she said.

Natalka obliged. This position helped lift and displace the spleen forward. Rebecca reached over and placed her right hand under Natalka's left side, forcing the spleen forward even further, while the fingers of her left hand gently pressed down, searching for an edge.

Natalka groaned quietly.

"I'm sorry," Rebecca said. "Almost done. Another deep breath."

Rebecca moved her fingers along the edge of the largest spleen she had ever felt — all the way down to the pelvic brim and over to the right side of the abdomen. Her hopes diminished. She refused to be optimistic and then face the worst. The world was a strange and terrible place. She had already found that out the hard way. Why did she keep hoping for better?

After Natalka left, Rebecca stepped into the little corner of the office where they collected blood and urine samples. A cupboard above the counter was filled with large glass jars that held dipsticks, gauze pads, disposable lancets, disposable gloves, sterile sample bottles. On one side of the counter stood a microscope and glass slides.

Rebecca used a dropper to remove a droplet of blood from the sample she had taken from Natalka. She touched the bead of blood to a glass slide, then took another slide and, angling it against the first one, moved it slowly along the glass to draw the blood flat across it. She let it dry, then fixed it with a stain. After diluting it with water and letting it dry again, she examined it under the microscope. She didn't often go through this procedure, mostly when an immediate decision had to be made about treatment and she needed information before lab results would come back.

This was different. She doubted there was anything she could do that would dramatically alter the course of Natalka's illness. She could call it scientific curiosity, but she knew better. She had gotten involved, and that was always dangerous emotionally.

She squinted into the microscope. She understood the confusion of Natalka's Polish doctor. Among the red and white blood cells and platelets there were none of the blast cells associated with leukemia. And when she put another drop of blood into the counting slide, she found Natalka's white blood cells were below normal. Not the astronomical count usually found in leukemia. That didn't rule out the diagnosis, however. She knew better than to hope for that. Before her next patient, she looked up "Splenomegaly" in her pathology textbook.

That evening over dinner, his blue eyes smiling, her father said, "I can't believe you're abandoning us for a count. And not even Jewish." He was a tall, wiry man with a nose that was too long for his face. "How do you know he's a real count?"

"Sha!" her mother said, passing potatoes to Uncle Henry, who was always invited for Friday night dinner.

"Well, us hoi polloi usually want to see documents before we scrape and bow. Don't you think, Henry?" He waved a chicken-laden fork at Rebecca's uncle, a small man with the same light brown, wavy hair as Flo.

"I'd be happy with a family tree," Henry said.

"You always were the fussy one," said her father. Then to Rebecca, "I'm sure your uncle has a book where you can look up the count."

Henry was a high school history teacher with encyclopaedic interests and an extensive home library. "I'm flattered by your confidence in me, Mitch, but the count, himself, is the only one who might have such a book. Unless he comes from a very illustrious family."

"I'll bet the count's heard this one," her father said. "How can you tell a Polish airline?"

She gazed at her father, wondering whether telling jokes could be classified as an addiction. "How?"

"It's the only one with hair under its wing."

Her mother changed the subject. "Have you

heard from Nesha?" she asked, helping herself to some green beans.

"He's got a client who's keeping him busy," Rebecca said.

Her mother gave her the look that said, So, what does it all mean? Rebecca shrugged. Because she didn't know. There was something about Michael, some European charm she hadn't encountered before. She *was* impressed by the title. And the novel he was working on. Maybe she was attracted to artists, what could she say?

Later on, Rebecca found a parking spot on a quiet street lined with duplexes a few blocks north of St. Clair Avenue. Night had just fallen; the heat of the day was dissipating into the dark. A fresher air cooled her arms, lifting sweat from the back of her neck. It was still warm enough for her olive green cotton pants and little black top. She walked along the brightly lit sidewalk of Lawton Boulevard, past pretty lawns where end-of-summer geraniums, impatiens, and alyssum slept in the shadows. She could see Yonge Street up ahead.

She jaywalked across Yonge, threading her way through some cars slowing down for the light at St. Clair. She headed toward the red neon sign.

Fran's was a throwback to the fifties, with its high-backed padded booths, jukeboxes, and arborite tables. The waitresses tended to be dumpy, middle-aged women with bad perms and friendly dispositions.

Only a half-dozen tables were occupied when Rebecca stepped inside. Michael stood up from a booth partway down the restaurant, a confident arm raised in the air. She smiled and walked toward him. He looked out of place there, with his elegant taupe blazer and tanned skin. Too continental for Fran's, escargot to their chicken potpie. He was nursing a glass of white wine. She would never have thought of ordering wine at Fran's.

"I'm so glad you could come," he said, waiting for her to sit down opposite him in the booth.

He lifted an index finger and raised his head imperiously. A waitress appeared in a flash. Her round eyes fixed coquettishly on Michael, her dentures ajar, waiting for his word. He nodded slightly at Rebecca.

"I'll have an iced tea," she said.

"Yes, ma'am," the waitress said, managing another look at Michael before turning around and heading for the kitchen.

When the waitress had gone, he said, "You saw Natalka today. How was she?"

She didn't want to be rude and mention patient confidentiality, so she said, "She's holding her own. She's very brave."

He nodded absently. "Poles are known for their bravery. They often have nothing else. Will she be all right?"

The question was not new to her. Only this time she was stumped for an answer. She wasn't usually personally involved. "I don't know."

He seemed to wait for more, nodded again. "I'm sorry. It's not my business." He sipped his wine and studied her face, a smile playing on his lips. "You know, there's something about your face that looks Polish."

"Is that good?"

"Polish women are the most beautiful in Europe. Jewish women — they are the dark beauties of Poland."

Wildly flattered, but embarrassed, she said, "My mother was born in Warsaw but came here when she was a little girl."

"I knew it. I can see it in the cheekbones, the almond shape of your eyes."

He was still observing her when the waitress placed a tall glass of iced tea in front of her.

"Do you have children?" he asked.

"No."

"I have a son who looks like me. For this I'm both exhilarated and dismayed. Exhilarated because he will become me when I am gone. Dismayed because he didn't inherit his mother's nose."

"And where is his mother?"

"She remarried and moved to upstate New York."

She looked at the steady blue eyes and strong pointed chin. "I'm sure he must be very handsome." She felt swept up in a cross-cultural trance. She would never have said such a thing to a native Canadian. She was also not going to mention his hands, one of which was draped loosely around his wine glass.

"Does he live with you?" she asked.

He shook his head. "Edward's studying journalism in Ottawa. He's a very smart boy. Very talented. I don't say this just because I'm his father." He gave a sour little smile. "I miss him very much. Do you want to have children?"

The question caught her off guard. "I'd like to someday, yes."

"Was that question too personal? I'm sorry."

She politely dismissed the suggestion with a tiny wave of her hand.

"I find Canadians very shy. Poles are very frank with one other. We meet someone for the first time and in an hour we know everything about each other."

She grinned at him, charmed by his openness.

"I would certainly have been asked about my hands by now."

She sighed. "All right. You have remarkable hands. I've never seen hexadactyly outside a textbook. May I see?" She put her hand on the table palm up.

He placed his hand in hers, stretching out his six fingers with cool assurance. "It runs in the family."

"You have six toes too?"

He nodded.

Her other hand moved his fingers gently apart to check the spaces between. "What's unusual is that they're symmetrical. Often, hexadactyly — or poly-dactyly — means an extra thumb or an extra pinky finger. They usually look like an afterthought. Often they're surgically removed at birth. But you have the extra one in the middle so it's hard to tell unless you count. It looks completely normal. You must have a devilish time trying to find gloves."

"Shoes are worse."

She smiled, his warm hand still in hers. "Did you ever consider surgery on your feet?"

"No, Doctor. Luckily I can afford expensive shoes."

He bent forward over the table and turned his hand so that his fingers curled loosely around hers. "So why did you become a doctor?"

She sighed, choosing her words with care. "I was idealistic when I was young. I thought I could make a difference."

"And now?"

"I'm no longer young. And now I have to satisfy myself with small contributions. Delivering a baby. Discovering the root of someone's pain."

"Those are not small. If I could do what you do, I would very satisfied with my life. You belong to the most honourable profession."

"I'm not — Thank you," she said, trying to accept the compliment graciously. "And you? You aren't satisfied with your life? Writing is also an honourable profession."

"I write to try to resurrect my family. Poles have long memories. They live in the past, and I'm no exception. I've never gotten over the death of my parents, and with this novel, I try to find the secrets of my father's family.

"I didn't know you were writing about your family. Did your parents die in the war?"

"Surprisingly, they managed to survive the war. They died six months later. One of their own people betrayed them."

"What happened?" she said.

"Do you really want to hear?"

"I wouldn't ask if I didn't."

He took a breath. "Before the war, my parents, more my mother really, managed an estate for a very wealthy family — they're called magnates in Poland. My parents lived very well in a beautiful large house in exchange for managing the estate, which was really a huge farm. My Aunt Klara and her family also lived with us. It was like a feudal system. So — magnates on top, then my parents, then beneath them, some other families who were in charge of the peasants working in the fields. Halina's parents were one of those families. This is how I know her."

"Her parents worked for your parents."

"They all worked for the magnate, but it was a hierarchy. Then the war came. My parents suffered, but they managed to survive. Aunt Klara was taken away in a transport — she had the bad luck to be in town on market day when the Nazis arrived to deport people. She came back after the war, but her husband and two sons had died in a camp. Meanwhile, I'd spent five years in the forests fighting with the partisans. Only half the estate was still standing, the land ravaged, but my parents were lucky. Until the Soviets took over.

"The winter after the war, we had nothing. A few vegetables — seed potatoes mostly — and we barely lived off those. People were getting typhus from the water. I was twenty. Skinny as a rake from constant starvation. But I was happy just to be home with my family." He stopped suddenly. "But you don't want to hear all this."

"I'm very interested. Please go on."

"One day, a Soviet delegation arrived at our estate and arrested us for collaborating with the Nazis. I'd spent every day for five years risking my life fighting the Nazis. The charges were absurd, but it was no use. Someone had denounced us. I didn't know who. That was all it took in those days. For someone to say we were anti-Communist. They even said we'd given out anti-government leaflets. Completely false. But it didn't matter. Of course, with us gone, it was easier to nationalize the estate." His gaze drifted away.

"And then?" she asked.

"Then they forced us into a boxcar on a train filled with people they were trying to get rid of. Men who had fought with the *Armia Krajowa*, especially. People who owned land, workers who complained, anyone who had been denounced by a neighbour. The train was unheated and the winter was unbearably cold. It was mid-February and we travelled east for three weeks in an unheated train. Many people died during the journey. I'll never forget how cold it was. When we got to the camp —" He shook his head. "I can't describe it ... it was hell on earth. My parents were dead within a year."

He finally let go of her hand and picked up his glass, gulping down his wine. Raised his finger for the waitress again.

"They took you to Siberia?"

He nodded. "It took me five years to escape. I was barely alive when I came back. Aunt Klara nursed me back to health. And I saw Halina again. She was visiting her parents for the summer with her little girl. She'd been very fond of my father."

"Did you ever find out who denounced you?"

He finished another glass of wine. "I was in hiding. If I went around asking questions, the secret police would've found me. Not a day goes by that I don't curse him. But life goes on." The lines around his mouth hardened and he looked more his age.

"How did you end up in Canada?"

He leaned his elbows on the table and made a steeple with his fingers. "Halina told me that Janek had made a lot of money in Canada. She wrote to him and told him I was coming and that it was his patriotic duty to give me a job. She remembered my parents — especially my father. She was working for Orbis by then, so it wasn't hard for her to get me the papers I needed to leave the country. I had nothing to stay for. If Janek welcomed me, fine. If not, I had survived worse."

"So Halina, a card-carrying Communist, helped you escape the Communist regime."

"Politics are a farce in Poland. She's a Communist for convenience, not ideology."

"So what do you do for Janek?" she said, avoiding the subject of the strike.

He smiled. "I'm his social secretary. I make sure his meetings go smoothly. That nobody leaves mad."

"I'll bet that's not easy."

He shrugged. "I've learned a lot about business from him over the years. He's a hard man; not many people could do what he does."

"Maybe they have more scruples." She regretted the words as soon as they left her mouth. "I'm sorry, I've been listening to the radio. The strikers are very angry."

"They have a valid point of view," he said, sipping his wine. "But they wouldn't have jobs if he didn't create the company. They've been making good wages, supporting their families for years on the money he paid them." He rubbed his eyes. "Yes, yes, I know. He was too anxious to get his company off the ground. Some things were overlooked. Safety issues. Things will have to change. I wouldn't want to be in his position."

Enough about Janek. "How do find time to write?" she said.

His steady blue eyes watched her. "I make time. I stopped bringing my work home with me. Janek's not so happy about that, but he likes the idea of the book so he stays off my back. Now it's like a drug for me. When I'm writing my book, it takes me very far away. I go back more than two hundred years: 1750 is just yesterday. The people I'm writing about are historical characters; they actually existed. The one I'm most interested in is the last king of Poland, Stanislaw Poniatowski. My mother always told me that our family line goes back to him. His mother was a Czartoryski — one of the leading Polish families — and they will all have a role in the book. They are more real to me than most of the people I meet. I don't usually tell people this," he leaned over the table, "but there's a secret at the heart of the story, a wonderful, terrible secret. What's important is that it contradicts written history, and my publisher is excited about that."

"Contradicts written history?"

"I've discovered something quite extraordinary. Rather by accident while I was doing research on the king. He was a sensitive artistic man who loved women. And they loved him back. He had a host of mistresses, and that was my problem. They all had children by him. I knew one of them was my ancestor. So I got the list of them and checked them until I was blue in the face, but they were all accounted for. None of them was my great-great-great-grandmother. So I developed a theory. More than a theory. I believe it's true." He smiled sheepishly.

"It's not important to the world. Just to me. And the scholars who'll have to rewrite the textbooks. That's what I started off with. To shed light on my family, shake the family tree and find some royal apples. But after all my reading, I've found something different, a new world. It's their innocence that appeals to me. Despite the wars, the corruption, their world was blameless compared to ours. They could never imagine what the world has become. In 1750 there was still hope. That's what we've lost. Hope."

She hardly knew what to say to such pessimism. He had certainly seen too much.

"Surely there's always hope."

He gave a small, tired smile. "Yes, of course. There must always be hope. We tell ourselves that in desperation because how else could we go on. But two hundred years ago, people were just waking up. Imagine a child entering puberty: he looks around and everything is changed. Suddenly he begins to understand things. This was the Enlightenment. Our modern sensibilities were born then, the idea that everyone has the right to life and happiness."

"That sounds very democratic for a count," she said, teasing him with a smile.

"Janek is the one who tells people I'm a count. It's good for business. He wants to impress the people on Bay Street with my name on the board of directors. It gives him a certain cachet."

He needs it, she thought.

"He's quite anxious for me to finish the book. I'm working on the last chapter. Once it's published he'll revel in the publicity. He's very conscious of how people see him, and he wants to show all the snobs in the financial world he's just as good as they are. Better."

No, she thought, *I won't tell him I detest the man.* Instead, she said, "Is your publisher waiting for it too?"

"Yes, but before he gives me a contract, he insists I show him proof of my version of history. Halina's brought something from Poland that'll give me crucial information."

"What is it?"

He gave her a cagey smile. "A gift that Poniatowski gave to my great-great-great-grandmother. I'll be happy to show it to you when Halina gives it to me."

After leaving Fran's they strolled along St. Clair toward Yonge Street.

"Where did you park?" he asked.

"On the other side," she peered across Yonge, "a few streets over."

"I'll walk you to your car."

"Where did you park?" She suspected he had parked in one of the nearby lots.

"Doesn't matter," he said.

He took her elbow in his hand as if they were crossing an elegant ballroom and guided her across the street on the green light. She felt curiously underdressed beside him in her cotton pants and top, even with the lacy black sweater she'd thrown over her shoulders. He had let go of her elbow and every now and then as they walked along the side street his arm bumped softly against hers.

"Do you mind if I ask you — how did your husband die?"

She glanced sideways at him. Perhaps she had overrated openness. "He was diabetic. His kidneys failed."

"I'm so sorry," he said. "When?"

"A year ago. In two weeks it'll be a year."

"Was he a lot older?"

"He was thirty-three."

They walked in silence for a few minutes.

"What was he like?"

"He was an artist. He had a very good eye."

"He painted?"

"He used oils mostly. He was starting to work with acrylics — they dry instantly and you've got to be fast with them. He knew he was running out of time."

"You still miss him. A year is very little. A year is no time at all."

"People expect me to have moved on. They think a year is enough."

He took her arm and looped it through his as if it were the most natural thing in the world. "People who haven't gone through it don't understand. This kind of pain doesn't go away."

She stopped and turned to him, her breath suddenly ragged. "It *has* to go away. I can't live like this."

The blue of his eyes had turned navy, the ends of his mouth stiffened. He lifted his hand and stroked her hair. "Time will help. Time will dull the pain. And Sarah. You're lucky you have Sarah to help you through it."

Tears sprang to her eyes. Idiotic tears. "I can't talk to her about it. I think she blames me. I didn't catch it in time. The diabetes." She swiped viciously at a tear sliding down her cheek.

The same hand that had stroked her hair now touched her back and tentatively pressed her forward into an embrace. A cautious, unaccustomed movement, as if it had been a long time since he'd held a woman. In the middle of the dark sidewalk, his arms stretched around hers, uncertain and protective at the same time.

"It wasn't your fault," he said. "You shouldn't blame yourself."

chapter eight

Michael took St. Clair Avenue home. It was a fair distance from his neck of the woods, but traffic was light after eleven and he was exuberant. Rebecca had felt so right in his arms, formidable yet diffident, vulnerable, melancholy, but authoritative. A bundle of contradictions. The knowing way she had examined his six-fingered hand without revulsion, the attention she'd paid to his words, the sad light in her wise brown eyes. And he was embarrassed to say it, but her Jewishness tantalized him. He had known beautiful Jewish women in his time, but none he would have considered for himself. None who had intrigued him enough to cross over the boundaries of culture and religion. Not that he was religious at all. He never went to church, not even on the holidays. He hadn't asked her about her faith. Yet he felt the chasm between them; he was ready, no eager, to leap across.

She was much younger than he, but she seemed to find him attractive. He was still in good shape, he mused.

He was on the wrong side of fifty, but he still had all his hair, and though he had filled out since his younger days, he had kept slim and watched what he ate. Yes, she could find him desirable, her eyes showed him that.

As he drove along St. Clair past Dufferin, his nose began to twitch. The stench was coming. It rose in the air like a spectre, wraith-like at first, blocks from the source. Then, at Keele Street, *wham!* The full fury of the smell infiltrated the car, his nostrils, his brain, as he passed the stockyards. During the day the long, low wooden buildings, like cattle cars, stretched for what seemed miles along the south side of St. Clair. But at night, the stink of blood and sinew, the shadows between streetlamps, turned them into the desultory trains that rolled through wartime Poland filled with people destined for death. He remembered walking with his father near the estate early in the war, both wary as a train lumbered past, his father whispering about the inevitability of human cargo. They were blessedly ignorant then of the train that would take them away after the war, deep into the Siberian wasteland where Michael would watch both his parents die. He had been pulled back to his youth this week with Halina's arrival. His past was never far behind him, but he found himself sinking unwillingly into moments he had quite forgotten. The manor house outside Kraków, 1940. His father beaming as Natalka was baptized.

The Nazis had outlawed public baptisms for two years, since their occupation, so just a handful of people had been invited to the secret ceremony. The war was encroaching steadily from the city, and it was prudent to be furtive.

His mother and father standing in as godparents. Halina with her luscious blonde hair and tasteful city suit gazing in worship at Natalka, who fidgeted and whimpered in her godfather's arms during the whole ceremony. Janek, the baby's father, was barely mentioned. He had joined the Polish Home Army shortly after the invasion and no one had heard from him since. The baby was nearly a year old, too big for the christening dress that had been handed down from Aunt Klara's daughter. So Michael's mother had one of the peasant women sew a christening dress out of a lacy shawl for her. A silken wisp of Natalka's hair strayed from under the bonnet as she wriggled and sobbed in the arms that held her.

The priest, dressed in his alb and chasuble, paid no attention to the fuss. A fringe of white hair encircled his scalp He spoke slowly, pronouncing every word but without expression: "Natalka, what do you ask of the Church of God?"

Michael wondered if the priest knew about his father and Halina. If he did, he made no indication. Michael glanced at his mother. Her thick brown hair was pinned at the nape of her neck. She was still beautiful, her features delicate, like his own. Her large grey eyes didn't stray from the priest; betrayed nothing. Michael couldn't fathom it. Why didn't she fight?

Michael's father answered, "*Fidem.*" Faith.

What is faith to you, Michael wondered, marvelling at his father's composure. His nerve.

The priest traced the sign of the cross with his thumb on the baby's forehead and chest, saying, "*Accipe signum Crucis tam in fronte, quam in corde ...* Receive the sign of the cross upon your forehead and upon your heart. And this sign of the holy Cross which we put upon your forehead, do thou, foul spirit, never dare to violate. Through Christ our Lord. Amen. Evil spirit, get thee gone, for God's judgment is upon thee."

If only the devils that were abroad could be gotten rid of so easily, Michael thought.

"Natalka, do you renounce Satan?"

His father answered, "*Abrenuntio*." I do renounce him.

"And all his works?"

"*Abrenuntio*."

"And all his pomps?"

"*Abrenuntio*."

"Natalka, do you believe in God the Father, almighty creator of heaven and earth?"

His father answered, "*Credo*." I do believe.

"Do you believe in Jesus Christ, his only son, our Lord, who was born into this world and who suffered for us?"

"*Credo*."

The priest took Natalka from her godfather's arms and held her over the baptismal font. The baby gave a mournful cry. Then the priest took the sacred water and poured it three times over her head in the form of a cross.

"Natalka, I baptize thee in the name of the Father and of the Son and of the Holy Ghost."

With his thumb, the priest anointed the baby's forehead in the form of a cross.

"Peace be with you. Amen."

But peace never came. Foul spirits had arrived in German uniforms and brought their own version of hell. A sense of foreboding hung over the quiet celebration in his parents' house after the service. Halina's parents bowing and scraping to his, nibbling carefully on the food laid out on the banquet table, though they were hungry. Halina knew who to latch on to. Everyone was suffering, but Michael's parents, who managed the estate, could demand their share of eggs and milk and potatoes from the peasants to avoid starvation. Halina had always known which side her bread was buttered on. She'd arrived with an eight-month-old baby and immediately gravitated toward the estate manager. But why had it been so important for her to baptize Natalka? She'd never been a religious woman, that was obvious. And she was putting everyone at risk with the request. If someone had had the inclination to betray them, they could all have been dragged away to be shot. Michael remembered how his father had made a point of paying more attention to the baby than to her mother, but Michael understood (as did everyone else there) that in the heart of the night his father would share Halina's bed.

Michael found it hard to forgive her. She had saved his life later when he'd been forced to flee and live in the forest. But she had humiliated his mother. She hadn't done that by herself. His father had a history of other women. Drinking, gambling, and women, a prerogative of the aristocrat, money or no. The only difference between her and the others was that Michael knew Halina. He would have to work harder at forgetting the past. It did no one any good to dredge up old grievances. Life went on.

He drove down Baby Point Road toward home. The street was perfectly quiet at this hour, a few lights on behind curtains. As he pulled into his driveway he noticed a car with vintage fins from the sixties parked in front of his house. If he hadn't been so distracted, it would have raised alarm bells. He opened the garage door using his remote, then drove in.

The air was brisk at midnight compared to the balmy day. He hoped the sun would shine tomorrow so that his guests could go swimming. He would ply them with wine; that would warm them up in case the weather didn't cooperate. He was about to fit his key into the lock when steps sounded behind him. He swung around, taken by surprise.

"Who's there?" he called out.

A tall man moved up his walk toward him in the dark.

"What do you want?" He turned back to the door, frantically trying to push his key in when the man spoke.

"Hello, Mr. Oginski."

The key moved. The door was unlocked. Now what? If he opened the door the man could force his way inside. Michael would stand his ground.

"What do you want?"

The man was tall but thin, in a black T-shirt with a plaid shirt thrown over. His face was too large for the rest of him, with a pasty complexion, curly dark hair beneath the porch light.

"I know it's late, Mr. O, but I been waiting. I need to talk to you. I'm Claude Simard." He said this as if it would mean something to Michael.

When Michael didn't respond, he said, "I'm the one wrote the letter. I been waiting a long time."

Michael remembered the letter, but it had been addressed to his office. How had he found out where Michael lived?

"It's a little late for visitors," Michael said. "Why don't you come back tomorrow?"

The man began to cough. Despite his size, he wasn't in good shape. His large white face turned red and disfigured as he continued to cough. He pulled a handkerchief out of his pants pocket and held it over his mouth.

It wasn't an act. The man was a miner and, as Michael recalled from the letter, unwell. He hesitated, but Simard continued to sputter into his handkerchief. Chiding himself for paranoia, he led the man inside, bringing him to the kitchen where he poured a glass of water. The man gulped it down and finally stopped coughing. Wiped his face with the handkerchief. His hazel eyes shone with effort.

"You all right?"

"Happens all the time," he said. "Can't work no more. On disability. That's why I'm here."

It occurred to Michael that the coughing fit had been very convenient and now he'd let the man into the house.

Simard stuffed the handkerchief into a back pocket and studied Michael. "You know, I used to be a sturdy guy, muscles in my arms and a bit of a beer belly here." He patted his flat stomach. "But I have to tell you, Mr. Oginski. I'm dying. It's my lungs."

So here it was. Right on his doorstep. Finally. "I'm sorry," Michael said.

"Sorry ain't enough. I can't support my family on Workman's Comp." The man's eyes widened in anger, accused Michael. "I need *help*."

"Look, I don't think you understand. There's not much I can do, Mr. ..."

The man banged his hand down on the kitchen table. "You can start by telling the truth! All them years the company lied to us. They told us the air was safe. We was going down into that mine day in, day out, year after year. And every minute we was breathing in that air, it was killing us. I'm a dead man and the company killed me."

The man's eyes burned in his head, and Michael felt ashamed under their glare. "Nobody knew in those days," he said. "We were learning as we went along."

"They knew ten years ago!" the man said. "They knew twenty years ago. They just wouldn't spend the money to put down another shaft. Right from the start all he wanted was to get stinking rich. He put the shaft right through the ore deposit so when we crushed it and brought it up, we breathed in all the dust. No other company did that. You must know. You're supposed to dig the shaft alongside the deposit so the workers aren't right in there with the dust and crap. How much would it eat into his profits to put in another shaft? How much is a man's life worth?"

Michael looked away. There was nothing he could say. The man may have had a point, but he, himself, had had little say in Baron's business, let alone the design or running of the mine. When he'd first starting working for Janek he'd spent some time up north with prospectors, checking out claims. But for over twenty years, since they had hit it big with uranium, Michael had worked in Toronto in a cushy office far from the mines and the miners. How was he going to get this man out of his house?

Simard tilted his head on an angle. "You don't remember me, do you? I was one of the juniors at the union table years ago when I could still stomach that kind of stuff. At the King Eddy Hotel. Jeez, my eyes bugged out when I got in there. I'm a real small-town guy. Never seen anything like it. Those chandeliers! Never seen so many mine managers snarling neither. They were real hard-asses. All except you. You were the only one that looked human."

That was exactly why Michael hadn't lasted in negotiations with the union. Janek insisted on hard noses when dealing with the United Steelworkers. Don't budge an inch. They'll take a mile. Janek usually won. Even when he lost, he won. Like when he had to pay the workers more, the government coughed up the difference because they needed the uranium to sell to the American military. Janek managed to profit even from the Cold War. He liked to say he had a horseshoe up his ass. Crude but accurate.

"But maybe I was wrong about you," the man said. "You were just as bad as they were. Maybe worse. You knew better, but you didn't do nothing."

Michael looked into the man's large white face, wishing he could say something that would make him go away.

"I'm desperate," the man said. "You're my only hope." He looked around the kitchen, through the entrance to the dining room. "Nice house you got. Lots of nice stuff. Do you know what it's like, not to know if you can feed your family tomorrow? You've got to help me. I'm not leaving till you help me."

The phone rang shrilly, sudden in the tense air. Michael didn't know who was calling him at midnight, but he was grateful for the distraction. The man's hazel eyes stayed on him as he moved gingerly toward the far wall to reach the phone.

"Michael? *To jest* Michael?" A woman's hurried voice.

He had to switch gears to answer in Polish. "*Tak … Halina?*"

"I have something to tell you," she said in Polish. "Very important. Wait, I hear something. Just a minute." She left the phone for an instant. "Can't talk now. I will call later." She hung up.

"Yes." Michael continued in English into the drone of the dial tone. "You're coming over now? I understand. Yes, of course, that's fine. I'll be waiting." He hung up the receiver with a great show of concern.

"I'm sorry," he said to the man. "You'll have to go."

He drew his wallet from his pants pocket and peeled off four twenty-dollar bills. He held them out to the man. "I'll talk to Baron. Can't promise you anything."

The man stared at the money, then at Michael until he became very uncomfortable.

"You think you can buy me off like that?"

chapter nine

Rebecca was surprised at how easy it had been to slide behind the wheel of the Camaro and drive away as if it were 1969 again. Funny how the car brought it all back: planning out their wedding, her last year of medical school, David setting up a studio in their new apartment. Life was just beginning. The Camaro had been a present from her in-laws. David drove her down to class in it. The car hadn't changed much, a bit of wear on the driver's seat. Only everything else had changed.

She glanced at Sarah beside her in the flowered cotton skirt and blouse. She also looked the same, but Rebecca knew better, recognized the painful rearranging of a psyche through some mirror image. Another reason to stay away — avoid herself in Sarah's eyes.

Rebecca had arrived at her mother-in-law's house early Saturday afternoon, wearing a bathing suit under her shorts and top. She hadn't gone swimming for two years and had felt a stab of elation just pulling the suit on, the remnant of memory from carefree days on Georgian Bay. Halina was sleeping off a late night with Janek. Rebecca had asked no questions, didn't really want to know. So the three of them went on without her. Sarah said she was tired — had worn herself out baking poppy seed cookies to take with them, the perfect guest — and would Rebecca drive them to Michael's house. The two-seater Jag was not an option. Natalka climbed into the back of the Camaro.

Rebecca drove west along St. Clair, the afternoon sun blazing down on the roof of the car. She turned on the vents and opened her window a bit, waiting for directions from her navigator.

Sarah opened up the orange Perly's map book on her lap. "You can stay on St. Clair all the way to Jane, then make a left turn. It's just a few blocks south of there." She opened her window part way. "Is it too windy?" she asked Natalka, half-turning to the back.

"No, it's fine."

Rebecca glanced in her rearview mirror. Natalka had pinned her white hair up in the back, but some loose strands flew around her face. Their eyes met. "It's *fine*," she said to Rebecca's unasked question.

Shop followed shop along the straight line of St. Clair Avenue, where so many Italians had emigrated after the war that Toronto was home to the largest community outside of Italy. Colourful, confident stores laid end to end sold wedding dresses, shoes, fabrics, leather goods, and pizza; apartments ranged above. All the way to Keele Street, then a gradual diminishing of style, a shift of ethnicity. Car lots, gas stations, wider spaces with less purpose, a coffee shop with aimless clientele.

Then, without warning, the stench. Like being thrown into water. Rebecca gasped for air. She could hardly believe it could get worse, but as they drove it got harder to breathe.

Sarah flipped open the Perly's and studied the page. "The stockyards," she said, holding one hand over her nose and mouth.

They both rolled up their windows, and Rebecca turned off the vent that brought air in from the outside. It suddenly got very hot in the car. She looked in the mirror to see Natalka holding a handkerchief over her nose and mouth.

They passed Canada Packers on the north side of the street, a red-bricked warehouse of a building. More meat packers on the south side, all the same square boxes of brick, white trucks parked in front.

"Must be those," Sarah said, pointing to the south side of the street.

Rebecca noticed her mother-in-law stiffen and followed her finger. To their left, a hundred feet in from the street and fenced in by a tower of chain link, ran an endless stretch of what looked like red, oversized garage doors. They so closely resembled cattle cars that she could imagine Sarah's distress, the wartime memories they must be unlocking. Sarah never talked about those years, but Rebecca had learned from David how painful they had been.

Were the stockyard doors painted red so the blood wouldn't show? The entranceways to death went on and on for half a mile or so, while Rebecca drove the car over ancient criss-crossed railway tracks embedded in the road. They must've brought the animals to their final destination long before the new tracks were laid down on the south side of the stockyards, more convenient to bring them directly to the slaughterhouses.

"Turn left at Jane," Sarah said through the hand over her mouth. "The next lights."

They passed plain semi-detached houses, their porches littered with cartons and worn-out sofas, some pots

festooned with petunias. The smell dissipated and they
both opened their windows again to chase out the stale
air. Shops began on the east side, became quite smart and
trendy suddenly. Rebecca wondered where an elegant
man like Michael would live in such a neighbourhood.

"It'll be the next street on your right," Sarah said.

Rebecca slowed down and searched for the sign:
Baby Point Road. The prominent family that had lent
the street its name was French, the "ba" pronounced
with a short vowel, like sheep bleating. One James Baby
became a judge in the eighteenth century, later commanded a militia in the war of 1812, according to her
book on historic Toronto. Over the years he bought and
was granted thousands of acres in Upper Canada, as it
was called then, including this area in the west end.

Rebecca made a right turn into an enclave of large,
luxurious houses, of which there had been no hint from
the main street. She could have been in Rosedale, only the
street was wider and the houses set on larger lots. The
road wound further and further, a treasure trove of houses, no two alike, past a centre boulevard that split the
street and led them down a road where the homes must
have backed onto the ravine, because suddenly nothing
could be seen beyond them but sky. The Humber River
would be coursing through the valley of that ravine,
where, according to her book, an ancient Iroquois village
once stood, the southern end of a portage that linked
Lake Ontario to Lake Simcoe and Georgian Bay.

"Almost there," Sarah said as the car crawled
along. "It's that one."

They stopped in front of a many-gabled house that
looked as though it had been plucked from the English
countryside. The rough limestone walls were studded
with mullioned windows that caught the sun in their
leaded panes. There was a wide chimney and a sweep-

ing roof. Rebecca felt as if she'd gone back a few hundred years, though the house was probably built in the 1940s like the others on the street.

The three of them walked along the flagstone to the front door carrying their various bags stuffed with towels and bathing suits.

"What a beautiful house!" said Sarah.

"Like from a fairy tale," Natalka said.

Rebecca rang the doorbell. They waited. And waited. She rang again.

She looked behind them at the street. Not a soul stirred.

"Maybe he's already in the back," she said.

A high wooden fence surrounded the backyard, an entrance gate near the side of the house. Rebecca played with the latch and found it was unlocked. She swung the gate open and led the others in.

Bushes of deep pink phlox grew against the stone wall, their airy blooms nodding forward, touching the women's legs as they passed. The edge of the swimming pool winked amid the glistening white concrete. Rebecca caught a heady whiff of chlorine, a smell she always associated with happier times in bygone pools.

"Michael!" Rebecca called out. She caught Sarah's look of surprise at her use of his first name. No doubt she would put it down to Canadian familiarity. Rebecca would have to explain later.

The water in the oblong pool was a pale turquoise, the surface dappled by a wisp of breeze that made the sun bearable.

"Michael!" Rebecca sang out.

Stepping toward the house, she could see through the window that the kitchen was empty. A silence fell, the breeze stilled, and the rays of sun blazed down on them without mercy.

Rebecca turned toward the water, suddenly smooth as glass. A reflection there drew her, only it wasn't a reflection. Could it be a shadow? She squinted through the haze of sun and saw an outline at the bottom of the pool.

"Oh my God!" she gasped.

Kicking off her sandals, she took a deep breath, then jumped feet first into the water. It was a shock, the sudden change of dimension, silent water pressing in on all sides.

She kicked her feet frantically until she reached him: Michael lay face down on the floor of the pool wearing blue bathing trunks and a pair of goggles. His hair was waving in the water. She grabbed it in her fist to lift his head up — his face was blank, his mouth open. She looped an arm under his and lifted his body. With her free arm she began to stroke hard, pushing the water away. She wasn't sure she would have the strength, but she kicked and kicked her feet, shoving the water aside, and found herself shooting up in the direction of the surface. It had only been seconds, but her lungs were empty and screaming for air. She had to keep going, she had to get him out. She only needed to surface before her lungs burst.

She sensed, rather than heard, a nearby breach of the water. Someone else breaking the surface, creating waves.

Suddenly an arm reached for her, a slender but determined arm pulled her up into the world again. Sarah.

Rebecca gasped for air.

"Grab the pole!" Sarah shouted.

With her free hand, Rebecca lunged at the pole Natalka was balancing over the water. She let herself be towed into the shallow end of the pool, Michael hooked under her arm.

The three of them struggled to get him out of the water. Sarah and Natalka each took a shoulder, Rebecca carried him by the feet. They managed to get him to the stairs of the shallow end of the pool then lifted him step by step, trying to keep from dragging him along the concrete. Finally they deposited him gently by the edge of the pool.

She stood coughing and gasping for air. The sky was a perfect blue. She had never seen it so blue before.

"Are you crazy?" Sarah cried. "What are you, a cowboy — risking your life like that? You could've been killed!"

Sarah's dripping clothes and hair stuck to her body, her head small as a cat's.

Rebecca's chest heaved while she tried to catch her breath. She could only gesture toward Michael like a trophy.

"He's dead anyway!" Sarah said.

Rebecca shook her head, crouched over him. "Michael!" she shouted, breathless. "Can you hear me?"

There was no response.

"Call for help!" she said to Sarah.

Sarah hurried to the house.

Rebecca rolled him onto his side, pressing down on his back to push out any water in his lungs. *A,B,C,* she remembered. Airway, breathing, circulation. She turned him onto his back again, then placed one hand beneath his head to tilt it up and lift his chin, a manoeuvre that would remove his tongue from the back of his throat if it were blocking his airway. She noticed a dark bruise at the edge of his jaw. What had happened? A heart attack? The sculpted mouth was gone; only thin blue lips remained. She ignored the goggles, leaned her ear to his face. Was he breathing? Was his chest rising and falling?

No sound. No movement.

Kneeling beside him, she pinched his nostrils together. She took a quick, conscious breath, let it out again, bracing herself for the intimacy. She was glad of the goggles as she bent over, then covered his lips with hers, breathing into his mouth at a normal rate. That was when she tasted it. Alcohol. Nothing particular, like scotch or rum. It was probably vodka, the drink of choice if you didn't want people to smell liquor on your breath from a conversational distance. The whole scenario suddenly made more sense. Adrenaline still buzzed through her chest, only now it fuelled her anger while she breathed into his mouth. *You stupid bastard*, she thought. *Who are you anyway? I don't know the first thing about you. Except that you've thrown your life away.*

Okay, she thought, *okay*. Concentrate. Breathe. Wait a beat for him to breathe out. Breathe into his mouth. A beat to breathe out. This is how a person lives. A breath in, a breath out. So simple. Yet every cell in the body requires it. It only looks simple. Breath in, breath out. So that oxygen can infuse the blood to course through the organs and keep the engine of the body running. This is how we stay alive.

She placed her fingers against his neck, checking for a pulse at his carotid artery. Christ! Nothing!

Okay. Chest compressions. She counted two fingers from the bottom of his sternum, then positioned the heel of her right hand there, the heel of her left hand over her right, interlacing the fingers. Strong, smooth compression with the left hand, faster than one per second, the heel of the right in constant contact with the sternum. Pump, pump, pump, pump. She was his heart now, his only hope, if he had any hope left. It didn't look good. His skin was clammy, taking on a waxy look. But one never knew, with drowning victims, when they would suddenly sputter back to life, water erupting from their mouths. She had no way of knowing how long he had been in the water. She looked at his lifeless face, the goggles that gave it a surreal sense of normalcy, the wet brown hair flattened to his cheeks.

She kept pumping, breathing into his mouth, pumping, breathing into his mouth. After about ten minutes she asked, "Do either of you know CPR?"

"I'm sorry," Sarah said. Then, "I'm going to take off his goggles, all right?" She asked this softly, the way one spoke to an unreasonable child whose behaviour was unpredictable. "I can't stand looking at them."

Rebecca glanced at the goggles for the first time. "Speedo" was stamped on the plastic piece between the eyes. Upside down.

Sarah carefully drew them up over his head.

Rebecca lifted one of his eyelids. His pupil was dilated. It was over.

She suddenly became aware of the sharp concrete against her skin. She pulled her wet top off over her bathing suit and stuffed in under her knees.

A siren approached in the distance, its urgent wail incongruous in the perfect afternoon. Sarah ran to the gate to direct them.

A minute later she was leading in two firemen in blue short sleeves carrying portable medical equipment.

"Okay, ma'am, we'll take over," one young man said to Rebecca, positioning himself over Michael to continue the procedure.

She sat back on her haunches to get out of the way. "He's gone," she said, glancing at Sarah.

"Let us be the judge of that," said the second man.

"I'm a doctor," she said, with resignation. "His pupils are fixed and dilated."

The first man continued the chest compressions while the other nodded his acknowledgement to her, then took Michael's blood pressure.

"We have to keep going until we get him to the hospital, Doctor."

"I understand," she said.

She stood up and wavered on her feet, dizzy from the stress, the heat, the shock of death. Exhaustion suddenly hit her like a wall. She couldn't move.

Two paramedics rushed into the backyard carrying a gurney. The firemen briefed them, but she couldn't hear through the noise of static in her head. It was as if she were tuned in to a radio on the fritz. She watched them heave Michael onto the gurney, while the fireman continued the CPR.

"What's happen?" A plump, grey-haired woman in an apron came running into the backyard. "Oh, Jesus!" She crossed herself, then her hands flew to her face and strings of Polish issued from her mouth in a wail.

Rebecca glanced at Sarah, hoping to get a translation, but her mother-in-law sighed with fatigue.

Instead, Sarah asked in English, "Are you a neighbour?"

"Just across street." She waved her hand toward the gate, then put her palm flat against her cheek in the universal gesture of woe. Her blue eyes never left Michael.

"How this happen?" she said. "I just here this morning. Bring food. I here every day bring food. He great man. *Great* man."

"It was probably an accident," Sarah said.

"Poor Edek! The son! He has son. Will be all alone now."

The paramedics were strapping Michael to the gurney, preparing to leave while the fireman kept pumping, pumping on his chest.

"You should take care of yourself, Doctor," one of the firemen said to Rebecca. "You're looking pale."

The paramedics started pushing the gurney toward the gate.

"Take her in the house," the fireman directed at Sarah. "Get a blanket for her — wrap her up before she goes into shock."

That was when Rebecca realized she was shivering.

Sarah put an arm around her waist and led her toward the house. The Polish woman followed the paramedics out of the yard. Sarah opened the French door into the kitchen and prodded Rebecca inside.

"Sit down. I'll go find a blanket."

Natalka followed with their bags.

Rebecca stared at the honey-coloured wooden cupboards, the oak floor. She could see Michael sitting in a chair at the small oak table. He was lifting a glass of vodka and toasting her. *Better luck next time*, he was saying, his sculpted lips smiling, his eyes alight.

"You are all right?" Natalka said.

"I'm very thirsty."

Rebecca stepped toward the sink and opened the logical cupboard to her right. In front of a row of drinking glasses stood a small crystal glass that looked like it belonged in a bar. She reached behind it and picked up a glass.

"I will do that," Natalka said. "You sit."

Rebecca's legs wobbled beneath her as she headed for a chair. Natalka handed her the glass. Water had never tasted so good.

Sarah came back with a maroon quilt. "Take off your things — they're all wet. Did you bring some other clothes?"

"Just underwear."

Her arm around Rebecca's waist, Sarah led her into the small bathroom down the hall. "Do you need some help?"

Rebecca shook her head and closed the door. She pulled off the wet shorts and bathing suit and wrapped a towel around her body. Then she caught herself in the mirror. Her dark hair was drying in frizzy patches around her white face. Dark circles pulled her eyes into her head. She had to lie down.

She tugged on the dry underpants and bra over her damp skin. Still shivering, she pulled the quilt over her shoulders.

Natalka was speaking Polish on the phone in the kitchen when Rebecca emerged from the bathroom. Probably telling Halina the bad news. Her voice rose in sudden agitation. Halina was taking it badly.

Rebecca followed the hall to a wainscotted study, where a desk stood by the window; behind it, a flowered chesterfield faced the fireplace. She lay down, enveloping herself in the quilt.

A great numbness descended on her, the kind she remembered from her internship when she'd gone without sleep for twenty straight hours full tilt at the emerg. David had tucked her in when she'd finally stumbled in the door of their small two-room flat. They lived in the married residence of the Mount Sinai Hospital then. It had been the happiest time of her life — too much to do, maybe, but the sense of accomplishment, the excitement of adapting everything she'd learned to treat real people, the importance of the work, and of course, David. None of it would've meant anything without him. Everything was possible with David beside her. No. That line of reasoning went nowhere. The implications were too barren to contemplate.

She dozed on and off. David knelt beside her, his flaming red hair and beard trembling near her face. The hair turned brown and became Michael's. He was leaning over her, trying to tell her something, his eyes blank and glassy. His mouth was moving but she couldn't hear what he was saying. Suddenly she was conscious of sound, a filament of noise that rolled out without turning into words. The noise was pulling her into consciousness. She resisted, but a man's voice insinuated itself.

"She's very tired," she heard Sarah say. "I can answer your questions."

Rebecca opened her eyes to find a uniformed policeman in the doorway of the room. She sat up, every muscle in her back complaining.

"You're Dr. Temple?"

She blinked, trying to focus.

"I'm sorry to disturb you, Doctor, I'm Constable Tiziano. I'm afraid I have bad news. Mr. Oginski was pronounced dead at the hospital."

She closed her eyes. She had known he was dead, had refused to accept it.

"Do you mind answering some questions?" He waited until she nodded, then came around to stand in front of the fireplace where she could see him. He was a stocky thirty, his round torso outlined beneath the blue uniform shirt.

"Did you see him fall into the pool?"

"He was lying on the bottom when we arrived."

The constable scribbled in a small notebook. "Do you know if he had any alcohol to drink today?"

The paramedics must've passed on their suspicions. The cop leaned on one hip, non-judgmental, a gatherer of data. Bloodless.

"I smelled it when I was trying to resuscitate him."

"A bad combination," the cop was saying, "alcohol and swimming. Three-quarters of drowning victims have had too much to drink. Did Mr. Oginski have a drinking problem?"

"I didn't really know him well enough to say." She remembered the glasses of wine in Fran's. "We just met last week. He was a friend of a friend." It would've been too complicated to explain.

"Your mother tells me you're the one who pulled him out."

"Mother-in-law," she said, put off by the mistake.

"Oh, beg your pardon." He scribbled in a notation. Revise data. "It was a very brave thing to do."

He was probably instructed to say that to anyone who had stupidly risked their life.

She was embarrassed by the compliment. "But pointless, apparently, since it was too late."

The cop ignored her comment, barrelled right along. "Was there anything unnatural in his behaviour when you saw him last? Was he depressed about anything?"

She knew where he was going. "Michael didn't kill himself, if that's what you're thinking. He was a vibrant man, interested in things."

The cop's pen waited above his notebook.

"He was writing a book," she continued. "A novel. He was really excited about it. He said he was almost finished. He didn't *kill* himself."

"So what do you think happened here?" The pen still waited, stalled.

She tightened the quilt around herself. "He could've had a heart attack."

"Did he have a heart problem?"

"I don't know."

The cop began to write in the notebook again. "There'll be an autopsy because he died at home. Anything's possible. But I can tell you every year we get a couple of calls where someone's had a few drinks, then feels like a dip in the water. The lucky ones are pulled out in time." He looked up at her. "What did he do for a living?"

"He worked for Baron Mines."

He licked his lips and solemnly wrote it down.

"Do you happen to know the next of kin?" he asked, his pen at the ready.

What was it he'd said in the restaurant? "He has a son studying in Ottawa," she said. "Edward. There's probably an address book somewhere." She waved behind herself at the desk.

He nodded his thanks. "Would you like me to take you to the hospital," he asked.

She stared blankly at him.

"To get yourself checked out. You've had an ordeal."

"Thanks, but I'm fine," she said. As if to illustrate, she swung her legs down to the floor.

When the cop had gone, Sarah appeared at the door. "I put your clothes into the dryer. They'll be ready in ten minutes or so, then we should go. Why don't you rest till then?" Sarah headed back to the kitchen.

Rebecca listened to the low murmuring of the two women in the distance. She was too agitated to lie down again. Pulling the quilt around her she stood up and stepped toward the fireplace.

On the mantel stood an array of framed photos, mostly old snapshots in black and white. The exception was a colour headshot of a young man, probably a graduation photo. Edward. A handsome younger version of Michael, with sandy hair and an appropriately earnest expression.

In a brown-tinted photo a handsome young couple grinned at the photographer from a doorway, the man's arm clasped around the woman's waist, a very pretty woman with her brown hair pinned on top of her head. Michael's parents. Next to it stood an old black-and-white studio shot of a girl, maybe sixteen, looking romantically off in some reverie. There was a resemblance to the man in the couple, and Rebecca guessed it was Michael's aunt. He had inherited the delicate curve of the brows and the strong nose from that side.

She scanned the last photo. An impossibly thin young boy standing warily among the trees, a rifle slung over his shoulder. She felt a tightening in her chest, her heart clenching into a fist. His life had been a hard struggle and now it was over. Maybe the question the cop posed wasn't so far off. Maybe there was a self-destructive urge in his drinking. Maybe he was having trouble making it through the day and was good at hiding it.

She moved toward the window. It amazed her that the sun was still shining. It seemed as if hours had gone by, yet the sky still held that mid-afternoon blue.

She turned toward the desk, a leather-inlaid mahogany. In the middle lay a thick binder. She opened the black cover and read the first page: "*The Stolen Princess*, by Michael Oginski."

Sophie
Voyage of Discovery
January 1744

The icy wind has followed our painful progress north along the Baltic coast. The shoreline is frozen, and beyond, reefs of ice drift in the leaden water. Where in heaven are we?

She read the first few pages and became transported. She felt Michael's breath in the character, his sensibility in the description of the landscape. She became inexplicably close to him at that moment. The neatly typed manuscript grew suddenly precious in her hands — it was all that was left of him. Now the book would never be finished.

He said he had almost two hundred pages and was nearly finished. She turned to the end: one hundred and forty pages. Eight chapters. That couldn't be right. He had said twelve chapters, she was sure it was twelve.

She flipped through all the pages from the beginning. There were only one hundred and forty. She glanced around the desktop. A dictionary, a thesaurus, a fancy pen in a marble holder. But no other pages. She pulled open the drawers one by one. Blank paper, pens, pencils, erasers, chequebooks, business cards — one from a publisher. Everything but.

Energized, she threw off the quilt and hurried out of the den into the hall. Sarah and Natalka were speaking in low voices in the kitchen as she jumped up the stairs on her toes.

The floor upstairs was covered in Persian carpets. She came upon the library first. Bookcases lined the walls. A brown leather sofa sat in front of a mullioned window. Some newspapers lay scattered on a coffee table. No pages of manuscript.

She noticed a filing cabinet in the corner. She pulled out the top shelf. Finally. A thick pile of handwritten pages had been deposited in the bottom. She lifted out half the pile, then the other half. There must've been three or four hundred pages made unreadable because of all the scratching out and written-over words. It looked like a rough draft. The last page was numbered 196 with a question mark. So where were the last sixty pages of the finished manuscript?

She entered his bedroom with misgivings. The walnut sleigh bed only made her remember he would never sleep there again under the high feathery duvet. She made a cursory check of his nightstand but found nothing.

Sitting down on his bed, she noticed a bit of pale turquoise slipping out beneath the pillow. She held the pyjamas up to the light and in the next beat pulled the top on in one smooth movement. The fabric felt silky on her arms, too intimate — he'd worn it next to his skin, and she wanted that right now, part of him that still felt alive, some of his smell still on it. Because she knew it wouldn't last. Nothing lasted. She told herself Michael would not want her wandering around his house in her underwear. She let her eyes travel through the room unhurried, trying to see what was really there through the fog in her brain. Between the ensuite bathroom and closet, a leather briefcase sat on the floor.

She put it on the bed and opened it. There was some Baron Mines stationery, business letters and documents. No thick sheaf of pages that signalled a manuscript.

Among a few badly typed letters, one handwritten page caught her eye with its splotchy words scrawled across the page. It was attached to an envelope with a paper clip. The letter was dated May 1979.

Mr. Oginski,

I am writing this letter because I am at the end of my rope. I worked in the Baron Mines at Bear Lake for 15 years. I can't work their no more as my lungs is shot. I developed the cancer of the lung! and people here say its because of the mine. It's not just me. Lots of men here got sick in their lungs. Its hell work- ing down there the air's thick like shit. How do you breath in shit? Some say the owners would not let us get sick like that. But I'm not one of them. So I am asking you. What are you going to do about it? We're getting sick in the lungs because the air is shit. John Baron shoud fry in hell but I told my buddies I'd talk

to you when I come to Toronto because
you're a more reasonable man. I'll be staying
at my sisters on the Danforth.

Claude Simard

She stood up straight, her back painful after the
strenuous CPR. Ahead, the ensuite bathroom tugged at
her curiosity. She stepped inside and opened the mirrored
door of the medicine cabinet. The usual aspirin and bandages. A few leftover anti-inflammatory drugs. A bottle of
Valium, nearly full. Nothing much of interest.

The last room was a guest bedroom. The son who
would never see his father again.

She started back down the stairs, uneasy. Sarah was
waiting for her at the bottom with her dry shorts and
blouse. She raised an eyebrow at the shirt.

"Are you all right?"

Rebecca nodded.

"You know, I think the policeman was right. Maybe
you should see someone. You don't look well."

"I'm fine, really." She fingered the silky hem of
Michael's pyjama shirt. "Okay, so I'm feeling a bit strange,
but I'll be all right."

She took the clothes from Sarah. "Look, something's wrong here," Rebecca said.

"I would say so."

"No, look."

Rebecca led her to the desk in the study. "The end
of Michael's manuscript is missing. There are only a
hundred and forty pages here. There should be nearly
two hundred."

Sarah flipped through the pages in the binder.
"How do you know?"

"He told me. He was almost finished."

"Maybe he was exaggerating. To impress you."

Rebecca shook her head. "There are hundreds of handwritten pages upstairs in his filing cabinet. Rough drafts maybe."

Sarah looked at the manuscript. "Well, it does seem to stop abruptly. Maybe he gave someone part of it to read."

Rebecca quickly threw on her shorts and top, then ran out the back door. She stood there, blinking into the sun. What was she looking for? A shirt matching Michael's swimming trunks was draped on the back of a patio chair. She sat down at the white vinyl table and stared across it. There were no glasses, no bottles. If he'd been drinking, why was there no evidence of it? She peered down at the concrete. Maybe he'd set a glass down at his feet.

A wave of perfume from the nearby border of alyssum rolled over her. She bent closer to fill her lungs with it, push out that other smell that should've been only a memory. No glass appeared, but the sun set a small patch of concrete aglow behind her chair. No, it wasn't the sun. Near the alyssum a cluster of tiny gold flecks of various shapes had arranged itself in a ragged mosaic on the concrete, as if a golden nugget had melted from the heat.

Under the other chair she spotted a pair of leather sandals, one thrust into the other, each toe stuffed into the opposite heel. She really knew nothing about Michael.

She headed inside to find his bar. In the dining room, little crystal shot glasses stood in a row in a cabinet. He had gathered together the usual components of a bar, an ice bucket (empty), a bottle of tonic water, seltzer water, half bottles of gin, scotch, and whiskey. But the vodka was nearly full up. And hidden behind the other bottles. Maybe it wasn't vodka he had been drinking. She could've been mistaken.

She stepped into the kitchen. Natalka sat gloomily at the table while Sarah stood at the glass door looking out into the backyard. Rebecca opened the cupboard door under the sink. A plastic bag half full of garbage hung inside a brown bin. On top lay a crumpled handkerchief, a blue and green plaid she couldn't imagine Michael owning. She pulled the bin out into the light to take a closer look. In the folds of the fabric the plaid was stained with blood. Maybe it wasn't Michael's handkerchief. She hurried upstairs to get the letter from his briefcase. Unwilling to offer explanations she went directly downstairs to her bag in the den and stuck the letter with its envelope inside.

Back in the kitchen, she felt Natalka's eyes on her as she pulled the bag of garbage out of the bin. She massaged the outside of the bag but couldn't feel the outline of a bottle. Maybe he'd already put it out. She found the garbage pail out the side door of the house. Two small plastic bags lay inside. Her fingers pressed on them as if they were someone's abdomen. No bottles.

Back inside, Sarah and Natalka sat at the breakfast table watching her wash her hands. "Let's go," Sarah said.

Rebecca went to the den to fetch the manuscript. Sarah watched her carry the binder under her arm but said nothing as they walked out to the car.

"I'll bring it back," Rebecca said.

They were just getting into the Camaro when a black limousine with tinted windows screeched to a halt behind them. Janek flew out of the driver's seat. He stopped at their car, a short, squat figure in a polo shirt.

"What happened?" he cried. "The police called me at home — there was an accident?"

His pomaded grey hair fell forward in spears. He looked like he had been in a scrape: the skin around one eye was dark, and a bruise mottled his cheek.

Rebecca faced the bulldog man. "I'm sorry," she said, "but Michael is dead. He drowned in the pool."

He stared at her, his eyes growing narrow. "Not possible. He was a good swimmer."

"He might've had something to drink. Did he drink vodka?"

"All Poles drink vodka."

"To excess?"

"He was an aristocrat. He didn't do nothing to excess. This is completely impossible. He was a strong, healthy man." His brown eyes bulged at her.

"You look like you've been in an accident yourself," she said. "Have you had that checked?" She pointed at his face.

He waved his hand in the air impatiently. "It was nothing." Then, eyes blazing, "You were here — why didn't you pull him out? Why didn't you save him?"

She stared at the bullying posture, the jowls swaying, felt bile rising in her, but could not bring herself to answer.

Sarah said, "He was dead when we got here."

He set squinty, critical eyes on Rebecca and said something to Sarah in Polish. Sarah turned abruptly from him and said to Rebecca, "Let's go."

The two women got into the car. Sarah was about to close her door when Janek caught it with his hand. He stooped to look in the back, where Natalka sat quietly.

He gave her no greeting, instead spat out in English, "Where's Halina?"

"She's at my house," Sarah said, anger lifting her voice.

"Then why doesn't she answer the goddamn phone?" he said.

Natalka's swan neck stiffened and anxiety rose in her eyes.

chapter ten

No one spoke in the car. Rebecca drove along St. Clair Avenue back to Sarah's house, the only sounds the engine humming, the radio buzzing beneath comprehension. The sun hung behind them, its heat receding in the late afternoon. It amazed Rebecca how the street, the sky with its high elusive clouds, looked the same as before. Nothing had changed: women shoppers still laughed on the sidewalks, kids licked ice cream cones in the shade of awnings.

Saturday afternoon traffic bunched up in Little Italy heading toward Dufferin Street. A red light stopped them at every block; pedestrians crossed laden with grocery bags.

Every now and then she glanced in the rearview mirror: Natalka gazed out the window with a blank stare.

Rebecca drove mechanically, the street, the stores a blur, the only clarity Michael at the bottom of the pool, her jumping in, kicking, kicking in slow motion to get to him, his hair floating around his dead face.

She pulled into Sarah's driveway, thankful for the automatic impulses that had kicked in to get them home. Sarah rushed out of the car and ran ahead to unlock the front door. Natalka, in no hurry, trailed inside after Rebecca.

"Halina!" Sarah called out at the foot of the stairs leading to the bedrooms.

No reply.

She climbed the stairs, Natalka watching. Rebecca took a quick look around from where she stood: everything appeared as they had left it.

After a minute Sarah returned to the top of the stairs. "She's not here."

Natalka sighed and began to climb; Rebecca followed.

Sarah had given them a room with a queen-sized bed. A valise stood in a corner. Everything looked in order.

"She's gone!" Sarah said, puzzlement in her voice.

Natalka stared at the made bed, her hands clasped in front of her. Wisps of white hair trailed from the bun at the back, framed her face.

"There're no signs of a struggle anywhere," Rebecca said. "Did she take anything with her? Some clothes?"

Natalka's small, elegant head trembled on the stalk of neck, her bravura gone. She had turned very pale.

"I don't know."

"Well, are any of the bags gone?"

Natalka glanced at the valise. "The smaller one is inside the bigger one."

Rebecca thought of all the years of squeezing together into a small space, the accommodation that must have become instinct in Poland.

"What did your mother say on the phone?"

Natalka avoided her eyes.

"At Michael's. You called her."

Natalka sat down on the bed, staring into the distance. "She was upset. She was shocked."

"Did she say she was going somewhere?"

"My mother is genius at having secrets. She's Communist, after all. But I suspected something wrong. I just didn't know what."

"Why would she leave?" Rebecca asked.

"She was afraid," said Natalka.

"Of what?"

She shrugged.

"What did she say on the phone?"

Natalka lowered her eyes, embarrassed. "We live in country where one must have suspicion to survive."

"What did she say?"

"She said, 'If he killed Michael, I am next.'"

Rebecca and Sarah exchanged glances.

"Did you tell her it was an accident?" Rebecca said.

"She would not be convinced."

"Did she say who she thought it might be?"

Natalka opened her mouth to answer when a pounding exploded at the door downstairs.

Sarah ran to answer it. The others followed.

Janek rushed into the living room out of breath, arms flailing. "Where is she?"

Without waiting for an answer he marched through the first floor into the kitchen, the den, his heavy footfalls resounding in the house. He retraced his steps to stand before them again, his fire hydrant body undisguised in the blue sports jacket.

"She's not here," Rebecca said with a firmness just short of rude.

He glared at her, his thick neck twisting to the stairs. "I'll find her!" he growled.

With surprising energy for a body that stout, he jumped up the stairs.

"Now just a minute ...!" Rebecca began.

The three women ran up after him. They watched from the hall as he trundled from room to room on his stubby legs, his jowls shaking with each step. Then he found the room with the luggage and his focus shifted.

Without hesitation he began pulling out drawers in the dresser, the nightstand, rifling through the clothes.

"I'm calling the police," Rebecca said. She turned to leave the room.

Natalka put a firm hand on her arm. "Please," she said. "Don't."

He picked up the valise and unzipped it. A smaller piece of luggage lay inside. He unzipped that too but it was empty. Disgusted, he threw it aside and surveyed the women, the mess he'd made, the drawers hanging out with sleeves and bras trailing over the sides.

"Where is it?" he demanded.

Now what? thought Rebecca.

"Excuse me?" Natalka asked.

"Don't play stupid," he said. "The compass. I know she brought it. So where is it?"

"I don't know."

"You're lying!" he shouted.

Natalka jumped at the sudden blast.

"We had an agreement!" he yelled. "I gave her money for the trip and she was supposed to bring it for us."

"For Michael," Natalka said quietly.

He sneered. "Oh, so now if Michael's dead, she thinks that's *it*? She doesn't have to give it to me?"

Natalka didn't react.

"Maybe *she* killed him."

Natalka's eyes widened slightly, but she was in control. "You know her better than that."

Rebecca couldn't stand by any longer. "It was an accident," she said. "Michael drowned."

He narrowed his eyes, as if she were a naive child.

"Mama was still here when we left for Michael's house," Natalka said. "She was exhausted from the whole night out. She didn't come back before dawn." She watched him until he fidgeted, shifted his weight from one foot to the other.

He stepped up to Natalka and grasped her arm tightly in his hand. "You tell her it's mine! If she thinks anything different — I'll find her."

Natalka pulled away from his grip, rubbing her arm. He glowered at them, then stamped down the stairs. The front door slammed.

The three women stood in the sudden silence that followed the echo of the door. Rebecca turned to Natalka, trying to frame a question that wouldn't upset her. Natalka saved her the effort.

"Mama was desperate to help me. She did nothing wrong."

"What is this compass he wants?" Sarah asked.

Natalka sat down on the bed and winced, her shoulders slouching forward. Rebecca knew the enlarged spleen would be tender. Natalka sighed before speaking.

"I have to explain. Mama knew Michael's aunt in Kraków. They kept in contact until the aunt died about ten years ago. Aunt Klara. She lost her family in the war, Michael went to Canada, so she took interest in us. She told Mama stories of the family, they came from very noble people. She told her about compass. It belonged to family once, but then ended up in museum in Kraków. She said it proved who they really were. When Klara died, Mama wrote Michael to break news to him. They began correspondence. He told her about his book, how he was trying find out information on his family. When we found out I was sick, when Mama realized we must come to the west, she offered compass to Michael."

"In exchange for bringing you here?" Rebecca asked.

Natalka nodded. "Michael was willing to pay for tickets, and we could stay in building Janek owned, but the treatment, doctors ... only Janek could afford such costs."

"But the compass was in a museum, you said? Did she offer it under false pretenses? Never really intending to bring it?"

Natalka blinked at Rebecca, glanced at Sarah. "Again, I must explain," she said. "Remember Mama works for Orbis, she arranges for workers' travel? She has other duties also — she arranges visas." Natalka stopped and watched them as if assessing their reaction to an important detail.

"You probably know travel restricted in Poland. The government afraid people not come back. Someone who prepares visas has much power. She ... befriended ... one of cleaners in the museum. Czartoryski Museum. Very well regarded museum in Kraków. From collection begun by Czartoryski family in eighteenth century. Anyway, this cleaner very unhappy. She had son who escaped to the west and she wanted see his children. So Mama promised her visa."

"In exchange for the compass," said Rebecca.

"You must understand — it was not on display. It was lying in carton in storage like thousands of other objects. They don't have room to put out everything. No one would miss it."

"So it's here?" Sarah said.

Natalka drew her arm across her abdomen and closed her eyes.

"Are you all right?" Rebecca asked.

She opened her eyes, gave Rebecca a hint of a nod. "Maybe she took it, I don't know."

"It was here?" Sarah said.

Natalka rubbed her eyes. "She hid it soon after we arrive. You were in kitchen."

"Then it must be in the living room," Sarah said

Natalka looked down at her feet, pressed her arm tightly against her stomach.

Rebecca waited through a moment of silence, until all hope of a response had died. She touched Sarah's arm lightly and led her to the door.

"Let's let Natalka get some rest," she said. Over her shoulder she added, "You should lie down and take a nap."

She closed the door to the bedroom and led Sarah down the stairs.

They stood in the centre of the living room glancing around.

"She might've told me where it was in a few more minutes," Sarah said.

"She wouldn't betray her mother."

"I left them in here that first day," said Sarah, lifting up the sofa cushions, poking around under the coffee table.

"That burglary the other night," Rebecca said, watching her mother-in-law checking out nooks and crannies. "Maybe that's what they were looking for."

Sarah straightened up, blinking at her. "If Halina isn't back tomorrow I'm calling the police."

Rebecca began to examine the room more carefully. "Whoever the intruder was, he didn't find what he was looking for."

"How do you know?"

"Natalka said maybe her mother took it. That means it was still here after the break-in."

"The bookcases were turned upside-down," Sarah said looking around the room.

"That doesn't mean she didn't put it there," Rebecca said.

She began with the top shelf of the first bookcase, pulling out two books at a time to check if anything was stashed behind. She went along the row of books methodically, then down to the next shelf.

Sarah watched for a minute before parking herself in front of the second case. She began to pull out two books at a time, checking behind. There were four cases, two with doors enclosing the bottom shelves, which made them harder to search.

Sarah groaned as she crouched down to go through the bottom of the fourth case.

"Go sit down," Rebecca said. "I'll finish this one."

"You know you're an old woman when people tell you to sit down." But she obeyed, wobbling to the sofa.

After a moment, she carefully pushed herself off and bent down to kneel in front of the chesterfield, peering beneath it. She placed her hand under its flat skirt and moved along the length of it on her knees. Disappointed, she stood up with a groan, smoothing out her skirt.

"You're right. I'm too old for this," she said.

Nevertheless she stepped behind the couch and took hold of the damask curtains, giving them a shake.

Rebecca sighed out loud and fell, exhausted, into the couch. Sarah plopped down beside her.

"I give up," Sarah said. "Maybe it isn't here."

"Never give up."

"But we've looked everywhere."

"Not everywhere."

Sarah followed her gaze across the room. They both approached the piano on tiptoes.

Sarah lifted the mahogany lid and propped it open. They both craned their necks to survey the workings inside, the felted levers that controlled the keys — not an inch was wasted. There were no gaps that could hold anything bigger than a finger.

Rebecca groped blindly beneath the keyboard, her fingers searching for hollows. Unsatisfied with that method, she crawled under the piano on her knees, ducking her head between her shoulder blades. She looked up at the unstained wooden framework. First one side, then the other. The wooden support beneath the keyboard stopped before it reached the end on the far left, forming a little cavity. She held her breath and thrust in her hand. Something moved. Her fingers touched something small and velvety.

"Do you see anything?" Sarah said, her voice floating from above.

Rebecca wrapped her fingers around the object and pulled. The gap in the wood was irregular, and it took several tries before she managed to coax the thing from its resting place.

When she emerged from under the piano she held in her hand a dark blue velvet bag pulled tight with a drawstring. Something hard-edged was inside.

"So let's see already," Sarah said.

She followed Rebecca to the dining table, where she deposited the bag.

"Michael said this thing would change the history books."

Sarah glanced at her with impatience. "Well then, let's have a look."

Rebecca loosened the drawstring, opening the bag. She reached in and drew out an octagonal gold box, about three inches long, trimmed with the most brilliant blue lapis lazuli she had ever seen.

"Wow!" she said.

Sarah took in a sudden breath.

The blue, which ran along the side panels and edging on the lid, seemed lit from within, an extraordinary blue like a twilight sky or a lake during a summer storm.

Rebecca lifted the lid. On a bed of purple velvet lay a small silver instrument, coffin-shaped, with roman numerals etched around the border in black.

"Why it's a little sundial," Rebecca said.

"And a compass," Sarah added.

A round glass eye took up half of the instrument. Inside, a tiny needle hovered at "Nord." A triangular piece of metal decorated like a bird lay attached across the length of the instrument, its narrow end pointing to the compass.

"This looks very old," Sarah said.

She lifted the thing out of its bed of velvet, then slowly drew up the bit of metal lying across it, so that it sat perpendicular to the base, the beak of the silver bird pointing to numbers ranging from forty to sixty. A shade fell across the black etched numerals.

Sarah turned it over. The back held the base of the little compass, a tiny silver flower. The silver back, smooth with age, was engraved with the names of cities beside a number: "Paris 49, Londres 50, Hambourg 54, Cracouie 50, Venise 45." At the bottom was "N.Bion. A. Paris."

Rebecca turned back to the box. Now she noticed the engraving on the inside of the lid:

Á Sophie,

Pour que tu puisses toujours me retrouver.

Staś

It was dated December 9, 1758.

Rebecca translated with her high school French. "'To Sophie, So that you ...' I'm not sure of the verb tense ... 'So you will always be able to find me again. Stas.'"

"That's a Polish name, short for Stanislaw," Sarah said. "It's pronounced with an 'sh' at the end. Like Stahsh."

Rebecca ran her finger absently over the engraved letters. "There was a Sophie in Michael's manuscript," she said.

Sarah stared at her, waiting. Rebecca was suddenly self-conscious.

"I read the first few pages at his house. Sophie was a young girl on her way to Russia."

On her open palm, Sarah balanced the silver ornament worn smooth with time. "So how does this change the history books?"

Rebecca brought Michael's black binder in from the car when she got home. Still in her shorts, she was shivering now that the sun had gone down. The middle of September was deceptive that way — bright hot sun in the afternoon and temperatures that dipped after dark. She threw a sweater around her shoulders but was too impatient to change into jeans.

Standing at the dining table, she threw open the manuscript. A new world was opening up to her, and she felt a frisson of excitement in her stomach.

She made herself some tea and nestled into the nubbly beige of the sofa in the den, the manuscript on her lap. She began to read.

chapter eleven

Sophie

Voyage of Discovery

January 1744

The icy wind has followed our painful progress north along the Baltic coast. The shoreline is frozen, and beyond, reefs of ice drift in the leaden water. Where in heaven are we? Since passing Danzig a few days ago, we have seen nothing outside our window for miles but lowering sky and ice grey fields. The watery sun has set early, and my stomach complains, and finally, finally we stop in the frozen rutted post road that has shaken us till we are all black and blue. M. de Lattorf opens the door of the carriage. I wish I could move. If I weren't so keenly anticipating what lies ahead of me, if my destiny did not shine before my eyes like a distant sun, I would weep with misery. We've been travelling for more than three weeks, each day more bitterly cold than the last, and all of us are exhausted. Poor de Lattorf hunches his shoulders against the cold and extends his gloved hand to me. But I can no longer feel my feet, they are so swollen. Mama doesn't concern herself. She has disappeared inside the door of the inn with Fräulein Kayn. At least it's too cold in the carriage for the elderly fräulein to tell her usual tales about the ghosts she has encountered.

"Mademoiselle," de Lattorf mutters.

I pull my woolen scarf aside from my eyes a fraction, but I cannot see his windblown face, only the gloved hand that now curves toward me in a question mark.

"I can't," I say through chattering teeth. "It's my feet —"

He ducks his head down through the door to take a look at me huddled beneath my woolen blanket. Apparently he understands since he climbs partway in and picks me up. His fur hat is crusted with beads of ice. He lifts me out through the door of the carriage as if I were an invalid child, and not a girl of fourteen. The way Papa used to carry little Willy. But Willy had a withered leg. It broke Mama's heart when he died. She wouldn't cry like that for me, I know.

M. de Lattorf carries me over the threshold of the inn and stops. We both blink and stare at the chaos of the place. Dirty children scramble and shout at each other in German; dogs, hens, a small pig, and an old man smoking a pipe, all settled on layers of filthy straw. On a bench in one corner, another old man, only this one looks clean, dressed in black with a curly grey beard; probably a guest. Two stout women prepare food at the grimy wooden table. Each way station has been worse than the last.

"*Pardon*," de Lattorf mutters as he steps gingerly between the bodies. He lowers me onto the dirt floor in front of the earthenware stove almost on top of a little girl with a sooty face. "*Pardon*," he says, and she moves her legs aside to make space.

I try to smile in appeasement, but my feet burn inside my boots. No matter. I will survive this. And the remainder of the journey, though the distance will be nearly a thousand miles. I try to picture the Duke's face when I arrive, but it's too noisy for imaginings.

Mama glowers at the mess, then at me. "What's the matter with you, Sophie?"

"My feet are frozen."

"Hedwig, take off Sophie's boots and rub her feet."

Mama stands erect near the table, arguing with one of the women about the accommodation. Apparently the rooms we were to use lie across an icy pasture unreachable by carriage, so we are to sleep in this bedlam with the family.

To her lady-in-waiting she says in French, "Look at the children huddled over there — I've never seen anything like it, lying one on top of the other like cabbages and turnips to keep warm."

Fräulein Kayn clucks in sympathy, then tries to soothe Mama. "Look, there is another guest here."

Mama turns to scrutinize the bearded old man dressed in black and wearing a broadly brimmed hat. He seems to have brought his own food and is calmly chewing on it in the corner while reading a book. Fräulein Kayn murmurs something to Mama that sounds like "Jew."

I observe him more carefully, intrigued. I have never seen a Jew before, have only heard them described as avaricious moneylenders. While Mama and Fräulein Kayn divert their attention elsewhere, the Jew's dark eyes suddenly turn to me, twinkling in the distance as if he has felt me watching. A shiver skips across my back, but I am not afraid.

Mama barks questions about dinner at the propri-
etress. She is angrier than usual, and I wonder if she is
cursing my decision to answer the royal summons and
make the journey. But she is just as ambitious for me as
I am. My position will reflect on her. Would she believe
me if I told her it was not ambition that drew me away
from my home forever, but destiny?

The servant tries to rub some life into my swollen
feet while I wolf down a stew that a month ago I would
have pushed away as barely edible, a preparation of grits
and turnips and murky ingredients I dare not guess at.

My only regret is Papa, for I know I shall never see
him again. Sweet, honest, good Papa. I think he only let
me go because I said I would come back if the situation
was not to my liking. It isn't as though I haven't met my
cousin the Duke, even if I was a mere ten, and he eleven
and still called Karl Ulrich. He was good-looking then, if
pale, and well-mannered to me, though he was ugly and
hot-tempered with his tutors. I heard rumours since that
he liked his wine too much and got drunk every night at
table. Four years have passed since then, and I feel no
aversion to the notion of marrying him, considering his
prospects. But I assured Papa that I would only make up
my mind once Mama and I had assessed matters.

I carry Papa's pages of instructions and advice in my
bag, but I know what they say. Above all, do not give up
your faith, Sophie. Remain Lutheran, no matter what. I
promised. What else could I do? It wasn't until we were
leaving that I suddenly saw how old he looked. It was
the worst moment of my life, when we parted. I dissolved into tears. Very unlike me.

I observe de Lattorf staring at the compass he uses
when we're on the road. He's probably half asleep. Out
of boredom, I try to engage him in a philosophical discussion begun the previous evening. "Do you still feel that

parents ought to teach their children to believe in God?"
I ask, amused at the fluttering of his eyelids. I was right;
he is near dozing. "Merely to ensure they behave in a
moral way?"

We have been debating this topic all week, and de
Lattorf sighs. "What else will keep them from stealing
from their neighbours and murdering their wives? God
is necessary to keep everyone honest."

"Yes, yes — if God did not exist, it would be necessary to invent Him." Voltaire's phrase has become the
catchword of modern society, but I wholeheartedly
believe it. "What about the idea of rational thought?" I
go on perversely, not yet ready for sleep. "If we replaced
ignorance and superstition with knowledge and rational thought, don't you think some people might behave
morally even without believing in God?"

"Some people, perhaps, Mademoiselle. But if you
truly believed you would go unpunished after this life,
no matter how despicable your actions, would you
behave well?"

"Monsieur!" I tease.

I recall a similar conversation not long ago with
Frederick of Prussia when he invited our family to his
court. None of us suspected his motives at the time. It
was an unexpected invitation and Papa was away on
command as he often was. While Mama made herself
gracious to the ladies in the court, she was shocked to
see Frederick summon me to sit beside him at table. He
said I was to call him "Fritz." This King who had shown
himself to be courageous, nay, formidable, according to
Papa, as soon as the crown fell to him on the death of
his father, Frederick William in 1740.

Everyone in Europe had assumed the flute-playing,
French-loving prince would be kind and malleable on the
throne. But Papa was called away almost immediately to

command troops on the border of Silesia. The whole continent in upheaval that year because the Emperor of Austria, Charles VI, also died in 1740, and his daughter, Maria-Theresa, was set to rule. Papa heaped scorn on her silly blonde head. It was the perfect time for Frederick to strike, he said, while Maria-Theresa was sorting out her friends. While her father's decrepit old generals were trying to decide whether to pledge their allegiance to the pretty young daughter. Frederick had to strike, had to take the opportunity that opened before him to return Silesia to its rightful place. The people there were Protestant, and should be ruled by a Protestant king. Wasn't that reason enough to remove it from the realm of the Catholic Maria-Theresa? When he'd come back from the campaign, Papa told us Frederick had given a masked ball for everyone's pleasure, including the Austrians, on an evening in December. The next day he set out at the head of the troops he had ordered built up along the border of Silesia. He met little resistance, especially from those who'd enjoyed themselves at the ball. And Prussia grew.

I was mindful of all this while for the next four hours Frederick and I discussed philosophy and art and compared our appraisals of all manner of things. He was surprised at my education and opinions but pleased that I had them. He sensed my discomfort at the proximity of my mother and ventured a comment about how when he was my age he had hated his father with passion, but now saw that in his single-mindedness his father had built an incomparable army and in his mindless cruelty had made Frederick strong. It had been but a few years since his father's death and the beginning of his own reign. In this cruelty from a parent, we were linked, and I felt closer to him. I reconciled myself that Mama would never love me, as his father had never loved him.

During this afternoon, which I shall never forget, the people around us must have marvelled at the King of Prussia spending so many hours conversing with a child. Yet I felt I understood him. I sensed the same sadness in him I knew in myself, the same certitude that happiness, the way other people experience it, would always elude me. Nevertheless he was charming and gracious and referred to his own unhappy situation only in the most oblique way.

"Sometimes one must do things one finds abhorrent," he said. "Take, for instance, marriage. For the likes of us, people in our position, marriage is a means to an end. There is little chance it will result in affection. For that kind of comfort one must turn elsewhere. I am telling you this because you are a spirited, intelligent girl. You remind me of myself at your age: do not develop foolish sentimental notions that will hinder your good judgment. You are young still. You can learn. Never let affection get in the way of your future."

I know in my bones that this invitation of a thousand miles through the deepest heart of winter is his doing. That he was testing me and that I passed the test.

There is Mama. She has laid herself down fully clothed on the bare wooden plank she ordered the innkeeper to bring her. They have installed me and Fräulein Kayn near the stove on an unimaginably filthy featherbed, leaving the children who ordinarily sleep there on the straw-laden floor. The elderly fräulein is snoring quietly when I feel movement near my elbow; I lift my head. Two tiny red eyes are just as startled when I scramble to sit up. The children nearby giggle and throw something at the rat. I gaze around, fully awake. Fräulein Kayn shifts but keeps snoring. In the faint light of the fire, I see, in the corner, the Jew leaning over his book, reading. Everyone else is sleeping.

I get up and manoeuvre through the prone bodies with swollen, painful feet. When I am still at a distance he looks up, smiles with high-coloured cheeks. I stop, suddenly shy. He motions to me with a small wave of his hand, then pats the spot on the bench beside him. I look around to see Mama sleeping fitfully on the wooden plank. I approach and sit down. He puts the black hat on over his skullcap.

"You cannot sleep, child? You are not accustomed to rats in your bed." His voice hums, like a soft melody. He is robust, his skin ruddy and threaded with tiny veins above the grey beard.

"May I ask what you are reading?" I say, aiming at politeness.

"Why, it is the philosophy of Spinoza, child."

"Spinoza? I thought I knew the names of all the philosophers. This one is unfamiliar."

"He was a Jew from Holland, not well known."

I try to reconcile the image of the Jew before me and the Jew on the page with the references to greedy moneylenders.

"And what distinguishes his philosophy?"

The man observes me, perhaps wondering at this question from a young girl. "Spinoza adopted a geometrical method to study the world."

"Geometrical?" I ask, perplexed.

"He felt human nature obeys fixed laws no less than do the figures of geometry. Therefore he wrote about human beings as though he were concerned with lines and planes and solids."

"How extraordinary!" I say. "To think of oneself as a triangle or a circle!" I suddenly feel very childish at this outburst.

"Spinoza wrote that it is the part of the wise man not to bewail nor to deride, but to understand."

I am chastened, but gently. I steer back toward politeness. "May I ask your name, sir?"

He bows his head with ceremony. "Rabbi Israel ben Eliezer, at your service."

He does not ask mine, but looks into my eyes, searching, searching. When he has satisfied himself that he has found what he is looking for, he says, "Would you like me to tell you a story?"

"I'm too old for stories," I say, surprised. "I'm not a child. I am on my way to the man I'm going to marry."

"Ahh." The rabbi nods. "Then I know just the story for you." His bushy grey eyebrows arch in a question.

"I can't sleep anyway," I say, and wait.

The old man shifts his hips to settle more comfortably on the bench. He takes a breath. "There once were two souls floating far above the earth, one male, one female. Though they were two separate souls, they had found each other eons ago and come together virtually as one, drifting along, outside of time. Finally the day came when they were allotted placements on earth — two families into which they would be born. The two families lived in distant villages, but the souls knew that one day they would meet again, even though as humans they would forget everything that had gone before. The girl was born into a family of craftsmen who fashioned barrels. They were called 'wet' barrels since they were used to transport liquid and therefore needed to be meticulously crafted out of dried oak.

"When she was of marriageable age, her parents sent her to a distant village to meet the son of a 'dry' cooper whose barrels could be made to less stringent standards because they needed to carry only dry goods. However, he was richer than the wet cooper since it took him less time to make more barrels. She was an adventuresome girl and looked forward to her new surroundings. Also, ever since she could remember, she had felt as if something were missing in her life. She loved her parents and her brothers and yet ... there was an empty space in her spirit that she couldn't explain. So she made the arduous journey and found the prosperous young cooper." The rabbi pauses.

"Was this the other soul, then?" I ask.

The rabbi's ruddy cheeks rise in a smile. "Oh, that life was that simple! But alas, the young cooper was as different from that soul as it was possible to be. The girl, however, did not remember how she had joyously drifted above the earth with her soulmate. So she married the young man, thus joining wet barrels with dry, and the business grew. Her husband preferred his wine to anything she or the work could offer, so she became the mistress of the shop.

"One day a young man came to the cooperage and asked for employment. He had left his village in a distant land to seek his fortune. As soon as she saw him, she felt a stirring in her soul, something completely new to her. This young man was just as taken with her. He didn't understand, himself, the draw he felt. One night when her husband drank himself into a stupor, she came to the young man. During the day they avoided each other. But at night each sought out the other.

"One night when they embraced, her hand brushed by a small bulky object in his breast pocket. She went to reach for it, but he caught her hand.

"'What are you hiding so close to your heart?' she asked.

"The young man wanted to have no secrets between them, since he loved her as he had never loved another. So he withdrew the tiny wooden box from his pocket and watched her lovely eyes cloud over with confusion as she lifted the lid and looked upon a single grain of wheat.

"'My father passed it on to me as his father passed it on to him and his father's father before him.'

"She moved her fingers toward the grain, preparing to lift it from its velvet lining. The young man, alarmed, snapped the lid shut. The puzzlement in her eyes became anger.

"'You have so little trust in me?'

"'It is a magic grain,' he said. 'We don't touch it. We revere it. We honour it from the depths of our hearts.'

"'I don't understand.'

"'It is a sign between us and the land, handed down through the centuries. We honour it because it has fed us and kept us alive, our entire family and all those dependent upon us.'

"'This tiny grain?' she said, as she lifted the lid again.

"'You must never touch it. My life, the lives of all my family, depend upon it.'

"Her face became absorbed in it, searching for the magic, so he put it away.

"One day a message arrived from the young man's village that his father was ill and he had to go home. He begged her to come with him, but they both knew that was impossible. She wept large tears and accused him of wanting to leave her.

"'You will never come back!' she cried. 'You've become tired of me!'

"He was beside himself with dismay, that he was the cause of grief to the only woman he had ever loved. 'How can I prove my devotion to you?' he asked.

"With tear-stained eyes she placed her hand on his breast pocket. His heart skipped. But he trusted her with his life. He handed her the tiny box, content that he could leave a part of himself with her. He made her promise that she would never touch it.

"When he had gone, she became busy with her work. More and more barrels were being made to fill the orders from far and wide. Many coopers now worked for her. Business was good; her customers trusted her. The tiny wooden box containing the magic grain she kept in her skirt pocket, a part of her love always near.

"The young man sent her letters begging her to leave her husband and come to him. His father was gravely ill and the young man was needed to run the large farm. He still loved and yearned for her, and when would she come?

"But how could she leave the cooperage that she had built up with her own two hands? He had no right, she thought, to ask her to leave behind the staves, the hoops, the oak that had to be dried just so. He sent her letters stained with his tears; she added them to her growing pile.

"One day when she had received the latest of a long line of letters begging her to leave everything she knew and loved, she despaired of seeing him again. She cursed the distance between them and his family obligations, and finally the magic of the grain in the tiny wooden box. Plucking the box from her pocket she stood there glaring at it. If it were magic, why didn't it stop her? If it were magic, why didn't it strike her dead? Gingerly she lifted the lid. The grain lay there, tiny, inconsequential, exactly like all the other grains she had ever seen in her life. It had been a lie like everything else he had told her. This grain was no more magic than the grains the farmers planted in the fields beyond the cooperage.

"She stepped outside into the yard. It was no use wasting it. At least in his absence, she might make use of the grain to grow some food for her workers. She held the box in her hand, waiting for the grain to speak to her. It was silent. Nor did it strike her down when she lifted it from its velvet lining. She held it between two fingers: it didn't feel like a magic grain. But she would test it. Bending over, she scooped up a handful of earth and deposited the grain beneath. She patted the soil down around it and marked the spot with a twig.

"The next day she looked out her window and was amazed to find that her yard had become a field of wheat swaying in the sun. No matter how much she harvested, more grew in its place the next day. She began to fill barrels with it and became even more prosperous.

"In the next letter she received from the young man, he wrote that his father had died. He was desperate to see her but he couldn't leave since now the entire burden of running the farm fell to him. In the next letter his writing had changed into a smaller, tighter script. He said a disease was attacking their crops and the future of the farm was uncertain. In his last letter the writing had become crabbed and splotchy. Locusts had eaten what little was left of their crops. All had been lost, his family scattered. What, he asked her, had become of his magic grain? She received no more letters.

"When he died, his soul did not seek out his long-lost love, and when she died, her soul could not find his. For the rest of eternity her soul searched and searched for him in vain."

The rabbi leans back on the bench, tired.

"What an unhappy tale!" I say. "She destroyed the man she loved and lost both their souls."

He observes me with mischievous eyes. "What would you have done?"

I am startled by his question. I would like to think I would have kept the grain safe forever, but that would not have brought the young man back. "I don't know," I say.

His eyes darken, but he says no more. I realize he wanted to hear something different from me, and I regret disappointing him. I have not yet learned to conceal my thoughts.

The story has affected me in a way I do not understand, and I am curious about the storyteller. "Forgive me, but you are an unusual visitor in such a place. To where do you travel?"

"Back to my home. A little town in the Carpathians."

"Why did you come here?"

"To see if you were real, my child. To see if my dream was true."

A shiver skips across my back, the kind Fräulein Kayn would describe as death. "And what did you dream?" I ask, though I am uneasy.

His eyes, which seem to see everything, close in order to see what isn't there.

"I dreamt you stood in an opulent room with velvet draperies hung over the windows and gilded portraits on the walls. You were surrounded by documents — they fluttered around you like birds, pleading with you to let them go. Once, you would have. But now, you caught each one and signed it, and with your signature you took away the freedom of my people. With one stroke of your quill you punished a nation."

I let out my breath, relieved. "But this cannot be true — I don't know your people."

"When you travel this week, look up into the night sky for a sign. You will know when you see it."

I hear a gurgle from the direction of the fire and turn to see Fräulein Kayn sitting up, fixing huge eyes on the rabbi. The fräulein, with her nonsensical belief in spirits, will devour these stories whole.

By the time I awake the following morning, he has vanished. "Did you see the rabbi leave?" I ask Mama who is already up.

"What rabbi?"

"The old man in the black hat sitting in that corner last night." We both look up to find the corner filled with straw and chickens strutting about.

Mama turns irritated eyes on me. "Between you and Fräulein Kayn I am surrounded by phantoms on this journey."

"The fräulein will remember," I say, puzzled.

The older woman watches the scowl on Mama's face and shakes her head.

For the next few days we travel long miles north along the Latvian coast. Mist shrouds the luminous grey marshes that surround us on all sides. We pass a few godforsaken hamlets where the beggarly villagers come to their doors wrapped in layers of rags. At the sight of our three unlikely carriages rolling through the ice in this bitter January, they all cross themselves and mutter prayers as if we are dead already. Each night as outriders lead us to our next lodgings, Fräulein Kayn peers up at the sky through the window of the carriage. She must have a crick in her neck by now.

On the third night we must stop in a village since inns and post houses have long disappeared. I am bracing myself for another night of fighting for space with dogs and rats, when, on alighting from the carriage, Fräulein Kayn gasps. I follow her gaze toward the clear black sky. There, high above us, a ball of fire streaks across the bowl of the heavens, its blue trail of stars flashing behind it, electrifying the night. I cannot take my eyes off it, even when the blazing tail fades into the pale stars of the night sky.

"A portent of evil!" Fräulein Kayn whispers.

"It's a comet!" I cry. "No more evil than the moon and stars."

"The devil is behind this, I tell you."

I don't believe in signs, yet I am troubled at the memory of the rabbi and his people and a future that seems incomprehensible to me.

We have been travelling for nearly five weeks now and I have quite forgotten what it feels like to not be frozen or jostled for endless hours over icy ruts that the roads have become. My visions of the Duke have evaporated into the dreary pall that passes for day in these parts, and for the first time I begin, myself, to wonder whether I have lost my senses coming on this journey. Mama sits across from me with her scarf pulled over her nose and cheeks, red and swollen from the cold, her eyes painfully closed.

My eyes fix on the silver expanse of marsh and I fear my brain is frozen as well. I have not the energy to put two thoughts together. A movement in the distance coaxes my eyes to shift into focus. What a sight! A rider is galloping towards us. He exchanges words with one of the servants in the first carriage, then turns around and gallops back the way he came. My heart begins to beat again as if there is a possibility that I might thaw out.

Within the hour another rider approaches. Our coach stops and a Colonel Vokheikov introduces himself. He has been sent to escort us across the frontier and on to the city of Riga. Mama sits up straighter as the handsome young officer rides beside us, warm steam expanding from his horse's nostrils. Blood begins to course through my body, slowly warming it from the inside out. I wonder if the ringing is in my ears, but Mama looks up at the same time. Yes, somewhere bells are pealing. And a sound like thunder. As we get closer I realize it is the sound of cannons. I am puzzled, but Mama's shoulders lift and she lets the scarf fall around her neck. She nods at me with a tight smile.

I am astonished at the people lining the road as we pass through. The whole town has come out to wave at us and cheer. Mama's smile loosens. Her neck becomes regal and bows benevolently to all admirers.

The empress has sent us warm sable coats with gold brocade and fur collars. But these are nothing compared to the apparition that lies before us: a fur-lined sleigh that contains not only a stove, but mattresses, and is so large a dozen horses must pull it. If this is a dream, I hope never to awaken. The comet was indeed an omen, but one of good. The rabbi's story of tragedy comes rushing to mind, but I can no longer recall the anxiety I felt earlier; it has faded like the cold. All I can remember is the fortunate girl, the heights she flew to, the power of her signature.

chapter twelve

Rebecca crouched in front of the black-eyed Susans in the backyard. She yanked at the tall grass that had insinuated itself between the long, fuzzy stalks. The flowerbeds were shaggy with weeds; dandelions and thistle sprouted in the loamy soil David had nurtured before he went blind. No annuals had been planted the spring after he died. Last spring. Yesterday. But over here dazzling red and yellow snapdragons had seeded themselves from last year's planting, and over there a lacy thread of alyssum, a reminder that eager life pushed its way through.

She stood up painfully and breathed the fresh September air. Her plan to spend the day weeding the garden was foolishly optimistic: her legs and back still ached from yesterday's exertion. And the images of the day replayed themselves: Michael's hair waving in the jewel-blue water, goggles tight against his face, the neighbour's chubby hands cradling her face, wagging back and forth. "Poor Edek, poor poor Edek. All alone now."

Edek. Edward. Rebecca had avoided thinking of him. The police would have notified him by now. Was he there, alone in the house? She knew what it was to lose someone. Like you've been punched in the stomach and all the breath's gone out of you. Michael would've wanted someone to check on the boy.

And maybe he'd know something. The "Sophie" chapter she'd read in Michael's manuscript last night answered nothing about the compass. She was drawn into the story of the high-born, clever young girl and the prophetic tale of the rabbi, but it raised more questions than it answered. Who was she? More to the point, who did she become? Because Rebecca could tell that the girl was heading toward some illustrious future. If Rebecca knew more history, she might have been able to guess. She would read the rest of the manuscript, but the end of it was missing. There would be no answers without those lost pages. Edward was her best lead.

By one-thirty she gave up on the garden and changed into khaki pants and a black cotton pullover. Driving down Avenue Road she headed toward the Gardiner Expressway. Traffic was light on a Sunday and she reached Baby Point Road in twenty minutes.

Michael's house looked the same, but there was a dark green Ford Mustang parked in the driveway. It must be Edward's. All at once she was reluctant to knock on the closed door. What if he were sleeping? What if she were invading his privacy?

Across the street the elderly neighbour who had run into Michael's backyard yesterday stood at the screen door of a large, red brick, two-storey house, gazing out. Rebecca got out of the car and climbed the flagstone steps toward her. She opened the door on Rebecca's approach.

"I'm sorry to bother you," Rebecca said, "but I wonder if I could speak to you for a few minutes."

"Who you are?"

"I'm Rebecca Temple. We met yesterday in Michael Oginski's backyard."

The woman levelled her small eyes at her. No sign of recognition.

"I was a friend of his."

The woman watched her with suspicion, her waist girded by a beige apron run amok with orange flowers. "I don't know nothing," she said.

"I just want to know if anyone visited Michael before we arrived." How was she going to convince this woman to talk to her? "I'm not sure it was an accident."

The woman's eyes grew large with alarm. She craned her neck to look behind herself, appeared to listen for something, then motioned to Rebecca that she was stepping outside. The door closed behind her. "We talk out here better."

The woman sat down on the top step gracefully, considering her girth. Rebecca sat down beside her.

"I live with daughter, grandchildren. Kids taking nap. I still can't believe about Pan Oginski. It is tragedy. He was great man. You were friend?"

Rebecca nodded.

"In Poland we would call him Jaśny Pan."

"What does that mean?"

She shrugged her round shoulders. "Lord. Excellency. Sign of respect for important man. Why you think was no accident?"

"I hope I'm wrong. There were just a few things that don't add up." She wasn't about to go into the story of Janek and the compass with this stranger.

"Mrs. ..." Rebecca hesitated. The woman watched

her but didn't volunteer a name. "Yesterday you said you brought Michael some food. What time was that?"

Her blue eyes glanced away, the broad face with its flat cheeks turned toward Michael's house. "Ten, I think."

"Were there any visitors with him when you got there?"

"No," she said. "He alone." Her grey hair was pinned into an unruly bun at the nape of her neck. "But someone come after."

"Who was it?"

Her large shoulder rose. "Don't know. Didn't see. But car parked in front later. Maybe hour."

"What did it look like?"

"Black. Nice car. Big."

"Was it a Cadillac?"

She shook her head. "I don't know cars." Her chin pointed to the house. "Maybe Edek know. He home now. Can ask him. Poor boy. To lose father. He alone now. Such a nice boy. I bring him supper later."

"That's very nice of you."

The woman knit her grey eyebrows together. "Terrible tragedy. Can't believe it."

Rebecca gazed across the street at Michael's English-cottage house with its stone facing and mullioned windows beneath all those gables. She wished she couldn't believe he was gone. Right now that was all she knew — that he was gone.

She walked across the street under the watchful eye of the neighbour and knocked on Michael's door. When it opened, she stood dumbfounded: a younger, thinner version of Michael in jeans and a black T-shirt wavered in the doorway. He was not as young as she expected. More middle twenties than late teens. Certainly no kid.

"You must be Edward," she said. "I hope I'm not disturbing you. I wanted to give you my condolences. Your father and I were friends."

The young man blinked into the light, his eyes red and swollen. "I'm a little dazed. What did you say your name was?"

"Rebecca Temple."

"You're the one who pulled him out of the pool?"

"How did …"

"The cop told me. But that's all he said." He opened the door wider. "Won't you come in? I really want to know everything. If you don't mind … could you stand going over it with me, exactly what happened?"

He led her into the study where yesterday she had lain sleeping. They sat down on the flowered sofa in front of the fireplace, their knees angled toward each other. He pushed some brown hair behind his ears nervously and watched her with solemn eyes.

"Your father said you're going to school in Ottawa."

He nodded.

"You're in journalism?"

Another nod.

"Your father was very proud of you."

He looked away, swallowing. "He was the one who persuaded me to go back. I dropped out for a few years."

That explained his age. She changed the subject. "When did you get here?"

He faced her again. "Late last night. I drove down the 401 like a bat out of hell. Couldn't see straight, nearly crashed up near Kingston. I kept hoping when I got here it wouldn't be true."

He was an astonishing likeness of his father, despite the pallor and the swollen eyes. He only needed filling out, some softening around the edges.

"Tell me what happened," he said.

How was she going to recount events without causing pain?

"I'm not sure what I can tell you," she said, "that you don't already know."

He leaned over watching her, his arms resting on his thighs. She hated this.

"He was already at the bottom of the pool when we got here."

He nodded, his eyes vacant. Was he really ready? She chose her words carefully.

"I jumped in and pulled him up to the surface. My mother-in-law and a friend were there and we got him out of the water to the side of the pool. I did CPR, I tried to resuscitate him ..."

He glanced at her and she wondered if he knew that meant mouth-to-mouth.

"The firemen came and took over the CPR."

"Firemen?"

"They're usually the first ones to arrive on the scene because they're close. You've probably got a local fire station near here."

He nodded.

"Then the ambulance came and took him to the hospital."

"Was he ...?"

"I think he was gone when I pulled him out. It's hard to tell if you don't know how long someone's been in the water. You don't want to give up too soon. But I think he was gone."

He stared into the air. "I thought he'd always be here. I can't believe he's ..." His eyes moistened with tears, but he blinked them back.

"Is anyone else here with you?"

He shook his head.

"Your mother?"

He looked down, played with his fingers. "She's in upstate New York. Got a new family. Step-kids to look after."

She sighed. At least when David died she had had people around her for support. "If you need help to … arrange the funeral. Or anything." She stuck her hand into her purse and retrieved a business card. "Here's my home number." She wrote it on the back and put the card on the coffee table.

He picked up the card and studied it. "You're a doctor." He observed her, his eyes the same blue as Michael's. "Did you … were you … going out with him?"

"We just met last week. He made quite an impression on me. I know it doesn't sound like much but … sometimes you meet someone and …"

He was still leaning on his thighs, looking up at her. "You're a little young for him."

She blushed. "He was very charming. I'd never met anyone like him."

He blinked back a sudden tear. "There *was* no one like him. And now he's gone. I went to the morgue this morning to see him." He turned away. "But it wasn't him. It was his body, but it wasn't *him*."

She remembered the empty shell that David's body had become. The agony of the moment she realized she would never see him again.

"They said they'd call me when they release … release the body." His head drooped forward.

She touched his shoulder softly and his face rose up, disfigured with grief. She put her arms around him and felt her own tears push at the corners of her eyes. For Michael. For David. He shook quietly for an instant, then loosened his arms around her, pulling away embarrassed.

"I can't believe this whole thing," he said. "I just don't understand … how did it happen?"

He asked this as if she had an answer.

"I've been trying to figure that out," she said. "So don't take this the wrong way but — your father might have been drinking before he drowned."

He shook his head. "That doesn't sound like him. He was careful when he went swimming."

She licked her lips. How to put it? "I smelled liquor on his breath when ... I tried to resuscitate him."

Edward frowned. "I used to have pool parties here and he'd tell us to swim first, drink after. Maybe you're mistaken."

She would wait to hear the autopsy results, but she kept this to herself.

"How'd he like working for John Baron?"

"Uncle Janek." For the first time Edward smiled, if crookedly. "What a character. Miserable bastard. But he gave Dad a job as soon as he got here from Poland. Dad arrived with nothing, so he owed him. And Dad never forgot that. But he didn't always like the way Uncle Janek operated. The company, I mean. He sure knows how to make money, though. Dad respected that. He respected his success."

"Any idea why they would argue?"

"What do you mean? There was an argument?"

"Baron showed up here yesterday when we were leaving. He had a good bruise on his face."

"So?"

"Your father had some minor bruising on his jaw. I'm wondering if they had a fight."

"If he *touched* my father, I'll ..."

"I'm just speculating here. Was there something they might've been fighting about?"

"Uncle Janek was his boss. Dad always gave in, even if it was something he didn't agree with. It was Janek's business, after all. And he isn't someone you want to argue with." He examined her. "You think Janek was here yesterday?"

"Your neighbour saw a large black car parked in front yesterday morning."

"Mrs. Woronska sees everything. Janek has a black Caddy."

"When did you last talk to your dad?"

"He called me night before last. Friday night. He'd just gotten his manuscript back from the typist and he was excited. He said he was going out soon and we'd talk on the weekend. We only spoke for a few minutes. I was waiting for a pizza, some guys were over. I thought I'd talk to him tomorrow. Never heard from him again. Saturday the police called." He put his hand up to his forehead, closed his eyes.

"You know, that book was so important to him," he said. "I never really paid attention to it. He was always talking about it. And now when I want to look at it, I can't find it. I've checked everywhere."

"Oh!" she said, feeling herself go red. "I'm so sorry. I took it home with me."

"You what?" His forehead furrowed with confusion.

"I just — I wanted to read it and I guess I wasn't thinking. I'm sorry, I'll bring it right back. It's just that — I wanted to talk to you about this — your father said he'd nearly finished the book and he had almost two hundred pages."

She felt ridiculously guilty. When it wasn't her fault. "Well, the thing is … I only found a hundred and forty pages. The end seems to be missing."

He watched her in silence and her embarrassment grew. She knew what he was thinking. "That's impossible," he said. "Dad said there were about two hundred pages. He was proud of that."

"I looked around to see if I could find the rest of the

book, but ..." She stopped, picturing herself in Michael's pyjama top. "Is it possible ... Is there a reason someone would want something in the book?"

"I don't know. Is there?" The skeptical tone of his voice put her on edge.

"Look," she said, anger replacing discomfiture. "If I had stolen the end of the book, why would I admit to taking the rest?"

His eyes softened and he looked away. "To confuse me?"

Her argument had hit its mark. "Are you that easily confused?"

"Apparently. Look, I'm sorry. I'm not thinking too straight."

"No, I'm sorry. I shouldn't have taken it."

He rubbed his forehead as if a headache had just come on.

"Have you read the whole book?" she asked.

"Just bits and pieces when I was still living at home. Sometimes he'd mail me stuff he was having trouble with. But I've been pretty swamped over the summer — the *Ottawa Citizen* hired me for four months — so he hasn't sent me anything for a while."

"Did he tell you what the secret is?" Edward gave her a puzzled look. "He said the book would reveal a secret about your family. That it would change the history books."

"You mean that we were descended from royalty? Is that what you mean?"

"Did he give you any specifics?"

"It was the last king of Poland. Poniatowski. Stanislaw Poniatowski. Somehow he was our ancestor. Dad was trying to figure out how, kind of like a family tree. But I never understood why it was so important. We live in Canada now. Royalty's a joke here. I'd be embarrassed to tell people I'm related to a king. I had this conversation with Dad a few times. We agreed to disagree."

He looked off into the distance. "You know, there's probably an explanation for the part that's missing. Maybe the guy who typed it made some huge mistake and Dad had to give it back to him to redo. Teodor. Teodor might have a copy of the whole thing. He's the one who typed it."

"Teodor?"

"He's a grad student at U. of T. Odd kind of guy."

"Do you have a number for him?"

Edward shook his head.

"Last name?"

"Sorry. My Polish is almost non-existent, but Dad said his last name was the Polish word for 'green.' Anyway, you can probably find him at the Slavic Department. They're in an old house on Sussex. Creaky old place. Dad used to pick up his stuff there after it was typed. I went with him once."

He raised his forefinger and said, "Hold on a minute."

She heard him pound up the stairs. When he returned he sat down beside her again, handing her a sheet of paper.

"There's an address on the letterhead. You can keep that."

It was a letter sent to John Baron.

"Maybe Baron will want this back," she said.

Edward gave her a crooked little smile. "Trust me. Uncle Janek kept passing these to Dad. There's more where that came from. This prof at the department was helping Dad with some research for the book. When the guy found out who Dad was working for, he started going after Uncle Janek for money. He's a real piece of work. Read the letter."

Dear Mr. Baron,

I want to take this opportunity on behalf
of myself and the whole Slavic Studies
Department to thank you from the bottom of
my heart for your very generous consideration
of this very important matter. As someone
who fought heroically for our Beloved
Poland, you understand the necessity of teaching the history of that Great Land to future
generations. I come to you in all humility as
someone whose life is devoted to the scholarly research of not only that ignominious period of which you know, when the land of our
forefathers was rent asunder, but also the glorious times, which the world has forgotten. I
will continue my untiring efforts to bring to
light every detail of our glorious history so
that students, and eventually the general public, will understand the importance and cen-
trality of our Beloved Country. I am confident
in saying that there is nothing more crucial at
this university at the present time than estab-
lishing the John Baron Chair in Polish Studies,
whose plans you have before you, whose very
future lies in your hands. Therefore your decision will determine how Canadians will
regard Poland, whether the New World will
grant the Old the esteem it so justly deserves.
With your extremely generous help we can
start to spread knowledge where now there is
only ignorance.

Yours, very sincerely
Professor Anton Hauer

She smiled and folded the letter, depositing it in her purse.

Sunday evening Rebecca picked up some fish and chips at a local restaurant for dinner. She couldn't be bothered cooking for herself. Sitting at her kitchen table, she nibbled at the food and read the second "Sophie" chapter.

chapter thirteen

Transformation

February 1744

W̶e sit covered in furs in our little sleigh-house, which must be drawn through the snowdrifts by a dozen horses. Mama looks out the window, smiling now that we are grandly accompanied by a squadron of cavalry and a detachment of foot soldiers. In four more days we reach St. Petersburg, a fine prospect where the river Neva enters the Gulf of Finland. I am told the Empress Elizabeth's father, Peter the Great, built the city on numerous islands connected by bridges, like the fabled city of Venice. Here, grand mansions line the frozen river and three broad avenues, at the head of which sits a tall, gold-spired structure, brilliant in the winter sun.

Our welcome is warm: cannons roar in the distance and bells peal as we arrive. A great mass of people have collected on the outdoor staircase of the Winter Palace. The Empress herself, and her nephew, the Grand Duke, Peter, are in Moscow, four hundred miles away, but her Great Chancellor, a stout, bearded man named Bestuzhev, and a number of courtiers greet us with pomp and ceremony — fourteen elephants perform for our amusement in the courtyard of the Palace. Though exhausted, Mama and I bow graciously when we are presented to scores of dignitaries. Sumptuous dinners are prepared in our honour.

Mama and I would like nothing better than to take to our beds, but the Prussian ambassador advises us to leave for Moscow as soon as possible in order to arrive in time for the Grand Duke Peter's sixteenth birthday. He tells Mama in private that Chancellor Bestuzhev is opposed to my marriage to Peter since I am King Frederick's choice and thus the union would represent an alliance of Russia and Prussia. The Chancellor would prefer closer ties to England. I am introduced to the world of intrigue.

In order to ingratiate ourselves with the Empress, Mama and I must once again ascend the steps of the royal sleigh. I try, in vain, to sleep. This time we are joined by a prodigious number of officials who fill thirty more sleighs, the whole long procession heading through the snow toward Moscow. We travel day and night at a frightening speed over the frozen wilderness, stopping only to change horses. Warmed by the stove and huddled beneath furs, at least we do not suffer from the cold. Yet this is a god-forsaken country I am so anxious to join.

In a matter of three jolting days we cover the four hundred miles to Moscow. There is little fanfare here for us as we ride through the narrow, crooked streets in the dark. The city has not the glamour of Petersburg and appears dingy. I am disappointed. We stop at a mansion lit with torches, where the Empress's adjutant general meets us. With little deliberation, he takes us through one grand room after another where hundreds of people are waiting to inspect us.

They bow low as we pass, the prince naming each in a low voice, which I can scarcely hear. I am quite dizzy with fatigue and nerves.

Finally, there he is — Peter. I hold my breath. He is taller than when I saw him last, yet very boyish still, with wispy blond hair, slight of figure. He greets Mama warmly and chatters in a high voice about how impatiently he has been waiting for us. His face is animated, his small eyes looking sideways at me. He is a child! I am not certain how I feel about him. I am... disappointed.

He waits with us in our rooms for the Empress to summon us. I notice he has no shoulders to speak of and a thin chest. It is late in the evening when the Empress is finally ready to receive us. We are led to the entrance of her bedroom.

I am struck dumb by her appearance when we meet: she is a monumental woman, extraordinarily tall and plump, dressed in a silver and gold gown with a wide hoop skirt. Brilliant blue eyes animate a beautiful face, a vision of elaborately piled auburn hair is set with diamonds.

After embracing Mama, she turns her eye on me. I am embarrassed by the scrutiny of this magnificent personage, this divinity, but after a few moments she smiles, and when she smiles, her face lights up the whole room. I have passed the first test.

That evening Peter dines with Mama and me.

"Do you remember the last time we met?" I say. "You were Karl Ulrich then."

"I still am," he says in his child's voice. "Only now I'm a soldier. One day I will have my own Prussian regiment and I'll drill them all morning and they'll march around the yard just as I say."

"A *Prussian* regiment?"

"Of course Prussian. I'm wearing a Prussian uniform, aren't I?" He puffs up what little chest he has under the blue wool.

I watch Mama from the corner of my eye. She is prodding at some meat on her plate.

"I suppose you have a Russian uniform as well?"

"Russian? Are you mad? You wouldn't catch me dead in a Russian uniform. It's a rag. It's a disgrace. Like the whole country." He pokes a forkful of potato into his mouth.

"But surely ..." I begin, then think better of it. "You've joined the Orthodox church, have you not?"

He chews, watching me with blank eyes. "My aunt insisted. She wanted to rename me after her father. I must have a Russian name, how else can I be the Tsar, you see. Even the churches are a disgrace. The priests are ridiculous in their black gowns and beards to their waists. And that stink of incense. Oh, and those bloody icons everywhere. My skin crawls when I'm forced to go. My aunt is very devout." He rolls his eyes to the ceiling. "Her mother was a peasant, you know. The country is filled with peasants. You must continue to call me Karl. Otherwise I shall not speak to you."

At the beginning of Lent the Empress leaves Moscow on a pilgrimage to a monastery fifty miles away where she will do penance and pray. Meanwhile, she has arranged for my instruction in the Orthodox faith to begin. I have anticipated the process but am nevertheless taken aback that my instructor is the Archimandrite, a severe but cultivated man. I suppose some minor priest would not have done. He is patient with me and answers my questions frankly. For my part, I fail to mention

Father's exhortations to me to never give up the Lutheran church.

I am in a turmoil of my own making. It is more difficult than I expected, this alteration of religion. Akin to trying to alter my heart.

I wake up one morning with a start: where am I? My skin is on fire. The room swims before me and my head aches. Are we still thrashing along the frozen rutted roads? No, I see high ceilings, long windows that let in a faint blue light. And someone stands by my bed. *Mama?* She is wringing her hands. *What are you doing here?* She doesn't hear me because I cannot form the words. They die on my tongue, which refuses to move. However, I am able to hear.

"Princess," an older man says to Mama, "I must bleed her or she will die." I recognize the voice of the Empress's Dutch physician, Boerhave. "Her blood is inflamed from the rough journey."

"No!" cries Mama. "Decidedly no! If you bleed her she will *surely* die."

"When the Empress returns tomorrow, she will decide on the treatment."

"She is *my* daughter."

I fall into a deep, warm sea where my head and limbs float. I am not in pain. I am not anything. The numbness is a relief. I no longer feel the distress from ... from what? From my new life? The lessons in how to live my new life? Can a German princess become a Russian Grand Duchess? There is so much to learn. The Russian language — earthy and lilting compared to the guttural German. The Orthodox faith — it is not the lessons that distress so much as Father's letters still arriving from the home that seems so far away now. I am certain I shall never see it again. The Lutheran faith I must leave behind like my home. Have I left behind my heart as well? No, because Father says God searches the heart and our secret desires and He cannot be deceived. Am I deceiving Him? Am I deceiving *me*? The Archimandrite who instructs me does not ask questions like these. Nor does he ask why I am marrying the boy soldier. We both know why.

I am being pulled from my warm, benumbed sea to wake again with a start. This time the Empress's large, beautiful face hovers close to mine, her eyes filled with concern. I am cradled in her ample arms.

"Dear Boerhave, it is working."

"Yes, Your Imperial Majesty. I shall bleed her some more in the evening."

I feel a pain in my foot; something is dripping, dripping close by. I picture the blood pooling in a basin.

"Dear, dear Sophie," she says, rocking me gently next to her large bosom. "You must be strong."

Still in her arms I sink back into that delightful numbing sea that takes away all pain. However, though my limbs float, my head is not as deep this time and I can hear whispering around me, the rustle of skirts moving past.

"Where's her mother?" someone murmurs.

"The Empress ordered her to her room. She argues against the bleeding."

Perhaps I am dreaming but I feel the Empress close by. I smell her perfume, like roses. Will she be my mother now?

When I open my eyes again, it is the Empress's mouth I see. At first it looks uncertain. Then the edges lift up into a smile. "Boerhave!" she cries. "She is awake!" The Empress gazes at me more fondly than my own mother ever has.

I struggle to sit up, helped by some ladies-in-waiting.

"Bring some food!" the Empress says. "She must eat."

"Only clear soup, Your Majesty," says Boerhave.

The Empress glowers at him. "How can she recover her strength with soup?"

"Only for today, Your Majesty," he says, bowing from the waist.

I feel great affection for her at this moment.

I have been ill for three weeks. Someone says it is spring.

Though still weak, I am soon hungry and eat everything set before me while sitting in bed. After a week of gobbling up every delicacy out of the royal kitchen, I begin my lessons anew, both the Russian language and theology. The date for my conversion is set. I am resolved to carry on.

Mama comes to see me, but the Empress is furious with her. She has discovered that Mama is meeting with the Prussian and French ambassadors. Worst of all, Chancellor Bestuzhev, who sides with the English against the French, has told her that Mama corresponds with King Frederick and relays to him the goings-on of the Russian court. The Empress will brook no spying or interference from either side, but at the moment leans toward the English. There is no end to the intrigue.

They continue in politeness before the court, but the Empress vilifies Mama to me in private. King Frederick continues to play a role in my life, writing to Father deliberate nonsense — that the differences between the Orthodox church and the Lutheran church are insignificant. He does not want to impede my progress in the Russian court, since I will be his friend. And well he knows his influence with Father. His king has promoted him to field marshal after nominating his daughter to marry the heir to the Russian throne. There is the little matter of religion. How can Father refuse to acquiesce to a conversion that apparently means so little?

At the end of June I am ready. I have committed to memory the confession of faith written by my instructor, the Archimandrite. Fifty pages of words that are not my own, but which become my own.

When I am led into the palace chapel I am dizzy from three days of fasting in preparation. The sanctuary is quite overwhelming, thousands of candle flames wavering, trying valiantly to reach into the shadows to illuminate the mosaics and sacred icons. As I kneel into the silk cushion, my crimson gown spread around me like a fan, the voices of the choir echo against the dim walls and pillars. The heavy fragrance of incense hangs in the gold air. My head spins.

I must repeat the words with conviction, and the Russian pronunciation with care. A multitude of spectators fills the chapel among the pillars. At first I hide my uneasiness behind a brave voice. But then something beneath my ribs lifts me up, like wings, and I hear my voice echoing among the stone walls, reaching out to the people and returning to me strengthened. Sophie is folded up within my heart like a map, her religion, her language, her parents. A new page begins, a new geography, where Sophie Augusta becomes Catherine Aleksayevna, whose clear, certain voice resonates among the astonished crowd.

The next morning I am to be betrothed to the Grand Duke. The Empress strides majestically before us into the cathedral beneath a great silver canopy held by eight officers. Peter and I follow. Once inside the Empress takes us by the hand and leads us to a dais in the centre of the church. Again a great assembly of spectators. After hours of exchanging vows of betrothal, kneeling and standing, standing and kneeling, bathed by the music of the choir, the Empress gives us our betrothal rings. We exchange them, Peter and I, and for the first time, I am addressed by my new title: Grand Duchess.

At first the new deference with which I am treated disturbs me. At the ball later that evening even people of rank bow and kneel and call me "Your Imperial Highness." My face aches from smiling. I am only fifteen years old but I am the second-highest ranking woman at the court. No one but the Empress and Peter may sit in my presence.

Lest I become too high and mighty, Peter brings me down to earth. His valet, Roumberg, fills his head with advice on how to treat a wife.

"After we are married," Peter says one day, "you shall not breathe unless I first give you permission. You shall say what I tell you to say and think what I tell you to think. A woman is her husband's possession, nothing more. In any case I shall have to beat you now and then. Roumberg knows of such things and he says a wife must be given a few blows to the head to remind her of her place."

I begin to fear our wedding night. I have come so far. So close to what I want. And what is that, I wonder at last. To please the Empress, a more affectionate mother than the one who bore me. To marry the man she has chosen to inherit her empire. To sit high among the stars. To shine.

During July the Empress leads her huge entourage, both court and household, into the countryside. Thousands of servants oversee a snaking train of carts filled with clothing and provisions, for she leaves nothing behind, not her gowns, not her icons, not her dogs.

Our noble procession denudes the countryside as we travel from town to town: all grain, livestock, cheese, fruit, and vegetables are devoured in a wide swath. The Empress enjoys herself with obvious ebullience. One day she hunts; another day she dances in peasant costume at a festival. The people worship her.

In August everything changes. The Empress puts on simple clothes, pulls on boots, and stamps along on foot to a shrine, a monastery, a convent. The whole court continues to follow now that she is a pilgrim, only they remain in their carriages, not quite so intent in their devotions. I marvel at the vastness of the land: the endless forests redolent of fir, the wheat fields swaying in the sun, the dewy meadows of chicory and daisies. I might have enjoyed it all if not for the presence in my carriage of Peter and Mama, the two never ceasing to find fault with each other and quarrelling without stop.

In October Peter becomes ill and is confined to his bed. At first I am relieved by his absence: no more talk of beatings or wifely obedience. But if he should die, my role here is finished. I am disquieted that I may be sent back to Anhalt-Zerbst, a German princess among many, all equally low of rank. To my relief Peter recovers. For a time.

A week before Christmas he becomes ill in earnest. It cannot be worse: he has smallpox. He is confined to his room with Dr. Boerhave and a few servants. No one is allowed in the room, but the Empress disregards the doctor's protests and nurses Peter herself.

I continue to study Russian. I also pray for Peter's recovery. Not entirely for unselfish reasons.

Peter is stronger than he appears, for after six weeks, he survives the smallpox. However in the battle for his life, the illness has scored some victories. His appearance has become hideous, his face still swollen and distorted with purplish scars from the pox. He wears a huge ridiculous wig since his own hair has been shaved off. How did this happen? How can I marry this revolting apparition?

His wispy hair grows back and his face returns to normal size, but he is no less vicious. His only saving grace is that he is not interested in me. On the dreaded wedding night I wait for him for hours with rising anxiety. I need not have worried. It is near morning when he staggers into the bedroom. Grunting in German, he falls dead drunk into the bed.

June 1746

The evening is finally drawing to a close and I am bored
to a stupor with all the noblewomen in attendance
around me. The weekly royal ball is opportunity for them
to gossip and spread rumours about who is carrying on
an affair with whom this week. Only half the nobles can
read, and none, it seems, are interested in discussing art
or philosophy.

Despite the high ceiling, the room is stifling hot and
swelters with dancers swathed in many layers of silk, the
air thick with sweat. Whenever I get up to dance, the
eyes of those around me are drawn to my waist. Some
aim at discretion behind their fans, but I know they are
watching and whispering. A year after my marriage
there is still no sign of a child. I am still thin and agile
and wretchedly unhappy. The Empress has become
impatient but I dare not confess to her that her nephew
does not try to make love to me. That we have never
made love. That he is, indeed, incapable of it. He is a
child in all ways including the physical sphere.

He does, however, know how to torment me.
There he comes with his narrow shoulders and plump
belly dressed in his blue Prussian uniform, still bearing
some scars from the pox. He is ready for the final salvo
of the evening.

Stopping within my earshot he says to his servant,
"Did you notice how pretty Fräulein Hesse is looking
tonight? Far prettier than my wife. In fact, my wife
looks inferior this evening, not at all pleasing."

He delights in his petty cruelty. Fräulein Hesse is his
current infatuation. Next week it will be another. Of
course he is incapable of doing anything about it.

The Empress's women prepare to find her a safe
room for the night. Her anxiety rises toward the end of

the evening when she must retire: will she survive another day? She sleeps in a different room each night to thwart the assassins that she is certain plot her death. Her scowling, muscled bodyguard lies at the foot of her bed. Even then she is afraid of the dark, afraid of being murdered in her sleep. She makes her women talk to her half the night, all the court gossip and rumours that stave off the dark. Do they repeat the murky intrigues of which I have caught whispers? That I am the chief spy, consorting with Frederick against the English faction? The Empress watches me with more and more suspicion, and I wonder which of the scheming courtiers have bent her ear. I no longer know whom to trust. I hear mutterings of "Traitor" behind my back. I have heard that the Empress suspects me of being a spy like Mama. Poor Mama, sent back to Germany in disgrace for her disobedience and disloyalty. The Empress's eyes accuse me of the same. Disobedience, disloyalty.

My head aches constantly. I steel myself against the pain. One day I can endure it no longer and I call in the court surgeon. He cuts a vein in both my arms to bleed me. The women around me go pale while the blood drips into a basin. He has just finished wrapping bandages round my arms, the vise of pain circling my forehead is starting to abate, when all of a sudden the door to my room flies open and in marches the Empress. Her eyes are wild. I have never seen her so furious.

"The secret is out!" she cries. "You have been seen together, you and your lover!"

The surgeon and all my servants flee the room, terrified, abandoning me to the Empress's wrath. How am I to defend myself?

"I have no lover," I say, trying to remain calm.

Her face scarlet, she shakes her fist at me and steps closer, her huge figure looming. I take several steps backward. She prepares herself to strike me; her arms aquiver.

"Don't lie to me! You have been *seen*! You are betraying your husband with Andrei Chernyshev. This is the reason you are not pregnant."

Peter's valet! Ridiculous. If I were going to betray Peter I would find someone more appealing.

The Empress presses closer. I keep stepping backward until finally there is nowhere left to go and her large body pins me to the wall.

"You cannot be a wife to Peter," she is shrieking in my face, "if you love someone else!"

My chest convulses and I start to weep uncontrollably. This is the mother I thought would love me. I cannot breathe through my tears.

"It is your own fault you have no child!" the Empress cries, so close to my face that her hot breath sears my skin.

My servants have rescued me after all. They have summoned Peter, who walks in coolly in his robe. The Empress abruptly steps back from me. Her face softens, becomes normal, and she speaks to Peter with affection. Suddenly she is gone.

Great Chancellor Bestuzhev, the man who advised the Empress against my marrying Peter, is up in arms. It seems that the only reason I have been brought to this godforsaken country is to bear a child and thus provide the empire with an heir to the throne. According to Bestuzhev, Peter and I are two wayward, spoiled children who need strict direction and discipline in order to fulfill our duty. Therefore, we are to be appointed guardians who will suffer no frivolity but will steer us toward our solemn obligations.

My heart falls when the Empress chooses as my chaperone her first cousin, Maria Choglokov, a pretty but humourless young woman who takes her assignment seriously indeed. Maria is tiresomely fertile herself, ever pregnant by her husband, Peter's new guardian. No doubt the Empress hopes Maria's fruitfulness will be catching, like a cold. Maria suffers no nonsense. No one in the household is allowed to speak with me on pain of being reported to the Empress as an intriguer. I am left in stony silence most of the time. With the result that during the day I am quite alone and find myself more and more in front of my mirror, my only company the young Kalmuk boy who arranges my hair so skillfully. I have grown weary of staring at my own long, thin face, my jaw still pronounced, but now trembling too often with tears.

Any time that I feel even a little light-hearted about something and forget to dissemble, Maria announces, "I'm going to make my report to the Empress!" I must learn to better conceal my thoughts.

The Empress insists Peter and I attend not only mass daily, but now we must also go to chapel for matins and vespers. Peter despises the church but is too much of a coward to protest. He is unwilling to bring down yet another rant from the Empress that she will disinherit him after all.

When her temper is unavoidable and he is in distress he seeks me out. At such times I take pity on him and pet him like a lapdog for I am the only person he can talk to without risking committing an offence. Though he does go on and on about grenadiers and artillery manoeuvres until I am bored to distraction. I am so bored that sometimes I humour him and let him make me into a soldier. He teaches me to march and obey field commands in my silk gown. Then he hands me a musket and orders me to stand guard at the door of his room with the heavy gun on my shoulder. It amuses him to leave me thus for hours.

Sometimes when he comes back to dismiss me, I smell wine on his breath. He does not bother to moderate his drinking but indulges in it both in public at the Empress's table and in private where bottles stand hidden in cupboards waiting for him. I have learned to avoid him after he has spent an evening of unbridled drinking with his servants.

The man who was supposed to tame Peter, Nicholas Choglokov, Maria's husband, has failed utterly to bring him under control. Together, the Choglokovs have not found a way to resolve the impenetrable task at hand: to bring about my pregnancy.

February 1748

I have just had a bad shock after delivery of a letter: my dear beloved father is dead. I shall never see him again, the ballast of my childhood. The blunt, upright, scrupulously honest man whose face I have trouble calling forth now, after a separation of four years. My tears start to flow and no one can comfort me. He had none of the guile or deceit that surrounds me here but was the most genuine of men. He acted and spoke in a straightforward manner that would be all but incomprehensible in this court.

My tears do not abate. I weep copiously for eight days, but then Maria Choglokov tells me that I have cried enough, that the Empress orders me to end my tears since I am a Grand Duchess and my father was not a king. I am allowed to wear mourning, but only for six weeks.

July 1752

The insolent chamberlain called Sergei Saltykov watches me from beneath black eyebrows and lashes when he thinks I do not see. He is arresting with his swarthy complexion, such a startling contrast to Peter's sickly white skin. Sergei is high-born like his wife, who is a lady at court. He attends every function and charms the Choglokovs with his compliments. I notice that my temple begins to throb when he enters the room. He is a known seducer — I have been warned about him, but he is relentless. He will not give up.

He must know, as does the entire court, that my marriage to Peter is a sham, that I am as virginal now as I was seven years ago when we married. Then Sergei also knows about the change of climate in the court. The Empress has had a bout of some illness of which she will not speak but which has made her all the more anxious about the succession. If she dies suddenly, what will become of the throne? There must be an heir, or all the rival factions at court will fall over each other to push Peter aside the moment the Empress is dead. Yet even she finally realizes that her nephew cannot father children. Her anger against him has been mounting.

One day, while passing the door of a room where she converses with an advisor, I overhear her say, "My nephew is a horror. May the devil take him!"

I am no longer watched for signs of flirtations with courtiers. Indeed, the Choglokovs, in an astonishing about-turn, encourage my attentions to Saltykov. They are quite impatient to leave us alone together. Since they take their orders from the Empress, it follows that the Empress has decided I must take a lover. She can wait no longer for an heir, and if my husband is unable to father a child, then someone else will have to.

The new desperation at court is not lost on Saltykov. He knows how to use it to his advantage. The Choglokovs arrange opportunities when Saltykov may seek me out without disturbance. A hunting party on an island in the Neva where only select courtiers are ferried for the day. While the others are off hunting hares in the field, Sergei pulls me playfully behind a thicket and confesses his ardour with long, honeyed phrases that reach into my heart. I am twenty-three years old and have never been made love to like a real woman.

His persistent attentions and declarations of love enthrall me. By September I succumb to his wooing. Within months I conceive a child.

In December the court sets out on the journey from Petersburg back to Moscow. The impatient drivers whip the horses over the rough, craggy roads at a frenzied pace. My carriage shakes and hurtles with a fury and I am thrown about without mercy. Before we arrive I am seized with pain and lose the child.

The Empress lodges me in a newly built wing of the Golovin Palace for my recovery. Its construction is so slipshod that the rats scuttle in and out of the already rotting wainscotting. That winter fires break out all over Moscow. One night, alone and ignored, as I have been since my return, I stand by the palace window to view the panorama of rooftops. I cannot believe my eyes: in the distance four — no, five — blazes are raging in different quarters of the city, sending up vicious flames, while smoke blooms into the black sky like a vengeful flower.

One spring day I enter Peter's apartments and am startled to see a giant rat hanging from a gallows constructed inside a cupboard. Peter leans nearby, his head tilted back as he gulps from a bottle of wine.

"You see," he says, wiping his mouth with the back of his hand, "this creature chewed into my favourite fortress and ate three of my best tin soldiers, though I scarcely think they tasted of much. A criminal act by any standards. Under the military code, the laws of war demand he must be executed and left on the gallows for three days as an example to other rats."

During the summer Sergei is inconstant and temperamental. I have trusted him, but he toys with my heart. I do not enjoy the games he seems intent on playing. Yet I must persevere if there is to be an heir to the throne.

That November the unthinkable happens. I am listening to Maria Choglokov in her salon describing a dress she is having made, when shouts rise in the corridor. All of a sudden Sergei and Leon Naryshkin fly into the room. They scream, "Fire! A wing of the palace is on fire!"

I rush to my own rooms, where my servants are already removing as much as they can carry. I venture into the hall, where dense smoke immediately invades my throat. Twenty feet away the balustrade of the grand staircase is on fire. I am struck dumb to see thousands of rats and mice file down the staircase in an orderly procession. The flames have spread rapidly from room to room, engulfing the worm-eaten wood in an instant. It is a picture of hell I pray I shall never see again. Maria and I run from the palace and find refuge in a carriage, from which vantage point we watch the devastation.

The fire burns for three hours. By nightfall there is nothing left of the magnificent Golovin Palace but an orange glow hovering over the smouldering, charred embers. While sitting benumbed in the carriage, gazing mutely at the walls as they crumble into nothing, I am filled with hopelessness. My life, like the palace, is collapsing into nothing.

January 1753

Six weeks after the destruction of the Golovin palace, a new palace has been erected by carpenters working furiously at the Empress's command. I must take my lead from her. I must not allow obstacles to bar my way.

Though the Empress puts a cheerful face forward at banquets and balls, her health is declining. She can no longer climb stairs on account of the weakness in her legs. Special lifts have been constructed in her palace to take her from one floor to another. I have heard rumours about secret dispatches sent by foreign ambassadors at the court who conjecture how the new regime will take over when the Empress dies. All the court begins to look upon me differently. They know I would assume a large role next to Peter in the succession. My one failing — I have no child. I must find a solution for that.

I set my sights on Saltykov, my inconstant love, and early in the new year I am once again pregnant with his child. This time I am resolved not to lose it.

chapter fourteen

Sarah had three singing lessons scheduled for Sunday afternoon, though she felt restless and distracted from the day before. Despite all her experience with dead bodies during the war, it was still a shock to see one. Also, her back muscles were aching from the effort of helping Rebecca pull Michael out of the pool. But it went against her grain to cancel a lesson.

She apologized to Natalka for being thus occupied, but the younger woman insisted she could entertain herself and that it would be a relief to have some time to just sit and read.

The first student stood near the piano as Sarah helped her warm up her voice. She plunked out a key on the piano for the young woman to begin. Fifteen minutes of vocal exercises.

"Feel the muscles in your mask area," Sarah said. "It's the sinuses that resonate." Sarah placed her thumb and forefinger on both sides of her nose beneath her eyes.

Sarah scrutinized the woman's posture. "Raise up your sternum. That frees your lungs to take in more air. Drop your shoulders. Stand like a dancer."

Sarah was drinking some water in the kitchen when the second young woman let herself in the front door. Sarah smiled at Natalka on her way into the living room.

When the last student left, Sarah sank onto the sofa, drained as usual after an afternoon of lessons. She was getting old. Who was she kidding? She *was* old.

Natalka called in from the kitchen. "You would like some tea?"

"I would, thank you."

Natalka brought in a tray with a teapot and two mugs, depositing it on the coffee table. She poured Sarah some tea, then sat down on the other end of the couch with her mug.

"You are very good teacher," she said, a new respect in her face. "Strict, but in kind way. You discipline, but you do not — how to say — you do not make the person small."

Sarah smiled, a little embarrassed. "Thank you, I'm flattered."

"My mother always encouraged music from when I was very little. She loves music, but she is not musician. She listens, she appreciates, but she doesn't feel it in her bones. Like we do."

Sarah felt very warm inside, to have a musician of Natalka's stature include her in "we."

"Do you give lessons?" she asked her.

Natalka sipped at her tea. "I had students before I got sick. Now I see I miss it — to share what you love with people that appreciate. I could not get through this without my music. When I am very depressed, I start to play and then it's better."

There was *a kinship among musicians,* Sarah thought. The connection she felt moved her to say to this almost stranger what she would've liked to say to Rebecca but never could.

"I lost my husband five years ago, then my son," Sarah said. "There's nothing worse than a parent outliving a child. I didn't think I would survive it. Of course, I couldn't sing. When your body is the instrument, you cannot sing if your soul is sick. The two are intricately connected. I was afraid I would never sing again. Then one day I heard Kathleen Ferrier sing one of those tragic English love songs in her contralto, and my heart opened up again. I realized the world was still beautiful. Music still caught at my throat — you know what I mean. None of that changed. Only I had changed."

Animation lit Natalka's small, oval face. "I understand completely. Everything for me changed also. Only music not changed. This I like — you can read notes on page of music and play on piano, then next person can read same notes and play same thing. This is structure, it is a comfort. If only other things are so reliable."

Sarah had dialed Rebecca's number several times that day to find out how she was, but no one answered. It was late in the afternoon before her daughter-in-law picked up the phone.

"I was starting to worry about you. Everything all right?"

"I was at Michael's house. I met Edward."

"His son?"

"I wanted to see if he was all right."

How had Rebecca gotten so close to a man she had

just met? She rarely showed such concern for her mother-in-law.

"And was he?" Sarah said, trying to keep the censure out of her voice.

"He was upset. But surviving. We talked about his father's manuscript. I made a copy if you want to read it after I'm finished."

"So you're enjoying it."

"It's very exciting. It sounds like the eighteenth century was tolerable if you were an aristocrat. Tonight I'm going to read about an English nobleman named Sir Charles. It's taking my mind off everything. How are you feeling, after yesterday?"

Okay, make me feel guilty, Sarah thought. "I'm a little sore. I pulled muscles I didn't know I had. How about you?"

"A little sore."

There was an awkward pause, the kind between two people who scrupulously avoid unknown territory lest they poke a sore spot.

"Did Halina come back?" Rebecca asked.

"No."

"Did you call the police?"

"Natalka wouldn't let me."

"Aren't you worried?"

"Of course. But I don't think calling the police will solve anything. I think she's gone of her own free will, so what would be the point?"

Rebecca breathed into the phone. "I just don't understand any of it. Nothing about this whole business makes any sense. She's left her daughter at a crucial time. Doesn't Natalka have an appointment to see the specialist this week?"

"Wednesday. I'll take her if Halina doesn't come back," Sarah said. "It's at Mount Sinai?"

"Yes. It's Dr. Koboy. I'll speak to you before then."

Halina did not come back on Sunday. There was still no word from her on Monday.

The early sun slanted through the patio doors in the kitchen and lit a halo around Natalka's white hair, swept up into a chignon. Sarah stared at her, wrapped her hands around the coffee mug without lifting it.

"Does your mother know anyone else in Toronto?"

Natalka sipped at her coffee. "No."

If she were worried about her mother, she didn't show it. "Did she say *anything* about where she was going?"

Natalka gave a small shrug, watching her coffee intently.

"What about the Polish Consulate?" Sarah said, desperate. "Did she ever mention the Consulate?"

The younger woman snapped to attention, her head angled on the slender stalk of neck. She looked away quickly, giving the impression of trying to remember. "I don't think so. Not sure."

"Well, it's the only place I can think of," Sarah said. "I'm going to drive over there and see if she's contacted anyone." She felt she needed to do something, but sensed a tension rise between them.

Sarah brought out the Toronto phone book and found the Consulate General of Poland. It was an address on the Lakeshore. Unfamiliar territory, but she would find it.

She poured her coffee down the sink and looked over at Natalka, still sitting at the kitchen table. "Are you going to come?"

The woman observed her thoughtfully. "No," she said. "And if you go, you must be careful what you say. Not make them suspicious."

"Suspicious of what?"

"If you say Mama gone, they think she wants to defect."

Sarah stopped moving, focusing all her attention. "Is that a possibility?"

Natalka blinked. "No, no. My daughter is still in Poland ... Would be trouble."

With misgivings Sarah drove down Bathurst to the Gardiner Expressway and got off at Lakeshore Road. A grey layer of cloud had expanded to fill the horizon. By the time she parked the car on a side street off the Lakeshore, a soft rain was misting the air.

She strode quickly under her umbrella, approaching a large mansion that housed the Polish Consulate. The elaborate wrought iron gate in the front was locked and a sign pointed her to the side entrance. She walked along the fence that stretched the length of the building. Finally she came to a narrower gate that must once have been meant for tradespeople and servants. This swung open. Was she doing the right thing? Why hadn't Natalka come?

Still under her umbrella she stepped along a narrow walk all the way to the back of the mansion until she reached the rear entrance. Opening the door, she was astonished to find herself at the end of a long line of people waiting to approach a wicket.

All signs were printed in Polish. Sarah felt her muscles go tense. Though there were two wickets, almost everyone lined up in front of the window beneath a sign that read, "Drop off documents." Only three people stood before the other window, where the sign read, "Pick up documents."

She excused herself to manoeuvre around the line of people standing near the door and stepped toward the other wicket.

The people standing at each window spoke loudly in Polish to the female attendants who sat behind a glass partition looking bored and impatient. Their responses were inaudible from where Sarah stood. The men and women standing around her murmured in Polish to their companions. Her neck felt like a board. It had been over thirty years since she'd been surrounded by people speaking Polish, and it was unsettling. The words themselves sounded sweet to her ears, but the memories of other speakers, the betrayals —

"My niece is joining the Felician Sisters," a woman in the next line was saying to her friend. She wore a shapeless brown raincoat around her ample body. Her grey hair was permed into tight curls.

"Little Jadwiga? Really?"

"I begged my sister to forbid her, but the poor girl is very plain and will never attract a man."

Sarah glanced at the large wart on the woman's cheek and suppressed a smile.

"Then maybe it's for the best. At least she'll do some good. I hear the Sisters help the poor."

"She wants to work with children. Probably never have any of her own."

"You know, the Sisters have a nice house downtown. She'll be taken care of."

An elegantly dressed woman in an olive green linen skirt and jacket stepped up to the next wicket. Unlike the others, she had spoken her request in a low voice while Sarah had been distracted by the conversation of her neighbours.

"Can I please see your documents?"

The woman passed her papers under the glass.

"This is not enough. You need the proper documents."

"But I have everything I'm supposed to."

"Not approved!" The attendant shoved her papers back.

"But why?" The woman's voice had risen, plaintive now.

"This stamp not correct." The attendant gestured to someone out of sight.

A door Sarah hadn't noticed before opened beside the wickets and a tall, spectacled man appeared. He stood aside waiting for the woman to enter. She hesitated a moment, looked at the people behind her in line, and stepped slowly through the door.

The man in front of Sarah picked up his documents from the attendant and marched away. It was Sarah's turn.

The middle-aged blond woman stared at her with blank eyes. "*Prosze Pany?*"

Sarah began speaking in English. She hadn't planned to, couldn't help the English words that escaped her mouth.

"I'm looking for a friend who arrived from Poland last week. I thought maybe she came here. If I tell you her name —"

"I'm sorry but we can't help you," the woman said in heavily accented English. "We are not here for that."

"I'm concerned about her because she didn't leave an address where I can reach her. So if she did contact you —"

"We don't keep names on file like that."

How could she make this woman take her seriously, make her understand?

"Look, she's an important person in the Party. She works for Orbis. All I want to know —"

The woman's eyes took on some light. "Wait a minute."

She turned away toward someone out of Sarah's line of vision, in the direction of the same door behind which the elegant but paper-less woman had vanished. Some muttering in Polish too low to hear, not meant to be heard.

The hairs on Sarah's arms began to bristle. An uneasiness she couldn't explain settled on her like scratchy wool. She remembered Natalka's warning, the alarm in her posture. Maybe this wasn't such a good idea.

The mysterious door on the other side of the wickets began to open. Before the blond attendant had turned her head back to face her, Sarah bolted through the line of people and out the back door.

Sarah groaned and turned over in her sleep. It had been a gruesome few days, and her bed would have been a welcome respite if only her mind would stay where her body was. But she began to fall, fall through the decades into Ulica Miodowa, the narrow canyon between buildings that leaned toward each other to listen to her breathing. *You won't find them here*, the voices murmured. *Long gone. Don't you know anything?* they snickered. *Over here. Come over here.* She glided toward the voices, such familiar voices, across Ulica Dajwor, past darkened shops, under the bridge, following a high brick wall to where an iron gate slowly opened.

You've finally found us, they laughed. She drifted through the gate, such a familiar gate, and then she saw them: gravestones heaved and pitted like crooked teeth, Stars of David emblazoned on their granite chests, telling her — telling her —

With tremendous effort she willed her body around. The stars twirled above her head, changed places in the great bowl of sky as she turned and floated out the gate.

Through Ulica Szeroka, the wide square, empty now, where the ghosts of Jewish merchants echoed on the cobblestones in front of the ancient buildings. The shades of horses and wagons, clip-clop, clip-clop. Rayzele in her arms, weeping, sighing. The reddish hair in a downy curl on her forehead. Baby hair. *Hush, little sweetheart. They won't find you. I'll never let them find you.*

No more than a turn of her head — she's in Ulica Grodzka and ... Rayzele, where is Rayzele? Darkness all around like ink. Drowning in shadows. *Where is my little darling?* Everything black. But there, what is that? A light up ahead. Above a door. A soft weeping.

She glides toward the door, so familiar, she knows that door, but it won't stay still. The closer she comes, the further it retreats. It's shrinking. She must reach the door, she must. She pushes herself. If she could only go faster the door would stop. But it keeps shrinking, threatens to dissolve into the dark. Her heart is racing, flying, she cannot go on, the door is just out of reach.

Rayzele! she cries out.

And there, suddenly looming above her — the door. The familiar old wood, thick, cold. She pushes it. It yields. The towering door creaks open. Her heart beats in her ears, rattling, drumming in her ears. A shank of light filters into the black street, too bright for her to look at. She averts her eyes like Moses before the bush that burns: But she must look. She must. Though it is painful to behold, she pushes the door further. The wedge of light grows, a spreading triangle. Her eyes close tight from pain, but she must look.

When she opens her eyes, she is awake and thirty-four years have swept by.

chapter fifteen

Sir Charles

For King and Country

August 18, 1746

Our grasp on life is tenuous. If anyone doubts it, let him stop at Tower Hill during the hour of execution. Although I travel to London for Parliament often enough, the Tower never fails to impress, especially the White Tower, some ninety feet high to the battlements. It's built of dark, rough-hewn ragstone, the corners and windows of which are edged with finely cut pale Caen stone. The four turrets are topped with onion-shaped caps that glisten in the August sun.

Henry Fox and I chat as amiably as if we are still in Holland House, where Lady Caroline is, no doubt, telling cook what she wants served for dinner. As members of government, we are placed in the Transport

Office next door to the two rooms that have been prepared for the two unfortunate Lords in view of the chopping block. The crowd hums in the distance, making us raise our voices.

The air is tense with anticipation. I have never been good at waiting and feel the need of a little mischief. I whisper to Fox, "If you had been born a Scot, dear Fox, would you have followed the Bonnie Prince into Culloden?"

Fox swivels his bewigged head around to ensure that no one has heard me. But the din of the mob beyond has veiled my words. "You are a dangerous friend, Sir Charles. I will consider the question as a sign of bad nerves, in light of what we're about to witness. Though I can't satisfy your morbid curiousity as I am sure that neither of us would ever've had the bad taste to be born a Scot. Wales is bad enough."

I snicker at his reference to my birthplace. "You avoid the question, Fox," I murmur. "Would you still give allegiance to our Hanoverian King, or would you bow down to the handsomest prince who ever took breath? Even if he is a Papist? Have you heard the song of late about the Bonnie Prince? 'Speed bonnie boat like a bird on the wing...'" I sing it under my breath. "Now that's a real British king! No matter that his mother is Polish and he lives in France." I watch Henry for reaction — but he knows me too well — there *is* none. A bit of a sigh, a slight tremble of the powdered curls at my whimsical treason.

"A prince in exile is always more appealing than the king who rules," he whispers. "A distant Stuart can be as romantic as a lost love. But let him set foot on English soil and raise his banner, and watch how quickly the fairy dust falls away. What will be left is a flesh and bones bully who will like nothing better than to invite the Pope to join him by the throne. No, I will stay with the king I know.

King George is our rightful and legal sovereign, even if he speaks English with a German accent."

"Then you admit he favours Hanover above us," I say.

"I admit nothing whilst we sit ten yards from the scaffold that holds the block. Ask me again in Holland House after we've drunk some port."

It is a full year since the Young Pretender, Prince Charles Edward Stuart, set up his standard in Glenfinnan and took possession of Edinburgh. There were months of panic while the rebel army advanced through England triumphant and unchecked. People could scarcely believe what was happening. I, myself, voted in Parliament to allow some Dukes and Lords to organize special regiments for service against the rebels. We need hardly have worried for they are a contentious lot and by Christmas had descended into quarrelsome parties.

And now it has come to this. The squaring of accounts.

The figure of Lord Kilmarnock appears across Tower Hill, walking with half-hearted steps before the mourning coach, which follows him, as does his horse. He looks very genteel, dressed in black, his own fair hair without powder. The Sheriffs walk before him; a clergyman supports him on one side with his arm, a sympathetic teacher named Foster on the other.

When Lord Balmerino appears walking upon Tower Hill towards the Transport Office, where we sit, I declare I can hardly believe it is the same fellow I saw at the Bar of the House of Lords, shabby-looking and old then, in a worn suit of clothes and a bad wig. Now here he is dressed in the Pretender's regimentals, blue trimmed with red, a good tied wig, and a well-cocked hat. He walks firmly, supported by nobody. Two clergymen walk behind with nothing to do. He looks more like an officer upon guard than a prisoner.

At first they are both brought to the rooms right next to ours. Lord Balmerino asks to speak to Lord Kilmarnock, which is granted. We can hear everything, since they are within a yard of our door.

"Lord Kilmarnock," he says, "had you heard ever that there were orders before the Battle of Culloden to put all the English prisoners to death? I fear rumours and lies are raised against Prince Charles."

To which Lord Kilmarnock replies, "I knew of no such orders at the time, not being let in on such secrets. But now I have heard so from undoubted authority, and upon my honour I believe 'tis true."

"No," says Balmerino. "You are misled. I believe no such thing." He walks out of the room.

Later, he meets with Lord Kilmarnock upon the stairs of the Tower. They embrace. Lord Balmerino says to the younger man, "I wish I could die for us both." Lord Kilmarnock falls upon his neck.

The first to go is Lord Kilmarnock. Yet supported by the two men on either side, he walks to the scaffold, which is erected some ten yards from the door. He stands and prays with Foster, who is very affected and embraces him often. After twenty minutes he begins to undress. Jack Ketch asks his forgiveness, which he grants. Then he declares to the few people on the scaffold that he repents his actions most sincerely and that he will bless and pray for King George with his last breath. He ignores the spectators, who cannot number less than one hundred thousand, but who are held at a distance of fifty yards from the scaffold by horse and foot soldiers. The noise rising from them is like the roar of the sea, indistinct but vast.

He tucks his hair under a night cap. Then he kneels down before the block, a horror of a thing with two hollows, one for the breast to rest upon and another to receive the chin so the neck lies upon a rise. He kneels upon a cushion. But he becomes very uneasy, rising from the block, pulling off his waistcoat, kneeling yet again and rising yet again. After showing much anxiety he kneels down finally for good and tells Jack Ketch he will drop a handkerchief for the sign. He prays for several minutes, then lets the handkerchief fall. The obstinate hum of the crowd suddenly stops. Jack Ketch lifts the axe and strikes off his head at one blow, all but a bit of skin. I cannot turn away as the head falls into a piece of scarlet cloth held by four men on the other side of the block. My stomach lurches into my mouth and I wonder if any cause is worth dying for, or whether either of them would have followed their path if they knew where it would lead. Now the stage is covered with new sawdust to hide the blood and the block is covered with black cloth. The crowd murmurs again, the sound emanating into the warm summer air like steam.

Very different is the behaviour of Lord Balmerino, who goes to die with greater indifference than I go to dinner. He comes out and first peers at the spectators. Then after mounting the scaffold he approaches his coffin, which lies there, saying, "I must see whether they have put my title right." Once assuring himself, he throws his hat upon it and pulls out his spectacles in order to read some words to the people on the scaffold. The speech is very treasonable.

"If I had a thousand lives, I would lay them all down for the same glorious cause that I engaged in. How could I or anybody refuse to join with such a sweet Prince as Prince Charles?"

The executioner asks for his pardon, which he grants. Then he asks how many blows he gave Lord Kilmarnock.

"One," he answers.

"Oh!" says the Lord. "That will do well for me." Then he gives Jack Ketch all the coins he has, three guineas.

Going to the other side of the stage to look at his horse, he sees the warder that attended him in the Tower. He pulls off his peruke, then calls up the warder and makes him a present of it. He puts on a cap made of Scotch plaid and pulls off his coat. Then he embraces two friends so cheerfully that I can hear the smack of his kisses up to where I sit with Fox. He turns to the two clergymen to whom he has not yet spoken a word, and thanks them for attending him, that they had done all they could for him. From thence he walks to the block and kneels on the wrong side of it. When told, he rises nimbly up and goes immediately on the other. Jack Ketch, his black mask on, strides toward a box on t'other side of the stage to fetch the axe, the same as a carpenter's. The condemned man follows him with his eyes, then calls out to him, asking to see it. The Lord takes the axe and feels it with his own hands. He returns it to Jack Ketch, saying his sign would be when he lifts up his right arm. Then he puts his head down upon the block. His face never pales, nor does he show the least shadow of fear. In a quarter of a minute he tosses his right arm up with the greatest calmness. Again, an ominous silence falls upon the crowd. Jack Ketch swings the axe down and severs his head. The first blow does the business, but two more are required.

When we get back to Holland House in Kensington, Lady Caroline is quite put out that we are not interested in dinner.

That night I dream of Winnington. Except that by some miracle he is still alive, my dear, dear friend, strolling the grounds of my beloved Coldbrook with me as if he had never been ill. In my heart I know it's a lie, but I am so grateful that he is there with me that I am elated and fairly jump along the grass. "Thomas, my old friend, I have missed you more than I can say." He does not respond but in the way of dreams I know he is equally happy to see me. A deer approaches him — he has always loved the deer on our grounds — and he stops. That's when I notice that his head is only hanging on by a thread. Then the whole story floods back over me and I remember everything, his illness, the impossible news of his death, his waxy face in the coffin, a face I have loved since boyhood. If you could die so easily, dear Winnington, what hope is there for me? Nothing is the same, nor ever will be again. Dear Winnington, I wish I could have died for you.

I do not come downstairs until lunchtime. Lady Caroline has the good grace to refrain from mentioning my absence at breakfast. That is because she is Fox's wife, not mine, and she has not Frances's rancour nor her wifely interest in me. That is why Frances, God save us, lives elsewhere while I sojourn with the Foxes when Parliament, or anything else for that matter, brings me to London.

Lady Caroline does, however, venture to say, "It is barbaric enough to execute someone, but to make it into a public spectacle! I fear we have not gone far enough from the Dark Ages."

"My lady," says Fox, "as much as I agree with you, I feel we must put traitors to death in full view of the throngs to show them what lies in store for them if they choose such a path. Otherwise I fear our country will ever be at the mercy of ruthless men and will never know peace."

"I am sure you are right, Sir," she says, throwing me a secret look. "Only I am grateful my presence there is not required."

"It is the most terrible thing I have ever seen," I say, for that is the truth. "Yet I know not what else could be done with two Lords who plot the death of the King. And the Bonnie Prince yet abroad, still plotting."

"After the slaughter of Culloden," says she, "I hardly think the poor Prince has enough supporters left to scrape together another army."

"I did not suspect Jacobite sympathies in you, Lady Caroline," I say.

"My sympathies are with innocents who are put to the sword."

The country is torn between pride in the Duke of Cumberland (the King's brother) for his victory at Culloden, and loathing at his methods, the bloodletting after the battle, the chasing down and murder of every Scot in the vicinity, including women and children.

"Just so," I say, relieved that my battles are in Parliament and not in the field.

"A package came for you, Sir Charles," Lady Caroline says. "Delivered by a subaltern of the Marines, I believe."

It waits for me on a small silver tray in the dining room. The letter is addressed to The Paymaster of the Marines. It is a commission that has given me much trouble, one that I will soon relinquish.

The Foxes watch me open the letter with interest.

Dear Sir Charles,

Please accept a small token of our gratitude for your efforts on our behalf. Thanks to your help, the men have received their first pay in two years. They have not done with drinking to your health in the evenings and have found a way to show their appreciation by presenting you with this gift, which was acquired on their last voyage.

Your servant, Lieutenant Samuel Blocker,
4th Regiment of the Marines

I am quite overcome, but manage to unwrap the package. Inside lies a blue velvet bag. I pull open the drawstring and insert my thumb and forefinger, retrieving a small silver sundial, half of which is taken up by a round compass embedded beneath glass. The whole thing is not more than three inches long, in the octagonal shape of a coffin. A handsome little piece with the pointer for the sundial fashioned out of silver in the form of a bird's beak.

"Why Williams, you have an admirer!" Fox says coming up behind me.

"Eleven hundred admirers," I say, showing him the letter.

"I take it you finally solved the puzzle of the two masters for your Marines."

Lady Caroline joins her husband. "I beg your pardon, Sir Charles. I imagined a female admirer grateful for your poetry."

I bow politely. "You flatter me, dear lady. Despite my modest reputation as a versifier, this gift has a more prosaic source. Since I am Paymaster of the Marines it falls to me to take charge of their pay. But till recently I have been helpless to straighten out accounts for these poor lads who, through no fault of their own, suffered because they joined the Marines rather than the army or navy. It really is too complex to relate ..."

"Oh, Sir Charles," Lady Caroline says, "don't leave us in mid-tale. Tell us why a whole regiment is in your debt."

"Not just one regiment, Lady Caroline," Fox interrupts. "All the regiments. The whole of the Marines."

I must smile. "If I tell the whole wretched story, you will see what a bore it is and how small was my part in the solution. Here it is at your insistence: A regiment of soldiers is paid only after it is mustered. In order to be mustered the whole regiment must come together. No problem for the army or the navy. But the Marines belong to both the land and sea forces at the same time, under two masters so to speak: the Secretary-at-War while ashore, and the Lord High Admiral when at sea. An anomalous position, as you can imagine. Once they are on the sea, the lads are split up among various ships. Therefore they cannot be mustered, and if they cannot be mustered, they cannot be paid. A very unsatisfactory situation, which caused many hardships among the men. My paltry role was to write to Sir William Yonge when he was Secretary-at-War, describing the whole sorry affair and pleading on their behalf."

"So here is your reward," Fox says. "How prophetic of them to know you would be needing a compass."

"I won't be going before the winter, my dears. You shall have the pleasure of my company till then."

"Yet I don't see why you must go," says Lady Caroline, feigning a pout. "I know how travelling disagrees with you. Every time you must journey in a coach you suffer fever."

"And a swelled face and a stomach turned to jelly. That is because an indolent, high-fed body such as mine knows of no motion, though my mind is in constant exercise."

Fox turns his narrow eye on me. "Have you not heard Copernicus has discovered that the sun stands still in London? Everywhere else 'tis damps and vapours. Why would you think of leaving?"

"I am sure I shall regret it," I say, with a happy flutter in my heart at even the thought of leaving. I do not fool them, nor mean to.

Lady Caroline leans over and plants an impulsive kiss on my cheek. "Sir Charles, you are our best friend and we are always in your debt."

I smile at her large grey eyes. She is so beautiful, a worthy partner for my friend. To say nothing of being the great-granddaughter of Charles II. "It's been two long years since I made enemies of your parents by hosting your wedding. You have more than repaid me with your friendship."

Fox places a hand on my arm. "We can never repay you for your loyalty when we most needed it. You took upon yourself a heavy load."

"But I have gained the respect of all the romantics in England," I say quite happily. "At least all those who are not friends of the Duke and Duchess of Richmond. I do not repent my role in your marriage. There is nothing I enjoy better than to play the controversial host and smooth the progress of true love. My worst sin was not informing the parson whom he had the privilege of marrying. Do you remember how quickly it all went? I wonder if he ever connected your quiet wedding with the furor that burst forth when it was discovered that the daughter of the Duke and Duchess had married a commoner."

"You and Marlborough were the only ones at our wedding," says Fox. "You're like a brother to me."

"Believe me, dear Fox, nobody but Lady Caroline can love you better than I do."

I embrace him as if I am on the point of departure. "You and my children are all I will regret leaving. Everything else is gall and wormwood to me."

Fox and I were both devastated by Winnington's death, only Fox had Lady Caroline to console him. I found myself, all at once, questioning my entire life. I was thirty-eight, a minor official in government, a poet whose words would no longer come, alone too often in the evenings. I adored my two girls, but they were with their mother, who never forgave me for neglecting her. And I, in turn, never forgave her for not forgiving me. My solution was escape. I begged the King to send me abroad.

"I'm hoping for Dresden, Fox. I have heard the court is strange and the people disagreeable. But the place itself has a reputation for beauty. The King of Poland has spent an unseemly amount of his treasury collecting the finest paintings, the opera is the best in Europe, and grand churches are being built in the baroque style. I shall have to kiss hands at court, of course, but perhaps I will come across an agreeable one that belongs to a German countess."

"I will whisper your name in people's ears," Fox says. "The King couldn't have a better minister to represent him." He nods at the compass, still in my hand. "This gift comes at an auspicious moment. It will help you find your way."

Dresden, June 1747
My dear Fox,

I have received a most cordial reception on my arrival in Dresden. 'Tis impossible to tell you how well I am with the King of Poland. There is no distinction or civility that he does not show me. I eat with him twice, sometimes three times a week. I am of all his parties that I like to be of, and those I don't, I always make fun of, which pleases him. He has sometimes talked to me for an hour without saying one word to the French Ambassador who stood by me, and which I think a little impudent of His Majesty, who receives a pension from France. In short, it is impossible for a Minister to be better at a foreign court than I am here.

The King of Poland (for he is known by that title more than the Elector of Saxony) is very healthy despite his fifty-three years, though he now grows too corpulent. His pleasures consist of hunting, music, pictures, and smoking tobacco. While the King, his father, lived, he managed his own private affairs with great economy and applied himself to public business with great diligence. But since his accession to the crown, Count Brühl has taken over management and has always endeavoured to alienate the King from business, in which he has succeeded too well. Even in his pleasures, the King is the worst-served Prince in Europe; for though his expenses in dogs and horses are prodigious, yet, during the time of my being there, he had not one hound that could hunt, nor three horses in his stable fit to be mounted.

Count Brühl's power and favour are absolute. While in the court of the King, his father, the Count rose from being a page in two years to become Privy Councillor, Ministre de Conference, and Great Master of the Wardrobe. His house is a palace. He has every vice and expense that would each of them singly undo any other person: gambling, horses, books, pictures, and a mistress. To this end he freely takes bribes for crown appointments and services rendered.

In spite of all this, the magnificence of the city itself makes visitors here for the first time wander about with their necks sore and their jaws low. I begin to believe all I ever read in the fairy tales, Arabian Nights, etc. to be very true. The churches and state buildings are baroque in style but built on such extravagant scale that they take one's breath clean away. It is hardly surprising to find the Saxons writhing under a grievous burden in taxation. No farmer could expect to sell the produce of his land without paying sixty percent of the value to the government. Yet the court is content to spend £100,000 on the purchase of the Duke of Modena's collection of pictures — to say nothing of double that amount on the recent royal marriages — unmindful of the hardships which the Prussian invasion of 1745 had inflicted on the inhabitants of the country.

Dresden, November 1747
My dear Fox,

Despite the gaiety of the court, I fear I am unwell. My spirits have been brought low by my anxiety not only for my health, but also about money. Or rather the lack thereof. Living in Dresden is proving to be very dear and I have already put in a request for an increase in my allowance, which I must have in order to remain any longer. It has become impossibly cold here and I await the onslaught of winter with dismay.

I fear for my health, and in this regard, I implore you, my dear Fox, to whisper in the right ears so that I may be moved from here. I have always, as you know, coveted the post at Turin, which will be vacant soon. The Italian climate would cure my ills, of that I am certain, and I would be just as useful to the King. I hope I shall not be sent to a German court; all the rest are equally indifferent. But not having the language here, makes Germany very disagreeable to me. I throw myself on your mercy in this matter. The hope of one day seeing my children and you is the only agreeable thought that I have refuge to.

When you write of the cheerful hours we spent together, Winnington, you, and I, you put me in mind of an agreeable dream I once had. For at this time I cannot bring myself to believe that I really ever was so happy.

December 1748
My dear Fox,

I fear I shall never see a more southern clime than Brighton
despite your greatest efforts on my behalf. If Cumberland
asks that Lord Rochfort be sent to Turin, then I cannot
oppose his wishes, no matter how vexing those wishes
may be. I ask you, as Secretary-at-War, to impress upon
the court that Dresden is the dearest spot in all of Europe
and it is impossible for me to stay without a substantial
increase in pay. Could not the rank of Plenipotentiary now
be accorded to me?

April 1749
My dear Fox,

Rumour has it in Dresden that Prince Charles Edward
Stuart has arrived in Poland. Since I have urgent instructions from home to send news of his whereabouts as I
learn them, I am doing so with the proviso that all sorts
of stories are being put about. One of these is that the
Prince is in Paris incognito. Another account has him in
Venice, where a marriage is being negotiated for him with
a certain Princess Radziwill, a very plain child not twelve
years old. It is not bad enough that we must ever protect
ourselves against outside enemies, but the constant anxiety of duelling with an enemy from within is too much.

May 1749
My dear Fox,

I own I am flattered with the King's thinking me capable
to serve him in Prussia despite the difficulties any

Englishman would encounter in that court. Of course, I accept with pleasure. I am greatly honoured that the King sees fit to raise me to the rank of Plenipotentiary. But my dear friend, I must tell you some of the consequences that attend my going to Berlin. I know I shall have a jealous and suspicious Prince to deal with who cannot bear to have his own actions pried into, while at the same time leaves no stone unturned nor any means unemployed to penetrate into those of other peoples', particularly of the Foreign Ministers residing at his court, whom he looks upon as spies of the most dangerous sort and treats them as such. Because of Prussia's intimate connection to France, I believe at this instant I have the honour of being as ill with His Prussian Majesty as any Minister in Europe.

Please be so kind as to tell your sister that I accept her kind offer of the sacrifice of her second son to my service. Ensure her that I will not allow Harry to starve or live out of doors whilst in my employ and that his education on the continent will more than make up for his paltry allowance.

Berlin, October 1750
My dear Fox,

My brief stay in the Prussian court has served only to confirm what I hitherto maintained — that an Englishman will find himself unwelcome and suffer indignities at the hands of the King.

I have known for a month that his Prussian Majesty has made up his mind to get me removed. I am shunned and avoided by everyone at court, most people having orders not to visit me. I am looked upon as a dangerous spy and an enemy to the King's views and treated accordingly. I had rather be a post horse with a fat man on my back than Frederick's First Minister, or his brother, or his wife. He has abolished all distinctions. There is nothing here but an absolute Prince and a People all equally miserable, all equally trembling before him.

The only agreeable event I can relate is a fortuitous acquaintanceship with young Count Poniatowski, whose older brother I met in Dresden. The young Count has an exceptionally gifted mind paired with a genuine heart and I expect, in the fullness of time, he will be a great man in Poland.

chapter sixteen

Rebecca felt herself floating in some bubble that was navigating its way between the ages. She was living in 1979 but felt that at any moment she would slip back two hundred years. On her way to the office she marvelled at the cars on the road and at the same time felt their transience. 1750 had passed. They had lived their lives much as Rebecca was living hers. In her eavesdropping on their lives she could see things had not changed all that much. *I cannot bring myself to believe that I really ever was so happy.* She understood that. Only too well.

She was conscious of time passing Monday morning and kept checking her watch as it crept toward twelve. She would probably have worked right through lunch every day but Iris had long ago taken it upon herself to structure her employer's time more sensibly. Thus, no patients were scheduled between one and two. Iris would prevail upon her to take a break and eat something. Partly to placate Iris, she often brought a small plastic container of leftovers from home, a salad, some fruit, a bagel with tuna. Sometimes Iris headed for Chinatown a block away at Dundas and brought back some General Tso prawns or chicken in peanut sauce. They would spoon it over rice on the plates they kept in the cupboard above the small fridge jammed with drug samples. Then they would eat at their desks near the cabinets packed with colour-coded patient files.

On Monday Rebecca brought an apple and a pear in a paper bag.

At one o'clock Iris picked up her purse and headed for the door. "I'm peckish for some Chinese food. What can I bring back for you?"

"Thanks, but I'm not hungry."

Iris's round face scowled. "You have to eat."

Rebecca picked up her paper bag with the fruit. "I brought something."

Iris peeked inside, wriggled her nose. "That'll be dessert. What about some sweet and sour chicken?"

"Really, I couldn't." Rebecca gave a half-hearted smile, knowing she didn't fool Iris. Eating was still difficult sometimes. She was fashionably thinner, without trying, now that David was gone. He'd liked the meat on her bones. *You're a lot of woman*, he'd said. Then a Groucho Marx flapping of the eyebrows. Red eyebrows. Orange hair. There was no reason to eat anymore.

But she did have something else to do.

As soon as Iris left, Rebecca escaped into her private office. She reached into her purse and took out the card the cop had left with her on Saturday.

"Eleven Division." A man's voice.

"Constable Tiziano please."

"I'll see if he's here."

A moment later, "Tiziano."

"It's Dr. Rebecca Temple. We met Saturday at Michael Oginski's house ..."

"Yes, I remember," he cut her off. "What can I do for you?"

"I thought you might have some news about the autopsy. I'm a little concerned ..."

"We don't give out that kind of information to the general public, Doctor. And anyway, we don't work that fast around here."

"I'm hardly the general public, Constable. I was a friend of his and I'd like some reassurance that his death was an accident."

"Do you have any information to the contrary?" he said with no emotion she could detect. A cop asking questions, piling up answers to sort out later.

"No," she said.

"Do you have any reason to suspect foul play?"

She hesitated, wondering herself why she couldn't let it alone. "Some things at the house just don't seem right."

"Go on."

"He was writing a book and the end of it's missing."

Silence.

She knew how ridiculous it sounded. At any rate, she wasn't going to admit she'd gone through his house looking for the rest of it.

"Anything else?"

"I just want to know why it happened. If he had a heart attack — well, it would clear everything up."

"Look, Doctor, I appreciate you knew the deceased, but we have a policy here and it doesn't include sharing information. We're pretty busy here and —"

"I guess I'll have to call Detective Wanless at Twenty-two Division. He'll know what to do."

A hesitant pause. "You know Detective Wanless?"

"I helped him on a case last spring. He and I are great pals."

The former was true, the latter could charitably be called an exaggeration. She hoped Tiziano wouldn't call her bluff. Wanless was a by-the-book cop who had not believed her patient had been murdered last April until Rebecca had nearly lost her own life.

"All I want to know is if he had a heart attack. To verify my own conclusions."

He breathed into the phone. "This is just between us, Doctor. Call me later, after five. No promises."

Rebecca ate her pear and stuffed the apple into the pocket of her black crinkle-cotton skirt. Throwing off her sandals, she put on the running shoes she had bought last spring when it had become apparent that her body was seizing up from lack of use. She had shut down after David's death, and the running shoes were a symbol of rejoining the human race. She could never use that pun, but it amused her to say it to herself. Maybe she *was* her father's daughter. Six months later, she was still in lousy shape, but better than when she had started.

She walked briskly up Beverley Street, the sun warm on her bare arms. At this rate she could get there in ten minutes. Maybe find the grad student and get some answers.

The larger houses she passed had been mansions built by successful businessmen in the late nineteenth century. Not so long ago, when she compared the stories of the eighteenth century she had become immersed in. Many of the humbler houses on Beverley were rented to gaggles of students from the university, four or six to a house. How she envied them their relatively carefree lives.

She crossed College Street where Beverley became St. George and more obviously university territory. The ivy-covered buildings on the east side formed the outside perimeter of King's College Circle. Behind them, invisible from the street, grew a large grass round where students lounged or played soccer. Around this idyllic centre were arranged picturesque grey brick piles that defied architectural classification. How many times had she and David, while undergrads, sat down in front of the Sigmund Samuel Library watching young men in shorts lunging at a ball? Staring at the round was akin to sitting on a beach mesmerized by a lake. There was a calming effect no one could explain. She had spent her young adult life here and reckoned it was the most beautiful place on earth.

Heading toward the new part of the university, she turned left at the Sidney Smith Building, a white brick monolith honeycombed with square rooms lit by fluorescent lights that had induced stupefaction in her when she had the bad luck to have a class scheduled there. She marched up Huron Street, the whole block filled with Sidney Smith. She finally left it behind at Harbord Street. According to the address on the letter Edward had given her, the Slavic Studies department was on Sussex Street a few blocks north of Harbord.

The building turned out to be a drab, three-storey brown brick, probably an apartment in a former life. The sign on the plaque near the door listed the Italian Studies Department, First Floor, Hispanic Studies Department, Second Floor, Slavic Studies Department, Third Floor. Pitted concrete stairs and an old iron railing led up to a metal door. She pushed it open to find herself in a beige hall, a concrete staircase to her left, a hallway of offices to her right. No elevator, of course. Just her luck. Well, she had her running shoes on.

She hadn't broken a sweat yet. The second floor was a cinch despite the burnt-out light bulb in the stairwell, the unswept corners. It was that last staircase that did it. By the time she got to the top she was winded. She didn't care how ugly the place was. Okay, so she should do this more often. Maybe she'd make the Slavic Studies Department a daily destination. Though the décor was depressingly beige and the mustiness invading her chest smelled of dust. Maybe she could find a third floor somewhere prettier. This one was the same layout as the first floor. She stepped into the hallway of offices and came to a door where the lettering on the translucent window announced "Slavic Studies Department, Chairman, Prof. Gregor Stoyanovich."

Opening the door, she saw a small, round-shouldered woman of indeterminate age toiling over a typewriter. Her brown hair stuck to her forehead, shiny with sweat, and Rebecca realized her own heat wasn't solely a result of her exertion; it was stifling on this floor, with the sun beating on the roof inches above.

The woman looked up without interest, barely glancing from her work. Rebecca was in no mood to be ignored.

"I'm looking for a graduate student named Teodor." She was about to explain she didn't know his last name, when the woman pointed out the door.

"End of the hall."

"Thank you," Rebecca said, closing the door behind her.

She turned left and started down the hall. Before she could wonder which door it would be, she spotted the figure seated at the end of the hall. Literally. A small table holding a typewriter had been set up, partially blocking the stairs at that end of the building. A thin, blond young man with a very pointy nose sat stooped over the keys, typing with painstaking care. He didn't look up as she approached.

"Are you Teodor?" she asked.

He looked up at her through metal-rimmed spectacles, his brow furrowed. He had stopped typing but his fingers stayed poised over the keys. "Yes?"

"Are you the student who did the typing for Michael Oginski?"

The question seemed to catch him by surprise and he moved his hands away from the typewriter, resting them on his thighs. "Yes?"

"I was a friend of his. I just wanted to ask you a few questions."

"Oh." He breathed out with relief. His colourless eyes darted to the open door she had passed. "I was shocked to hear," he said so softly that she thought he must truly have been upset. His voice, however, remained quiet. "But my job with him was finished. I gave him the manuscript already." Despite the low tone, there was a nasal quality to his voice that made it sound whiney.

"Do you remember how many pages you typed?"

"One hundred ninety-five. I charge by the page. Is there a problem?" He squinted at her behind the glasses.

"I'm just wondering if you kept a copy," she said. "We can only find one hundred and forty pages of the manuscript."

"I assure you I gave him one hundred and ninety-five pages," he said with some force, his voice suddenly louder than before.

"I'm sure you did," she said, wondering what he thought she was accusing him of. "I wasn't implying that you didn't. I only thought you might've made a copy."

He frowned at her. "I only make copies if the person asks. It's a headache with the carbons. People can photocopy if they want."

There was an awkward moment.

"What did you think of his book?" she asked, to break the tension.

His eyes darted back to her face, examining it for motive. "Did he tell you to ask me that?"

"Who?"

"You know, just because I liked the book ... I am a good student — a good researcher — and I resent him going behind my back and bringing in people to ... to interrogate me!"

"I don't know what you're talking about."

He watched her a moment over his long nose. "I won't give him any excuse. I worked hard to get where I am. My thesis is solid. He knows that. Tell him I'll go above his head if he doesn't accept it this time." Patches of flush rose in his pale cheeks.

"I'm sorry, but I really don't know what you're talking about."

She heard a shuffling behind her. The young man's pale eyes suddenly widened. He shot up, the legs of his chair scraping backwards along the floor.

A bear of a man appeared in the doorway of the closest office. Full cheeks rose above a meticulously clipped moustache and beard. His thick brown hair sprang from his head in controlled waves.

"Teodor, have you finished the section I gave you?"

The student's mouth fell open. "Professor Hauer, it is a complex issue. It will take me a few days to prepare ..."

So this was the professor whose overblown letter lay in her handbag. He grimaced at Teodor, then gave her a squinty smile as if trying to place her. He was handsome in his tweed jacket, well scrubbed and fastidious. Somehow cool in all the heat.

"I apologize for taking up your student's time," she said. "I was a friend of Michael Oginski's."

"Terrible tragedy," he said without missing a beat, as if he had been following their conversation from inside his office. "Always a tragedy when someone dies before their time. I, too, was a friend. Dr. Anton Hauer, Professor of Polish Studies. Please," he pointed a hand toward the door, "won't you come into my office."

He shot Teodor a nasty parting look while graciously holding out his arm for her to enter. She was glad for the chance to escape those angry, pale eyes.

The small office was lit by a floor lamp whose bulb was hidden behind a gold-coloured fringed shade. A small window. A knotted wool rug in shades of gold and ivory covered the old linoleum floor. There was a European feel to the room. Professor Hauer closed the door that had previously stood open and pulled out a straight wooden chair for her, hovering until she was seated.

"Would you like some coffee? I just made a fresh pot."

"Thank you, no." She was going to melt.

"Would you prefer something cold? A glass of water?"

"I'd love one."

He stepped behind his desk to a small table where a drip coffeemaker stood beside a pitcher of water. He handed her a glass, then sat down at his desk. Books were stacked neatly in a case within arm's length of his chair.

"You must excuse Teodor," said Hauer. "He has trouble keeping up with the work and consequently he becomes easily upset. He tends to exaggerate things and sometimes I think, well ..." He shook his head. "I think he imagines things."

"He's a very nervous young man," she said.

"He has reason to be. His work is not up to standard. But let's not waste our breath on him. You came about poor Count Oginski." His dark eyes sparkled at her, took her in.

"If you don't mind my asking, how did you two know each other?" she asked.

He raised his eyebrows, scratched the back of his neck. "The Count came to me when he started writing his book. He was a very charming man and I was eager to help. I don't think he understood how much work was involved. I sat with him so many times, telling him about the period, the people. I tried to help him as much as I could. He was a count, after all." He gave her a crooked smile, his eyes still gleaming at her. "And in the end, the book was —" He shook his head portentously.

He paused and looked off to the side in a teasing way that annoyed her, since she knew he had every intention of explaining.

"Was what, Professor?" she asked, playing his game "The book was what?"

"It was a *disaster*."

She was taken aback. "Why do you say that?"

He folded his clean pink hands on the desk; his eyes returned to her face. "He was not an academic. He had no academic training. Or credentials. And he tried to write a book that required rigorous scholarship, discipline. He was just not up to it."

Behind him the soft light of the lamp suffused the ancient grey paint. He had tried to allay the shabbiness of the office but had only succeeded in calling attention to it. She wondered whether the university shared his own high opinion of his scholarship.

"I have to disagree," she said, surprised at the anger building up in her. "I've read a few chapters and I'm sure he never meant it to be a scholarly work. I'm enjoying it immensely."

"With all due respect, you are not working in the field, Miss —"

"Dr. Temple."

He stopped short and took a better look. He had been talking *at* her before and now appeared to finally see her.

"You are at the university?"

"I'm a physician."

He raised his dark eyebrows. "Well," he said, smiling with tight lips, a puzzled respect. "Do not misunderstand. He was a great aristocrat. You could see it as soon as he walked into the room. Tall, distinguished. Very impressive. I'm sorry to say the book — the book is a fiction."

"He told me he was going to reveal a secret about his family that would upset historians. Did he discuss that with you?"

He gave her a disdainful smile, cocking his great brown head on an angle. "A secret that would upset historians?" He arched an eyebrow. "I have to explain something to you, dear Doctor. History is the highest of disciplines. It requires many years of intensive study, research, erudition. It is not something that can be rattled off in one book by an amateur. As much as I admired the Count, his book is not history, so how can it upset historians? It is a novel. Good for the beach."

"So you don't know what he was referring to?"

"I helped him in the beginning. With the research, and so on. I haven't had much contact with him recently."

"So you wouldn't know where the end of his manuscript is?"

He looked at her blankly.

"Teodor says he typed almost two hundred pages for Michael but we can only find a hundred and forty."

"Ah. Teodor. With Teodor anything is possible. I'm sorry I can't help you there."

"You think he's lying about having the manuscript?"

Hauer shrugged. "He's a very odd fellow." His brown eyes narrowed. "He has some ... psychological problems. I should've trusted my instincts when I first met him. He told me about his family in Poland. Disturbed people. Apparently his father took his own life. I should've seen the signs. But he was on his best behaviour and he fooled me. He wanted to study Poland.

How could I know? So I took him on. There are not so many students who want to study Poland."

"But about the manuscript ..."

"He *is* having trouble with his thesis. Maybe he plans to use the Count's material in some way."

"Wouldn't you recognize that, since you're familiar with both works? Wouldn't he have to show the thesis to you as his supervisor?"

"Yes, of course, dear Doctor. But he is *desperate*."

"Professor Hauer, I'm not convinced that Michael's death was an accident."

His eyebrows flew up. "You think Teodor —"

"I'm not accusing anyone."

"What do the police say?"

"They're doing an autopsy. I think they're leaning toward the accident theory."

"It said in the paper that he drowned. That friends found him in the pool."

It was so hot in the building. How could he stand it, in his tweed jacket? "He'd invited all of us to his house that day."

"You were there when it happened?"

She shook her head. "We arrived too late."

"So you were the ones who found him."

In her profession she was used to people's morbid curiosity. It bothered her nonetheless.

"I understand there were friends from Poland?"

She nodded.

"He mentioned a compass that belonged to his family in Poland. That he would like to get his hands on it. I always doubted its existence." He seemed to be waiting.

It was time to change the subject. She decided to take some liberties with the truth.

"He told me about the project you're working on, setting up the Chair in Polish Studies."

He bowed his head as if she had just mentioned the name of God. "It is my most fervent goal. I have directed all my energies toward it." He looked off into the distance behind her. "It will transform Polish studies in this country."

"And how will you do that?"

His eyes popped open. "*Me*? Dear Doctor! I am not lobbying for *myself*. The position of Chair is open to the best qualified candidate."

"I just assumed …"

"No, no, no. Of course I would be deeply honoured if later I am chosen. But that will not be up to me ultimately. The Chair is bigger than any one person. And for now, I must see to the publishing of my book, a seminal history of Poland, in English."

He reached over to the shelf and picked off a thick volume. He placed it on the desk in front of her triumphantly. The black dust jacket bore red and white lettering in Polish, which she couldn't read. By Dr. Anton Hauer. She flipped through to be polite. Some very dated black and white photos of castles and battles flashed by. She turned it over. On the back, a small photo in the bottom corner of the dust jacket revealed a much younger Dr. Hauer, clean-shaven except for a thin moustache, brooding for the camera.

"In Polish universities," he said, leaning forward, "this book is required reading."

"I guess I'll have to wait for the English version," she said. "Have you translated it yourself?"

"Yes, yes, it's all ready to go."

"When is it coming out?"

His face clouded over, his body stiffened in the chair. "There's a delay," he said. "Publishers move so slowly. They don't really understand my book. There's a new editor and he simply misses the point. He thinks history should be dramatic and exciting — and it is, but not the way he thinks. You know, these young editors brought up on television. The facts aren't always dramatic but they're real and that's history. For instance, the three partitions of Poland ..."

She looked at her watch to signal the end of her visit. "I'm sorry," she said, "but I have to go."

He watched her more intently. "Where are my manners? Another glass of water?"

She stood up. "Thank you, but I'm running behind. I have to get back to my office."

He stood up. "It was a pleasure to meet you, Doctor. Perhaps you can come back for another visit."

In two long strides he reached the door before she could open it. "Here's my card. Do you have one?"

Without enthusiasm she reached into her purse for a card.

He leaned in front of her to turn the door knob. The aroma of balm on a thick head of hair.

In the hall she turned back to look at Teodor, see if there was anything in his face that would betray him. He in turn was watching Hauer, who blithely ignored him. The student's face was disfigured with an unsettling mixture of fear and loathing.

chapter seventeen

Stanislaw

A Fateful Meeting

Warsaw, 1749

I feel the gentle pressure of my body on the featherbed as if it is someone else lying here and I am floating above, watching. What a foolish young man that is, hating the autumn light that creeps through the window. He has never understood anything, even less now. Educated, yes, learned beyond reason, but true understanding — how can he understand anything when he has never had a real friend. What does all his knowledge and rational thinking gain him beyond a puzzlement with the world that has chased him into this room, this bed. His tutors cannot help him now. His *Maman* draws the curtains each morning to show him that the world waits outside and each morning he closes his eyes against the light and the world.

"I am afraid for him, Staśek," Maman whispers by the door outside the room, but I can hear. My senses have become acute after endless days of lying here with my eyes shut. "He recovers from one illness and falls prey to the next. And he is not trying any longer. He doesn't want to get better."

"He is a strong boy, Konya, do not upset yourself." His voice is steady, but I know Papa is worried. He is an old soldier and doesn't allow himself the luxury of showing fear. "He is too much inside himself, Konya. Brooding on philosophy and art makes him melancholy, and melancholy brings him to … this. He would benefit from the company of young men who ride. The air would do him good."

Maman disagrees wordlessly. It was she who kept me solitary from the beginning of my childhood. My books were my companions. Her duty was to oversee my education and ensure that I grew into a fitting member of the *Familia*. Other children were foolish and unschooled and would corrupt my forming mind. I cannot say she was wrong. I can say only that my education was joyless, for I was never allowed the time to be a child. It is as if one took the month of April out of the year.

I will not blame my present illness on my upbringing, yet there was another time when I was twelve and on the verge of manhood. By then I was being educated by the very liberal Theatine Fathers in the spirit of the Enlightenment. Count Keyserling, an old family friend, gave me lessons in logic and mathematics, a Freemason taught me military studies, and my spiritual instructor believed in predestination. Was it any wonder that my mind became overloaded with fashionable concepts and I had a breakdown at that tender age, struggling with the basic contradiction: how to resolve the idea of predestination with the question of free will?

If all is decided ahead of time and fate is predetermined, what is the point of trying to do *anything*? Any action one takes is futile and pointless, and the wise man accepts his lot with resignation. Yet we seem to live our lives making decisions as if they are ours to make. Over the years, my cloud of confusion has floated skywards, and even now at eighteen I sense its presence but it no longer troubles me. Then what is this ennui that has grasped me in its tentacles until I feel I cannot breathe? No, it is not confusion. It is … meaninglessness. What is the point? If I am meant to keep breathing, I suppose I shall. But for what? Despite Maman's piety, she has not managed to pass her faith on to me. But the idea of fate, a corollary of her religion, has somehow entered my soul and found an unlikely home. Logic seems to be of no avail; no rational word I tell myself will penetrate my childhood lessons.

One evening while I lie here pretending to be dead, I hear a second male voice, Count Keyserling, whispering outside my door. "My dear Count Poniatowski, while I was Minister in Berlin, I made the acquaintance of an exceptional physician, Dr. Lieberkühn. He has worked wonders where others have failed. Send the boy to Berlin so that he can be placed under this doctor's care."

"But to go alone to a strange city …" Maman begins.

"I am certain that our mutual friend, Count Bülow, will keep an eye on him while he is away from home."

What is the point, Count Keyserling, I would say if I could speak. We cannot change anything. Yet perhaps that is part of the plan, that I go to the Prussian capital to search for my destiny.

I imagine Maman looking over at me, sighing that her favourite child should be taken from her.

Dr. Lieberkühn is indeed a remarkable physician, part chemist, part magician. I spend most of the winter and spring in his tender care. Perhaps because he wants nothing from me, I respond. Then to garner his approval, I will my body to heal itself. Even so, I cannot say that in his hands alone lies the secret of my recovery. Escape from home has played its part since it has pulled me out of the tedium of Polish politics that never fails to oppress me whilst in the stern employ of my uncle Michael. But perhaps the greatest credit for my newfound spirits ought to go to a stranger, the British Minister in Berlin, a man I have never set eyes on before.

We have all come to dine at the house of Count Bülow, who presents me to one illustrious guest at a time.

"Sir Charles Hanbury-Williams, this is Count Stanislaw Poniatowski, the son of an old friend." The Englishman is a large, well-dressed man wearing an expensive wig.

"I recently made the acquaintance of your brother Kazimierz," he says, "and we became great friends. There is quite a difference in ages between you, I see. You're more Digby's age." He turns to the young man beside him. "Count, I'd like you to meet the nephew of a dear friend, Harry Digby, who is also my secretary. You two will get on famously."

Both their faces beam at me with such open friendliness that I feel at ease at once. It is the most cheerful reception I have received since arriving in Berlin months before.

When we go to table, Sir Charles sits down on my right, Digby on my left. The older man refuses nothing that is set before him, expressing such exuberant wit at the sight of the soup, the duck, the pudding, that all around him are in high spirits. A prodigious appetite accompanies his wit.

At first he prods me with the usual questions about my stay in Berlin — have I had the opportunity to admire the view of the river Spree, or ride upon the *grand alleé* of Unter den Linden, the magnificent main avenue lined on both sides with linden trees in full leaf? Have I seen the deer in the Tiergarten? Once he has heard the frankness of my answers — yes, the river, the trees, the deer are all they should be, but Berlin seems a drab place where the men are perpetually absent on active service while the ladies suffer from a surfeit of Voltaire — he begins to favour me with asides that our neighbours are not meant to hear.

"What is your impression of the great Frederick?" he asks, as if my opinion is the one he has been waiting for.

I wonder how far my frankness can go. "His court is not what I expected, though he, himself, is the cleverest of men."

Draining his wineglass he replies, "Do not hesitate to tell me your true thoughts, young Count — I can tell you have them — for I am bored with insipid, invariably magnanimous opinions."

Count Bülow and M. Gross, the Russian Minister, are engaged in their own conversation. I must admit I am flattered by Sir Charles's attention and try to impress.

"I have met with Frederick twice and both times I've found him looking haggard and anxious. His eyes are dark from fatigue and his clothes in need of washing. He is always trying to be more brilliant than everyone else and has the embarrassed air of a man who fears he's failing."

Sir Charles watches me with interest. "You are an astute observer — your conclusions happen to exactly coincide with my own. I find Frederick the completest tyrant that God ever sent as a scourge to an offending people. His ambition and treachery know no bounds. He thinks nothing of plunging all of Europe into bloody war." He quickly peers around. "Count Bülow has given us a holiday from the Prussians this evening, leaving them off the guest list tonight."

Harry Digby adds, "Yet Frederick is held in affection by many of the common people, Sir Charles. They call him *unser Fritz*, our Fritz."

Sir Charles sniffs at this but keeps his voice low. "The basest of rulers have their followers. But do not doubt that he is an absolute Prince — his people tremble before him and detest his iron government. Why, no man can sell an estate, marry a child, or go out of this town, without special leave."

Count Bülow suddenly turns his attention to us. "Sir Charles, I hear you were presented to the Queen Mother last night."

My table companion delivers a smile. "Charming woman, Her Sacred Majesty, Sophia. I cannot complain of my reception there — to be sure she is our Sovereign's sister. She welcomed me warmly at her residence, Mon Bijou — indeed a jewel on the banks of the Spree. We spent some agreeable hours walking in the gardens, then she did me the honour of asking me to stay to supper. The lady is adept at cards and won forty florins from me."

"I hear that you, also, are adept at cards, Sir Charles," Count Bülow says. "I salute your generosity."

"I salute your diplomacy," M. Gross adds with a wink.

"I'm afraid my diplomacy has not won over the son," says Sir Charles. "It is unfortunate the mother has no influence with him. I hear he resides so much at Potsdam on account of her presence in Berlin. When a son does not love his mother, I cannot expect deference from his court, though King George be his uncle. Did I say? — the Prussian Minister tried to provoke me with an insult to the King, days after my arrival. They have been even worse to poor M. Gross because he represents Muskovy. He is ignored at court, sometimes rudely on account of the enmity between Frederick and the Empress Elizabeth."

M. Gross shuffles nervously in his seat, but Sir Charles continues.

"His Prussian Majesty cannot bear powerful women since they're not apt to throw themselves at his feet. Needless to say, the Empress despises him back. As a gentleman I cannot repeat the names that have burst from his mouth when he speaks of the Tsarina."

M. Gross changes the subject. "Sir Charles, have you encountered any of the Jacobite colony living in Berlin? I hear there's quite a nest of them here."

Harry Digby notices my look of puzzlement and whispers, "Those who follow the Prince Charles Edward Stuart, the Catholic heir to King James. They plot to overthrow King George."

"Indeed," Sir Charles says, "I have been warned to avoid the Scotsman George Keith for that very reason, and when I met him at the Prussian Minister's house the other evening, I put on a sullen dignity and ate my pudding and held my tongue."

"I believe he has a brother James," Count Bülow says.

Sir Charles gives an ironic smile. "*He* is a different matter. As Field-Marshal he may be useful company for he must know the whereabouts of the elusive Prince Charles. Once he is said to be in Venice, next someone has spotted him in France. I will spend an evening drinking punch with James and his Livonian mistress. Her home is Riga, and therefore under the ken of Muskovy."

M. Gross's eyebrow goes up.

"We would really learn something of the Prince's movements if the Tsarina could be induced to have the Livonian mistress summoned to Petersburg where —

how shall I put it — measures could be taken to make her speak."

I hear several intakes of breath around the table. Sir Charles takes them in stride, almost relishes the shock, I believe. He continues.

"Such is beyond the realm of diplomacy and I shudder to imagine ... But I believe that the fair lady is recipient of all the Field-Marshal's secrets. What say you, M. Gross? Your Tsarina does not shrink from using spies."

M. Gross chooses his words carefully. "The internal affairs of sovereign nations are beyond the ken of the Empress," he says, "and she studiously avoids meddling for fear of embarrassing herself."

"Yes, of course," Sir Charles mutters, winking furtively toward Harry and me.

Unhappily, soon after Sir Charles's arrival in Berlin, it is time for me to return to Warsaw. The *Familia* is busy preparing for the Polish *Diet*, which will sit in August. They insist on me standing for election but I find the whole business tedious. There has not been a *Diet* in recent memory that has managed to rise above party divisions long enough to pass any legislation. So it is with this one. Polish rule of law allows any one man one veto, to dissolve parliament. A fierce jealousy among the nobles has placed foreign kings on the Polish throne for too long. Poles would rather kneel to an outsider than trust one of their own, who would be a rival. The whole business is a travesty and embarrassment on the world stage and the source of my disaffection with any role in government.

The same day parliament is dissolved, Sir Charles and Harry Digby arrive in Warsaw, to my delight.

Though I need no incentive, the *Familia* has encouraged me to cultivate Sir Charles as the representative of England, a country whose support they covet. It is easy to court Sir Charles because of his wit and generous dis-position. I call on him in the mornings and take him to lunch with my uncle August Czartoryski or to dinner with my sister at the Branicki Palace. He has made fast friends with my father, who has impressed him with his energy at nearly four score years.

Sir Charles is called back to Berlin in September. I am very sorry to see him leave and promise to send him regular missives. Soon enough I receive a letter from him, which begins, "*Mon cher Palatinello,*" a reference to my father's title as Palatine of Mazovia. He regales me with tidbits of gossip he has collected from his meet-ing with Voltaire, recently arrived in Potsdam at Frederick's invitation. I well remember the little palace at Sans Souci where the French poet is now a guest — the splendid architecture, with its central dome and end-less terraced gardens, sparkled in the sun, but the royal apartments were scruffy and mean. The King's grey-hounds were allowed to roam at will and tore to shreds any silk upholstery or curtains that put up resistance as they made their rounds. And His Prussian Majesty holds a tight fist on his purse, but I understand Voltaire — whom Sir Charles calls a vain genius — would not budge from Paris before he had received in his hand the money for the journey.

By March 1751, after suffering many indignities in Frederick's court, Sir Charles is called to Dresden, the seat of Saxony, where he served several years before. It is partly on that account that my family decides to send me there to see the renowned court from which King Augustus rules not only Saxony, but Poland. I set out for Leipzig, where Augustus and his retinue are paying their customary visit to the Fair. The King is good enough to invite me for the hunting season to Huburtsburg, his country palace a few miles out of Dresden.

I wander among the throng of courtiers, foreign ministers, and officers of state. Diffident in such a crowd, I nod and smile at those faces that are familiar. Yet most are strangers to me.

"Count Poniatowski!" a voice bellows out.

Sir Charles, his large form clothed in fine silks, makes his way toward me, his face affable and smiling. I am overjoyed to see him and we embrace like father and son. Harry Digby, who is at his elbow, embraces me with equal warmth.

They take me aside and immediately set me smiling. "Thank heavens you are here, young Count," says Sir Charles. "Apart from Digby, you are the only other person with whom I can speak frankly." He peers around with all innocence. "What is your opinion of Augustus's Queen?" he asks.

I lower my voice. "I have barely seen Maria-Josepha but have heard she is very religious."

"Indeed. But you must not dissimulate with me, young Count. Her Majesty is very devout, but not a bit the better for her devotions. She does nothing but commit small sins and begs forgiveness for them. She is ugly beyond painting and malicious beyond expression." This muttered for our ears only.

I find that, for the corpulent Augustus, "hunting" consists of swallowing an ample lunch in the forest, followed by a leisurely carriage ride with his Queen to meet the hunters at the kill. Since I am a less than ardent sportsman, I follow Count Brühl, the First Minister, who, led by clever huntsmen without being at the tail of the hounds, always takes the best paths and is in at the death. Count Brühl, an implacable schemer, does not escape Sir Charles's pithy observations.

One evening, one of many, Sir Charles, Digby, and I sip some *Goldwasser* before retiring. I hold up the glass, watching the flecks of gold settle in the drink, a costly vodka made in Danzig.

Sir Charles seems equally entranced by the liquid. "I am told this precious little brew is an infusion of extracts of angelica, gentian, valerian, juniper berries, and on and on and on. Yet all we dullards can see is the gold flakes. We are blinded by the gold. And none, I dare say, so much as Brühl." Sir Charles takes another swallow. "His vanity is beyond all bounds and his expense has no limits; neither does the King of Poland set any to it, for he permits him to take whatever he pleases out of the revenues of Saxony."

"He is said to have lost immense sums at play," says Digby. "And the extravagance of his clothes!"

Sir Charles leans forward and, though we are alone, lowers his voice. "Each morning he selects a different suit which must be worn with a particular watch, snuffbox, stick, and dagger. His abominable taste matches his reputation for insincerity. His answers are usually very obliging, but there is no dependence to be made upon them."

"But you must admit he makes them in high spirits," Digby says.

"If you had as many wigs and diamonds in your closet, young Count, would your spirits improve?"

"Do you find my spirits wanting?" I ask, feigning reproach.

"If you will permit me to be honest, as a friend, even as an uncle — you tend toward a melancholy that you are too young to own."

His eyes show concern, and I cannot be offended.

"You are in the prime of your life," he continues, "a nobleman with the best connections and education, in a beautiful place in a beautiful season — and in time you will have the power to act."

"Then you do not believe in fate?" I say. "In pre-destination of events?"

Sir Charles and Digby exchange glances.

"My dear Count," he begins, "you must always take matters into your own hands. You must always control your own destiny. *That* is your fate — to act. The only thing predestined is this." He pulls from his pocket a handsome silver device with a small round compass embedded within it.

"North is destined always to be north, regardless of what we may do. Imagine at the time of reckoning you stand before God and He asks, 'What did you accomplish in your life, how did you make the world better?' Will you answer: 'I sat and waited for my destiny to unfold'?"

The vodka has dulled my senses and brought a glow into the cheeks of my companions. I wonder if we would have been so frank before the bottle was drunk.

"I've struggled with this basic contradiction since boyhood. I'm afraid the battle has affected my spirits and sometimes … a despondency takes hold of me that I cannot control. Do not scold me on this account because at those times it matters little that I am in a beautiful place in a beautiful season. Have you read *Paradise Lost* where Milton says, 'The mind is its own place and can make a Heaven of Hell, a Hell of Heaven'?"

"I am always impressed with your education," says Sir Charles, "but perhaps you have pored over enough books and ought now to turn your attention to the ladies."

"My mother will not thank you for that assessment."

Sir Charles dispatches another glass of wine. "Then I will not trouble her with it."

The six weeks spent in Saxony are among the most enjoyable in my memory. More so due to the friendly company and frivolity of Sir Charles and Digby. Yes, frivolity. A quality sadly lacking in my family.

Alas, we go our separate ways again. The beginning of 1752 finds me in the throes of despondency fuelled by the futility of Polish politics. Only the regular letters from my English friends lift my spirits. In the summer I am elected to the *Diet*, which is to meet in autumn at Grodno — a primitive, filthy place. But it is well known that King Augustus hates having to go to Lithuania and will find somebody to sabotage the proceedings with a veto so he can go home as quickly as possible. This is, in fact, what happens. No sooner have I made my maiden speech in parliament than a deputy, who has no doubt been given a present by Augustus, stands up and vetoes the session.

The only brightness in my life comes from my cousin Elzbieta, with whom I have developed a close and tender friendship. But my uncle frowns upon our familiarity. It seems that as the power of the Czartoryskis has grown, so too their conception of their own importance. The Poniatowskis are treated as poor cousins, and no longer suitable to marry. Uncle arranges for Elzbieta to marry into one of the richest families in Poland in the spring.

In March 1753 I am compensated for my broken heart by being sent on a long tour abroad. In Vienna, my first stop, I happily encounter Sir Charles, whom I have come to regard as a second father. He and Digby show me another side to the gloomy Vienna I recall on my last visit, a grey, oppressive place on account of the Empress Maria-Theresa, whose court reflects her humourless piety. The presence of friends changes everything. Her court is no less gloomy; it merely has less influence on me.

When we move on to Dresden I am charmed by the city. We walk three abreast through the square of the Altmarkt, where the tall, narrow buildings fit together like teeth. Yellow and green, the Baroque houses glow in the summer evening sun. People are strolling and stopping to chat with neighbours now that commerce has ended for the day.

It is too early for the opera so we head for a look at the Elbe from a sweeping terrace they have named "Brühlsche Terrace" in honour of Count Brühl, who, for all intents and purposes, rules Saxony for King Augustus, who would rather play the ceremonial sovereign. Perched high above the river, we breathe in the smell of summer, a blend of calm water and roses in the nearby garden. From where we stand we can see the massive but graceful span of Augustusbrücke, which bridges the river, joining the two sections of the city.

We turn in the direction of the Zwinger, a monumental Baroque structure that resembles an open-air banquet hall.

"Many an extravagant party has been set here, I'm told," says Sir Charles. "A young Augustus was married here in legendary pomp and ceremony some thirty years ago. I dare say it's held up better than he has."

We can see the palatial wings of sandstone enclosing a central courtyard large enough to parade an army, but filled with lawns and pools and ornamental fountains. Wide staircases lead to galleries of paintings I have only dreamt of.

"I am quite overwhelmed," I say, gaping at the colossal proportions of the place, everywhere a riot of stone garlands and nymphs.

"Best you do not appear so to any but us," Sir Charles quips.

I smile foolishly. "I cannot help marvelling at the wealth that has constructed such buildings and bought such collections of art, when my own country is so ignored by the same sovereign. He does not do his duty to us."

"I am told he does not step into Poland except to attend the *Diet*," Sir Charles says.

"He is in and out within two weeks. He pays someone to stand up and veto the session, then he flees the country to come back here, or to Huburtsburg."

We walk toward the Theatreplatz. "The Magnates in your country do not seem to mind," Sir Charles says.

"They prefer to quarrel among themselves," I say, "without the interference of a foreign ruler. They care only about their own fiefdoms. But things must change if the country is to go forward. Things must change."

"That is what I like to hear!" Sir Charles beams at Digby. "Our young nobleman is ready to assert himself."

I blush with pride.

We mingle with the wigged and perfumed crowd entering the theatre, all of us eager to see this new opera by Handel, *Giulio Cesare*.

"You've heard about the first act?" I murmur to Digby. He shrugs. "They carry a severed head out on the stage."

His eyes blink and show interest in opera for the first time. Sir Charles booms out a laugh that startles those around us who turn sideways and purse lips at the disturbance.

We head for the box of the Maréchal du Saxe, Augustus's half-brother. A large, florid man in dress uniform, he greets us warmly, kissing each of us in turn on both cheeks, then introduces us to his mistress.

As we move away, Sir Charles whispers to me, "See if he doesn't start a discourse on his campaign in Flanders."

The two older ladies sitting in the back appear so impressed with the Maréchal in his uniform that they could not flutter their eyelids more if he had conquered all of Europe and not just Flanders.

"Madame de Bouvier, you probably recall the situation in 1745 when I led the French troops in the successful battle of …"

The orchestra begins to tune up and we step toward the front where our seats await us, out of earshot of Flanders. Still standing beside my friends, I am enjoying the sweetly discordant sounds of the instruments before the performance when a flurry of movement distracts me. Before I can turn, I am rudely shoved aside by a tall, expensively dressed young man who nearly knocks me off my feet. I lose my balance, but Sir Charles catches my arm and keeps me from stumbling to the floor.

"There! Wait till you see the beginning," the brutish young man tells his companion, another fellow. "They're going to bring a severed head out on the stage!"

My chest swells with rage. I must control my breathing in order to speak. "Do you fancy yourself in a stable?" I cry with indignation. "That you push away gentle folk who had their place before you?"

All the chattering around us stops. Everything goes quiet.

The young aristocrat barely looks at me, only sneers to his friend.

"Answer me this instant, or you are no gentleman."

Turned toward the stage, he brushes his fair hair aside with a disdainful hand.

"You *will* answer me, either here or on the field with swords."

"There is no call for a fit of apoplexy," he says finally.

"Now look here," the Maréchal steps up to the fellow. "No need to resort to violence. I saw the whole thing and you owe the Count an apology. Count, this is Prince Wilhelm of Lichtenstein, a young man in need of some manners."

The handsome offender sighs and shakes his head slightly. "I meant no harm. It was merely the excitement of seeing the head."

The Maréchal clears his throa,t waiting, as is everyone.

The young man glances at me with distaste. "I regret ... any offence ..."

He is saved by the opening strains of the orchestra and retreats haughtily to a seat on the side with his friend.

Sir Charles leans toward me. "I admire your fortitude, dear Count. You are ready for anything."

I am heartened by these words but can hardly speak from anger. My heart is beating in my ears more loudly than the drum, as the curtains slide open to reveal the stage.

We all watch intently when the Egyptian military leader walks on stage carrying a basket. The horror becomes apparent when he informs Cornelia that inside the basket lies the head of her husband, Pompey, Caesar's partner in government. Amid all the flailing of arms and exuberant arias I come to the disappointing realization that only the horror will be apparent, not the head, which remains provocative but invisible in the basket.

Years later, when I look back on that night, I detect a pattern that has etched itself upon my life while I was looking I know not where: no matter how much energy or fury I bring to living, those events I anticipate the most will get away from me. The things I want most shape my life by their absence. Like Pompey's head in the opera, they never appear.

chapter eighteen

That afternoon, in two separate examining rooms that adjoined her private office, Rebecca took care of patients who arrived with heart palpitations, sprained ankles, skin rashes, sore throats, and fuzzy tongues. She took a lot of blood pressures and listened to a lot of chests. By five o'clock, she took a minute between patients to call Constable Tiziano.

"This isn't official, Doctor," he said, "I don't want this to go no further."

He waited.

"I won't tell anyone, Constable."

"Okay. Pathologist says preliminary findings showed cause of death as drowning. No heart attack."

"No heart attack?" An electric shock went off in her body. No time for it to sink in. He went on.

"No trauma to the head. Some bruising and scratches on the face. Some bruising on the knuckles."

"Knuckles?"

"Could've happened after he fell into the pool. Struggling to get out."

"You've seen this before in drownings?"

"No."

"Wouldn't he get bruising on his knuckles if he'd hit someone?"

"That's what the pathologist said."

She could feel her anger rising. "Well, then he fought with somebody before his death and …"

"And seems to have won. There's not much on his face, a few scratches on his arms that could've happened in the pool."

"But I think I know who he fought with."

"Yes?"

"John Baron had bruises on his face that afternoon. He's an awful little man, rude and belligerent …"

"We'd all like to put rude, belligerent men behind bars."

So he was human after all.

"Do you have proof that they had an altercation?"

"No."

"Um-hum. Oh, and one more thing. His shoulder was dislocated."

"His shoulder was dislocated?" She knew she sounded like an echo but she was having trouble taking it all in. The picture of Michael lying on the concrete beside the pool flashed before her.

"What does the pathologist say about that?"

"It might've happened when you pulled him out."

"Yes," she said. All right. Maybe. "What about alcohol?"

"Alcohol and Valium in the blood."

"Valium?" she said. "How much Valium?"

"Enough to knock him out. Especially since he'd had a few drinks. Guy probably never knew what hit him."

"But that takes a *lot* of Valium. Why would he take enough to knock himself out when he was expecting guests?"

"I don't have to tell you, Doctor, if he was used to taking the stuff, he'd need more and more. Do you know if he had a habit?"

"I'd be surprised if he did."

"But you can't rule it out?" She was still thinking about it when he said, "Was he upset about something?"

"He didn't kill himself." Even as she said this, a little voice inside her head began to whisper, *You hardly knew him, how can you be sure?*

"Well, did anyone threaten him?"

She thought of Claude Simard's letter. She thought of Teodor. "No."

"Well, it doesn't add up to a struggle. If there's nothing else to go on, it'll probably go on the books as an accident. Death by misadventure we call it."

"What about —" What was she thinking? "What about his feet? Were there any scratches on his feet?"

"They would've reported that."

Rebecca hung up. She felt nauseated. She had been hoping all along for a heart attack. Things would have been clear-cut then. An accident. But this changed everything. She went into the next examining room to take stitches out of a young basketball player's knee.

At 6:30 she said goodbye to her last patient. After Iris had left for the day, she pulled the envelope from her purse and reread the letter from Claude Simard. Her stomach growled as she nibbled from the store of roasted almonds she kept in a bag in her desk drawer. She remembered the apple in her skirt pocket and pulled it out.

She thought of the handkerchief in Michael's garbage bin. It wasn't that Michael would not carry a handkerchief. He would never own one that shade of plaid. What if Simard had come to Michael's house before they arrived? Should she have told Tiziano about the letter? There was no threat in it, just desperation. He even called Michael a good man; how could that be construed as a threat? She didn't want to implicate him before she had any real information. The guy's story was tragic enough without her making trouble for him. Yet she couldn't just ignore the letter, the handkerchief. Even if it was too soon to tell Tiziano.

She was really hungry now. There were lots of good restaurants on the Danforth. Greek town. She found the return address on the envelope in her Perly's street guide. It was past the trendy part of the Danforth, where it headed toward seedy.

She drove east to Gerrard Street then turned north on Broadview to reach the Danforth. She could have gone along Bloor Street, which turned into the Danforth as you drove east, but traffic on Bloor crept at a snail's pace any time of the day.

Danforth Avenue was busy at dinnertime. The weather was still fine, and people sat outside at tables under striped awnings at the mainly Greek restaurants. On her way back she would get some takeout moussaka.

The upscale restaurants ended and gave way to small, colourless stores where cheap outdated toys and kitchenware lay behind dusty display windows. She found Rhodes Avenue and made a right turn. The street was lined with war-vintage houses that looked their age. She stopped in front of a small, semi-detached, two-storey house covered in clapboard. The tiny lawn was studded with dandelions.

What was she doing here? She just needed to know one thing: did Claude Simard push Michael into the pool?

She walked up the sagging wooden stairs to the front door and knocked. There was a din of some kind going on inside. Bags of garbage relaxed in the corner of the veranda. Strips of white paint peeled down the lintel around the door and nearby window.

She knocked again, this time louder.

Finally the door opened. A television murmured inside. The smell of cabbage wafted over her. A little girl of about eight, wearing a pink dress two sizes too large, stood watching her. Before Rebecca could say anything, the girl yelled out, "Mam!"

A harried voice from inside called back, "Tell them to go away, Mary!"

The little girl blinked but didn't move. Her rather plain face was smudged with dirt. She held the door tightly to her side, blocking any view of the interior.

"I'm looking for Claude Simard," Rebecca said as loudly as she could without screaming. Maybe someone would hear her over the TV.

A woman in her forties approached the door. She wore a shiny black skirt and white blouse, her brown hair tied back in a stringy ponytail. "Oh, yeah?" she said. "What for?"

"I want to ask him some questions. About his job."

"This got to do with the strike?"

"Sort of."

The woman scrutinized Rebecca a moment, took in her matching linen skirt and blouse, the high-heeled sandals. She turned her head away from the door and yelled into the house, "Claude! Someone to see you. And I gotta go. I'm late for work."

She vanished inside while the girl stood guard at the door. A minute later the woman squeezed through the doorway and hurried down the steps. Rebecca watched her head up the street toward the Danforth. Probably a waitress uniform.

The little girl stared at Rebecca, twirling a strand of dark greasy hair around a finger.

"Is Claude your father?" Rebecca asked.

The girl shook her head.

"Your uncle?"

She nodded.

"Get away from there, Mary," a man's voice commanded from behind. A large hand reached to open the door wider and the little girl flew back.

A tall thin man with a bit of a stoop beneath a black t-shirt watched her with lacklustre eyes. "D'I know you?"

"I was a friend of Michael Oginski's."

He shifted his weight from one foot to the other, shoved one hand into his jeans pocket. "Yeah? It's too bad what happened to him."

"How did you know?"

"Word gets around."

"Did you send him this?" She held up the envelope with the office address scrawled on the front.

The man swallowed, cleared his throat. "What if I did?"

"Hey, Claude!" a man's voice cried out from inside. "You're missing the wrestling."

She continued. "Did you go to his house on Saturday?"

"I got company. Gotta go."

"Did you go to his house on Saturday?"

His head pulled back and he began to cough, sending his large cheeks shaking. "No," he said between hacks. "Why would I?"

He pulled out a handkerchief from his pocket and spat into it.

She stared at the blue and green plaid. "I know you were there," she said. "You left one of your handkerchiefs behind."

"Hey Claude! You gotta see this guy move." The

voice from inside. "He fought with Mohammed Ali that time, remember?"

Claude quickly stuffed the plaid square back into his pocket, then cocked his head toward the house. "So Miss ..."

"Dr. Temple."

He stared at her. "So, Doc. You wanna beer?"

She followed him down a dark hall toward the electronic din of a crowd hungry for blood. In the living room a man around Claude's age sat on the edge of a threadbare mock-Scandinavian sofa, wearing a Yankees cap. He shoved his long, grey hair behind his ears when he saw Rebecca.

"Hey, doll, have a seat. You'll see some damned fine wrestling."

"Shut up, George," said Claude.

He led her through the living room, past George, into a tiny adjacent kitchen separated only by a half height wall. The roar of the TV crowd continued.

"What's it to you where I was?" Claude said, not asking her to sit down in one of the two vinyl-upholstered chairs.

"I'm not sure the drowning was an accident."

"You think I —" He gaped at her and started to cough again. "Look at me! Do I look like I could ... I can barely carry myself around. Okay, I was there. But it was Friday night."

"What happened?"

"Nothin' happened. I just wanted to see if he could help me. I can't work no more. I'm dyin' of cancer and it's John Baron's doing. I thought he could help me out."

She looked at his red-rimmed eyes. He had taken the handkerchief out again and held it in a large fist. Large hands. How much strength did it take to —

"Why didn't you go to Baron himself?"

"Baron's the devil. Wouldn't ask him for nothin'. Besides, you can't get into that building if you look like a miner. They got guards on them doors."

"How did you find Michael's address?"

"He's in the book. Baron ain't."

"So you got to Michael's house. Then what happened?"

"I was just startin' to make my case, hardly more'n a few minutes. All of a sudden the phone rings. Sounds like someone's coming over and when he hangs up, he says he don't have time now. He'll get back to me. Pulls some twenties outta his wallet and hands 'em over. I tell him he can't buy me off like that. Then I left."

"You were angry."

"Sure I was angry."

His face suddenly registered her implication. "But nothing happened."

All at once George loomed beside her, the odour of sweat. He was Claude's height, only upright so he seemed taller.

"Got another beer, Claude?"

Claude opened the fridge door and took out two bottles from a whole shelf of bottles. He held one out to Rebecca.

"No thanks."

George prodded off the cap and took a swig. "Everything okay, Claude?" He looked pointedly at Rebecca.

Claude opened his own bottle and gestured toward her. "She thinks I killed somebody."

George grinned. "Did you?"

"You know I wouldn't hurt a fly," said Claude, winking at him.

"Yeah, you ain't got nothing against flies, but what about the rest of us? You tell her about your temper?"

"He's just foolin' around," said Claude. "He knows I wouldn't hurt a fly. Nothin' bigger either."

"Yeah, sure," said George. "Claude here wouldn't hurt a fly." George lifted the bottle in a sign of departure. "'Scuse me. I gotta go watch two guys beat the shit out of each other."

Rebecca waited until George had sat down in the living room again. Then she said to Claude, "Did you two fight? I mean physically?"

"No."

"Did he hit you?"

He peered at her. "No."

"Could you tell who was on the phone?"

"Some woman."

"A woman?"

A smile played along his lips. "I guess he was cheating on you."

"We weren't …" She threw him a censuring look. "Did you get a name?"

Simard scratched his head. "Helena?"

Rebecca caught her breath. "Halina?"

"Maybe."

"And he said she was coming over?" He nodded. "What time was it?"

He looked toward the ceiling, thinking. "Midnight, thereabouts."

She stared at him. He stared back. Why would he lie about this?

"Do you remember any of the conversation?"

He turned away. "Nothing special. Something like: 'You're coming over? Okay.'"

"How did Michael seem to you?"

"What d'you mean?"

How could she put this? "Did he look drunk?"

"Drunk? Hell no."

"Did he look ... drugged?"

Simard grimaced at her. "I don't know what yer getting at, lady, but he was just normal."

He looked down at her hand. "Can I have my letter back now?"

She shoved it back into her purse. "I'll let you know."

Rebecca found a parking spot on the stretch of the Danforth where you could walk from one Greek restaurant to another checking out menus. She ordered some moussaka to go at the counter of the first one she came to. The waiter told her she was welcome to wait at the bar for the five minutes it would take. Instead, she stepped out to the pay phone on the sidewalk. It was 7:30. Maybe Tiziano would still be on duty.

"Eleven Division."

"Could I speak to Constable Tiziano."

"Who's calling?"

"Dr. Temple."

There was a click, then someone picking up. "Yes, Doctor, what can I do for you?"

"I've got some new information you'll be interested in. A woman visited Michael the night before he died. Now she's disappeared."

"Has she been reported missing?"

"She's not exactly missing. We just don't know where she is."

"You're kidding, right?"

Not the enthusiastic response she'd hoped for. "She's visiting from Poland with her daughter. They're suspicious of authority so we haven't called the police. But I don't trust her. Doesn't it make you wonder, her disappearing just after Michael's death?"

She waited. Silence. "I don't have the luxury of 'wondering,' Doctor. I'm too busy doing police work. Look, it doesn't change anything. Without signs of a struggle, it's going down as an accident."

She took a breath. "Well, Constable, I have to tell you I'm very uncomfortable with the amount of Valium found in his blood. I think I would've noticed if he was addicted. And if he weren't addicted, he wouldn't have taken that much at one time."

"You'd be surprised at how well people can hide things. It's not something you advertise. You know how many alcoholics there are out there and you'd never know it to look at them? And let's say you're right, he wasn't an addict. Maybe he just wanted to take something for his nerves and he underestimated it and took more than he needed. Then before the stuff took effect, he went into the pool, and before you know it ..."

"Isn't it possible someone drugged him?"

"Look, Doctor, I don't want to be rude, but you should leave the policing to the police."

"I'm perfectly happy to leave it to the police. I think you should start by speaking to Halina."

Pause. "Does she have any reason to want to harm Mr. Oginski?"

"I don't know. Isn't that your job to find out?"

An audible sigh. "Do you have any idea how many alcohol-related drownings there are each year? They're heartbreakers, and I know how you feel. You knew the guy and that makes it worse. But I see it all the time. I know it's hard to accept, but sometimes that's all we can do."

That night Rebecca slept fitfully. The moussaka had been delicious but too heavy for her system, which was still upset from the weekend. Every time she felt herself falling into blessed unconsciousness, some demon would make her turn over and she would be roused yet again into a headachy stupor. This went on until she looked up at a suddenly blue sky and found herself straddling Michael again, pushing down on his chest, pump, pump, pump. She breathed into his mouth, breath in, breath out. This time his eyes were wide open under the goggles. He was staring at her while she worked on him, which made her nervous and glad of the goggles, "Speedo" upside down. Nose not quite right. He blinked behind the transparent plastic of the goggles, his eyes as blue as the sky.

Rebecca sat bolt upright in bed, gasping for air, astonished at the darkness of her room. It was night, the blue sky was gone, and Michael was dead. But the goddamn goggles! The Speedo logo *had* been upside down. Did that mean the goggles were upside down? The plastic bridge across the nose too low on his face. She glanced at her clock radio. Nearly three. Too late to call anyone. She would wait until the morning.

After a few hours of shallow sleep, she sat up in bed and read further into Michael's manuscript, a chapter made up mostly of letters. When was the last time she had written a letter?

By seven o'clock she could wait no longer. Maybe he would be up now. She dialed the number.

"Hallo?"

He sounded half asleep. She had woken him up. "Edward?"

"Who's this?"

"It's Rebecca. Dr. Temple. I'm sorry to call so early, but I have to ask you something." She heard him breathing into the phone. "Do you use goggles when you swim?"

"Goggles? What time is it?"

"It's seven. Look, about the goggles. Does it matter if they're upside down?"

"I don't understand. What're you asking me?"

"Would you ever put your goggles on upside down?"

He waited a moment. "Oh," he said. "No."

"Why?"

"Why? Well, they won't work upside down. Water will get inside."

"How?"

"There's a tiny space along the bottom edge. The water'll get through if they're not worn right." He breathed loudly. "Is this something to do with my father?"

"No. Look, I'm sorry I got you up. It was just something I was wondering about."

She hung up, embarrassed. It had been short-sighted of her to raise the issue with him. Not unless she had something real to go on. Tiziano would probably say that Michael had been too drunk to put the goggles on right side up. But the Michael she had met was impeccable. His clothes, his manners, his language. Michael would never have put his goggles on upside down. Everything about that day was wrong.

chapter nineteen

The Go-Between

April 16, 1755
Mon cher Castelanino, (now that your father has been promoted to Castellan of Kraków)

When we were last in Warsaw I made a promise that if I ever went to Russia you would accompany me there. Your mother will be delighted to be rid of you, then, for it is my cheerful duty to tell you I have been named ambassador to St. Petersburg and I am in need of a secretary. Here is our opportunity to live in the same city for longer than a week. And imagine when that city is Petersburg! I don't have to tell you (your *cher Maman*, the Countess, will cheerfully perform that office) the opportunities for education and otherwise to be found in the Russian court.

My health has unfortunately been troublesome

and I have had an attack of fever, which leaves me weak and delays my departure for Russia. I hope to arrive there by June. I have written one of the British residents there asking him to look out for a house where we may be lodged.

Your humble servant,
Sir Charles H.-W.

London, May 12
Dear Sir Charles,

I hope it is understood that your first and most important duty in the Russian court is the business of the subsidy treaty. His Majesty is most anxious to finish the business once and for all, especially since storm clouds from the direction of Prussia loom on the horizon. In the event of an attack on Hanover, the King's cherished Electorate, the Empress Elizabeth is willing to furnish 50,000 troops to invade Prussia in exchange for a subsidy of £400,000. Your advice has been incorporated into the treaty, that is, that by a secret article, four annual payments of £100,000 above the subsidy would be given on the understanding that troops would be available in position, ready and waiting to strike at a moment's notice if England, its dominions, or allies were attacked. As you say, this would prove a valuable deterrent to the designs of Prussia and her French allies. As you know, your predecessor was unable to bring the treaty to a conclusion. It is my fervent hope that you will be more successful.

Your servant
Lord Holdernesse, Secretary of State

St. Petersburg, June 20
Dear Lord Holdernesse,

I am mindful of the pitfalls of doing business in Russia but have great hopes for the treaty because of my familiar footing with the Great Chancellor Bestuzhev. As you know, nothing can be achieved here without bribery. Thus after throwing out early hints of English gratitude for his assistance, I have offered Bestuzhev himself £10,000 if the convention with England can be brought to a successful termination. After inviting myself to his house for dinner, I am joyful to report that he has agreed to the sums in your instructions. Now the papers must be delivered to the Empress, who is, unfortunately, in the country, where she is disinclined to do any business. I fear this spells certain delay.

Your humble servant,
Sir Charles H.-W.

St. Petersburg, June 25
My dear Fox,

I am lodged in a very fine house on the river Neva, as fine a river as the Thames. It is a pity that it does not run above six months of the year. But then in winter I hear it makes the finest street in Europe. Though the situation of the mansion is delightful, facing the river opposite the Winter Palace, it is unfortunately bare from wall to wall without a chair or stool in it. Furniture and chimney-pieces are being sent from England, and Lord Chesterfield has seen fit to provide me with goldfish, though I am told they will not survive here. I am endeavouring to make it very comfortable, for there is not much society here and one is obliged to live very much at home.

I have had my first audience with the Tsarina and she is very gracious to me. She is still handsome and thinks so. However, her health is failing and she is said to suffer from dropsy and asthma and to tire easily. When I saw her, she was afflicted with a cough that would not abate. Her favourite, Ivan Shuvalov, is partial to France, as is his brother, Alexander, the head of the Secret Chancery.

I have also been presented to the Young Court, as the Grand Duke and Duchess, Peter and Catherine, are called. Never was a match more ill-suited. Peter is the Empress's nephew, son of her sister Anne. Both his parents are dead, and she has adopted him as her heir. Yet he is sickly, as well as sullen, morose, and illiterate. He is also vicious beyond his years and shows no signs of growing up. He plays with tin soldiers half a day and the other half with dolls. Beside him, Catherine sparkles with health and the joy of living. Her parents are Prince Christian, now deceased, and Princess Johanna of Anhalt-Zerbst.

Catherine is twenty-six years old and reads widely; she shows ambition and does not fear giving strong opinions. Since her coming into the country she has by every method in her power endeavoured to gain the affection of the nation. She has learned the Russian language and has a great knowledge of this empire. The Grand Duke's one saving grace is that he has confidence in his wife. He tells people that tho' he does not understand things himself, yet his wife understands everything.

The pair has been married for ten years and do not live together, but have their own followers. I am told Peter has affairs with the maids-of-honour and Catherine has her admirers. One of these was a handsome young gentleman in waiting with whom she fell in love. Last year she bore a son, Paul, reputed to be his. Indeed Peter is said to be unable to beget children. The little boy is looked after by the Empress and her servants, Catherine seeing him but rarely. The young couple lives chiefly at Oranienbaum, a Royal Palace overlooking the Gulf of Finland at little distance from the capital.

I must say that I am astounded at the prodigality of the Russian court, which is even more extravagant than Versailles. The Tsarina's palaces are filled with a multitude of sweeping salons lit by the costliest crystal chandeliers. The rooms, the nobles, the Tsarina all sparkle with gold and gems the like of which I have never seen.

In the course of several long discussions I have had with the Grand Duchess Catherine (in my position I find myself seated beside her at banquets) she has remarked with some bitterness upon the debt into which she has fallen because of her high expenses at court. Would I, as the English Ambassador, she asked in all confidence, be willing to lend her money — a substantial amount — to help her alleviate that debt in exchange for information that would prove useful to our government. I have already agreed upon the loan, confident that through her agency I may learn about the goings-on in the Russian court. I am looking forward to playing a strong part in the present reign, and in the event of the Empress Elizabeth's death and the accession of her niece, I feel I am assured of cementing an alliance between England and Russia.

So that I do not embarrass myself in the opulence of the court, I have had to order new clothes to be made at my own expense. Even so, my new brocades and velvets will be shabby in comparison.

My young friend, Count Poniatowski, arrives next week. I am greatly looking forward to merry conversation with him at the expense of the court.

Your humble servant,
H.-W.

St. Petersburg, August 7
My dear Fox,

The other day, young Count Poniatowski and I rode in our carriage from Petersburg to the Palace in Oranienbaum, the summer residence of the Young Court. The occasion was the fête in honour of the Grand Duke's name day. The fresh scent of the grass, the wondrous blue sky, put me in a fine mood. The early evening sun turned the air golden. Some poetic turns of phrase sought birth in my head but were stillborn in the throes of the exhilaration that anticipated the festivities.

During the evening my young friend, the Count, distinguished himself on the dance floor. I am too old for such violent exercise but was content to exchange exaggerated pleasantries with Chancellor Bestuzhev and the various ambassadors in the court. During my diplomatic forays, from time to time I watched the young Count cut a dashing figure as he danced a minuet. I was not the only one who watched him. The Grand Duchess seemed to have him in her sights as he stepped this way and that around his partner with catlike grace. Without meaning to, I caught her eye, and she bowed her head with a look of mischief.

Later I was delighted to find myself once again seated beside her at the banquet. She is surpassingly cultivated with an enchanting manner. Between the soup and the meat we established that we had in common a predilection for the works of Montesquieu, Diderot, Racine, and above all, Voltaire.

"I saw Voltaire on stage in one of his own plays and I can report to Your Highness that he acted with great spirit. Though I must also report that in person he is a small man with uncombed hair." I looked over the assembled courtiers. "And more poorly dressed than your lowliest servant."

She chuckled with delight then threw a glance over the many tables around us. "You arrived with a young man," she said. "I was quite diverted watching him dance. A very pleasant-looking young man. I believe he is seated over there."

I saw my young friend in animated conversation with Count Naryshkin sitting next to him.

"That is young Count Poniatowski, Your Highness," I said, happily surprised at her interest in my protégé. "His family is prominent in Polish society. His mother was Countess Czartoryska before her marriage."

"I have heard of the family. They are reputed to be the most cultivated people in Poland."

"The young Count has had an impressive education. I believe one day he will be an important man in his country."

I sipped wine from my glass as Chancellor Bestuzhev approached the Grand Duchess. Tho' I was grateful for his sympathies to the English interest (and thus to me) I saw he was an odd apparition among the perfectly groomed courtiers, with too much black curly hair, his teeth but a few brownish stumps in his mouth.

He bent to Her Highness's other ear and whispered hoarsely, something about a Count Lehndrov who sat just beyond. A tall, dark-haired man stood and bowed in our direction. Handsome enough, but there was a shrewdness in his face. Not to compare with the blond sweetness of my young friend who looked like a lord.

She bowed her head slightly and whispered back to Bestuzhev something that included the words "too tired." I assumed the Chancellor was doing his part to entertain the Grand Duchess. Though she didn't mention my young friend again, her eyes repeatedly wandered in his direction right up until the serving of dessert.

Your humble servant,
H.-W.

St. Petersburg, September 30
My dear Fox,

You will be proud of me when I tell you I have become matchmaker between Russia and Poland. If I can only be of service to my country (and my friends) I am happy. Unfortunately for me, Poland is overwhelming shy and will not believe in Russian interest. I make it my job to whisper each day in Poland's ear in the hope that he will finally see the light. Would that it were my only job in this cauldron of intrigue and perchance these many months would not have passed by with so little development.

Perhaps nothing will come of it after all, but the personalities in question have everything in common, including intellect and taste, but they also complement each other, one being vivacious and daring, the other labouring under a tendency toward moroseness. I fear I too have become prey to this tendency and sometimes am overwhelmed by a great dullness that overtakes me. At such times every reasonable thought is pushed from my head and a weight descends upon my chest.

For example in the matter of the subsidy treaty, where nothing has proceeded apace. The Tsarina, induced by the faction favourable to France, asked for more money from our King's treasury for her troops' assistance against Prussia and France. I held out no hope for any increase but suggested certain rearrangements of the dates of payment and a few other minor points of difference and lo and behold, it was settled! I must tell you I feared lest it should be buried in oblivion and entirely forgot in a corner of the Empress's closet. But at long last she signed and the papers have been sent off to the King. There have been so many delays in this matter that the vast distance the messenger must ride between Russia and England is but a minor obstacle.

A new danger has appeared in the person of a Scottish gentleman, Mackenzie Douglas, who has come to Russia claiming to study the working of mines. As an English subject arriving in St. Petersburg, he has come to me in order to pay his respects to the British Ambassador. But I have not forgotten making the acquaintance in Dresden of his cousin, a rank Jacobite who had not the sense to conceal it. Therefore I am ready for this Mr. Douglas, a Jacobite spy whom I have been warned is in the secret service of the French, dispatched here to win over concessions from the Tsarina, thereby pushing out the English influence at court. I have no doubt he was sent by the Bonnie Prince himself, who is still enjoying the hospitality of King Louis at Versailles, both of them dreaming of the day when they might overthrow King George.

But I am too old for this business. My stomach troubles continue, I have a weakness on my left side and a giddiness in my head. No Alderman of London has less of wit, humour, invention, or verses than I.

Your humble servant,
H.-W.

December 2
My dear Fox,

I have had a letter from Holdernesse that sets off alarm

bells in my head. Is there any truth to the intimation that there is a treaty in the works between England and Prussia? Such a thing would be impossible to explain to the Empress after my strenuous efforts to persuade her to sign the treaty with us *against* Prussia. Is that why it has taken nearly a month for the messenger to arrive back from England with the subsidy treaty papers signed by King George? I fear I will be caught in the middle of such an arrangement, with the Empress loath to trust me with much of anything again.

My rising anxiety in this direction may explain the unsettling incident of the other day. One afternoon last week the young Count and I became lost while exploring an unfamiliar part of the city. The confusion brought on a sudden attack of giddiness and no one was more surprised than I when I fell down in the street. My young friend implored the crowd that had gathered around us for a physician. Dear Fox, I was carried by five men like a side of pork down some distant and narrow alley and into a small house. I lay there unable to move, thinking perhaps I was already dead, it was so dark and the air filled with smoke. *I have finally gone to the devil*, I thought, and to prove it, there he was — an old man with a long, grey beard dressed entirely in black, both robe and peculiar hat. Not the picture of Satan I expected. No horns, no tail.

He turned out to be not the devil but a magician of sorts (I do believe he may have been a Jew) for after inquiring about my afflictions and examining my body, he brewed over a fire a potion of some exotic concoction that he placed in front of my nose for me to imbibe. I thought to refuse, but then concluded I could feel no worse and it could but kill me, so I sipped the brew down.

As you can tell, my dear Fox, I still live and breathe. And I can truly say that I have never had such a deep sleep. When I awoke, the young Count peered at me with much anxiety and became calm only when I sat up and remarked that I felt like a new man. I was willing to give the old healer anything he wanted in payment. But all he asked for was this: to remember him when the time came.

What time was that, I inquired. I would know, he said, and would say no more. I left him some pounds and marked well in my mind the alley where stood the little house so that if the need arose I might return.

Dear friend, England seems very far away indeed. My duties have become onerous to me and I long for the peaceful happy hours I spent with you and Lady Caroline at Holland House.

Your humble servant,
H.-W.

It is long after dinner. The servants have retired. The December winds howl outside and my bones ache from the cold as I search the house for the young Count. I find him in the study, reading by the fire.

"You're still here!" I say, approaching with purpose. I will not let him stay snugly in the warmth of the house tonight. I have been thinking how to broach the subject and have decided on attack.

He looks up from his book. "I beg your pardon."

"You haven't left for Naryshkin's house yet."

"I'm sure I don't know what you mean."

"I heard him invite you to one of his soirées. 'Tis an honour you ought not refuse."

My young friend waves the suggestion away and pretends to continue reading. I have gone too easy on him. This time I will press him without mercy.

"It would be the politic thing to do, to go where you

have been invited by a gentleman of the royal bedchamber. You could make a good entrance if you went now."

"I have no desire for a romantic entanglement with some lady-in-waiting. Who will next week set her heart on some other gentleman at court. I detest such games."

"But Count," say I, "it is not a lady-in-waiting who keeps her eye out for you. It is the Grand Duchess herself."

He cocks his head at me. "So you have said, dear Sir Charles. But I am sure you exaggerate her interest. She is so far above me I cannot believe she would single me out from such a handsome court."

"Tell me if I am wrong, dear Count. You have come to Russia under my protection in order to learn about the world?"

He nods politely, a bemused smile on his lips. "And I have nothing but gratitude for ..."

"As much as I am fond of gratitude," I say, "it is results I want. There is work to be done here. And pleasant work it is, too. She is an enchanting woman — you will not suffer there."

"You are weary of my company," he says with a sigh.

"It would not hurt to become the friend of a future Tsarina. Even if her husband rules — which I have grave doubts about — she will be the strength behind him."

"Precisely why she would not interest herself in a lowly Polish nobleman."

I open my eyes wide to show him my frustration. "You do not give yourself enough credit, dear Count. There is no other young man at court with your intelligence or culture. She spied it immediately. You had best trust my instincts about this. I am the more experienced man and I smell interest. You would do both your country and mine a service to engage her."

"So you send me to be a diplomat."

"I do not send, but encourage you. If I were but a little younger I would not consider you at all. But it is you she admires and it is you who must go to Naryshkin's. And if in the course of your friendship you obtain for your country the sympathy of an empress, I do not see the harm in that."

chapter twenty

Rebecca stood in the shower trying to wake up. She was entranced by the people Michael had brought to life in his book. As she had been entranced by the writer. Despite the age difference, despite the cultural difference, they had made a connection. Any spare time she had was spent reading his manuscript. She tried to push back the images of death and pictured his blue eyes animated in the restaurant, his arms bringing her close in that restrained embrace on the dark street when she needed consoling. He was simply an extraordinary man. Almost regal with his Old World charm, a gentleman of the old school, yet unpretentious, good-natured. Was that why she couldn't let it go, the death by misadventure verdict? She seemed to be the only one who questioned it. Tiziano was so blinkered by precedence in the normal scheme of things that he was ready to dismiss the niggling questions of Halina's disappearance, Simard's visit, the missing manuscript, the

Valium that shouldn't have been in his body, John
Baron's bruises.

Well maybe when everything was said and done, all
those loose ends would fall into line and point the way
to accidental death, but until that happened her mind
worked the pieces of the puzzle incessantly. As a physician she unraveled the mysteries of her patients' illness-
es daily. Michael's death was pressing in a different way.
She could no longer help him, but she could give him the
dignity of the truth.

Before leaving for the office that morning Rebecca
phoned the number on Michael's business card.

"Baron Mines."

"Could I speak to John Baron please?"

"Hold, please."

"John Baron's office.

"Could I speak to John Baron?"

"Mr. Baron's not taking any calls today," said a
woman's officious voice.

"I wanted to speak to him about Michael Oginski."

"He's not giving any interviews."

"I just wanted to ask him some questions."

"He's not speaking to reporters," she said with
impatience. "All the papers know that by now, so tell
everyone to stop calling."

"I'm not a reporter. My name is Dr. Rebecca Temple.
I've met him socially."

"You people will try anything, won't you?"

The line went dead.

That morning the results of Natalka's blood tests
arrived. They confirmed Rebecca's preliminary findings.

Instead of an elevated count of white blood cells, as she would have expected in chronic leukemia, they were the opposite. Below normal. As were her red blood cells. She was anemic. And her platelets were reduced, which accounted for the nosebleeds that would not stop. Her liver enzymes were mildly elevated, but that was no surprise since her liver was slightly enlarged. She would have to wait for the hematologist's report. Natalka was seeing him tomorrow.

No wonder her Polish doctor was confused about the diagnosis. Clearly this was a very sick woman, but the waters were muddy. She would pass the information on to Dr. Koboy, who would probably want a bone marrow sample. For now there was nothing more she could do.

Her last patient of the morning left at twelve-fifteen. Rebecca grabbed her shoulder bag and stepped past Iris sitting behind the counter.

"Going for lunch?" Iris asked.

"Got a little errand to do," she said. "My pager's on if you need me."

She drove south heading toward Bay Street. You could barely see the sky between the high rises of the financial district. People were blown along the sidewalks in the wind tunnels created by the corridors of buildings. Parking was scarce but she was lucky and found a spot at a meter that someone was vacating.

In the distance the Baron Mines Building was a dark slab of granite that would have stood proudly on any upscale street in London or New York. It looked as if no expense had been spared. The black stone facing shone in the drab light as if it had just been polished.

She had forgotten about the pickets. In front of the massive glass entry doors about a dozen men in shirt-sleeves and baseball caps held up homemade signs and shuffled around in a desultory circle. One of them was Claude Simard. She hoped he wouldn't see her. His sign read, "Baron Mines is killing us."

Walking toward them, she gazed at the side of the building: there must have been an entrance other than the front. But a gate built along that wall concealed any means of entry behind it.

She stayed outside the circle of pickets, marching toward the door on an angle, trying not to make eye contact with the miners. She was nearly there.

"Baron Mines doesn't care," read the sign closest to her.

"Hey, Doc!" someone yelled. "Shoulda known you were with them." Claude Simard stepped out of the circle to come closer. "I guess you can't trust doctors neither. You fooled me all right."

The men within earshot turned to look at her. She felt her face go hot.

"I've never been here before," she said.

Simard's large pasty face broke into a bitter smile. "You don't have to convince me. I don't care. Tell it to the Judge." He pointed his index finger to the dishwater sky.

"You're a religious man then, are you?"

His rheumy eyes watched her. "I know them that's done evil will be punished. We all get what's comin' to us. In the end."

The man had a knack for issuing statements laden with innuendo. Sounding like threats. What did he mean anyway? Michael got what he deserved because he worked for Baron? Was he threatening her? Maybe it was a confession of guilt. She'd watched him, lean and stooped, trudging along in the circle of pickets; he didn't appear to have the strength to kill someone. But rage is funny that way; it might deliver strength in the right circumstances.

She felt him watching her back as she stepped through the huge glass doors. Inside was a different world. Marble everywhere. Great speckled slabs of it on the floor. Pillars of marble towered two storeys high. Over the sweeping granite entranceway, in gold block lettering: Baron Mines.

Three men in suits stood in a short line in front of her, stopped by a guard.

"Name?" he asked the first person. Scribbled down the information in a notebook. "Suite?"

Rebecca hurriedly read the names of occupants listed in gold on a nearby plaque behind glass. Baron Mines took up the top floors of the twenty-storey building. The rest of the tenants seemed to be financial companies.

Her turn came and she stepped forward.

"Name?"

"Dr. Rebecca Temple."

The guard glanced at her a moment, wrote it down. "Suite?"

"Lovatt and Prue Investments."

He nodded and she headed for the bank of elevators. A group of businessmen got off.

"Why don't you join us at a club?" one of them was saying. "We can have a drink before lunch and ..."

She stepped into the elevator. Pressing the button for the twentieth floor, she hoped Baron took a later lunch.

The door opened into the oak-panelled foyer of Baron Mines. A huge chandelier hung from the centre of a high ceiling, its crystal tears sparkling like stars. Rebecca stepped onto the deep red broadloom, the heels of her shoes sinking into the plush. Behind a long marble counter sat a striking young woman. She looked up at Rebecca's approach, her blond hair sleek against high cheekbones.

"I'd like to see John Baron," Rebecca said.

The woman looked down at some pages on her desk. "Do you have an appointment?"

"No," she said. "But he'll want to see me. I was a friend of Michael Oginski's"

The blonde was waiting, unimpressed.

"And I have some news about his daughter," Rebecca said.

The receptionist lifted an eyebrow. She watched Rebecca, plainly wanting to ask but not daring. Did people know about Natalka?

"Just a moment," she said. She lifted the receiver and murmured something into the phone.

Replacing the receiver, the gatekeeper said, "Mr. Baron's secretary will be right out."

A handsome woman in her thirties appeared, her crisp brown hair styled like the Queen's. "This way," she said, and led Rebecca down the hall, a small, peremptory figure in a light blue suit.

They passed a closed door on the right that read, "Michael Oginski." A lump formed in Rebecca's throat.

The Queen opened an oak door inscribed with Baron's name in gold letters. Rebecca followed her further down a short hall. She knocked on an unmarked door. A grumble came from inside, and she pushed the door open, standing aside for Rebecca to enter.

Baron sat eating alone at a round, linen-covered table, surrounded by elegant crockery and crystal glasses. Behind him on the burnished oak panelling hung a huge oil painting, maybe six feet long, of some ancient European battle, in a heavy rococo gold frame. It was quite wonderful. Rebecca was impressed. Until she saw what he was eating, in this private dining room. With his left hand he spooned some baked beans into his mouth, with his right he picked up a piece of wiener and stuffed it in.

He looked up finally, his mouth full of food, and motioned her to the chair opposite him. She sat down, getting a whiff of the red roses arranged in a crystal vase in the centre of the table. He pressed a button on the phone beside him while he chewed.

A waiter in a white jacket appeared instantly. "Yes, sir?"

"Bring another dish for the lady." He gulped down some beer from the foamy glass in front of him.

"Oh," Rebecca said with surprise. "Thank you, no."

"You think it's not good enough? My chef makes the best beans in Toronto. These aren't from a can."

"I'm sure they're wonderful," she lied, "but I've already eaten."

"You'll try some." Then, "Bring her a dish!" he snapped, dismissing the waiter with a flick of his hand.

He gave her a false, conciliatory smile. "I saw you admiring my painting. It's the Battle of Grunwald, very famous painting by Matejko. The big one's in Warsaw in the museum. Takes up a whole room. Magnificent! Matejko did this one first, sort of like practice. Best painter in Poland. Cost me lots of money. You heard of Grunwald?"

She shook her head.

"Most important battle of all time. 1410. But Canadians are ignorant of European history." He jabbed his fork into the air. "Schools are not teaching. I will tell you about this so you know. For years German knights were spreading across Europe, then they came to Poland, massacring everyone in the towns. This battle," he pointed over his shoulder, "German Crusaders had black crosses on their chests — I still remember from school, all Polish children learn this — they defeated soldiers all over Europe, their leaders were famous. In the middle you see one on a horse just before the

Poles kill him. This was huge battle, maybe a hundred thousand men. Everyone in Europe thought the Germans would win. But the Polish king used his head and defeated them. The Germans," he squinted at her, "are always killing us."

"It's a very impressive painting," she said. But not to her taste. The dark canvas seethed with men in black armour thrusting swords, a wild confusion of bodies blending into each other beneath the hooves of rearing horses; in the dark green background clouds swirled, dust rose to the mottled sky. It was the stuff of nightmare.

Rebecca fidgeted in her chair. "I wanted to talk to you about Michael Oginski."

"A fine man," he said, poking a piece of wiener in his mouth. "The best man I know. A real aristocrat."

The bruise on his cheek had faded, but she could still see the spotty outline.

"Do you know if he had a problem with depression?"

"Michael? Bah! What's this about?" He took a gulp of his beer.

"I'm having trouble believing Michael's death was an accident," she said, trying to gauge his reaction. "The policeman asked me whether he'd been upset about something. I didn't know him well enough to say. He thought if Michael had been upset enough, he might deliberately have ..." She trailed off, having difficulty putting it into words.

Baron's thick dark eyebrows angled together. "Ridiculous!" he thundered. He stared at her during a minute when his thoughts seemed elsewhere. "He wouldn't do that. He was a gentleman. Gentlemen don't kill themselves like that. If he was going to do it, he'd shoot himself!"

She was appalled but tried to keep it out of her face.

After a light knock on the door, the waiter glided over the red broadloom and placed a dish of wieners and beans in front of her. With a flourish he arranged a white linen napkin on her lap and some silver cutlery on either side of the dish.

"What would the lady like to drink?" he said.

"Water will be fine."

He stepped toward a corner where an ornate wooden counter stood lined with liquor bottles; he brought her a crystal pitcher of water and a cut crystal glass.

Once the door closed behind the waiter, she continued. "Well then, if he didn't … kill himself, there are two possibilities left." She ignored the dish in front of her, though it smelled good. "One, it was a terrible accident. He had a few drinks then decided to go into the pool and maybe he lost his footing … maybe he went under and was too drunk to save himself. Or two," she paused for effect, "someone killed him."

He shook his head, the grey hair stiff with pomade. "Who would want to kill him? Try the beans." He held his beer glass in the air waiting for her to comply.

She hated herself for giving in to a bully, but she needed his cooperation. She lifted a forkful of beans to her lips. They were delicious. A hint of maple syrup.

"Ummm," she said, nodding her head with approval.

She ate for a minute, hoping to lull him into complacency. He was poking a pinky finger into his ear when she said, "How did you get those bruises?"

"What you talking about?"

"You had very noticeable bruises on your face when I saw you at Michael's on Saturday."

His head bobbed slowly as he watched her, the jaw tightening behind the jowls. "I had fight with a miner. They're animals."

"One of the miners out front?" He nodded. "Did you call the police?"

He shrugged. "Guy ran away. I wouldn't recognize him."

If a miner had hit him, she thought, *he would've had the cops crawling over the lot of them until the culprit was found.*

"What if I told you a neighbour saw your car at Michael's house Saturday morning?"

"Ridiculous! Lots of cars look like mine."

"What did you fight about? Why did he hit you?"

His expression didn't change, but some strategy seemed to shift behind his eyes. "You know, I'm powerful man. You have no right asking questions. What? You think I kill him?"

"Did you?"

He threw his spoon down onto his plate, the clattering against bone china startling in the quiet room. "*Psa kref!* You don't know what you talking. I loved him like brother. One from those low-life miners hit me. I come to house first time when you there."

He played well at indignation but his grammar was slipping.

"Did he fall into the pool while you were there?"

"Now you insulting me," he said, pushing himself away from the table.

She wasn't finished with him. "I have some lab results back from your daughter's tests," she said.

He stood up, a short stubby man holding his head at a cocky angle. "I don't have daughter."

Leaving the plate of beans half eaten, she followed him down the hall toward his office. "Mr. Baron, don't you want to know how she is?"

"You don't understand," he said ahead of her, waving one hand in the air without turning. "She isn't mine."

He opened the door to his office and marched in. Since he hadn't closed the door behind him, she pressed on. The Queen in her blue suit followed Rebecca with her eyes.

Baron disappeared through a further door, also left open. She took this as permission and stepped inside. She was dismayed but not surprised by more oak panelling. A maroon, butter-soft leather sofa. Hunting lodge décor.

Baron strolled around an antique oak desk inlaid with leather and settled into a brown leather armchair.

"About Natalka," she said, standing in the entrance.

"You know, I'm not telling my wife about the whole thing because would upset her. I have family here."

A photo of his blond wife and, presumably, a son stood on the polished surface of the desk.

"It's not good, Halina coming like this."

"She came because Natalka is very ill. Did she explain that to you?"

"I know what she wants. Is good time for her to remember me. She wants me to pay. Natalka not my daughter but I will pay. Because that's how I am."

"Natalka thinks she's your daughter."

He motioned her with an imperious finger to take the upholstered chair in front of the desk. She approached and sat down with a little thud, the seat lower than she had expected. Looking up, she saw that Baron was much higher in his chair than he had any right to be. She'd heard of executives who cut down the legs of visitors' chairs while mounting their own on raised platforms. As a result she was forced to crane her neck to look up at him.

He folded his hands together on the desk and tilted his head for emphasis. "We had little time together. Only married a month before the war."

Maybe she could derail him. "Did you have a happy marriage?"

"Happy? Nobody thought then to be happy, not to be happy. We lived. Like everybody. We knew something was coming, so just before the Germans invaded we got married. When it happened, I knew I had no choice — I went underground and joined the *Armia Krajowa*, the Home Army. Some of us sent to England. We fought together with the Royal Air Force. We saved their asses lots of times. Finally when we came back — everything was different. I dreamed of Halina for six years, six years I didn't see her. And when I get home, there she was with a five-year-old brat."

"She could've become pregnant before you left."

"You don't know Halina. Like alley cat. She'll crawl into bed with anyone. You don't think she found men in those six years? She didn't like be without a man. Girl never look like me."

"She could still be your daughter."

His eyes became slits. "This is what Halina tells. But I know better. A friend of mine — Tomasz — see her just before she leave Kraków to go to parents in the country. She wasn't pregnant. It was 1940. When she say Natalka was born. I don't believe word that comes from her mouth."

A shadow of a smile played on his lips. "She could be killer. This I believe. She could kill Michael."

Rebecca gazed up at him. He really was a piece of work. But Halina *had* vanished. Was she really afraid of someone, as Natalka had implied? It had crossed Rebecca's mind that Halina could have pushed Michael into the pool.

"What motive would she have?"

He shook his head ominously. "Terrible things happened in old country. She was not blameless. Maybe she didn't want him to find out the truth."

After closing up the office Rebecca drove to Baby Point Road again. Michael's manuscript lay on the passenger seat of her car. She had photocopied the pages so that she could finish reading it, but she would return the original to Edward and try to hide her embarrassment.

Though she got tangled in rush hour traffic on the Gardiner Expressway, it really wasn't very far.

She marched up the stairs to the many-gabled house and rang the bell. Edward opened the door, the early evening light illuminating his face. She caught her breath — he looked so much like Michael, the long aristocratic nose, the sculpted mouth, the blue eyes that saw everything. But were strangely unfocused at the moment.

His hair was longer and disheveled. The buttons of his shirt were undone, showing a few sprigs of brown curls on his chest.

"Hi," he said, a goofy smile lighting his face.

Had he been drinking? "I wanted to return this," she said, handing him the binder.

He opened the cover and flipped to a page. "Yeah," he nodded, holding the binder open on both arms. "I remember some of this."

"Everything all right?" she asked.

He nodded absently, his eyes still on the page.

"I'll be going then." She turned to leave.

"Don't go," he said. He closed the binder. "Please come in."

She smelled it as soon as she walked inside, that sweet, pungent, weedy smell she remembered from her university days. A few of her friends had sung the praises of marijuana, had given her a joint to convert her, the stiff, proper medical student. The thing had had no effect on her whatsoever. She'd never felt the high that her friends had gone on about, and had felt cheated.

When Edward led her into the den, she couldn't help looking out the window toward the pool. It looked so peaceful out there now. They sat down on the couch. His eyes flitted about the room.

"I don't know if the police have been in touch with you," she said, "but the pathologist found alcohol and Valium in your father's blood."

His eyes tried to focus on her. "I don't understand it. The world has gone crazy. Or maybe I didn't know him like I thought."

"Is there anyone you can think of who might've wanted to harm him?"

His eyes widened. "He was just a nice guy. You think someone might've …"

"I saw John Baron today."

He cocked his head. "Uncle Janek. He loved my father. He's going to take care of all the funeral arrangements."

"That's very thoughtful of him." There must be a side to Baron she didn't know. "Did your father tell you about Halina?"

"The Polish lady. She fed him during the war. She was coming to Toronto and he was going to see her again."

"Did he tell you about the compass she was bringing, that it would help him with his book?"

"He might've mentioned it. I wasn't as interested as I should've been. Busy with school."

"Baron thinks Halina could've killed your father."

Edward stood up unsteadily and walked to the window that looked out on the pool. "Janek has always been a little paranoid. Nobody killed my father. Everybody loved him."

"You know, someone could've drugged him, then, when he was unconscious, dragged him to the pool."

He turned around and looked at her with pity in his eyes. He was certainly Michael's son.

"Sometimes you have to accept things as they are. There was no sign of a struggle. It was an accident. Look, come into the kitchen. Mrs. Woronska brought over enough cabbage rolls to feed an army." He waited for her to stand up then led her into the kitchen.

While he set some plates down on the table, Rebecca stood at the patio door looking out at the pool.

"On Saturday there was a pair of your father's shoes under the patio table. Are they still there?" She turned to find him staring at her.

"I haven't gone out there."

She slid open the patio door and stepped out. The sky had clouded over toward dusk and turned everything a deeper shade of itself. The grass was a rich green; the water in the pool had turned an innocent turquoise, as if it hadn't sucked the air out of a man three days earlier. And the shoes. The shoes yet lay beneath the table, the toe of each stuffed into the heel of the other, some absent-minded ritual that created the shadowy silhouette of an animal about to pounce.

She shuddered and bent down to pick up the shoes. They were lightweight brown leather sandals with full heels. She pulled them apart to examine them.

"What are you looking for?" he asked.

"Look at the heels."

There were vertical scratch lines along the leather on the backs of both shoes.

"Yeah?"

"He had no scratch marks on his feet. If someone dragged him under the arms to get him to the pool while he was unconscious, there would've been scratches on his feet. Unless he was wearing shoes."

"Scratch marks on the shoes," he said, without expression. He turned them around in his hands. "These aren't new shoes. Maybe the scratches are old."

"Maybe," she said. "But I don't know how anyone could've gotten them wearing the shoes under normal conditions."

Edward sat down on a patio chair and put the shoes on over his socks. He slouched back in the chair, stretched out his legs, and rubbed his heels along the concrete. Then he took them off and handed them back to her.

She stared at the sandals. "Yeah, fine," she said.

He served her cabbage rolls in tomato sauce from a large pot simmering on the stove. It was the second time that day that a man had offered to feed her.

She hadn't realized she was hungry. "These are delicious," she said, cutting into her third cabbage roll.

When they were finished eating, Edward took her into the den where he made a fire with some logs in the fireplace. They sat down in comfortable silence on the sofa, gazing into the flames that leapt at first, then diminished into flamelets.

"Would you like a joint?" he asked.

"No thanks. I have to drive home."

"Someone waiting for you there?"

"No."

He put his arm on the back of the sofa behind her head. "I'm so bloody tired. I've never been this tired. You know, there's extra bedrooms upstairs if you want to smoke a bit and stay over."

She could see him watching her from the corner of her eye. "I should go. You're tired and I've got an early day tomorrow ..."

"You really a doctor?"

She smiled and turned to find his blue eyes scrutinizing her. "You don't believe a word I've said, do you?"

"You're so beautiful ..."

Angling his head slowly he bent toward her, closer, closer, in slow motion, she saw it coming but couldn't pull away, wouldn't pull away. His lips, soft, full, covered hers with sudden warmth, pressed hers until she found the energy to pull away.

His eyes were closed. He winced and opened them a crack. "I thought doctors were supposed to make you feel better." He closed his eyes and his head fell back. He was fast asleep.

So much for her sex appeal. She lifted his legs onto the sofa, evened out the embers in the fireplace, and locked the door on her way out.

It was past midnight and Rebecca couldn't sleep. Wary about taking unnecessary medication, she usually gritted her teeth and ignored anxiety, even pain. But since David's death, she had kept a bottle of tranquilizers — technically muscle relaxants — for those times she needed something to help her sleep. She broke the tiny pill in half and swallowed it. Then she sat in bed with her lamp shining on Michael's manuscript and read the next chapter, "The Beginning of Love."

chapter twenty-one

The Beginning of Love

December 1755

It is late when I creep out of my apartments in the clothes I feel most comfortable in, the ones I've borrowed from my little Kalmuk hairdresser. Breeches, a ruffled shirt, and a jacket, with a dark cape thrown over for warmth. My long hair is pinned under the tricorn. During the day I would fool no one. But in the dark I can stride through the streets to Naryshkin's mansion, unnoticed on a winter's night. A bracing walk of a mile or so along the river. I attract no attention dressed as a man. I must confess, however, I enjoy it too much. The freedom, the power. Even my step is stronger and I begin to feel that I will be able to do what is necessary when the time comes.

Naryshkin's sister greets me in the salon. I remove my tricorn and let my hair fall loose over my shoulders.

Here, like last week and the week before, eight or ten young friends from court are assembled, mostly in pairs. There is a characteristic low murmur, sometimes the peak of a familiar voice. The corpulent, good-natured Naryshkin is holding forth with a joke as usual. The individuals rarely change, only the arrangement of pairs. They each take a moment to give me an informal bow of the head before they return to their wooing. They are accustomed to my men's clothes and no longer blink at the sight of them as they once did.

Ten minutes after my arrival, Naryshkin's sister greets a new guest. I am teasing a young countess about the attributes of her latest choice of lover when my eyes are drawn to the door. There stands the comely young man I have seen with Hanbury-Williams. Extraordinary, intelligent eyes take everything in. Take me in. He appears somewhat uncertain — perhaps my ruffled shirt and breeches baffle him — but his lovely bow-shaped lips hint at a smile.

Naryshkin brings him to where I stand. "Count Stanislaw Poniatowski, Your Highness," he says. The low murmur stops abruptly.

I offer him my hand. His eyes drop shyly as he bows, kisses it. His fingers are long and slender, graceful for a man. His face has such delicate features, yet a strong nose. I admire the contradiction.

"Your friend, Hanbury-Williams, speaks very highly of you," I say. I make a point of turning my face to the small group so that they may carry on as usual.

"He is a dear friend and mentor," says he with a slight smile. "He advises and I listen."

"He is a wise man of the world and you are fortunate in his friendship."

"I hope, Your Highness, I will be as fortunate in yours." He locks me in his arresting brown eyes, and I am entranced. If the others are watching, let them all go to the devil.

"We are all friends here," I say, drinking in his milky white skin. "You may call me Sophie."

His long lashes sweep down, hiding his beautiful eyes for an instant. I have embarrassed him with my familiarity. Oddly enough, I delight in his shyness. It is a refreshing change from the conceited self-assurance of the louts who frequent the court.

"I am honoured," he murmurs.

"And what may I call you?"

"My friends call me Stanislaw."

I lower my eyes and incline my head at the exchange of familiarity.

"I compliment you on your attire," he says, mischief in his eyes as they sweep down to my breeches. "It is wickedly becoming."

I have had my effect on him. I am well satisfied.

"Why, I thank you, sir. It is the price I pay to leave the palace unobserved. Pray, come, meet my friends." I lead him toward the fashionable young men and women who, of a sudden, turn to each other with more animation than is their usual wont. Even then, I begin to plot such scenes as my friends will never take part in.

He and I spend the evening discussing Montesquieu and Diderot, bandying about clever words, sometimes lobbing them at each other. I am quite entranced by him, drinking in the heart-shaped face, the brown eyes that sparkle at me with quiet intelligence and mischief together, the graceful mouth.

For his part, he barely takes his eyes off me, inclining his head as I speak as if each word from my mouth is a jewel he must capture. At the end of the evening I am quite heady with his attention.

When it is time to go, he offers to accompany me home.

"You look extraordinary in those clothes," he whispers, eyeing me sideways as we leave Naryshkin's. "Even lovelier than in a ball gown."

I take his arm as we stroll back toward the palace in the dark. The night is very brisk and our breaths become visible clouds rising in the air.

I take him in a side door to which I have the key. Inside the dim hall we are suddenly diffident with each other.

"Meet me here tomorrow," I murmur. "Instead of Naryshkin's."

His eyes widen, unsure. Do I see excitement as well?

I bend toward him and kiss his cheek softly. "I'll wait for you at midnight."

And before he has time to answer, I fly away.

The whole of the next day I am filled with anticipation for the evening: Will he come? Is he as enchanted with me as I am with him? It is no good looking at a book or exchanging serious words with anyone. I am truly distracted.

At midnight I creep along the hallway toward the back entrance, carrying a candle. No one is about. My heart is fluttering and makes me quite giddy.

I pull back my shoulders, preparing for his absence. Holding the candle aloft I creak open the door. In the dimness I see no one before me. I can taste the disappointment.

Then an abrupt movement! A figure leans in a corner of the doorway. I bite my lip to keep from shouting for joy. It is *him*, arms wrapped across his chest for warmth. He straightens up and approaches until the light from the candle reveals him. His eyes shine at me with a warmth that spreads around my heart.

I open wide the door, the chill air rushing about me. He steps inside, the fresh scent of the cold night clinging to him.

"Is it very cold?" I say, trying to keep the elation from rising in my voice.

He removes his hat to reveal the wondrous blond hair tied back. "Very cold," he says. Playfully he touches my face with freezing fingers. "Cold as Siberia."

I exaggerate a shiver. "I will warm you," I say and take his chilled hands between mine, rubbing them softly.

"Siberia is where I will be sent if your husband finds me."

"Are you afraid?" I ask.

"I tremble with fear."

His hands are soft between mine. "But is it my husband you fear? Perhaps you fear me."

"Do I have reason to fear you? Are you a dangerous woman?"

"I am when I am crossed."

"Then I will be sure not to cross you." He smiles into my face like a cherub and my heart rises toward him.

I step up close to him and lift my chin so that I may stare into his eyes, golden in the shadows. He bends his face slowly toward mine. My throat goes dry. At long last his lips touch mine, sending a flame that spreads through my body.

I take him by the hand and lead him to my apartments.

The first time we make love is a revelation. I admit I have not the experience of some, but that a man can be tender and at the same time strong, stalwart yet generous, is a joyful discovery. Tho' I have taken him into my bed, we spend half the night in discussion of philosophy, literature, and our respective countries. To my astonishment, he finds my opinions of interest and seeks to find the basis for them. No man before has been curious about my convictions.

From then on we meet as frequently as is possible. At times we transfer our liaisons from the palace to Naryshkin's house. In this routine, I undress for the night and my most trusted chambermaid lights a candle on the windowsill to signal that all is clear to Naryshkin, who waits outside.

He is a boisterous clown and has devised his own signal.

"Miaow!" I hear. A much louder cry than any cat could utter.

At this I leap from my bed and pull on the breeches and jacket that have become second nature to me. Naryshkin hires a modest droshky that will not arouse interest to drive us back to his house. There my Polish love awaits me.

Lovemaking alternates with serious discussion. Even after several months his eyes shine while I ramble on.

"This is why Voltaire is the man of the century," I say. "With but his pen he combats the enemies of mankind: ignorance, superstition, the tyranny of the church, the abuse of power ..."

"May I say, Your Highness," he taps me under the chin, "for someone in your exalted position you have a surprisingly enlightened attitude. I hope you are able to maintain those opinions when you are Empress." He leans back upon my pillows, one arm behind his head.

"I intend to keep what I want," I say, narrowing my eyes at him suggestively.

"And is the list of things you want very long?" he says, pulling me down toward him with his free hand.

"Not very long," I say. "It starts and ends with you."

I kiss his sweet bow lips. A flutter in the pit of my stomach.

"I perceive that's a lie," he says, "but a very tender one." He pushes a strand of hair from my cheek. "What else will you want? When you are Empress."

I examine his heart-shaped face to see if he truly wants to hear. The curiosity in his delectable eyes convinces me. I lean against his chest, at ease.

"My premier concern — that Russia be not left behind. The tolerance and reason that are sweeping through Europe must visit here. Russia is a great empire, but it must change."

"Do you imply," he says impishly, "that Russia suffers from a lack of reason and tolerance?"

"I do not imply. I shout! But who would bother to listen? Reason and tolerance are commodities the court has little use for. Power and greed are the only coin of the realm."

"Strong words for an Empress in waiting. Perhaps things will change when the crown comes to rest at last upon your head."

I turn and find his eyes to see if he jests. He is all seriousness.

"I will never succumb to power and greed," I say.

He smiles. "I believe you, but I am curious about specifics, Your Highness," he says. "How will you visit reason and tolerance on this barbarous land?"

I pull myself up on an elbow so that I can see his face. He cocks his head, waiting for me to expound. I see the admiration in his eyes. I revel in it. With him at my side I could achieve almost anything.

"For one, we must establish just laws and enforce them humanely. There must be no arbitrary rule, but legal procedures must govern the exercise of power."

"Hear, hear!" he says, clapping his hand against my arm.

I am encouraged to continue. "We must build schools and educate everyone, to teach them to reason and think judiciously."

"Bravo!" he says. "You are a marvel." He pulls me down to him again. "You are a goddess. Give me leave to worship you." His tone is ironic, but his eyes!

"I do not require worship. No one has ever worshipped me."

"I can hardly credit that. But if that be true, then I shall be the first. Tho' you may not require it, you deserve it."

"Worship is all very well," I say, "but it seems a cold thing, directed at statues and altars. What of love?"

His eyes soften and threaten to run over. "What of love? I shall tell you." He pulls me to him with resolve. "You have made me forget that Siberia exists. I have never loved as I love you now. I will love you till I die."

His lips melt mine, and in a sweet delirium, I lose myself in his arms.

Later, when I sleep, I dream of coopers and barrels, two souls who once were one, now drifting ever further apart in some dark ether, and the face of a rabbi with tears standing in his eyes.

In March the air softens. The streets are still piled with snow, but the sun stays longer in the sky and glistens with more brilliancy on the river ice. My ladies have remarked on the new colour in my complexion. Only a trusted few know of my liaison. My Polish lover and I have been so discreet in our trysts that neither the Empress nor Chancellor Bestuzhev has any inkling. Besides, they are both singularly occupied with foreign matters.

Presently the Empress rages about the treaty. She is out of humour that England has signed with Prussia. Perhaps we should not be surprised, since Frederick is

King George's nephew and King George's chief concern has always been his city, Hanover. Poor Sir Charles is the object of the Empress's pique since it was he who prevailed upon her to sign the subsidy treaty in which Russian troops would protect Hanover against Frederick. And now Hanover kisses hands with Frederick!

I heard the Empress tell one of the courtiers, "Hanbury-Williams has grown to be a Prussian and meddles too much with Prussian affairs."

She *hates* Frederick, who delights in spreading outrageously obscene jokes about her and her lovers throughout Europe and who in his correspondence repeatedly calls her a slut. I have owed much to him in the past, but his actions were not unselfish, even when I was fourteen, and I feel no compunction to defend him.

After everything, the Empress complains openly of being deceived by King George. My Polish love is also lately frowned upon by dint of his connection to Sir Charles. The Count is thought to be an English agent working against the Russian interest. No wonder there is great confusion in the court — what the English call a muddle. The French faction is encouraged and becomes bold. Great Chancellor Bestuzhev, with his English sympathies, is slipping from grace. With Austria drifting closer to France, and the alliance cemented between England and Prussia, war between France and England is inevitable. Russia must choose sides, and it appears certain that the Empress will come down on the French side. The earth is moving beneath our feet and none of us knows where we will end up.

In July, my life is turned upside down. My Polish love sits on the edge of my bed, his face long. I sense trouble and remain standing.

"My parents have asked me to go home in time for the *Diet*," he says. "There's a position I will stand for in Livonia."

Have I been waiting for this all along? For the axe to fall? I must survive this, tho' my happiness absolutely depends on him. My stomach lurches; my head throbs with pain.

"You must give me leave, or I will not go."

I tremble at the prospect of the empty space that will fill my heart when he leaves, but I will not add to his sadness. I know he is not in a position to refuse. "Of course you must go if your parents bid it."

"Everything is so difficult here now," he says. "You see how Sir Charles is treated. It will be worse when war breaks out in earnest."

"It pains me greatly," I say. "We both love him, to be sure."

"And I am his protégé. Therefore I am seen as an English spy by the court. Under these circumstances, it is better for you, also, if I leave Petersburg. Your position will be harmed if you are connected to me. We will be found out sooner or later."

I turn my face from him. "The Empress begins to hear rumours," I say, a numbness creeping around my heart.

"It was inevitable," he says, rising from his seat on the bed.

I stand transfixed, unable to hide my distress. He takes me in his arms tentatively, strokes my hair, trying to console me.

"You'll see, my little Royal Highness, I will be back in a trice. I will come back tho' hell stands in my way."

chapter twenty-two

In the middle of Wednesday afternoon, Iris knocked on the examining room door where Rebecca was looking down a little girl's throat.

"Sarah's on the phone," Iris said through the door, surprise lifting her voice. "She's at the hospital."

Rebecca excused herself to the young patient and her mother and stepped into her private office. Her mother-in-law never called her at the office.

"Sarah? Are you all right?"

"It's Natalka. I'm sorry, I'm a little upset. She's all right now but ... the doctor sent her down to get her blood taken ..."

"Dr. Koboy?" She had almost forgotten Natalka's appointment with the hematologist.

"But then it wouldn't stop bleeding. So he said she should stay overnight."

"Did they stop the bleeding?"

"Yes. She's fine now. Just nervous. She said this

happened before. She said sometimes she had nose-bleeds that wouldn't stop. It's very nerve-wracking."

Sarah had been through enough with David. She didn't need to get emotionally involved with another family's illness. Especially one with a rotten prognosis. Bleeding was one of the symptoms of leukemia. On the other hand, it was also a symptom of a legion of other disorders.

"Let's wait till we hear from the hematologist," Rebecca said.

"I've got to go home," Sarah said. "I've got a student coming for a lesson after school. I just wanted to let you know she's here."

"You haven't heard from Halina?"

"No."

After she hung up, Rebecca wondered, where *was* Halina? She had left Sarah holding the bag with Natalka. Didn't she care about her daughter? She had certainly given the impression of caring. But what did Rebecca really know about her? Maybe she was just a good actress. Rebecca wondered if she could be that wrong about someone. She prided herself on her ability to assess people, but maybe the cultural divide changed all the rules. Maybe she ought to stick to assessing the people who walked into her office and whose bodies she could probe with her instruments. For all she knew, John Baron was right and Halina had killed Michael.

Rebecca finished out the afternoon in the office. It was after six when her last patient left. She slunk past Iris to avoid any long explanations, then marched down the stairs and out the front entrance of her building, her olive-coloured suit jacket over her arm. The hospital was a ten-minute walk away. She crossed Beverley Street, heading east on D'Arcy, glad for the chance to get out.

It was still light, but the energy of the day waned with the sun. A stillness hung in the air, a harbinger of fatigue. She resisted it.

In five minutes she had crossed McCaul and walked up to Elm Street. Her chest went tight as she marched past the hospital residence on Elm where she had lived with David while interning at Mount Sinai hospital. One of the happiest years she could remember. Small two-room apartment, galley kitchen. Nowhere for the TV but in front of the bed. David in the bed when she had a few hours off. Who could have known they would have so little time.

She came up to Murray Street, the back entrance of the hospital, still lost in David's arms. Her energy was flagging. She'd had a small sandwich for lunch hours ago, and though she didn't really feel hungry, she recognized that empty space in her stomach that pulled the strings to the rest of her.

She settled for a half-pint carton of chocolate milk from the coffee shop on the first floor of the hospital. She hated milk and could only face it when it came gooey-sweet and brown. Standing near the glass wall of the shop, she sucked up energy through the straw, watching the crowds rush up and down the corridor. After tossing the carton into a trash can, she headed toward the elevators.

Her mind had gone pleasantly blank watching the light above the elevator descend from floor to floor, signalling its approach. Two elevators arrived at the same time, and she was about to step into one, surrounded by the other passengers, when someone getting off the next elevator caught her eye. Out of context she almost didn't recognize her. A blonde profile walking briskly toward the front door of the hospital in low pumps and a grey suit. It was Halina.

Instantly Rebecca swivelled her body amid the throng of people moving into the elevator. "Excuse me!" she said.

The momentum of the crowd pulled her along like a river. "Pardon me!" she said, pushing her way backwards, raising some scowls on people behind her trying to get on the elevator.

She escaped and rushed out the front door. People filled the wide sidewalks on their way home from work. She narrowed her eyes, looking north, then south, watching for the white-blonde hair, the grey jacket. She stared at a line of people waiting for the light at Elm Street. When the light changed, a grey suit stepped forward, separating from the crowd. It was her. She was heading south along University Avenue. Somehow she must have found out about Natalka and was now returning to her lair.

Rebecca was too far away to call out. And if she saw Rebecca she might bolt. The woman may have been over sixty but she was in good shape.

Rebecca followed her down University to Dundas. Halina showed no signs of slowing down. She kept walking until Queen Street loomed up ahead. At Queen, Halina turned right. Rebecca followed at a discreet distance. People were milling about after work, meeting friends on street corners, smoking in front of restaurants.

They passed Beverley Street, still continuing west. When Halina was partway across Spadina Avenue, the light changed and stranded Rebecca on the wrong side of the street. She tapped her toes on the curb at the edge of the noisy traffic while her quarry marched obliviously into the distance.

Cars, trucks, trolleys streamed in front of her. She squinted through the gasoline vapours, trying to keep the grey suit in her sights. Finally the red light turned

green. She bounded across the street, avoiding the
streetcar tracks. She was shooting toward the sidewalk
when a car inching into a right turn on the red nearly
collided with her. She glared at the startled woman driving, then resumed the chase.

Except when she looked up, her quarry was gone.
She rushed past shop after shop selling fabric; *schmata*
stores, her mother called them. Had Halina gone into
one of them? Rebecca glanced through each window as
she flew past. Nothing. She must have turned a corner.
When Rebecca reached Augusta Avenue, she turned
right. Still nothing. No, not nothing.

A few buildings up from Queen, behind a tall
wrought iron fence, stood an imposing mansion that
looked out of place on this street of small, semi-
detached houses. A pale gingerbread trimmed the rich
brown brick that erupted into many gables; contrasting
cream-coloured bricks edged the corners of each wall. A
grand tower soared from the centre toward the dusky
sky. One of the front windows had been replaced by
stained glass, a spare modern design with a large cross
at its centre. But what gave Rebecca hope was the shrine
in the backyard: a painted plaster Madonna in a blue
robe, her arms spread beneficently. Perhaps Halina had
found some kind of retreat. Rebecca opened the gate
and stepped toward the heavy wooden door.

Her hand reached for the doorbell. In that moment
she thought, *What am I doing here?* Did she really
believe that John Baron was accusing Halina for any
other reason than to get Rebecca off his scent?

The door opened. Rebecca was at a loss for words
at the sight of the diminutive elderly woman who stood
before her. She was dressed in a nun's habit, a starched
white headband fronting a black wimple that covered
her hair. A large gold cross hung around her neck over

the floor length black dress. She smiled shyly, her head on a slight inquisitive tilt.

"I'm looking for Halina," Rebecca stammered. She realized she didn't remember Halina's last name.

"Who are you?" the woman said in accented English. Her plump face shone white against the backdrop of black. Pale downy hair grew on her upper lip.

"I'm her daughter's doctor."

"Something wrong? She sick?"

"She's in the hospital." Rebecca neglected to mention Halina already knew that.

The woman nodded with concern and turned aside to let Rebecca in. "Please wait."

The nun began to climb the oak staircase as if each step was an effort.

A lamp had been turned on in the fading light of the hall. The walls were half panelled in dark oak, the upper half of the room filled with pictures of Jesus and Pope John Paul II. The scenes of the crucifixion made Rebecca uneasy. All those nails in the hands. The depiction of torture and death seemed an odd image for people to worship. Was that really what God wanted? For people to suffer?

On a small table she found brochures about the Felician Sisters, a group started in Poland by Sister Mary Angela in 1855. A convent. It seemed a strange place for a Communist to hide. Natalka had said her mother was not a good Party member.

After a few minutes, the nun stepped slowly down the stairs, followed by Halina. The nun continued walking and disappeared into a room off to the side.

Still in a grey skirt and white blouse, Halina watched Rebecca nervously, her hands clasped tightly in front.

"Everyone's been worried about you," Rebecca said.

She looked with hard eyes at Rebecca. "Did Janek send you?"

"Of course not. Why would you think ...?"

"How did you know I am here?"

"I followed you from the hospital. I was just on my way up to see Natalka."

She looked behind Rebecca at the door. "How you know Janek did not follow you here?"

"Why should he?"

She stared dumbfounded at Rebecca. "Because he kill Michael and now he want to kill me."

Was that the real reason she had fled? Or was the show of fear just good acting. "Baron says it was you who killed Michael."

Halina blinked several times, but her face did not betray her thoughts. She played the game well. "Of course he say this. You believe him?"

"I know you called Michael the night before he died."

"So?"

"You said you were coming over."

Halina looked momentarily confused. "No."

"You didn't go to Michael's house that night?"

"No. I call him on phone, but Janek comes into room and I hang up."

"Where were you?"

Halina's pale cheeks turned pink. "He has apartment. You must understand — he is helping us. I need be good to him for Natalka."

It was Rebecca's turn to be embarrassed. "Your private life is none of my business."

Halina turned away self-consciously.

"But why did you phone him?"

Halina glanced toward the room into which the nun had disappeared. She led Rebecca into an opposite corner of the hall. "I want to warn him."

"About what?"

She crossed her arms over her chest. "I say something stupid to Janek. It is my fault. I want to scare him to give me money for hospital. I know what he did after war and I say I will tell Michael. Of course I will *not* tell, but Janek blows up. He not listen no more."

"What did he do after the war?"

Halina's face turned stony. "It is terrible. Better to forget."

"I need to understand what happened."

Halina closed her eyes. "Janek denounced Michael's parents after war. Michael never know. Because of Janek, they are sent to gulag and die. Janek hate Michael's father, Piotr, because I love him. Janek was jealous."

Rebecca felt nauseated. So it was Janek who had destroyed Michael's family. Who had sent them to Siberia to their deaths. Who had blithely gone on with his life in Canada as if they had never existed. What must he have thought when Michael came to him for a job after he had managed to escape his parents' fate? After all those years to find out. No wonder Michael had hit him hard enough to leave bruises.

"Piotr was handsome man," she said with unaccustomed wistfulness. "He love me too. Janek thought Piotr was Natalka's father."

Rebecca held her breath. "Was he?"

Halina shook her head.

Didn't Michael say he had first met Halina when she came to the countryside with her baby? If Michael's father had sired Natalka, wouldn't Michael have known her earlier? Could the lovers have hidden such a liaison during the war? Rebecca was inclined to believe Halina on this one thing.

"Why would Janek kill Michael?" Rebecca asked.

"Maybe it was accident. I don't know. Janek go there to explain. He was thinking I tell Michael already.

He thinks Michael knows. So probably he say, himself, what he did, then Michael is finding out. This must be shock for Michael. He must be furious. Janek has bad temper. Probably they fight."

"How do you know he went to Michael's?"

Halina glanced nervously toward the room at the other end of the hall. "I am with Janek all night. In the apartment. He leave in morning, ten o'clock. Bad mood. He say he go to straighten things with Michael."

"Did you speak to Janek after that?"

Halina shook her head. "I go to Sarah's house in taxi. I am sleeping when everybody go to Michael's. Then Natalka call me later from his house — she say Michael is dead. I am afraid to speak to Janek after this."

"Are you sure about the time that Janek left? Ten?"

"I go to Sarah same time."

That left a time gap. Had they argued for two hours and then Baron had somehow drowned Michael in the pool? Because Michael had not been dead that long when Rebecca fished him out of the water. Had Michael become despondent after discovering that he had been working for decades for the man responsible for his parents' death? So despondent that he had swallowed Valium with a couple of shots of something and jumped into the pool? No. The goggles said no. Someone in the depths of despair about to kill himself does not stop to put on goggles.

Rebecca stood in the doorway of Natalka's hospital room, tired, confused. She carried a bag of goodies from the coffee shop together with two cardboard cups of tea anchored in a disposable tray. Her head ached from thinking. John Baron, according to some, was the devil, but had he killed Michael? Indeed, had *anyone* killed Michael? The more Rebecca knew, the less she understood.

They had placed Natalka in a semi-private room. She lay in the bed closest to the door, leaning back on her pillows with her eyes closed. Her white hair lay unpinned around her long neck, her pale skin wan in the fluorescent light.

Rebecca was about to place the bag on the night-stand and leave unannounced when Natalka opened her eyes. As soon as she saw Rebecca her face lit up. Her skin took on some colour as she sat up. Rebecca approached, standing by the bed.

"I'm so happy to see you," Natalka said, putting her hand out.

Rebecca took the hand, which held on without letting go. "How are you feeling?"

Natalka smiled. "Not so bad. Could be worse." She angled her head toward the other patient in the room. She was elderly and attached to an IV. No visitor.

"It sounds like the doctor just wanted to make sure you were stable. Sarah said they couldn't stop the bleeding."

"I don't know why the doctor was worried," Natalka said. "I have lots of blood left."

Rebecca smiled.

"It is nice to see familiar face. You are tired?"

So it showed. "It's been a long day." She wasn't going to trouble her with news of her mother.

"I brought you some tea," Rebecca said, placing the little tray on the night table. She pulled a chair close to the bed then fished out her dinner, an egg salad sandwich, and for the patient, a small pack of digestive cookies and an apple.

"You're a good doctor," Natalka said scowling. "You bring only healthy food."

Natalka sipped her tea, watching with interest as Rebecca bit into the sandwich.

Rebecca took the other half of the sandwich out of its plastic sleeve and handed it to her. Natalka grinned and offered Rebecca a cookie.

They were chewing happily when a figure appeared at the door. Marty Koboy, Rebecca's favourite professor in medical school, approached and placed his hand on her arm in greeting. Standing up, she towered over him, though she was average height. His build was small but athletic. He always said, "Good things come in small packages." His ability to put everyone at ease endeared him to all his students. His thick black hair was now peppered with grey. The tiny broken veins in his cheeks made them look rosy.

"I'm sorry I had to incarcerate your patient, Rebecca, but she was bleeding all over the floor." He said this loud enough for Natalka to hear.

The patient smiled.

He stepped close to the bed. "Did you finally stop bleeding?" Gingerly he lifted up her hand with one of his, taking her pulse with the other.

She blushed. "I am fine. Maybe I can go home now?"

"Is this such a terrible place?" he said. "Look, *I'm* still here. I'm just leaving to go home and I can't wait to get back tomorrow."

She shrugged at Rebecca, as if wanting an advocate.

"Anyway," he said, "you're going to have another test tomorrow. We're going to get a sample of your bone marrow."

Rebecca cringed but kept her face blank.

"It's not the most pleasant test in the world. But it will confirm my diagnosis. Then we'll know what to do."

"Do you think I have leukemia, Doctor?"

"I'll have more information for you tomorrow. Let's just say I'm cautiously optimistic."

Natalka's face brightened. She brought her hand to her mouth, hiding a smile.

He cocked his head and patted her arm. "Now don't you bleed anymore."

Rebecca followed him out the door. They stepped away from the room, out of earshot. "Doctor, don't you think she has leukemia?"

He grimaced. "No," he said. "But I can see why there might be confusion. The lady is luckier than that. I think she has Gaucher's Disease."

"Gaucher's?" Rebecca recalled the name but not the details.

"It's a rare bird. I've never actually seen a case. It's a lipid storage disease, a deficiency in the glucocerebrosidase enzyme that affects the spleen, as you've seen. It can be fatal, but mostly when it presents in childhood. It's not a pleasant disease, but she'll survive. She'll have to have a partial splenectomy. And there's some experimental work being done to replace the enzyme, mostly in the States. She might be able to get on a list. But like I said, I need to look at the bone marrow to confirm." He observed Rebecca more closely. "Is she a relative?"

"No. Why?"

"Gaucher's is familial, and I noticed she was here with your mother before," he said.

Rebecca recoiled. "That was my mother-in-law."

He gave a knowing smile. "Well, the young lady's as charming as you are. I thought you might be related."

Rebecca was exhausted from her insomnia over the past week. She climbed into bed early with a cup of hot chocolate and opened Michael's manuscript to the second last chapter, titled "The Flesh is Weak." It started with a letter from Sir Charles to Catherine. Rebecca was getting very fond of the English diplomat and felt uneasy about his future.

chapter twenty-three

The Flesh is Weak

Sunday, August 18, 1756
Your Highness,

I am born, Madame, to obey you. You ask me for
news of our friend. I send it to you at once,
Poniatowski's letter, forwarded by a faithful English
merchant, sent to me by his confidential servant from
Riga. Be assured, Madame, that my own business
here goes very badly. They will not accept the
£100,000 sterling in the subsidy, which would be the
first payment of four, and without their acceptance I
look upon the treaty as broken. The Great Chancellor
Bestuzhev either does not, or is determined not to,
understand me. After all our trouble, in both time
and effort, the faction that supports France has the
upper hand.

I assure you that our whole business with the treaty may be ruined by this stupidity. This is very annoying to me, and puts me in a very bad temper with all the world but you.

As to the plotting of the faction favourable to France, I am delighted to see the masterly way in which you fathom their artifices and despise their weakness. My advice to you on the whole affair is to sit quiet, to let them come to you without ever giving any decided answer about anything. Experience counts for everything in business — that is what gives knowledge; thus an adviser and a doctor without practice will only make a mess of things and murder patients.

Henry the Great began his letters to Sully, "*Mon Ami.*" I shall feel very proud if you will do the same.

Your humble servant,
Hanbury-Williams

Thursday, August 22
Dear Sir Charles,

Thank you for your friendship towards me, *mon ami* — since that is the title which you suggest I use. Be so good as to forward this sealed letter to our absent friend, the Count. The request that he makes you, to send him word that I love him, emboldens me to tell you that you are confirming for him a truth of truths.

Let me tell you that from no one but you would I readily without complaint accept the numerous flatteries that you shower on me. But from you, I take them as proof of friendship. I am annoyed that your affairs are so perpetually held up, but am very flattered that your bad temper is diminished as far as I am concerned. When shall

I be able to put you in a good one? Meanwhile my good wishes and my affection are always with you.

C.

Tuesday, August 27
Your Highness,

I must now speak to you about your money. It is my privilege to help you settle your expenses in court. This is what you should do, and what I shall do.

After I settle the account with the banker, I shall send word to you how much remains in my hands; and you will draw that sum by Naryshkin as you require it, from time to time, for my own security demands that no one should ever be able to prove that I procured you money. After that, I will send you the bond which you have to sign for my Master, the King; you should copy it in your own handwriting from the original.

I hope that this plan will please you. I shall try all my life to please you and to help you. I own that it hurts me to think that the Great Chancellor Bestuzhev believes that your protection is only extended to me because of Poniatowski.

I assure you, Madame, that insignificant as I am, I would not live with the greatest prince in the world on such a footing. My friendship is of no great value and my devotion is a small affair, but such as they are, I am not lavish with them; and I can honestly say that up till now no one in this world has suffered from having placed confidence in me.

I pride myself on being an honest man, and I hope in time to convince you of it. This is how I shall set about it. I shall never be troublesome to you, I shall faithfully guard

your secrets, I shall tell you nothing but the truth. I shall
help you in all that in my power lies, and never shall I flatter you. Your esteem is my ambition, because I believe that
the man who obtains it is worthy to possess it.

Your obedient servant
Hanbury-Williams

Wednesday, September 4
Dear Sir Charles,

From the moment I had the pleasure of making your
acquaintance, I conceived a real regard for you, quite
independent of any other connection, seeing that my association with your protégé, the Count, only came into
being seven months later.

    You are not insignificant — you are a *grand seigneur*
as far as merit and honesty are concerned. Your friendship and devotion are without price, and I congratulate
myself on having acquired your confidence.

    But have you no news of Count Poniatowski? I had
hoped that by now there would be some talk of his return.
As for your suggestion that for his safety it is necessary that
he secures a position when he comes back, I fully agree. It
is most reasonable that he return here as Minister from
Poland. I have been deliberating on how to achieve this. In
a few weeks he will be in Warsaw for the *Diet* where King
Augustus will preside. Someone must approach the King
on his behalf. In God's name give me your advice, for my
head reels. Abandon me not in my present distress.

C.

Sunday, September 8
Your Highness,

My devotion to you, Madame, has no limits, save that
of a higher duty to my King and country. You ask for my
counsel and here it is: Poniatowski's return can only be
secured by the Chancellor Bestuzhev. I own that I am
much afraid that it is the latter who has provoked the
Empress against him — a horrible thought, but as he has
it in his power to assist us, we must not quarrel with
him. Therefore be firm but kind. Press him to show you
a scheme to secure the Count's return. I suggest an effusive letter to King Augustus.

Personally, I have nothing more to do here. Your
court loves France too well to think of England, double
treachery there while France offers sanctuary to the
Pretender who yet schemes to overthrow King George.
And no further word on the treaty. My worst fear is that
all my strenuous efforts have been in vain.

For you I will do anything. But prudence must guide
us, for treachery threatens. Above all, I persist that our
correspondence must remain an impenetrable secret
delivered by only the most trusted servants.

Good-bye, Madame, my pen falls from my hand. I
am tired out and none too well, with pains in my head,
but yours always.

Your humble servant,
Hanbury-Williams

Wednesday, September 15
Dear Sir Charles,

I thank you for all that you have said and done and am

only sorry that you are not well.

I implore you to neglect nothing which might hasten Poniatowski's return. You will oblige me in a very tender spot. I shall follow your counsel blindly. My heart and my head, notwithstanding the praise which it has pleased you to shower on them, are quite dejected. I shall press Chancellor Bestuzhev every day, even twice a day, for the return of the Count. I have already sent a rude letter to him. I am going to adopt your maxim, never to be on very good terms with him when I want anything.

I feel really vexed at his conduct toward you. To say nothing of his treachery and low cunning. An honest Chancellor would be a marvel.

A rumour has just reached me that King Frederick is marching into Saxony.

C.

Warsaw, Thursday, September 26
Mon Cher and respectable Ami!

I love you as my second father! It is an appellation which I owe you for so many reasons that I shall never change it. You can judge better than I can ever express how touched I am by all that you tell of the Grand Duchess in your letter. May God bless her and make her as happy as she deserves to be.

My parents received me more warmly than ever. They have guessed my reason for wanting to return to Russia and my mother is putting up roadblocks. Her religious scruples, which have become very strong, force her to say *non consentio*. When I pressed her more strongly to give her formal consent to my return, she told me with tears in her eyes that she foresaw that this affair would alienate my affection, upon which she had based all that was sweetest in life. I found myself in the most horrible predicament that I have ever had to face. I dashed my head against the walls, shrieking rather than weeping.

I earnestly beg you to write my parents and urge them to send me back because I am necessary to you. Anything. Only use your influence.

Almost the whole of my family are assembled, awaiting the result of the strange scene which is taking place in Saxony. The mail no longer reaches us from the court.

With no reliable intelligence, I can tell you nothing except that the King of Prussia has marched into Saxony and now occupies Dresden. Frederick is said to have acted in the cruellest manner toward the royal family, who are virtual prisoners in that city. There are unsavoury accounts of the destruction of Dresden, that Frederick has laid waste to most of it. When I recall the beauty of the place, my heart breaks.

As for the Polish *Diet*, if King Augustus does not arrive here for the first day, probably he will not come at all. Therefore I am stranded in Warsaw awaiting the outcome.

Adieu. They are hurrying me, for the messenger is leaving. Would that I could speak to you instead of writing. You recall the silver compass, which you gave me as a parting gift because I was foolish enough to admire it in your hand. I keep it with me always. If I have to, I shall use it to find my way back to you. It is a cursed thing to be parted from those one loves.

Your very humble and obedient servant,
Stanislaw Poniatowski

Tuesday, October 8
Your Highness,

Do not be discouraged by the Countess Poniatowska's
refusal to allow her son to return to Russia. She loves
him. She is intelligent, but very bigoted, and has elicited
from him a promise that should a marriage ever become
possible, he will insist on a ceremony in the Roman
church. She has a horror of the Orthodox faith and
knows in her heart that you will never repudiate it in
order to marry. After all, you cannot be sovereign in your
adopted country without adhering to the Orthodox
church. But I have more credit with her than anybody and
I shall use all of it on this occasion.

Be assured that I am as anxious for the return of
Poniatowski as you are, and that I shall work for it with the
Great Chancellor Bestuzhev; and I give you my word that
if he does not do it, I shall find some pretext to quarrel with
him. I shall make my court quarrel with him. He shall
never have a penny of the English pension I promised him.

Continue to press him; he is a very slippery eel. Write
him letters in a tone which threatens him with the loss of
your friendship in the present and your protection in the
future. He can do what you ask, if he pleases.

I am sure that you will be sorry to hear that I am not
at all well, and that my illness causes me such pain in my
head and stomach that I have much difficulty in writing
to you and that I cannot be present at court tonight. I
fear that my failure in what I came here to do — to
bring to a close the subsidy treaty — has made me ill. If
it is not too grand to say so, I have let down my King
and country and feel the weight of it upon me.

With regret, your humble servant,
Hanbury-Williams

Thursday. October 10
My dear Sir Charles,

I do not like your notes when they are an effort to you.
I am afraid of making your health worse. Rather dictate
your letters to someone. Your condition pains me
extremely. Perhaps I can lift your spirits by telling you
that I received a copy of the letter Chancellor Bestuzhev
has written to King Augustus. In it he is as effusive
as you would like, insisting that "... in the light
of the present critical position of affairs, an Envoy
Extraordinary should be sent here without delay from
the Kingdom of Poland whose presence would draw
closer the ties of friendship between the two countries."
He says that he has found "no one who can be more
pleasing to his court than Count Poniatowski, who has
won Her Imperial Majesty's favour and the goodwill of
the whole court."

What do you say to that? It seems to me fairly
satisfactory!

May God grant you good health, happiness and all
the blessings imaginable.

C.

Friday, November 1 (dictated)
Your Highness,

I am sorry, Madame, that your kindness to me will cause
you to learn with sorrow that my illness continues the
same. Dr. Condoidi assures me that he will pull me
through in time; but I doubt it, for my liver no longer
does its work, and my digestion is so ruined that I have
eaten nothing solid for nearly a month.

I am sorry that Count Poniatowski worries himself about me. I am his friend and will remain so, tho' we shall not see one another often, since we are Ministers of governments that are in opposing camps. We shall find a means of communicating our thoughts to one another, and I am so certain of his devotion to me that I think only of how to help him. I flatter myself that, one day, you, Madame, and the King of Prussia as your lieutenant, will make him the King of Poland.

You have told me, and I have no doubt of your sincerity, that you hold the King, my Master, in high esteem and that you love England. Russia makes a treaty with France; and at the same moment, France receives with open arms a Minister from the Pretender, in order to plan the invasion of Great Britain. If you were in your rightful place, you would not allow this. You would see all these things with your own eyes.

I hope you will look upon me entirely as a person who is bound to you by love and affection, and as one who will never allow you to do yourself harm in my interests. Adieu, Madame. May heaven preserve you.

Your obedient servant,
H.-W.

St. Petersburg, Wednesday, January 22, 1757
My dear Fox,

I am sorry to tell you that I am in very bad health and have been several times confined to my house with the result that I am no longer able to collect sufficient information to warrant me remaining at my position. Every step I take is watched very narrowly, my letters are opened, and some of the people who used to get me the best intelligence have been questioned why they go so often to my house, and advised not to make me such frequent visits.

I have no illusion as to the course which the Russian court will adopt — it is only a matter of time before they accede to the Treaty of Versailles and join France and their allies. I have no doubt that France has already bought Chancellor Bestuzhev. In light of the continuing intrigues of the French to replace our King with the Pretender, I will not be surprised to hear Bestuzhev exclaim that Bonnie Prince Charlie is the rightful ruler of England! Nobody that is not on the spot can have an idea of this court.

After having twice requested to be recalled, I am sorry to tell you what is serious and ridiculous at the same time, which is, that my disorder is just fallen into my legs, particularly my left leg, so that when I have just got our King's leave to go away from here, I have no legs to go upon.

Count Poniatowski has at last arrived, after all our efforts. I was well enough to be in court when he presented his credentials to the Empress. One of the Great Chancellor's conditions for the Count's return as Polish envoy was that we no longer live under the same roof and indeed associate only in matters of business since our governments are enemies. It is hard on the both of us, since our natural inclinations are affectionate.

I will under no circumstances stay another winter in the country. I can only imagine when you will receive this letter since from the moment when the Prussian army began its advance, the post routes were closed and messengers must make long detours.

I remain your humble servant,
H.-W.

chapter twenty-four

Rebecca was examining a mole on an elderly woman's face when Iris knocked on the door.

"Dr. Koboy on the phone."

"So it's official, Doctor. Miss Czarnowa has Gaucher's. What a charming lady — when I told her, she kissed my hand. You sure she's not related?"

Rebecca smiled with relief. "I'm very happy to hear that."

"She'll have to stay put for another day or so. We're going to do a blood transfusion and try to get her blood counts up. I'll keep you informed."

When Rebecca had a minute between patients, she looked up Gaucher's in her pathology text:

> ... a rare disorder of the reticuloendothelial system in which the enzyme glucocerebrosidase is deficient. The clinical features of inherited glucocerebrosidase deficiency were

first characterized by Philippe Charles Gaucher in Paris in 1882. He originally described a patient with massive enlargement of the spleen and liver and identified characteristic cells in the spleen that had an increased size and displaced nucleus. These "Gaucher cells," characterized by lipid-laden macrophages, were later also found in liver, bone marrow, and other tissues. Accumulation of Gaucher cells in the spleen results in splenomegaly. Also associated with Gaucher's — anaemia, leucopenia, reduced blood platelets, and skeletal involvement. Clinical symptoms vary widely ranging from disability in children to asymptomatic disease in the elderly. The disease is more severe when symptoms manifest in childhood than in adult onset.

Iris was on the phone arranging appointments for the next day when Rebecca walked past her desk on her way out. It was five-thirty. They waved to each other — Iris blew her a silent kiss with her pen hand — and Rebecca was down the stairs and out the door. It wasn't until she stepped toward her car in the little lot behind the medical building that she realized she wasn't going home. Halina's revelation had burdened her. Rebecca had suspected a struggle between Michael and Baron the day of the drowning. Only she couldn't have known the profound enmity behind that struggle. The disclosure of such betrayal changed her whole picture of that Saturday. It made the taking of vodka and Valium more likely, but it didn't explain why Michael was in the water.

Rebecca pulled onto Beverley Street and headed south. Baron was probably the last person to see

Michael alive. He had refused to consider Michael's death a suicide when she had suggested it. He also denied being there. This time she would do better. She would use the new information to disarm him. She hated playing games, but some people could not be dealt with any other way.

After parking her car at a meter, she marched up Bay Street toward the Baron Building. Business people in conservative suits were rushing along the sidewalk on their way home from work. She felt underdressed in khaki trousers and an olive green blazer over her camisole. The crowds were giving the area in front of Baron's building a wide berth.

The miners were still there in their jeans and plaid shirts, only something had changed. Two cops hovered across the street, intently watching the scruffy men argue amongst each other. Tensions had risen along with their voices. One man pushed another until he staggered backwards and started shouting obscenities. Rebecca slowed down, hesitant, searching for Claude Simard but not finding him. She straightened her shoulders, determined to muddle through. After all, she sympathized with their plight. Why should she be intimidated?

She concentrated on the hill of cigarette butts that rose behind a granite planter where some leaves struggled in the shade. But as soon as it was clear she was heading for the entrance, the miners pressed around her.

"I'm on your side," she said. "But I need to go into the building."

"Can't be on our side if you got business in there," said one heavy-set man.

Twenty faces glared at her, eyes bright with fury.

"Let me by, please," she said, her voice cooler than she felt.

The men didn't budge.

"Where's Claude?" she said, hoping a familiar name would have some influence.

The men began peering at one another furtively as if she had just discovered dirty pictures in their wallets.

"Let the lady through!" a voice bellowed from behind.

A column opened up between the plaid shirts and one of the cops from across the street pushed his way through. He took her by the elbow and led her to the entrance.

"Thank you," she said.

"Not the best time to be coming in here," he said, opening the front door for her.

She smiled sheepishly and headed for the elevator. There was no line of visitors this time, but the guard intercepted her and asked where she was going. It was a good thing she hadn't gone beyond the wall plaque bearing the list of suites.

"Reames, Lehrer and Moss," she said.

He nodded and let her go.

On the twentieth floor, the elevator opened to the grand foyer of Baron's offices. But this time there was no dishy blonde sitting behind the marble counter. Only two men in suits standing with their backs to her. It was only after Rebecca stepped out of the elevator and her vantage point changed that she knew she was in trouble. One of the men was tying up Baron's secretary in the chair. Her Queen Elizabeth hairdo had sprung some curls around the plaid handkerchief that they'd tied around her head by way of her mouth. The noise of the elevator door closing made the men's heads spin around.

Rebecca gasped.

Claude and George fixed their eyes on her. They had combed their hair, but with their lined, nervous faces, they looked like monkeys in suits.

"What're you doing here?" Rebecca said.

The two men looked at each other. George's face contorted into a malicious smirk.

"Look, Claude," he said in a low voice, "she's come to visit her boyfriend. Maybe check out his heart. No, wait, I forgot — he hasn't got one." He took a step toward her.

"How did you get up here?"

"Shh!" George said. "He doesn't know we're here."

"It was easy once we had the suits," Claude said quietly. "George here thought of it. Not a bad fit for the Sally Ann, eh?"

"Shut up, Claude."

George took a few more steps toward her. She was thinking it couldn't have been Bay Street types who'd cleaned out their closets because the grey suits were cheap and shiny. She put her hand out behind her to reach for the elevator button, but he lurched and grabbed her before she could find it.

"Come on, Claude, gimme a hand!"

Each man grabbed one of her elbows and started dragging her further into the office.

"What're you doing?" she cried, before George pressed his sweaty hand against her mouth.

She flailed her arms, but she was no match for the two of them. An awful picture rose in her mind that this was how they had pulled Michael into the pool. She threw a glance at Baron's secretary; her eyes bulged with terror.

"You people think you can just go on life as usual?" George removed his hand from her mouth and shook Rebecca by the shoulders until she was dizzy.

"You don't even know we're *alive*, do you?" he snarled in a hoarse whisper. "Well, we're fuckin' tired of pissin' around here waiting for God Awmighty to make up his mind that we're human too. We got rights, and he's gonna hear us out."

Claude began to cough in her ear, a phlegm-filled, wheezy cough that wouldn't stop.

Everything was spinning in front of her. She needed to get her head back. "I don't have anything to do with Baron. I was just coming to talk to him about —"

"I don't care, lady. It's your own fault you walked in on this. We might be able to use you."

Now that her head was slowing down, her pulse started to rush in her ears. "This isn't the way to deal with things," she said. "You're just going to get into trouble like this."

"You think we aren't in trouble? Claude here is dying. I'm not far behind. Baron knew the mine was killing us all along. He didn't give a shit if we were breathing in asbestos dust as long as he got his ore out. He got rich and we got cancer."

"Look, I'm a doctor. I understand what you're saying, and I agree he's a monster. But I had nothing to do with it ..."

"You know, lady, if I had a penny for everyone who said that — It ain't my fault you're dying. But we're dying anyway. And he wouldn't even let us in the building to speak our mind. That's why we had to dress up."

"You know," she said, "I came to talk to Baron about Michael Oginski's death. I thought he might have had something to do with it. But now I think you did."

Claude shook his head morosely. "I knew this was wrong, George."

"That's how much you know, lady," George said. "Hell, I never even met the guy."

"But Claude did. He was there the night before Michael died."

"Claude?" George snickered, a horsy rumble in the back of his throat. "Claude's not the killer type. Look at him. He's scared shitless."

Claude was watching her intently, as if he would learn something from her face.

"Okay, Claude, it's time."

"I don't know, George …"

"You're dying, Claude, and you still don't know? They've kicked us around for the last time. Just go down the hall and open the door. He doesn't know we're here. This is our last chance."

"How do you know he hasn't gone home?" she said.

"Listen," George said, cocking his head.

She heard the distant murmuring of a television.

"Secretary said he's watching the news."

Rebecca looked around and thought for a moment; all she needed to do was make a sudden leap past George. He must have sensed something because he grabbed her arms and pinned them behind her, her back against his chest. She could hear him breathing loudly. His lungs were damaged but he was bigger than she was. She couldn't move.

"Go, Claude! I'm right behind you."

Claude stared at them a moment, his large pasty face trembling. "No, *you* go first."

"Ah, Christ. Here. Grab hold of her so she don't get away."

Claude came up behind her and self-consciously took both her arms in his hands, holding them with an awkward firmness.

George strolled down the hall with a cocky step, his long, Brill-creamed hair stuck close to his head. Claude pushed her along in front of him in the same direction.

They stopped in front of the oak door with Baron's name on it. Now the TV announcer could be heard clearly.

"The Shah of Iran and his family have arrived in the

United States after Muslim revolutionaries overthrew his government earlier this year ..."

George placed his hand on the doorknob, turned it slowly, then opened the door. John Baron was leaning back in his huge leather chair, watching the television built into the wall.

George stepped inside. Claude hesitated before pushing Rebecca inside, following closely on her heels. Baron's round head flipped up as they barged in. His eyes moved quickly over the three of them, trying to size up the situation.

"Who the hell are you?"

"You don't recognize us all dressed up?" said George. "Picture us with our faces black and working our butts off in the mines."

He leaped to his feet, his face purple with rage. "What the fuck you low-lifes think you're doing? I'm going to call the cops up here ..." He pressed some buttons on his phone. "Helen! Helen, where are you?"

George lunged forward and pulled the phone from his hand then wrenched the cord clean out from the wall. He swept his arm viciously across the surface of the desk, throwing photos, memos, an onyx pen set crashing to the floor.

"You bastard!" he shouted. "You call us low-lifes, after what you did to us! We worked for you and you fucked us over big time in your office up here in the sky. Like we was nothin'."

"You *are* nothing."

George's narrow nose twitched. His nostrils flared. He ground the broken glass from the photos into the carpet with the heel of his shoe.

"You bloody bastard! You owe us. We're dying because of you. Your mine ruined our lungs. And you knew it all along."

"You didn't get sick in the mine," Baron said, shaking with fury. "You can't prove that."

"My doctor says it was the mine."

"They don't know nothing. I got a doctor that says it wasn't."

"This here's a doctor," George said, gritting his teeth as he turned around to find her. "Why don't you ask her? What happens when you work twenty years in a mine that ain't got enough air because of the asbestos dust? When there's only one shaft for cutting up the ore and the same shaft for breathing. Because God Awmighty here wouldn't spend the money for another shaft?"

She assumed it was a rhetorical question.

"The mine had to make a profit," Baron said, slamming his hand on the desk. "Otherwise you wouldn't have jobs."

"You made a profit on our backs. On our graves. We want compensation."

Baron's eyes narrowed in triumph. "Ah, so *that's* it," he smirked, his mouth on an angle. "It's always about money."

What right does he have to be self-righteous, she thought.

"You owe us compensation. We can't work no more. How are we supposed to feed our families?"

"You ain't getting a cent out of me, you scumbags. Not a red cent."

George spun around, his eyes crazy, searching for something. He grabbed a leather chair, lifted it off the ground, and threw it as far as he could, knocking over a small table that held a crystal vase of roses. The vase broke and spilled water and red petals on the beige broadloom.

"You maniac!" Baron shrieked.

George stared at the pieces of crystal, the wet stain where the water had spilled on the carpet. For a second she

thought, *He knows he's gone too far; thank God it's over.*
Then, almost in a trance, he reached into his pants pocket
and drew something out. She heard a sickening click.

"No, George," she said. "That's not the answer."

He looked up at her with surprise, as if he'd forgotten she was there. He started toward her, holding the
switchblade in front on an angle. She couldn't breathe.
Was it because she was already dead? She saw herself
lying on the floor beside the broken glass, bleeding to
death. Had he stabbed her yet?

"No, man!" said Claude. "Not her!"

He grabbed her from Claude and flipped her
around, pinning her arms behind her against his chest
with one hand, the other holding the switchblade
against her neck. Her legs began to wobble. She had to
flex her thigh muscles to keep her knees from buckling.

"Now you're in for it," Baron said.

"You think I care about any of that? I'm at the end
of my rope, mister. You need to do something and *now*.
You give us what we deserve or I kill her."

Suddenly everything went quiet. They were all holding their breaths.

Baron sneered. "I don't care about her. You can kill
her if you want."

"Why you goddamn bastard!" Claude spat out. He
marched around the side of the desk. "You don't give a
shit for no one but yourself!" he screamed. "That what
it takes to get to the top?"

He raised his arm in preparation to strike. He was
taller than Baron, but Baron was faster. He punched his
fist straight into Claude's stomach, making the bigger
man double over.

Claude emitted a low, moaning sound. She felt
George's grip on her tense up. The knife blade pricked
her skin. It was a standoff.

"I have something to trade," she said, her voice shaky. "Information Baron wants to keep under wraps. Nothing to do with the mines. This is a secret from Poland."

Baron turned to face her. She had his attention. "What the hell you talking?"

George swallowed. "Why should we care about that?"

"There are two possibilities," she continued, addressing herself to Baron. "One: I tell George and Claude the secret and they go to the papers. When they print it, the police will want to question you about Michael's death. Any hope of respectability you might've had will vanish. People will not want to know you. Your stock will plummet."

Baron blinked at her. "You're bluffing," he said. "You don't know nothing."

"I don't bluff," she said. "Halina told me what you did after the war."

Baron watched her, the wheels turning behind the eyes, strands of pomaded hair falling forward. "What difference it makes, after the war? Too long ago. I didn't kill Michael. I went there to explain. I tried to talk to him but he was furious. He wouldn't listen. He *hit* me for Chrissake!"

"And then?"

"Then I left."

"Hey," said George, "we're getting way off topic here."

"Which brings me to the second possibility: I keep the secret to myself and in exchange for my silence, Mr. Baron, you make a concession. You give these men fair compensation, like a pension they can support their families on. The kind of pension companies have that care about their employees."

Claude, his arm around his middle, looked up at her, confused.

"And if I don't agree, this animal here kills you?"

George loosened his hold on her and slowly moved the knife down to his side.

"If you won't agree, I give George a story he can take to the reporters out there. They'll get front page headlines for at least a week about your disregard for human life thirty-five years ago. Kind of fits in with today, doesn't it? You might call it a pattern."

It was a good thing he hadn't been outside lately. The reporters had lost interest in the strike; they had disappeared from the front of the building.

Baron's face was purple with rage. "What you trying to do to me?"

"I'm giving you the opportunity to do the right thing. Own up to your responsibilities. And if that doesn't convince you, think of the stock market. How fickle investors can be when they discover the founder of a company can't be trusted."

His jaw set hard. "I won't forget this. It's blackmail," he said. "I give two pensions. That's all."

"No!" said George. "That's not enough. Pensions for everyone that gets sick."

"That's ridiculous!" Baron cried. "I'll be ruined. I'm not made of money!"

"Sell some property," she said. "Rent out your chef. You're a resourceful man. I'm sure your army of accountants can figure it out. Meanwhile, George, why don't you write up a little contract to that effect so Mr. Baron can sign it. Before the cops come up and I'm tempted to spill the beans."

Baron plopped his squat body back down in the leather chair, dazed.

"What just happened?" Claude said.

Rebecca stepped away from her abductor. "You better go untie the secretary, George. She can help you with that contract."

That evening Rebecca sat in her den, still shaken from the events of the day. She put off going to bed, knowing sleep would not come. Instead, she opened Michael's manuscript to the last chapter, "Voyage of the Heart." Rebecca was saddened to be finishing the book, especially since it was not the end. And she would never know the end. If she took another tiny half-pill now, maybe she could still get a good night's sleep.

chapter twenty-five

Voyage of the Heart

January 1757

"Miaow!"

A delightful noise I haven't heard for months: Naryshkin is yowling beneath my window. Clever lad.

At the signal I jump from my bed in my breeches and ruffled shirt. I am nothing if not prepared. My sweet, tender love is finally *here*! I throw myself down the hallway on toes that barely touch the ground. It is late and everyone has retired for the night.

This afternoon at court amidst the crowd, our eyes met after so long and I felt as if my soul had found its home. His eyes grew bright at the sight of me and momentarily everyone vanished and we were alone. A peace settled over me such as I had not known for six months since last I had seen his face.

Fumbling with the key to the back door, I finally throw it open. While the winter wind howls at me, I search for the beloved figure. And there he stands in his dark cloak, his smile brilliant in the night. He dazzles me; tears leap to my eyes. Impatiently I pull him inside where it is warm. He sweeps off his hat to reveal a white wig he wears for disguise; very fetching, but it doesn't hold a candle to his own blond hair. The wig will be removed soon enough, I wager. Joyous anticipation leaps through my body. He takes me in his arms, pressing me close to him ardently as if he has never left.

"You are my first and only love," he whispers. "I will love you till I die."

We dare to meet two, sometimes three times a week with the help of Naryshkin and my most trusted chambermaid. Though Sir Charles has warned me of the danger of bringing the Count into my rooms, I confess I am unable to resist the temptation. It is more trouble to go to Naryshkin's, to say nothing of the danger should I go to the Count's mansion despite our precautions.

I have devised a complicated arrangement of screens and had them installed in my boudoir, where the Count can be concealed in case of unexpected visits. I am prepared.

One night I am lying in my love's arms when there is a sudden knock at the door. We both jump from the bed at once. I throw on a silk robe and the Count, terror on his face, ducks behind the screens. *Mon Dieu!* He has left his coat on the chair in full view! I toss it after him, tripping over my own feet.

I stand ramrod straight, shoulders back, head high. "Who is it?" I say imperiously.

"Alexander Shuvalov, Your Highness."

My heart sinks. We have been found out.

I steal a look behind myself: nothing is visible but the screens, which are covered in flowered silks. I move the closest screen on a tighter angle.

"Enter!" I say.

The door opens and in steps the most feared man at court, the head of the secret police. His black hair frames a large, cruel face, which is made hideous by a nervous tic on the right side when he concentrates on something. I must keep my composure.

"I deliver a message from the Empress," he says bowing, his eyes discreetly leaving my face to search the room behind me.

I pray the Count makes no sound.

The note is a ruse; it could have been delivered in the morning. The Empress invites me to see my son for a few minutes after lunch the following day. I am still holding my breath.

"A delightful array of screens," says Shuvalov, the tic convulsing his cheek. "And, if I may be so bold, what do you have behind them?"

I smile stiffly. He is fishing. "Why, that is where I keep my portable commode."

He stares at me a full moment, then the right side of his face goes into a hideous spasm. He asks me no more, but moves backward out of my room like a crab.

I don't see much of Sir Charles during that winter since he is ill and cannot leave his house. I send him a note to cheer him:

Monsieur,

What do I not owe to the providence which sent you here, like a guardian angel, to unite

me with you in ties of friendship? You will
see, if one day I wear the crown, that I shall
partially owe it to your counsels.

By the spring, I am relieved to find that his strength
must be returning for I receive a note I would consider
impertinent from anyone else: "The wish is very near
my heart, Madame, that your son should have a brother. Dare I ask if there is one on the way?"

It is too early for stirrings in the womb, but my
monthly bleeding has stopped and every morning brings
nausea. So, yes, dear Sir Charles, I will bear a love child.

During the summer, the war goes against King
Frederick. Our own Russian troops, led by one of my sup-
porters, Field-Marshal Apraxin, join the armies of the
Empress-Queen, Maria-Theresa. Together, they defeat the
Prussians in Bohemia. To my horror (to say nothing of the
chagrin of Sir Charles) the French occupy Hanover.
Despite her failing health, the Tsarina is triumphant and
strikes medals to commemorate the battles; she offers *Te
Deums* in the Cathedral. Once, on our way out from a
service, the crowd shouts, "To Berlin! To Berlin!" The
Empress waves cheerfully, and I force a smile.

Peter mopes about, not even trying to conceal his
misery at the downfall of his idol. He defiantly wears
the large ring sent him by the King of Prussia, which
bears his hero's likeness.

At the end of August, Field-Marshal Apraxin
defeats King Frederick's forces at Gross-Jägersdorf.
Both Chancellor Bestuzhev and I send secret letters to
him suggesting he not pursue his advantage but go easy
on the Prussians. Therefore the Field-Marshal allows
them to retreat in good order. Instead of advancing on
Berlin, the move all of Europe expects of him, Apraxin
withdraws to the Russian frontier.

The Austrian Ambassador is livid over Apraxin's retreat. The French faction in court has begun to spread rumours about treachery, and I am afraid that Sir Charles and Count Poniatowski bear the brunt of the court's indignation.

Sir Charles tells me he has been given leave to go back to England. I am stricken at the news. I have no better friend in court — his knowledge of the world, his wit, his sympathy for me and my possibilities. I give him my word that I will support the new British envoy, Lord Keith, but tell him that no one can ever take his place.

I am heavy with child in October and send him a final letter, stained with my tears, shortly before he leaves.

> My dear Sir Charles,
>
> I am in despair at being deprived of the pleasure which I should have had in seeing and talking freely to you. My heart is scarred by the harsh treatment that you have received, but my deepest gratitude will be for ever yours. May happier times allow me to prove its full extent!
>
> Farewell, my best, my dear Friend.

On December 9 I bear my second child, a daughter whom the Empress names after her sister, Peter's mother, Anna Petrovna. I am allowed barely a glimpse of her before the Empress whisks her away to her own apartments. A trusted lady in waiting later whispers to me that the baby has a rare anomaly — she has six fingers on each hand and six toes on each foot. Since she is otherwise healthy, I take it as a sign of good fortune, an extra endowment from God.

Early in the new year I receive shocking news: Chancellor Bestuzhev has been arrested. He has been implicated in the scandal of Field Marshall Apraxin's retreat, mostly on the meagre evidence presented by Shuvalov. I am terrified that I will be next. I cannot eat or sleep for days. Then it happens.

I am summoned in the middle of the night to the Empress's chambers. Shuvalov is there, and Peter, who has become my enemy. I fall to my knees in tears before her and beg her to send me back to my relatives in Germany. She is disarmed. Then she insists I stand up and face her.

"You have meddled in many things which have nothing to do with you," she says. "We have letters you wrote to Apraxin." She points to a gold basin behind her.

But I have had reports that all my letters were burned. "I wrote to congratulate him on the birth of his son."

"Chancellor Bestuzhev says there were many others," the Empress says, watching me closely.

"If Bestuzhev says that, then he lies."

"If he is lying about you, I will have to have him tortured."

I make no response but keep my composure.

For the next few hours, she interrogates me. At the side of the large room, Peter confers with Shuvalov in whispers, then shouts out angry accusations about my obstinacy and bad temper. The Empress listens to my reasoned answers and appears to be losing patience with him. She knows that once she is gone, Peter intends to dethrone me and replace me with his mistress. The Empress is weak from her last stroke. Who knows how long she will yet live? I force myself to stand straight and remain calm.

Finally the Empress lowers her voice and says, "Do not be distressed. My nephew is an idiot."

Count Poniatowski does not escape so easily. Among the Chancellor's things, a letter is found written by my beloved, thanking him for his assistance in securing the Count's position as envoy. At the time, Bestuzhev had acted on his own, without consulting the Empress. He is consequently called high-handed and treasonous, considering that Poniatowski was a protégé of Sir Charles, the English Ambassador, who is now the enemy's envoy.

The Count quickly writes a letter to King Augustus asking to be recalled, then he retires to his bed, feigning illness. After a while he receives word that he may depart his post when he is ready. The storm dies down. In the next few months he is forced out of retirement when dignitaries arrive from Dresden and must be escorted to the usual court functions.

To our delirious joy, the Count and I resume our trysts, usually in my rooms, putting off the day when he will leave. We could continue thus indefinitely, but we become careless and our enemies in the French camp take note of our movements. Had I but listened to Sir Charles! He advised us to meet anywhere but in my apartments. One night the Count is stopped outside my chamber by Peter's men and taken away for questioning. My husband has known about him for a year but only now creates a fuss. He knows that the Empress is weak and the time approaches when he will ascend to the throne. We will not rule together. I must decide now which direction to take when the time comes. I must be ready. I know in my heart that I will not stand by and allow Peter to banish me to a convent while he takes his mistress for his consort. I think not only of me, but of Russia.

On a sad day in autumn the Count departs for Warsaw, pledging with all his heart to seek the first opportunity to return. Before he leaves he presents me with a beautiful little silver sundial in which a compass is embedded. The golden box in which it lies is inscribed with a message that breaks my heart. "So that you may always find me again." Though we embrace with passion, I feel a shadow rising between us, the distant memory of a story of lost love that sometimes steals into my dreams in the night.

Kensington, London
January 16, 1759

Your Highness,

This is in answer to several letters Your Highness kindly sent to Sir Charles Hanbury-Williams and which have hitherto gone unanswered. It is my sad duty to report that Sir Charles is in no condition at present to respond to correspondence of any kind, owing to a debilitating mental condition. Because of this mental derangement, he has been confined to a private house under my care. It is my contention that madness is as manageable as many other disorders and must be approached with understanding.

I have been told by witnesses that this mental instability first showed itself while Sir Charles was on his way home from your country. He perseveres in talking of his failure in the Russian court, his anxiety over a lost treaty. I relate this, not in any laying of blame, but so that Your Highness may comprehend the irrational state of his mind. Since returning to England his condition worsened until his daughter was forced to give permission for his confinement.

We have seen some progress, and perhaps with time his mental faculties will improve. Until then, I thank you, on his behalf, for your kind interest. I remain

Your humble servant,
Dr. William Batty

chapter twenty-six

Rebecca only worked half days on Friday and had gone home at one o'clock, worn out. She didn't realize how much yesterday's hostage-taking had fatigued her until the examining room started to swim before her eyes while a patient was showing her his poison ivy rash.

Once home, she curled up on the couch in her den and finished reading the last chapter she had of *The Stolen Princess*. She was astonished at how close she felt to these people, her apprehension at the troubling letter from a Dr. William Batty who was treating Sir Charles for a "mental condition." It occurred to her that Dr. Batty might be the source of the expression used for people with a screw loose.

What did it all mean? Who was the stolen princess? She tried to remember what Michael had told her about his book. What stuck most in her mind was that something he had written in it contradicted the history books.

How would she know what was contradicted if she didn't know the history in the first place? He told her he was looking for his great-great-great-grandmother. Something like that. And that Stanislaw Poniatowski, who became King of Poland at some point, was the father of her child. It seemed obvious to Rebecca that he was writing about Catherine. Quite a sobering thought, that Michael could be the descendent of Catherine the Great. He said he had checked all the children of the king's many mistresses and that all the offspring were accounted for. What about his child with Catherine? Rebecca would have remembered if he had mentioned her. Why hadn't he? There was a conundrum there, and if she could unravel it, maybe she'd be closer to knowing what happened to Michael. Someone had taken the rest of the manuscript to make sure no one figured it out. Was that someone Teodor?

She dug up Professor Hauer's card and dialed the number.

The secretary answered. "Department of Slavic Studies."

"Could I speak to Teodor please?"

"Moment."

She heard the secretary shuffle away.

After a few minutes, a hesitant male voice answered, "Yes?"

"This is Rebecca Temple. I came to talk to you about Michael Oginski's manuscript a few days ago …"

"Yes?"

"Well, I've had a chance to read it since then and I need to speak to you about it. You remember we only found a hundred and forty pages — the rest are missing. You must know what happens in the end. I think the missing pages might have something to do with his death."

She heard an intake of breath. Was she getting close?

"This is a dangerous business," he whispered. "I can't talk now. I can't talk here. People listen ..."

"Well, what about some place else? Would you like to meet somewhere for coffee?" Some place in public should be safe.

"I ... That is possible."

"How about this afternoon?"

"I'm busy in the office. And tonight I'm busy."

"How about tomorrow morning?" Did he suspect?

He paused, breathed into the phone. "All right."

"Eleven okay?"

"There's a little café on Spadina just north of Harbord."

"What's it called?"

The dial tone hummed in her ear. She would find it.

That evening at her parents' house she was particularly interested in her mother's brother, Uncle Henry, whose teaching career she had never given much thought to before. He had remained a bachelor and came to dinner every Friday night, an integral part of the family. He and her mother shared a resemblance around the eyes, which were grey and animated. He was a small but fit man with a round head covered with springs of grey-blond hair. Rebecca waited until he had cut into his roast chicken.

"I'm reading a story about a young German girl named Sophie who travelled to Russia in 1744 to marry her cousin Karl."

"Why aren't you reading medical texts?" said her father, giving her the fish eye. "What for did I spend all that money sending you to medical school?"

"Quiet, Mitch," said Uncle Henry. "It's a trick question." He held a forkful of meat near his mouth and flashed a toothy smile. "To which I know the answer. Catherine the Great." In went the chicken.

"That's amazing," said Rebecca's mother, Flo. "You must be an awfully good history teacher. Don't you think so, Mitch?" She passed down a platter filled with broccoli and toasted almonds.

"'Awful' is the right word there," said her father, unable to resist. Both her mother and uncle had played straight man to Mitch's routine ever since Rebecca could remember.

"Have you heard of a Polish king named Poniatowski?"

He shook his curly head, spearing some roast potatoes with his fork. "I'm on shakier ground there. Poland was always overshadowed by the superpowers around her. Russia. Austria. Germany — or in those days, Prussia. Around the end of that century, if I remember correctly, they carved Poland up like a cake and divided it three ways among themselves: Russia on the east, Prussia on the west, and Austria on the south. Your grandparents came from the Austrian side. That's why we all had German last names."

Rebecca had never thought to ask why her mother's maiden name, Wagman, was German when her parents, Rebecca's grandparents, came from Poland.

"Not all of us had German names," said her father. "Temple comes from Templitsky. We were from the Russian side. It was a mixed marriage," he said, smiling mischievously at Flo.

Rebecca knew the derivation of her last name, but had never understood the context before.

"Catherine was not good for the Jews," Uncle Henry continued. "She was the one who created the Pale of Settlement."

"I've heard of that," Rebecca said, "but I never understood what it was."

"Ah." He nodded, his grey eyes glinting with implication. "Jews were not considered good for Russia — they were stubborn and wouldn't assimilate, and when Catherine acquired the eastern chunk of Poland in the partition, she inherited the large population of Jews that lived there. Everyone was afraid the Jews would leave the territory and spread out into Russia. So she decreed that all Jews, Polish and Russian alike, had to settle in the new area. The Pale. As in 'stake,' or 'picket.' They were especially eager to expel the Jews from cities like St. Petersburg and Moscow and sent them to live in villages in the new part where they couldn't own land or get higher education."

Rebecca felt betrayed, led on by the empathy she had felt for the character in Michael's story. She remembered the old rabbi's vision and foreshadowing of evil when Catherine was still Sophie on her way to meet her future husband.

Uncle Henry chewed on his potatoes, fixing an eye on her. "What's this sudden interest in European history?"

Rebecca took that moment to turn to her mother. "Chicken's really good tonight, Ma." She popped a piece in her mouth.

"Thanks, dear. And I'm glad to see you're taking an interest in something other than work."

"Don't listen to your mother," Mitch said, his mouth on an angle. "Medicine is interesting enough. History's passé."

Rebecca acknowledged the joke with a smirk. "But I am curious about a few things, Uncle Henry. For instance, how does history view Catherine?"

They all turned to Henry, who solemnly put down his fork and adopted his teacher's face.

"Catherine is seen as an ambitious, ruthless woman who had her husband murdered so that she could become empress of all the Russias."

"Murdered?" Rebecca said. "She didn't seem to be capable of that in the story I'm reading."

"Well, there's no evidence that she actually gave the order to kill him, but shortly after becoming emperor her husband was put into prison. Catherine's lover at the time, a popular Russian officer, helped her stage a coup. Once her husband was in prison, it wasn't long before he was killed. Though she denied it, people always murmured that her lover had done what she asked him to do. But afterwards, she appeared on her horse in a Russian soldier's uniform and people cheered."

"Her husband would've been a disastrous ruler," she said.

Her uncle smiled. "You *have* been reading. All in all, Catherine was an excellent empress. She tried to overhaul the whole legal system of Russia. She was sympathetic to the serfs and tried to better their lot, and most important of all, she won a great victory over Turkey in a war she was expected to lose. That was where she acquired her title. After that war Russia was considered one of the great powers."

"Did you know she had an affair with the Polish nobleman who became King of Poland? That she had his child?"

Henry's mouth pursed while he ruminated. "I don't know anything about that. It sounds like he was a footnote in her eventful life. And how much could she have cared for him if she made his country disappear?"

Rebecca recalled the tale the rabbi had told Sophie about the two souls who were eventually torn apart by the woman's ambition. It was so hard to fathom, the sweep of a life.

He spooned more potatoes onto his plate. "That's why history is so fascinating. We live our lives on the tip of an iceberg and only begin to understand why we're here when we splash around and look below."

"Gee, Henry, I never realized you knew so much," Mitch said. "Maybe you should be a teacher."

"Do you know who the Jacobites were, Uncle Henry?"

"The Jacobites, my dear, were followers of the Catholic King James of Scotland. The word comes from 'Jacobus,' the Latin for 'James.' His son and grandson were called Pretenders because they tried to take the throne from the reigning monarchs of England. Quite a to-do at the time."

Flo gazed at her younger brother with pride.

"If you're that interested," Henry said, "I've got some books on the period at home ..."

"Anyone want to hear a joke?" Mitch said, wiping his mouth with a napkin.

"... if you'd like to borrow anything."

"Thanks, Uncle Henry. What I'd really like to know is what happened to the child Catherine had with Poniatowski." That seemed to be the obvious place to look for Michael's great-great-great-grandmother.

"Do you remember the kid's name?"

"Anna."

"I'll check out my eighteenth-century shelf when I get home. How late can I call you?"

Rebecca grinned at his enthusiasm. "If you find something, let me know. Whenever."

Rebecca glided toward the light in the distance, her gown rustling as she moved, a gossamer silver trimmed with pearls and pink roses. People stepped demurely to a minuet around the high-ceilinged ballroom. Rebecca stopped at the doorway, knowing they would want to bow as she entered the room. Floating across the ballroom, she gave them the opportunity to admire her chestnut hair piled elaborately on top of her head, decorated with jewelled combs and aigrettes, her white skin glowing with rouge.

A new minuet starts up and Count Poniatowski stands before her, eager to begin the dance. He smiles with soft curved lips, his long hair waved and yellow above straight shoulders. She takes the hand he offers and steps into the music. The floor dazzles with light from crystal chandeliers. The courtiers bow to her as they pass by, sparks flying from their diamonds and gold.

"I am only sorry our dance ended so soon," he says.

Since they have just begun, she wonders at this, but when she looks up into his face, it's Michael, his blue eyes smiling at her. Her heart lifts and she opens her mouth to frame a question, a thousand questions, but her voice is stuck somewhere in her throat. Then an irksome noise begins.

A bell rings in her ear. Then his face, her gown, the room melt away. It rings again and she's awake.

"Hello."

"Did I wake you?"

Her brain rearranged itself into the present, her bedroom in Toronto, 1979. "It's okay, Uncle Henry. Did you find something?"

"Not good news. I looked up my biography of Catherine the Great and she did have a child named Anna by Stanislaw Poniatowski in December 1757. But the child died in the spring of 1759 when she was fourteen months old."

"Oh." Now Rebecca understood why Michael hadn't counted on the offspring from that side.

"Catherine didn't forget him, though," said Henry. "You piqued my curiosity and I read ahead. Shortly after she became empress, Augustus, the king of Poland, died. He was also Elector of Saxony, but that's another story. Anyway, there were a few candidates for the job of king, but Catherine sent Russian troops to Warsaw to make sure her ex-lover was chosen. She was the ruling power in those days and the man she chose to be king would become king. It seemed less a personal choice than a political one though. She wanted someone who would do her bidding. And who better than a man still besotted."

"What do you mean?"

"Poniatowski seems to have gone to his grave loving her."

"So first she made him king," said Rebecca, "and later she took away his kingdom."

"Just so."

She remembered the rabbi's story in Michael's book, the magic grain of wheat that the young man worshipped and the young woman failed to comprehend — Rebecca realized it was Poland.

A few minutes before eleven in the morning Rebecca found the University Café on Spadina Avenue just north of Harbord. She sat down at a table for two. Then she waited. She drank a cup of decaffeinated coffee. She watched customers come and go. And she waited.

By 11:30 she decided Teodor was not coming. Maybe he thought he could get her off his back by making an assignation he had no intention of keeping. She wasn't that easily put off. If he had killed Michael, she would find him. Except that she was at a disadvantage now because she didn't know his last name. The Slavic Studies office would be closed on Saturday. Just for good measure she called.

In the phone booth on the corner she listened to the signal ringing, ringing. Then she remembered something Edward had said about Teodor's last name.

She dialed Sarah's number.

"Hello?"

"Hi, Sarah, how are you?"

"Fine, dear, how are you?"

"This is going to sound strange but I need to know a word in Polish. The word for green."

There was a moment of silence, which Rebecca took to be surprise rather than thought.

"*Zielony*. The word for green is *zielony*."

"I'll explain it some other time. It's a long story. Could you spell it please?"

Once she had hung up, Rebecca pulled open the well-thumbed Toronto phone book attached by a chain to the booth. There were only two Zielonys in the book, only one with the initial T. She dialed the number. It rang five times before she pressed down the button and dialed again. Maybe he was on a flight back to Poland. She recognized his street address; it was just a few blocks away, walking distance to his office. Which made sense. She had to go back that way to her own office where she had left her car. But if he'd killed Michael, she wasn't going there alone.

Pushing another dime into the slot, she dialed again.

"Hi Iris. Are you busy?"

She walked slowly down Spadina Avenue and took a few side streets until she reached College Street. Hauer may've been a pompous clown, but what he said about Teodor rang true. It all fit. Especially now that he was avoiding her.

She came to a small street that ran south off College. Teodor lived in a low-rise apartment building identical to all the others on the street. Though she had the address, she didn't have the apartment number. Lucky for her, the names of the tenants were listed on the mailboxes. He was in the basement.

She hung back in the shadow of a spreading chestnut tree on the corner. Finally, Iris drove up in her silver Pontiac. She parked at a meter on College Street.

"Did you ring the bell?" Iris asked, her blond hair swept up in waves off her neck. Even in casual khaki trousers and a print blouse she looked tailored. Rebecca had briefed her on the phone and Iris was ready to go.

She rang the buzzer for the basement. No response. She rang again. Nobody was coming in or out; it was very quiet for a Saturday.

"Wait here!" Iris said with the same authority that had made her indispensable in the office. She marched around the side of the building in her low-heeled pumps.

A moment later, Iris called out. Rebecca stepped around the corner and found her assistant grinning as she held the back door open for her. It had been left propped ajar with a piece of wood. Someone must have wanted fresh air.

They stepped down the linoleum-covered stairs toward Teodor's apartment. The same linoleum covered the floor of the hallway, worn, but clean. It didn't look like the home of a killer. But evil was banal, wasn't it?

Iris knocked on his door. They waited. She knocked again, an impatient clamour in the quiet hall. Did he think they would just go away?

"We know you're in there!" Iris said. "Open the door."

Maybe *Iris* knew he was in there. But Rebecca thought he'd probably skipped town, once he realized she suspected him. And she didn't want Iris to break down the door. Then she noticed it was not firmly set in, the way it would be if it were locked. She tried the handle and it turned easily.

She pushed the door open. "Teodor?"

The apartment was dark inside, as if the curtains were still drawn from the night. A musty basement odour escaped into the hall.

They stepped into the front entranceway and both gasped together. In the centre of the living room, a body hung suspended from a rope around its neck. The other end was attached to a light fixture. Rebecca found the light switch. Iris looked away. It was Teodor. His eyes were bulging, his neck a mottled purple. His skin had the waxy appearance of someone who'd been dead for a while.

Iris stayed rooted to the spot. Rebecca approached gingerly, looking around. She touched one of his hands. It was ice cold and a bit stiff. Rigor mortis had come and gone. He had probably been dead all night. An overturned stool lay beneath him.

She found a phone in the kitchen and called the police. Iris retreated back into the hall to wait for the cops to arrive. Rebecca avoided looking at the body hanging in the middle of the room while she prowled around with great care, being sure not to touch anything. On a desk near the window lay an orderly sheaf of papers. She stood beside it and read the top sheet. She recognized the type, the uneven pressure of some of the letters, the slight break in the letter "o" —it was the same as Michael's manuscript:

> My life is unbearable. I cannot go on. I'm sorry about Count Oginski, I shouldn't have done it. But he took away my future. He made history into popular culture, debasing

it into a cheap novel. Everything I worked so hard for, it all seemed so senseless. I thought if I could use some of his research — but it is impossible. My thesis is a shambles and will never be accepted. My failure is too much to endure.

The initials, "T.Z." were written by hand at the bottom.

She read it over again. *I'm sorry about Count Oginski. I shouldn't have done it.* There it was. He had killed Michael. Why, she wasn't quite sure. He blamed Michael for ruining his thesis. Hauer had said he had trouble keeping up with the work, that he was desperate. Michael had been a scapegoat for an unstable mind. Following in his father's footsteps. He seemed paranoid about Hauer; maybe he had been living in some delusional system that she never got the opportunity to observe.

A bell went off in her head. She stared at the pile of paper beneath the suicide note. It wasn't thick enough to be the rest of the manuscript, but it was something.

She didn't want to touch the note so she bent over and blew it gently until it moved partly away. Peeking from beneath, the page read, "The Stolen Princess, February 1759." So there it was.

Constable Woolrich arrived first, a lean, fair-haired young man who assumed a business-like manner while speaking to Rebecca and Iris but who seemed shaken by the corpse in the living room. Standing in the hall, his back turned to the open door, he dutifully wrote down in his notebook the story Rebecca told him of Michael's death and how it seemed connected to Teodor. She mentioned the suicide note.

"A detective will be by shortly," said the constable. "He'll sort out all of that."

Within the hour, Detective Frohman arrived, followed by forensic people in white coveralls. Still in the hallway, she repeated everything to the detective, a portly, middle-aged man with brush-cut hair who smelled vaguely of stale cigarette smoke.

When she mentioned the letter, he stuck his head in the doorway.

"Hey Phil," he called to one of the forensic guys, "dust the letter on the desk, will ya?"

"You've been a big help, Doctor." He turned to Iris. "Ma'am. Now if you've given the constable your addresses and phone numbers, you're free to go."

Rebecca remembered the small pile of papers beneath the letter.

"Would I be able to ... I mean, would it be all right if I took the pages sitting there on the desk? Once you've finished your investigation. They're part of a manuscript that Teodor took from Mr. Oginski and I'd like to give them back to his son." After she had photocopied and read them.

"You'll have to wait till forensics is finished, Doctor. That'll still be a while. Do you know who his next of kin is?"

"No, I hardly knew him. But you could ask his supervisor. Anton Hauer. I have his office number."

He copied the number down from the card she retrieved from her wallet.

The forensic team worked quietly in the shadow of the body suspended from the ceiling. After the coroner arrived and had a chance to examine the body *in situ*, Teodor was at last cut down and laid out on the floor. As a physician she had seen death in many forms, but violent death was rare in her practice and never failed to shock her. Iris was uncharacteristically quiet. Her hair still swept up from her face, though her features had fallen.

Once outside, Rebecca breathed in great gulps of fresh air. Iris looked like a deer caught in the headlights.

Rebecca felt guilty for asking her to come. She walked Iris to her car. "How about dinner tonight? We'll go out for Chinese."

Iris gave her a baleful look. "For a change I have no appetite."

Rebecca tried to smile, gazed numbly at the leafy linden trees. "It'll come back by tonight. Think of it this way: Teodor felt guilty for killing Michael and chose to end his own life. It doesn't make things any more palatable, but it does put them into perspective." She put her hand gently on Iris's arm. "Meet me at the office at seven o'clock and we'll stroll over to Spadina Gardens." Iris's favourite restaurant.

"I'll drive you to your car," Iris said, without expression.

"No, that's all right. It's just a few blocks. I'd like to walk."

She watched Iris, looking dazed, step into her Pontiac and drive off.

Rebecca turned south. The afternoon sun warmed the Victorian stone houses of Beverley Street, just like yesterday. As if nothing had changed. As if Teodor was too small to count in the scheme of things.

Her empty office seemed curiously peaceful in light of the afternoon's events. Suddenly her head became too heavy for her neck. She eased into the leather chair behind her desk and put her head down to rest on her arms.

An hour and a half later she startled awake. She blinked at her watch: 3:30.

In the bathroom she splashed cold water on her face, catching herself in the mirror. Her dark hair lay in unruly waves around her face, a pale, unwholesome apparition. She had missed lunch and began to feel the gnawing of an empty stomach.

In the drawer of her desk she found an old Three Musketeers bar and took a few bites. Some roasted almonds kept it company until she chewed them up. After downing a glass of water, she set out for Teodor's apartment again.

When she arrived, a few people were leaving the building and let her in the front door. There was yellow police tape across the apartment door but no constable guarding, which, she assumed, meant they had finished their preliminary investigation. She kicked herself for falling asleep. They had probably locked the door. Well, they had probably tried, but it didn't quite fit into the doorframe. She turned the handle, and to her surprise, it gave way.

Ducking under the tape, she stepped into the apartment. The body was gone, but an unsavoury odour lingered. From the distance she could see the pages on the desk. They had been left behind. Lucky her.

She should probably get permission from the cops, but that would take time. She picked up the pile of paper reverently and estimated the number of pages: only about ten. A chapter. It was titled "Escape and Rescue." Where was the rest of the manuscript? If Teodor had killed Michael, the manuscript had to be here.

She began pulling open the drawers of the desk. There *was* a manuscript, a thick one in a binder, but it was Teodor's thesis, titled, "The Disappearance of Poland: Life during Partition." It was riddled with red editorial markings, entire pages dismissed with jagged, irritated lines, presumably made by Hauer. The middle drawer held file folders filled with copious notes in Teodor's hand. In the bottom drawer she found a handwritten letter:

Dear Count Oginski,

I wanted to let you know how much I enjoyed
reading your manuscript. It is a masterpiece!
You made history come alive, writing about
the real people who created events. We historians start with events and try to discover why
they happened and only incidentally talk
about the people. I wanted to tell you how
much your book has influenced my work and
come to make me view "history" in a different way. Do not be concerned about the scholarly approach of some academics who —

How two-faced he was! Or just conflicted. He hated
Michael's book. He loved Michael's book. Very unstable. A fragile personality.

Then a shock came over her. It was her phone call
that had pushed him over the edge! Her wanting to talk
to him about Michael. He realized she knew. And he
couldn't face the consequences. He was fastening the
noose around his neck while she was having a pleasant
dinner at her parents' house. If she hadn't called him ...

She distracted herself by continuing to search for
the manuscript. It was a bachelor apartment with a pull-
out couch where he must have slept. The closet and the
dresser in the corner contained only his drab, simple
clothes, corduroy trousers and washed-out shirts.

She couldn't think straight. Her stomach was growl-
ing and she needed to pay attention to it. Maybe some
Chinese takeout. The thought of food nauseated her in the
middle of this pathetic apartment, the chaos of a life lost,
the possibility that the life had been lost with her help.

Picking up the chapter of *The Stolen Princess*, she
tiptoed out of the apartment.

chapter twenty-seven

Escape and Rescue

February 1759

I stare at the paper with the official seal, but my eyes blur before me. No, it's the words that blur. An elegant hand tracing watery insects across the page. Damn my head! I give it a good shake. No, that is worse. The words run together into a pool as if the ink they had been printed with suddenly became liquid again and drowned all meaning.

"Young Tom," I say, "be so kind as to read this to me."

Tom is the son of a trusted servant at Coldbrook, my house in Wales. I have watched him grow into a kind, if dull, young man whose duty it has become to tend to me. He takes his responsibilities seriously and at times I must remind him who is master.

"Why, Sir Charles," he says astonished, "it's from the King!

"Yes, of course!" I say impatiently. "He's in danger and needs saving. I have offered to sacrifice myself. I will return to my post in Russia where the Pretender is planning his next strike."

"Bonnie Prince Charlie?" he says, cocking his head at me with half-witted incredulity.

"When does he say I might go?" I ask, trying not to be rude, but the truth is I am losing patience.

Tom turns back to the letter. His brows shift together like little sparrows. I warrant there is as much understanding behind them as well.

He continues to read. "I'm afraid, Sir Charles, he says you may not." Tom looks up. I grimace. "He says you have served him gallantly in the past. But now others must carry on and you are to attend to your health."

I shake my head. He has got it wrong.

"But when can I *go*?" I say quite beside myself. "Look more closely and find the date."

Tom is thick as a post, it is true. An attribute rampant among servants. A good soul, but thick, and as I cannot read the letter myself, I must gather its meaning between the lines, so to speak. The King does not wish it to get out that his old foe, the Pretender, has new plans afoot to strike at the Kingdom. The letter is written in code and I must decipher it.

"Read me precisely what it says," I say.

Tom scowls at me. He is a tall stripling, and his scowl might strike fear into one who did not know him. But my own Fanny helped teach him to read as a boy, and his gratitude extends to her father.

He clears his throat and begins.

Sir Charles,

You have served us brilliantly during your sojourn in Russia, going above and beyond the call of duty on behalf of King and Country. We yet have friends in that court on account of your prodigious work. Now after all your stalwart efforts, it is time to allow others to carry on the burden of a posting in a country with whom we are in a difficult war.

We are told of your illness and advise that you turn all of your attention toward it. With fervent wishes for your return to good health,

George II Rex

Tom looks up, eyes popping with wonder. "The King's gratitude! He is full of praise for you, Sir Charles. I am very proud to know you." He bends his knee and bows down.

"Up, boy! Up!" I shake my head at his dullness. "We must put our heads together, Tom, for this letter is written in code. When he says we yet have friends in Russia, he means me to go back and use them to our advantage."

Tom shakes his head slowly. "But sir, I don't think …"

"And when he says for others to carry on the burden of a posting, he means that I should be left free of that burden and go not as an envoy but as — as a friend of the court. A *spy*. I would be more useful that way. It is obvious."

Tom turns back to the letter. "I'm not sure of …"

"You are blind, Tom! When he writes 'a difficult war' it means we are losing. King Frederick is on the run from the French, the Austrians, and the Russians, and Frederick is our ally. That is my job — to sue for peace with the Empress. The longer the war continues, the more chance there is that France will help Prince Charles Edward Stuart invade England. That is the real danger. The Jacobites, led by the avaricious Pretender."

Tom screws up his eyes, holding the paper closer.

"Do not bother searching the letter for more, young Tom, for you have not deciphered code as I have. You must trust me in this. The king sends me to Russia and I choose you to accompany me." I beam at him, pleased with myself for offering him this opportunity.

Tom's eyes grow round. "But ... but I have never left England. There's my mother ..."

"Your mother will burst with pride!" I smile with indulgence, and then memory. "I have seen such things as you cannot imagine. You will never have such occasion again. Say nothing to your family, for this is a secret mission."

Tom appears uncertain, yet animated. "Perhaps you forget, Sir Charles, I am bidden to see that you do not leave this house. The doctor says you are not yourself."

I purse my lips and aim at him my most compelling face. "I am more myself now than I have been for months. The rest and exercise the good doctor prescribed have cured me. You are a witness that I do not jabber on like before; my thoughts are perfectly lucid. How can you chance the future of England? If I am right, you will be a hero. If I am wrong, you will return a wiser man filled with adventures."

His eyes dart with excitement. I have hooked him! "If we are to go," he says, "I must notify Dr. Batty."

"Under no circumstances!" I cry. "No one is to know. Our King's life depends upon it! What would your family say if your carelessness were responsible for the death of the King?"

Tom stares at me, horror in his eyes. He shakes his head with much vehemence. "I'll say nothing," he murmurs.

"If someone is curious about our packing of bags, we shall say we are off to Bath for the waters."

"Yes, but …"

"You must arrange our transport, Tom, for I will be suspect, but I will tell you all. You need only follow my instructions. It is a devilish long way and we must prepare. First, you will need to hire a coach that will take us to Yarmouth. There we will embark on a ship bound for Hamburg." I stop at the anxiety written on his face. "Do not gape at me so! Are you a patriotic Englishman?"

Tom stares at me, befuddled, but tenders a nod.

"Capital!" I cry. "Do you love your King?"

A heartier nod.

"Excellent! Now, we must be very circumspect and keep our own counsel. Not a word to anyone, else the mission will fail. Understood?"

Tom blinks. "Yes, sir."

"Good. Where was I? Oh, yes. After Hamburg, we will be at the mercy of the weather. If there is not too much ice we might perchance set sail through the Baltic Sea. Otherwise we must hire a coach for the remainder of the journey. It will be quite an ordeal. I assure you I will be ill for weeks during the voyage, but when the King calls upon one, well, there's nothing else for it. Now, young Tom, have you any money?"

Tom's face darkens.

"No, of course you don't. Forgive my asking. I shall collect expenses afterwards from a grateful government. In the mean time I have some money hidden here, which I have told no one about. But it will require a great deal

more. You will take me to the bank, where I shall draw
upon my account ..."

One day along the long road of our journey I glance out
the window of our coach and see him whom I most fear.
Tom notes my distress and peers out at the bleak countryside where I am turned.

"What is it, Sir Charles?"

"Do you not see him?" I ask astonished. "He rides a
tremendous white horse. A great handsome fellow, wide
of shoulder, his own yellow hair beneath the tricorn."

"Where, Sir Charles? I see but snow upon a hill."

"The Pretender's regimentals, blue trimmed with
red. A cutlass at his side." Not to alarm the boy, I
refrain from adding, *at the ready for our slaying.*

Tom screws up his eyes for a better look. I must
mollify him.

"Do not agitate yourself further, Tom. He has
turned away. Perhaps I was mistaken."

In the following days when next the rider appears
out my window, I say nothing. The Prince, sitting tall
and grand in his saddle, has me in his sights, his brilliant blue eyes flashing danger, but I am resolved to
carry on. I will not be threatened in this shameless
way by the traitorous Scot. Yet his treachery has sunk
to a shocking level, for even on the ship crossing the
North Sea to Hamburg, I see him yet astride his
tremendous stallion. Only this time he rides the blue
waves like a vision from hell, gnashing his teeth to
strike fear into me. To be sure he has joined in a pact
with the Devil, as well as France, and will be a fear-
some enemy.

It is nearly spring when at last we enter St. Petersburg. The ice yet lies thick in the river, but a clear blue sky sweeps high above the golden spire of the Admiralty. Three of the city's great avenues radiate outwards from before this historic building, one, Nevsky Prospekt, upon which we travel.

The driver stops in front of my old mansion. How strange it is to be here again! What memories, both fine and bitter, fight to overtake me. I instruct young Tom to wait with the carriage while I seek out my Lord Keith, who has taken over the house.

His servant announces my presence and my Lord tumbles out of his study, all amazement. It is mid-afternoon, and I have no doubt awakened him from dozing over some dull papers.

"I am astounded!" he says, buttoning his waistcoat. "How came you? I have had no news — you are very unexpected!"

"A fine greeting," I say, "after such a long journey. I am on a secret mission from the King. There will be no message about it — that is all I can say. How goes the court?"

"I understood you were not well ..."

"My condition was greatly exaggerated. As you can see, I am quite recovered. What news from the court?"

My Lord Keith observes me while scratching his bald head. "Very curious," he says. "As for the court, things are very bad for us. The French hold sway over the Empress and she will not see me. I am welcome only in the Young Court, where the Grand Duchess Catherine is still gracious to me. Sad news there. The little Grand Duchess Anna is deathly ill and is not expected to live."

I am shaken to the quick. I think of my own two daughters, now safely grown. "A fate no parent should have to endure."

"Her mother is beside herself," Keith continues, "and laments that she has not been allowed to live with her own children. Now the Empress gives Anna to her mother when it is too late. The French faction uses the illness against us and spreads rumours that the child is poisoned by an English sympathizer."

My mouth goes sudden dry. Scales drop from my eyes. This, then, is it. I am astounded that it is laid out in such simple terms. It all hinges on the child. The child has been poisoned by the French, who are using her illness against us. Prince Charles Edward Stuart is behind this, of that I am certain.

My mind races to concoct a plan. "I must see the Grand Duchess Catherine," I say to Keith. "You must get a message to her."

"It is impossible! You are no longer in an official capacity here."

"She would be very vexed if she knew I was here and you didn't do everything in your power to bring me to her. I was her trusted adviser once. And I have a message from the King."

He squints unhappily at me. "Yes, of course."

That evening I wait for her by the back door, the one that Count Poniatowski used to tell me about. At the appointed time it creaks open and there she stands, thinner than I recall, sorrow written in the lines of her face. Her shoulders stoop; her hair is undressed.

She bids me inside, and once in the hall I attempt to bow, but she hurls herself into my arms.

"Your Highness," I whisper, patting her back while she sobs on my shoulder.

"I cannot bear it!" she weeps out the words. "My little baby is dying."

"What of the rumour of the poison?"

She shakes her head. "I cannot say. I can hardly fathom it. That anyone would murder a child! What good does it do anyone?"

I do not trouble her with my theories. "May I see her?"

She wipes her tears with a handkerchief. "A letter came from an English doctor. He said you were … unwell."

"He said I was mad. But we're all a little mad, aren't we? Especially if we have a heart and yet must deal with the world."

Her face smoothes into a smile, a hint of the lady I remember. She picks up a candle and leads me down the hall. She opens a darkened room, holding the candle aloft to shed some light. A servant lies asleep near the small bed, where a tiny figure reclines under a coverlet. Little Anna is but fourteen months.

I approach, standing over the sleeping baby. On a table near the bed, candlelight reflects off the little silver compass I gave the Count when first he had been sent away. I touch it to see if it is real.

"I keep it here for good luck," she says. "I thought an angel might use it to find her way and then come and save my poor Anna."

I watch the little chest barely rise with each ragged breath. Her eyelids do not move. I feel her forehead. Hot to the touch. The Grand Duchess sobs quietly behind me. I feel powerless. Yet there is something. I have not come all this way to stand by while the treacherous Pretender works his evil. This was why he tried to prevent me, so that I could not be the agent of the child's salvation. In my mind's eye I picture the alleyway in the city where stands a little house and inside that house an old man dressed all in black standing by the fire boiling potions. *Remember me when the time comes.*

"I am your angel," I say. "You must let me help her."

The Grand Duchess looks up from her handkerchief. "It is too late."

"It is only too late when one gives up. There is a physician I know who works miracles."

"The court physician is the best in Russia ... if *he* despairs ..."

"You always trusted me, Your Highness. Trust me now."

She holds the candle aloft near my face to examine me. My eyes convince her. "I have nothing left to lose," she says. "We will go at once!"

"You must stay here," I say. "I will take the child's servant."

"I insist on coming!" she says.

I take her hand, as if I am talking to my daughter. "Your Highness, you will be the next Tsarina one day. Perhaps one day soon. If someone is trying to harm the child, think how much more eager they will be to harm you. I will not risk it."

She sighs with agitation. "Madame Dembrova," she says to the woman rubbing the sleep from her eyes. "Sir Charles is taking the little Grand Duchess out of the palace. You will accompany them."

"Here," she says to me, "take the compass." She places it in a pretty gold box that lies nearby. "For luck."

chapter twenty-eight

There it was, laid out before Rebecca like a road map. Only the road in question stretched not through space but through time. The contradiction of written history Michael said he had unearthed. Anna Petrovna, the daughter of Catherine and Poniatowski, didn't die. Sir Charles must have taken her to the mysterious Jewish doctor, who had somehow saved her. But then why did history record her death? Because her family believed she had died? Because Sir Charles had told them she had died and never took her back? He had made Catherine stay behind. He could presumably have said the baby was dead — there would have been no surprise there — and concocted some story about having to bury her quickly because of the fear of contagion. After all, smallpox was rampant then.

So Sir Charles had kidnapped her! But why? He was clearly deranged. Had he believed he was saving the child from enemies at court?

But all that was conjecture. How could she find out, now that Teodor could no longer tell her? She fished the card out of her purse and, on the off chance, dialed the number. It was five o'clock on a Saturday evening. She let it ring a few times and was about to hang up when a man's voice answered.

"Slavic Studies."

"Professor Hauer?"

"Speaking."

His slight accent was not unappealing. "It's Rebecca Temple. I'm so glad I caught you."

"Well, I was just about to phone you. The police called and told me about poor Teodor. They said you found the body."

"I'm afraid so."

"Well, I'm sorry it had to be you. It must've been a shock. What a terrible, terrible tragedy."

"Yes. Well." What was there to say? "You worked with him. Did he seem despondent enough to take his own life?"

"He was a very strange young man. I cannot say how despondent one needs to be. I think I mentioned his father also took his own life? I *can* say he was distressed about his thesis. Which was shaky and not up to standard. Perhaps if he had chosen some other career."

She thought of the unfinished letter of praise to Michael. Perhaps that was where the friction lay between the professor and the student, the difference in philosophy.

"Did the police tell you about the suicide note?"

"No."

"He seems to be confessing to Michael Oginski's murder."

There was a pause. "Good God! Who would've thought him capable of such a thing?"

"I expected to find the rest of Michael's manuscript in

Teodor's apartment, but there was only one chapter. I was wondering, Professor, if I could ask you about some details in the story. I think I've found the discrepancy Michael was talking about, the contradiction of written history."

"May I remind you that Count Oginski was writing a book of fiction," he said, his voice pitched higher with irritation. "So by definition, it is *all* a contradiction of history."

"I disagree, Professor. I think his book is a telling of real history as if it were fiction. The characters and events are historical; he's just given them back their personalities. He's written them on a human level and brought out the drama."

"My dear Doctor, history is a demanding vocation. It is not like writing a romance novel. One cannot suddenly change the facts when one is so inclined. When the Count presumed to turn an important event upside down, he was no longer writing history, but fiction."

"Are you talking about Anna Petrovna, Catherine's daughter with Poniatowski?"

"Yes, yes, Doctor," he said with exasperation. "I see you've been doing your homework. The Count spoke to me about this as if he had discovered some new material instead of just conjuring it all up."

"You mean the part where Sir Charles saves the baby?"

"Purely fiction. The history is well documented. The baby died."

So the child did survive in the book.

"Though I do give him credit for his artistic talent — it's a well-written fabrication."

Stubborn man. "What if I told you there is an artifact that might prove otherwise? A compass."

"I would say it was another fiction he used to acquire a publishing contract."

"He wasn't that sort of man," she said, affronted. "And he never saw the compass. He said the story was repeated in his family, that the compass would prove they were descendents of royalty."

"Nonsense! The whole thing's a sham ..."

"I've seen it."

"What do you mean? Seen what?"

"The little silver sundial with a compass set in it. There's a box with an inscription in French."

Finally, an uncertain pause. "Well, well. Should I believe you?"

"It's inscribed to Sophie from Staś."

A breath in. Silence while he was thinking. "Even if you're telling the truth, it doesn't change anything. A compass is just a compass. Unless ... unless you found something else."

"Something else? What do you mean?"

"It doesn't matter. Even if you found it, he could've planted it. Or had it planted."

What was he talking about? "There's nowhere to put anything in it."

"Well, then, you see it's more fiction. As I said before. The Count told me about ... information that the compass would give up. I suppose to tantalize me the way he tantalized his publisher."

"What kind of information was he talking about?"

"I hesitate to say for fear of promulgating a lie."

"Did he tell you where to find the ... information?"

Another pause. "I might be able to uncover what was there. But I'd have to see the object for myself."

Her turn to hesitate. She remembered every facet of the box and compass. It seemed impossible that anything could be hidden within either piece. She knew she wouldn't find it on her own.

"I can show it to you. Tonight."

A deep sigh. "Shall I come to your house?"

She was meeting Iris at the office at seven. Inflicting the story on her again. What would she do without Iris? "How about my office? Around seven."

She drove to Sarah's, wondering what she would say to persuade her mother-in-law that there was no harm in taking the compass from the house. To her relief, when she arrived, Sarah was out. Though she had never used it, Rebecca still carried David's old key to the house he had grown up in.

She let herself in and immediately went to the piano. Crouching beneath it, she dropped to her knees and felt above her head with her fingers. The box lay just where she had left it, snug in a corner under the keyboard.

Rebecca drove back down to her office, thankful that Sarah had not come home before she could escape with the compass. She would return it later.

There was no one in the building on a Saturday night. She arrived a few minutes early and headed for her private office, where she placed the box with the compass in her desk, beside the half-eaten Three Musketeers bar.

Hauer arrived before Iris. In the quiet building she could hear his footsteps coming up the stairs to her second-floor office.

She moved into the waiting room just as he came through the door. She had forgotten how large he was. His mouth smiled in the aperture between the neatly clipped moustache and beard. The thick dark hair was tamed with some pomade. He wore the same tweed jacket from the other day.

"Doctor." He nodded, his round brown eyes observing her. Under one arm, he carried something in a brown paper bag.

He pulled out a bottle, held it up for her approval. "Special Gdansk vodka with flakes of real gold. I thought we should have a drink to the memory of poor Teodor, whose family is overseas."

She led him into her inner office and went to fetch two drinking glasses from a cupboard above the small fridge.

He stood in front of her desk, gazing into the bottle, whose contents were clear with tiny flakes of gold settled on the bottom. "This is a Polish speciality produced for hundreds of years in the port of Gdansk." He poured one glass. "It was a favourite of Augustus the Strong, who was responsible for the grandeur of Dresden. It also helps the digestion."

He started pouring the second glass but took that moment to look up at her and spilled some on the desk.

"Oh, I'm so sorry. Clumsy of me."

She left to get some paper towels from one of the examining rooms. He insisted on cleaning the spill himself. When everything was dry again, she sat down behind her desk. Hauer, seated in front, lifted his glass and waited for her to lift hers.

"To poor Teodor. Let's hope he's happier now." He took a good swig from his glass.

She peered at the gold flakes drifting in her glass. So this was *Goldwasser*. She remembered it from the manuscript. Very pretty. She took a sip. She wasn't much of a drinker. Vodka usually had to be mixed with something like orange juice to tempt her. But this was different. This took her back to another century.

"How do you like it?" he asked, downing the rest of his glass.

She smiled and took a few more sips. The historical attraction was irresistible. It went down warm.

"Now, the compass?" he said, sitting forward.

He didn't waste any time. She opened the drawer and pulled out the blue velvet bag. His eyes were on her as she placed it on the desk and drew out the gold box.

He took in a sudden breath. She understood that. Apart from the elaborate carving on the gold, the sides of the box had been fitted with translucent panels of lapis lazuli, a twilight blue. Breathtakingly beautiful. He picked it up and turned it around in his large pink hands. He seemed more interested in the box than the treasure inside. Finally, he lifted the gold lid and picked the compass up from its velvet bed, placing it in one of his palms.

"Ah," he said. "Very handsome."

He had barely looked at it before he put it down. He turned his attention back to the box, closely examining the inside of the lid. "Yes, here's the inscription," he said, as if it were of no account. Then propping the lid open against one hand, he began to press the underside firmly with the fingers of the other.

"Now just a minute," she said. "That's a delicate …"

Had she heard a tiny click?

His fingers pulled at something. A thin sheet of gold expanded from the inside of the lid to reveal a hidden compartment. She bent forward for a better look. He drew out a folded piece of yellowed paper.

"Good God!" she said.

Carefully he unfolded the thick paper. She jumped up and came around to look over his shoulder. That was when she felt the effect of the vodka, the dizziness. But between the heavy creases of the paper she could make out a letter written in French in a crabbed disturbed hand. Dated November 1, it began, "*Ma chère Contesse Oginska.*"

"My French isn't very good," she said. "How's yours?"

"Exceptional," he said. "I'll translate."

My dear Countess Oginska,

I was very saddened to learn of the death of your cousin, Countess Konstancja Poniatowska, the mother of my dear friend, Stanislaw Poniatowski. It has been eight long months since the Countess recruited your generous assistance in the rescue of an heiress of Russia. I trust little Anna Petrovna is well. I had several letters from the Countess informing me that the child is a beauty and thrives in your house. She never failed to thank me for making it possible for her granddaughter to be raised in the Roman church. It was Providence that brought little Anna to you after your own daughter was taken from you by cruel fate.

You have been entrusted with a solemn duty: to keep safe a Princess Royal from the machinations of evil men who would use her to gain power. The Pretender and his Jacobite allies, including the French, will stop at nothing, not even the death of a Russian princess, to usurp the throne of England. For this reason, you must keep her identity hidden until such time that the French influence at the Russian court has waned and she can take her rightful place. Her mother will rejoice when all is revealed. It pains me to keep the secret from her, but even she does not have the means to keep her daughter safe in Russia. One day she will be grateful.

It is my misfortune that I will never see that day for I am not long for this world. I have done my duty to my country though my country has never understood the extent of it. My loyalty and patriotism go unrecognized and unrewarded. The King, whom I have always loved, has turned his face against me. I am very weary and can endure no longer.

Now that Countess Poniatowska is dead, only you and I are privy to the secret. And after tomorrow, only you will remain, dear Countess, for I have made my decision. Therefore here is my advice: the war yet rages in Europe. When peace comes, as eventually it must, it is your duty to take little Anna Petrovna back to her mother and reveal her identity. It will not be difficult to convince her mother because of the abnormality of the six fingers on each hand. Her Highness will know her daughter at once. Tell her I regret the pain it must have caused her but that I knew no other way to ensure the child's safety.

Adieu, dear Countess. God bless you and the princess.

Sir Charles Hanbury-Williams

Rebecca closed her eyes and felt herself sway from the history that had suddenly swept over her. An unmistakeable bridge had fallen into place between then and now, between 1759 and 1979. A time that had seemed so lost in the haze of distance now lay just beyond the door. After everything, Sir Charles had killed himself.

"It's overwhelming," she said, staring over his shoulder at the yellowed paper. "Sir Charles kidnapped the princess after she recovered and took her to Poland to Countess Poniatowska, knowing she would want the child raised Catholic. The Countess gave her to her childless cousin Oginska. Who never followed Sir Charles's advice! She never gave the girl back. Instead, she hid the letter in the compass box. Maybe she told her on her deathbed. Somehow the family suspected. I'm only sorry that Michael didn't get a chance to see the letter."

Hauer gave her an abrupt look and folded up the letter, replacing it in the secret compartment in the lid of the box. "It's all speculation. I have a colleague who'll be able to say whether this letter is authentic or not. I'll show it to him on Monday." He put the box with the compass into his jacket pocket and stood up.

She wavered, suddenly small beside him. And very tired. "I have no doubt about its authenticity. I'll have to take it back now."

"You should leave this to the experts. I will let you know if it's real."

"I already know it's real. Can I have it back now please?"

"I was hoping you wouldn't be stubborn about it. I was hoping you'd be reasonable."

"Look, Professor, it's not mine to give. I'm probably already in trouble for taking it out of the house. I'll have to insist on you giving it back."

"Does someone know you've taken it?"

"No …"

"I'm very much relieved."

"I appreciate your concern. But I still need it back."

He stared down at her with an expression that chilled her, his eyes intense but vacant. Something undefined had shifted in his attitude. He leaned toward her.

"I'm afraid I can't do that."

"Why not?"

His dark eyebrows rose like wings and he closed his eyes. "Because the publisher must never see it. The Count's book must never be published."

She fell into the chair he had vacated, suddenly dizzy.

A distant gold shadow came to mind: a smudged flame in the cement near the patio table in Michael's backyard. The gold flakes from a drink that was poured out.

"This is what you gave Michael, isn't it?"

She could hardly hold her head up. It kept rolling down onto her chest.

"Your noble Count! He stole my publisher! To whom I introduced him! A common thief." His round eyes had grown larger, darted around the room.

She tried to think. He must have poured two drinks doctored with some sedative on Michael's patio, emptying his own onto the ground when his victim wasn't looking. What had he put into her drink when she went out to get the paper towels? Valium? The drug would work quickly on her empty stomach.

"I was going to be their Polish expert. The book of Polish interest they publish every three years." He paced the floor in front of her, agitated. "I needed this book. If I didn't publish in English this year, that was it. The university would let me go. After all the help and information I gave him — I even lent him my research material. And what did he do? He betrayed me. He approached my publisher with a novel on Poland and waved his ancestry in their face." His spittle landed on her cheek.

"Catherine the Great! The great whore of history. Stanislaw Augustus! The snivelling fool who lost Poland. Yes, Your Highness. No, Your Imperial Majesty. The book was nothing! It was a fairy tale. But the company wanted to say they had published a direct relative of

Catherine the Great. How could they choose that drivel over my work? Do you have any idea how long I've been writing my book? The research! The scholarship!"

"You killed him because he took your publisher?"

"You don't understand," he said, shaking his large bear head. "He took away my future. I searched and searched and finally I found a publisher who was interested in Polish history. In English. The university won't renew my contract unless I publish a book in English."

"There are other universities," she said.

"It's the only one in the country with a Slavic Studies program."

"The U.S.?"

"It's the same there — no university wants me without a book in English. I couldn't get a green card. I won't go back to Poland. You must see I had no choice. It was his own fault. He brought it on himself."

"What about Teodor? Did he bring it on himself too?"

A skewed smile appeared on his lips. "What a bungler he was. With his puny brain I'm surprised he figured it out, but it shows one can be shrewd without intellect. He said if I accepted his thesis he wouldn't tell the police his suspicions. Blackmail, pure and simple. Accept his thesis? It was a shambles. A piece of trash."

It was a shambles. In her haze, she thought, *The same wording as the suicide note.* Which Hauer had written on the typewriter in the office, after everyone had gone home.

"He worshipped the Count, absorbed his view of history. He was poisoned by it, the human-centric position. No objectivity. I *wouldn't* accept his thesis."

"And you overheard him on the phone. When I called to set up a meeting. You were afraid he was going to tell me." Her energy was ebbing. No strength to stand up.

"I couldn't allow that. He put me in an impossible position."

"You were the one who broke into Sarah's house."

"If I had found the compass, if I could've stopped him from stealing my publisher, I wouldn't have had to ..."

Unsavoury details began falling into place. "He was unconscious from the drink and you had to take off his bathing jacket. That's how his arm became dislocated."

"There's no point, Doctor —"

"And you were the one who put his goggles on ... That was your mistake. They were upside down."

He smiled slyly. "I hardly think that matters now."

"They'll find out, you know. The police." She could barely move. There was a phone on her desk, but it was behind her now.

He chuckled. "I don't think so. There's not enough to connect me to the Count. And hardly anything to connect me to *you*."

She suddenly opened her eyes, unaware that they were closed. "What are you going to do with me? You're in a lot of trouble ... my assistant, Iris, is meeting me here ... any minute now ..."

"Don't upset yourself, Doctor. Nice try, trying to make me think someone's coming. It's going to look like an accident. I'm only sorry you didn't drink more. You'd be blissfully ignorant of what was happening. You see, I don't enjoy seeing people suffer. I'm not a bad person. I do what I must."

Ludicrous, she thought in her stupor. *What, then, is the definition of a bad person?* Keeping her eyes open was a problem.

"They'll find the drug in my system. They'll suspect something."

He smiled, "I've heard that doctors are susceptible to using drugs since they're so readily available. The police won't be surprised by their presence — they know what a temptation it is. After all, doctors are only human."

He had thought of everything.

"Resign yourself, Doctor. There is no help." He pulled the jack out of the wall and picked up the phone.

Where was Iris?

"Where are your supplies?" He turned toward the door. "No, don't get up, Doctor. I think I can find them." He left the room carrying the phone.

The idea of her getting up was ludicrous. Ludicrous was a good word. It fit so many things, changing shape to suit. Like odious. And monstrous. She knew she should be trying to get up, but her legs were jelly. Odious jelly. And he didn't like to see people suffer, so why should she get up? If she was going to die, she preferred not to suffer.

She roused herself. Had to stay awake. No closing of eyes. She tried to hear what he was doing. A vague splashing sound coming from one of the examining rooms. A familiar smell. Familiar but wrong. Something that shouldn't be splashing. Chemical. Isopropanol. Rubbing alcohol.

Stay awake! What was he doing with rubbing alcohol? How was she going to save herself if she didn't know what he was doing? If she couldn't move. If she couldn't think.

Think! An accident. Going to make it look like an accident. With lots of rubbing alcohol. Why alcohol? What were the properties of isopropanol? Antiseptic. Cleaning wounds. Topical use only. Was he going to make her drink it? Some accident. No, none of the above. It was *flammable*. He was going to start a fire. Good God! Setting up something in her examining room that would spark a fire. Weakening. Not enough energy to get out. Sit there and asphyxiate from the smoke. No. No, not like that. Would make sure of her death. Pull her into the room and set her on fire. That kind of accident plausible. Christ, *do* something.

Wake up! Mind over matter. Not going to let it happen. Brain too slow. Brain mush. Panic makes worse. Let instinct take over. Need to get sedative out of system. Remember basic medicine. Lift two fingers. Poke into mouth. Further, further back, as far as can reach. Gag. *Quietly*. Lean over. Vomit on floor.

Better. Better, but still groggy. What more? Adrenaline. Need adrenaline. Must get to drugs. Must get up.

One step at a time. Get up now. Push out of chair. Hold on to arm. Stand up. All right. Move faster. Faster! Back any minute.

Push leg forward. It goes! Hold onto desk. Stumble. Unbalanced. Hold wall. Creep to doorway. Careful. Mustn't see you. Tip head out just far enough: there in other room looking through cupboard. His back angled, won't see. Be quiet. Must be quiet. Sneak steps. Keep going round corner to supplies. Turtle slow. Light-headed.

So hard. So tired. Open cabinet. Pull out box of ampules — epinephrine. Slow motion. Must speed up or run out of time. Fumble with box. Clumsy. Pull out ampule. Get disposable syringe from glass jar. The intramuscular one, longer, quicker. Make sure one cc. Inject too much and dead. Rip paper wrapping with teeth. So hard. So *hard*. Breathing shallow. So tired.

Go on! Push syringe needle in epinephrine. Draw up, up. Too slow. Keep going. Faster. Okay, most in. Expel air from syringe. Now. Top of arm. Make sure no veins, no arteries. Blurred. Never mind. Plunge needle into skin. Push! All the way. Okay. Okay. Doing fine.

Now need minute for drug absorbed. Sound in hall. Steps. Him moving. Him coming! Not enough time! Coming round the corner. Do something. Instinct. Fall to floor. Play dead. Close hand. Hide needle in fist.

"Doctor, Doctor!" he said. "You must accept your fate."

Bending over. Arms under her shoulders, pulling, pulling backward. Dragged to other room. Breathing hard. Work for it, bastard.

Then she felt it. A crack of light. Then a window. Her heart began to beat faster, faster. Life began to flicker through her body. She could feel it growing, spreading, the drug coursing through her veins.

He dragged her into the examining room, where, by the smell of it, he had spilled the large bottle of rubbing alcohol. While he pulled her up in a chair, she surreptitiously opened an eyelid. He had turned on her high-intensity lamp. So that was it. His fire starter.

It was a small clamp-on lamp with a metal shade. He dropped it from a standing position into the pooled alcohol and watched it. Nothing. He bent his large frame over to lift it up. He turned the lamp around to examine it. Light pierced her eyes — she shut them tight.

She heard him drop the lamp into the alcohol again, harder this time. She opened an eye. He was bent over the lamp, the back of his large head in front of her. This was her chance. She opened her fist and raised her hand with the used syringe, the long intra-muscular needle. She summoned all her strength, aimed, and brought the needle down hard into the back of his neck.

"Uch!" He fell forward on the lamp. A crunching sound. "You bitch!"

Her legs were trying to push her out of the chair when his hand rose up and grabbed her arm tight.

He was up on one knee, his other hand reaching for the syringe, rooting for it to get it out of his neck. She tried to pull her arm away from his hand. She was still weak, no match for him. Now he had the syringe in his other hand. She watched with horror the rage in his eyes as he brought the needle down into her thigh, slashing, jabbing anywhere he could reach. She cried out in pain.

He stabbed indiscriminately at her leg, the arm she put out to defend herself with. She was bleeding from all the puncture wounds in her leg and arm. The blood! Blood flowed everywhere. She was beginning to pass out from the pain. It would be so easy now, to just let go. What was so important about her life, anyway, that it had to continue? Who would really miss her? Her parents. Her sister in Montreal, who she never saw anymore. Her Uncle Henry. If only she had had children, things would've been different. If only David hadn't died, things would've been … no. *No.* That was too easy. *She* would miss her. She wasn't ready to go yet.

He was so intent on jabbing the needle at her, he wavered on the knee he was balancing on. He didn't notice the flame beginning to flicker around the broken socket of the lamp.

With a great surge of energy, she lifted up her leg and knocked him off kilter so that he fell over onto the lamp. He shrieked and tried to stand up. One of his jacket flaps burst into a small flame. It had dragged into the alcohol when he had fallen over.

She took advantage of his surprise to jump up and make her way to the door. At the same time she realized that the syringe had broken in the struggle — the length of the needle was lodged in her arm. From the corner of her eye she saw something flare up on the examining table: the length of translucent paper on which patients lay. Then the pillow at the head of the table. The roll behind, from which the paper had been pulled, burst into flame. As she flew out the door, she heard a *whoosh* behind her. Then a chilling scream.

When she turned to look, Hauer's jacket was engulfed in flames. He bellowed and flapped his arms around, then fell to the floor and tried to roll.

Yes, she thought, with surprising objectivity. That was what one was supposed to do to extinguish the flames if one's clothes were on fire. But the surface area of the examining room floor was too small for a man his size. And a pool of alcohol fed the fire. Flames leaped from his body and roared to the ceiling. The examining table began to smoulder. He shifted back and forth on the floor for a few seconds, screaming. "Help me! Help me!"

Why should I, she thought, but ran to the other room to see what she could find. As she ran, she picked at the needle embedded in her arm, but it had broken at skin level — there was no end to pull at.

In the next room, she threw open the door beneath the examining table and pulled out a blanket. When she rushed back to where he lay, the room was filled with smoke. She could see the blanket would make no difference anymore. Nevertheless she threw it over the dying fire that still consumed him. The blanket snuffed out the remaining flame.

He was quiet now, his skin blackened, his breathing laboured, the odour of burnt flesh pungent in the air. She stared with horror through the smoke, as he lay dying. This was what he had planned for her. But for a tweak of fate, it could be her lying there.

She wasn't out of the woods yet. He must have hit an artery with the syringe because bright red blood was squirting out of her arm. She clamped her hand over the spot. That would stop soon enough — the needle in her arm distressed her more.

Suddenly her whole body started to shake. It was the after-effects of the adrenaline. She stumbled into the supply area and retrieved a long bandage. Tremors wracking her body, she struggled to wind it around the pumping wound on her arm. Dragging herself into the waiting room, she slumped down into a chair. She closed her eyes and tried to control the shaking. No. She would have to endure. There were some things one couldn't control.

"Rebecca!" Iris called out as she opened the door to the office. "You won't believe the trouble I've just had with my car ... Why do I smell smoke?" She stopped cold when she saw Rebecca.

"Dial 911," Rebecca said, the vision of Iris running toward her blurred through her tears.

chapter twenty-nine

Rebecca sat in an emergency cubicle at Mount Sinai Hospital, numbly watching a young resident make a small cut next to the needle shaft in her arm. That allowed his tweezers to gain a purchase on the tip of the needle and pull the damn thing out of her skin. He had injected the area with anaesthetic so that her arm, which looked like a pincushion, was as frozen as her brain. She had to give him credit for managing the delicate procedure while she continued to shake from the after-effects of the adrenalin. Long shudders took hold of her body when she least expected it.

The ambulance crew that had brought her in had dropped a few choice phrases to the staff: "little lady caught herself a killer," "don't mess with her, she's tougher than she looks," "went hand-to-hand combat with a burly six-footer and she won," et cetera. Every nurse who went by looked in to take a peek at her. The resident chattered on, asking her questions about her adventure, to which she gave one-word answers. She was peeved by his morbid curiosity. *Was the ER so dull?* she wondered.

She was trying to beat back the image of the burnt body in her office when Dr. Koboy poked his head into the cubicle. His blue eyes crinkled at the edges. "The whole hospital's talking about you, Doctor. They want to know where you learned to fight."

She gave him a weak smile. "In medical school."

"I guess I won't start any arguments with *you*." He gave her a mock grin, concern in the tentative line of his mouth.

She recognized the look and tried harder to smile at his five-foot-two frame. "How's your patient upstairs?"

"She's feeling fine. I think she can go home on Monday."

"I wanted to thank you for seeing her. I know you were doing me a favour."

"No, thank *you* for the referral. I've never seen Gaucher's before. Most of them are in the States. They have a much larger Jewish population."

"What do you mean?"

He gave her an odd look. "You're more likely to see a Jewish genetic disease where there's a substantial Jewish population."

"Jewish genetic disease?"

"I told you it was familial. I thought you knew."

On the elevator up to Natalka's floor, Rebecca wondered if she knew. She also wondered who the father had been. Janek may have been a monster, but maybe he was right about Halina. Maybe she *was* an alley cat.

In the semi-private room, Natalka sat up in the bed closest to the door. Sarah and Halina sat in chairs nearby. When Rebecca appeared in the doorway, Sarah jumped up.

"You look terrible. What happened to your arm?"

Bless her heart, Rebecca thought. *She noticed.* "It's a long story."

Sarah approached her, worry in her eyes.

Rebecca felt her mouth start to tremble and on impulse put her arms out to embrace her mother-in-law for the first time since David had died. A faint whiff of lily of the valley.

Sarah stroked her back. When they pulled away, Sarah dragged an empty chair from the corner and set it down on the opposite side of the bed for her. "Maybe one day you'll tell me one of your long stories. Meanwhile, sit down."

Rebecca smiled sheepishly at her and sat down. "There *is* something about Natalka's illness," she said.

There was a general intake of breath.

"No, no. Don't worry. Nothing bad. Just unusual."

She observed Natalka, wondering how the news would affect her. She must have been feeling better because she had put her hair up and applied a bit of lipstick.

"Apparently Gaucher's Disease, which is what Natalka has, is a Jewish genetic disorder. It runs mostly in Jewish families."

Natalka looked confused. It was Sarah who appeared stricken. Rebecca noticed her mouth open, her eyes bulge. Sarah turned abruptly to Halina beside her and said something to her in Polish. Halina answered in a stiff, insistent tone. Her pale skin turned a mottled red.

"What are they saying?" Rebecca asked Natalka.

Natalka lowered her eyes and quietly said, "Mama says she had Jewish lover."

"Hah!" Sarah cried. "Is that what she told you?"

Natalka looked from face to face, baffled.

"What was his name?" said Sarah, her voice raised. She glowered at Halina. "There *is* no name!"

Halina's eyes darted from woman to woman. "Avram," she said finally.

"Where did you meet?"

Rebecca had never seen her mother-in-law so upset. She was nearly hysterical.

"On train," Halina answered. "I met him on train."

Sarah clamped her fingers onto Halina's arm. The other woman stiffened but didn't pull away. "You're lying."

Halina shook her head with vehemence. "Avram. Avram ... Kiefkevich. He die in war."

Sarah's chest began to heave. She looked like she was going to have a heart attack. Rebecca grew alarmed.

"What did my baby die of?" Sarah cried.

"What baby?" said Rebecca. What had just happened? Had she missed something?

Sarah's fingers constricted on Halina's arm. "How did she die? You were never clear about that. Did she have fever? Did she cough? Did you take her to the doctor?"

Halina pulled away from Sarah's grip. "People died in war. Not enough food. No medicine. Babies died. Many babies."

Natalka said softly to Sarah, "What you are talking about? Please tell me."

Sarah lifted her head and took a breath. She glanced with distraction at Rebecca, then gazed out the window into the night.

"Near the beginning of the war, in February 1940, my little baby, Rayzele, was five months old."

Rebecca sat up, shocked. How could that be? David had never told her he'd had a sister. Had Sarah kept this secret for nearly forty years?

"The Germans were killing us. Every day people were dragged from their apartments and taken away in trucks. Or shot right in the street. If we had to die, my husband and I decided we would try to save Rayzele. There were few people we could trust. Halina used to work for my parents in their store. I looked up to her. I trusted her."

She glared at Halina, whose face trembled, her eyes shut tight.

"I asked her to take the baby. I didn't think we would survive the war. My husband and I got separated. I was sent to a labour camp outside Leipzig. The Germans were losing. I still remember the bombs dropping on the camp. All women. Ten thousand of us. The German guards took us out and made us walk through the fields. For weeks we trudged through the snow with nothing to eat. A death march in the middle of winter. The war was nearly over, but they wanted to kill us. When someone fell to the ground and couldn't go on, they shot her.

"One night, I'll never forget. Hundreds of allied planes flew over us for hours, all night, and dropped bombs on a target in the distance. They just kept coming and coming without stop. They dropped so many bombs they turned night into day, it was so bright. We were on higher ground and we could see the sky lighting up so far away and realized there must be utter devastation there. We thanked God the Germans were finally getting what they deserved. Later, we found out it was Dresden."

Rebecca felt a twinge in her heart at the name. She understood the retribution, the justice. Yet all the beauty of the ages destroyed. All the hope.

"The whole time I stayed alive so I could come back to Kraków and knock on your mother's door and ask for my Rayzele back."

Halina sat perfectly still with her eyes closed.

"When I finally got back to Poland and found your mother ... she said my baby had died."

Natalka gulped in a sharp breath. She turned to Halina.

"Mama?" Her voice was agitated. She said something to her in Polish.

Halina opened her eyes and murmured an answer. A short exchange. More questions, more answers.

Rebecca questioned Natalka with her eyes.

"She doesn't say how baby died."

Sarah stood up abruptly, the chair scraping the floor behind her. "Now I understand why," she said.

Natalka leaned back in her bed. "I don't understand anything."

"She didn't die," Sarah said. She glared at Halina with loathing. "*Did* she?"

Rebecca was awestruck and confused at the same time. David had had a sister. Who had died. Or not.

"What you are saying?" Natalka asked Sarah.

Sarah came to stand near the bed. She put her hand out to touch Natalka's head.

"What colour was your hair?"

"My *hair*?"

Rebecca gaped at Natalka's white hair. *She* knew what colour the woman's hair had been because she had examined her in the office. Her pubic hair was orange. She had been a redhead. Like David.

"Oh my God!" Rebecca gasped.

"I don't understand." Natalka shook her head. "I don't understand."

Halina stood up and began to shout. "You think it was easy? The war destroyed everything for me, too. For first time I had someone. What else I had? Janek leave me because of her. I gave up my own food for her." She looked at Natalka, tears in her eyes. "Someone loves me.

Loves *me* most. How I can give her up? I take care of her five years. Five *years*. And then you come back and want I should just give her away. Like cutting out my heart."

She wiped a tear away. "She make me so happy. And then, after everything, she get sick. And I know God is punishing me. I do everything — *everything* to bring her here. I cannot fight no more."

Halina ran out of the room, her hand over her mouth.

"Mama!" Natalka cried. "Mama!"

Sarah had gone pale and wavered where she stood. Rebecca balanced on the edge of her seat, ready to jump to her assistance.

Sarah sat down on the side of Natalka's bed. Her jaw was set in restraint. She took the younger woman's hand and drank in her face like a lover.

"How could she be so cruel?" she murmured to the air. "How could she? All these years I thought you were dead. All these years I mourned you." She stroked Natalka's hair.

"No," Natalka shook her head warily. "You are mistaken. How can it be?"

"She can't even face you. She can't face me. Because she stole your life from me. She stole all those years we never had together. They're lost forever."

Natalka blinked at her. "No," she said. "You must be mistaken. I'm sorry — so sorry — about your daughter, but has nothing to do with me. Halina is my mother. She is *good* mother."

"She *stole* you. If there is any justice, she'll be punished in hell."

Natalka shook her head, pulled her hand from Sarah's. "No! Stop! Then I am punished, too."

Sarah touched Natalka's face with wary fingers. "You were everything to me. I felt ... something right away. A connection. I couldn't explain. When you accompanied me on the piano and I sang ... We are connected in the soul."

Natalka crossed her arms over her chest. "It was someone else. I'm so sorry. But it was not me. Please, you must bring my mother back, tell her it is a mistake. That I love her very much and you have made a terrible, terrible mistake."

Rebecca watched her mother-in-law's face go from pale to white. Tears glistened in her eyes, which never left Natalka's face.

Rebecca didn't know she was dozing until the doorbell woke her. Her parents had arrived with fresh bagels and egg and tuna salad for a late morning brunch and had left over an hour ago. They'd been worried about her and wanted to see for themselves that she was all right. Afterwards, she had collapsed onto the couch in the den, her arm throbbing.

Holding her bandaged arm close against her waist, she dragged herself to the front door. When she opened it, Edward stood on the stoop holding a plastic container of food. He wore khaki trousers and a grey shirt, a light jacket slung over one arm. His straight sandy hair fell over one ear in a young way that touched her.

He smiled. "I wanted to thank you. The police told me what you did. That Hauer was the one who ..."

He couldn't seem to say it, but it had to be said. "He killed your father."

Edward looked down, swallowed. "I don't really understand. He looked so ... harmless."

"You mean he didn't look like a monster? No horns? He looked like the rest of us. Maybe he was."

Edward raised puzzled eyes at her.

Or maybe we're all monsters, she thought. In and out of her memory slid the blackened skin, the charred tweed jacket, arms protecting his chest, in vain. She had been *glad*. She was a doctor, a self-professed healer, and she had been glad. She was more human than she cared to admit, even to herself.

"Why did he do it?" said Edward.

"Self-preservation. In his own mind. A twisted sense of his own importance." Too human.

Edward cleared his throat self-consciously. "I'm driving back to Ottawa tonight and Mrs. Woronska gave me all these pierogies ... I thought maybe you'd like to share them." He held the container in front of him.

"Come in."

"They told me you were injured. How's your arm?"

"It hurts, but I'll live."

Once in the hall he said, "According to Mrs. Woronska's instructions, the pierogies should be fried in butter. And eaten with sour cream." He opened the plastic container to reveal a small jar of sour cream lying next to three neat rows of floured pierogies.

She led him into the kitchen.

"You sit down," he said, "and just tell me where everything is. Large frying pan?"

She pointed him to the cupboard. He opened the fridge and found the butter.

She smiled watching him tend to the food. It gave her a surprising sense of well-being, a man taking charge in her kitchen, the sizzle and smell of the potato and onion pierogies. He put the cover on the pan and turned the heat down.

Sitting across from her at the dark pine table, he reached into the jacket he had hung over the back of a chair. He pulled out the blackened remains of the gold box and set it in front of her.

"The police found this in Hauer's pocket. They said you told them it belonged to my family."

She blinked at the box, the corners melted and misshapen, the lapis lazuli covered in soot. "It was so beautiful," she said. "I wish you could've seen it. Have you opened it?"

He nodded, lifted the lid with some difficulty. Inside, the compass lay in a bed of ash. The silver was somewhat blackened, the latitude numbers all but illegible. But it had survived the flames; the needle still pointed north.

"Did you find anything else?"

"Like?"

She opened the lid back as far as it would go and pushed and prodded the way she had seen Hauer do. She stared at the blackened metal.

"It's no use. There was a hidden compartment under the lid. But the intense heat—it fused the pieces together. The letter must've burnt up."

"Letter?"

"The letter that proves you're descended from Catherine the Great."

He gaped at the box. "I thought Dad had made that up for the book. Or at least ... that he'd read something into the research that wasn't there. Like adding two and two and coming up with five."

"There was nothing wrong with his addition. The letter was from Sir Charles Hanbury-Williams, the English diplomat in your father's book."

"I remember him."

"It said that Catherine the Great and the Polish king, Stanislaw Poniatowski, had a child, Anna Petrovna. In the history books, she died. But according to the letter, she was saved by a mysterious Jewish doctor and taken to a cousin of Poniatowski's, a Countess

Oginska, to be brought up Catholic. The princess was your great-great-great-grandmother. I might be out one or more greats."

He watched her for more. "It's not exactly hard evidence."

She took his hand. "The little princess had an anomaly called hexadactyly. 'Hex' for six. Like your father. Like you." She spread out his six fingers in her palm.

He stared wordlessly at their hands together, then turned his until it held hers in a soft clasp. He lifted her hand to his lips and for a moment, the sandy-coloured hair falling forward belonged to Michael. He put her hand down sheepishly, but she was moved.

"It doesn't seem to matter without him," he said. "I'd give all of it if I could get him back."

"But it does matter. It's who you are," she said. "You have reason to be proud. Don't hide your light under a bushel. People will want to know you."

A corner of his mouth twitched. "I don't want people to be impressed with my ancestry. I want them to be impressed with my talent."

She smiled. "Your ancestry may open doors for your talent."

The only sound was the muted sizzling of dough on a low flame. She didn't want to push, but she couldn't let the subject drop. "It's too bad the book isn't finished. It was wonderful to read. I think other people would enjoy it too."

He studied her face. "You think I should try to get it published, don't you?" he said. "Cops said they found some more of the manuscript at Hauer's place."

"You'd have to finish it."

"I don't know," he said, shaking his head. "I don't know if I'm up to it. Though I've got all his notes. Tons of notes. He even made notes for the end, I found those.

Dozens of books of history and biography. Maybe I could finish it. I owe him that, don't I?"

"You owe it to yourself."

It would bring him closer to his father, she thought, but didn't say. A way of keeping his memory alive. Especially on those dark nights when he might stumble upon an idea he wanted to share and as he was heading for the phone, remembered he couldn't tell his father. For too long after David had died, she had started off to call him before remembering.

She would phone her own parents later and ask them some frivolous question, just for an excuse to hear their voices.

chapter thirty

Rebecca's family celebrated the Jewish New Year with a traditional heavy dinner at Flo and Mitch's house in north Toronto off Bayview Avenue. Rebecca's sister, Susan, had driven in from Montreal with her youngest son to be with her family. Susan's observant husband and the two older boys — "the rabbis," Mitch called them — had remained in Montreal with her in-laws.

Rebecca had tried to help her mother and sister with the preparations for dinner, but her arm still hurt and the bandages cut down on her mobility. She ended up sitting at the kitchen table happily entertaining four-year-old Jonathan. They both watched Flo and Susan from the rear as they chopped, stirred, and blended food on the counter.

"Who's that?" Rebecca asked the little boy, pointing at Flo.

"That's Bubbie," he said, his brown eyes shining.

Flo turned and gave them both a radiant smile.

"That's right," Rebecca said. "And who's *that*?" She pointed at Susan's back.

"That's my mommy!" he shrieked with delight.

"Right!" she said. "And guess what? Your bubbie is my mommy."

His eyes widened, the little face grew puzzled. "You're too old to have a mommy."

Rebecca grinned. "You're never too old to have a mommy."

"I'm tired," he said. "Aunt Rebecca, can I sit in your lap?"

She stroked his downy blonde hair. "I'd love for you to sit in my lap, sweetie, but my leg is injured."

"She has a boo-boo on her leg," Susan said, turning around to smile at them. "Show him, so he understands."

Rebecca had worn a light crinkly skirt because it was loose and comfortable on the wounds. She lifted the fabric up to reveal her thigh swathed in bandage.

"Ooohh," he said with delight.

Sarah and Natalka arrived after eight o'clock. When Natalka stepped into view, Rebecca's heart skipped a beat. She had been waiting. Natalka's white hair was twisted into a smooth funnel at the back, elongating the line of her swan neck. She looked the same as before, only now Rebecca was searching for something else: David. She found him in the shape of Natalka's brow, the direct green eyes.

Sarah handed Flo a large round honey cake on a covered plate. "Natalka helped me make it. It's her first honey cake."

"Sweet things for a sweet year," Natalka said, looking to Sarah for approval.

Sarah nodded at her and beamed.

Natalka seemed to have warmed up to her newly discovered mother after a week, thought Rebecca. A week and a cake.

Natalka took in the cathedral entranceway to the Temple home, the flowered damask furnishings that echoed the ochre in the thick broadloom, the wall tapestry that Flo had brought back from Amsterdam. Rebecca didn't take her eyes off her: the angle of Natalka's shoulders, the tentative smile in public, brought back David in a rush.

Rebecca admired the sea green jacket that Natalka wore over a matching dress. It didn't look like it had come out of the suitcase from Poland. Sarah must have taken her shopping. The colour brought roses to her complexion and reflected the green in her eyes. She would have been the image of grace if not for her illness. She held her new beige purse over the swollen area around her spleen.

Rebecca greeted Sarah with a kiss on the cheek. When she embraced Natalka, Rebecca whispered, "I have some news for you."

Before Natalka could respond, Sarah began introducing her to Flo, Mitch, Susan, and Uncle Henry. Rebecca wondered how much had been resolved between the two women. Though Sarah glowed in her presence, she didn't say "This is my daughter." She said, "This is Natalka."

"We're in for a treat later," said Flo. "I've asked Sarah and Natalka to play something for us tonight."

Rebecca observed her mother with surprise. She had engineered another opportunity for rapprochement — rehearsal.

Mitch took everyone's drink orders and disappeared into the dining room. Flo, Susan, and Uncle Henry retreated to the kitchen to finish the food preparations.

Rebecca led Sarah and Natalka to the far end of the living room near the upright piano, where a corner table held old pictures of the family. Natalka picked up a photo of Rebecca when she was six, wearing a frilly plaid dress.

"This is you?" Natalka asked, smiling, showing the picture to Sarah.

Rebecca nodded.

"So serious. You looked already like a doctor."

David had said the same thing about her childhood photos, that she had looked so solemn, like she was ready to take on the problems of humanity.

At least she had good news for Natalka. Lowering her voice, she said, "I have a message from Halina."

"She called you?" Natalka asked, glancing nervously at Sarah. "Where she is?"

"She went back to the convent downtown. She called this afternoon. I think she was too embarrassed to call Sarah's house."

Sarah stared at Natalka with wary eyes, looked away.

"She wants you to know she's going back to Poland. She's going to arrange for your daughter to come for a visit here."

Natalka's face lit up. "Anya? Coming here? This is wonderful." Her eyes quickly clouded over. "But how they will do it? Government will not let her go."

"Halina will tell them you're very sick and want to see your daughter once more. Before the end ..."

Both Natalka and Sarah took in a sharp breath.

"No, no, you're fine. It's just to persuade them," Rebecca said, placing a steadying hand on Natalka's arm. "But it's a good plan. She'll convince them that, once you're gone, the girl will have to come back to Poland to her father, the only parent she has left. Only once Anya's here, she won't go back to Poland. She'll stay here with her mother. And grandmother. Halina knows you'll both have a better life here."

Natalka's pale eyebrows curved together. "But she will lose job. Maybe worse."

"This is her idea. It's her choice."

Natalka bit her lip. "When she is going?"

"Sunday."

"This Sunday?"

Natalka turned to Sarah. "I don't want to upset you, but I must see her. I must ... thank her."

Sarah sighed and nodded. "We'll go down there tomorrow."

Mitch approached with their Dubonnet and the subject was changed.

Everyone sat down to dinner. Flo Temple served the *gefullte* fish first.

Natalka stared at the white oval lump on her plate. "No, thank you," she said. "I never had sweet fish. I don't really like fish at all."

"I should tell you," said Mitch, "I put a prize into one of the pieces of fish. But you have to cut into it to see if you're the winner."

Rebecca rolled her eyes at Flo, who didn't seem to notice.

Everyone watched Natalka push her fork warily into the ball of fish. "I think you're playing trick on me ..." She broke the fish into half, then quarters.

"Nothing inside?" Mitch said, disappointed. "Well, now that it's all in pieces, you may as well taste it. If you don't like it, we won't charge you."

Natalka smiled weakly and put a tiny piece in her mouth. She chewed. Then she stopped and smiled. "It's good."

A cheer went up around the table while she finished the rest of the fish.

When they had finished the beef brisket, Mitch raised his hand in the air to quiet the general tumult of conversation.

"Let's raise a glass to the chef. To Flo — a wonderful dinner, as usual."

Her mother grinned and basked in the attention.

"And to our beautiful and brilliant daughter, the doctor. Who managed to stay calm when confronted by a homicidal professor who gave a whole new meaning to the term 'publish or perish.'" Mitch threw her an apologetic kiss and everyone around the table tittered.

Served her right for telling him the story, Rebecca thought. Despite her struggle with the black humour, she felt surrounded by warmth.

Her mother leaned over and put her arms around her. "Thank God," Flo whispered.

Later, on her way to the kitchen with some dirty dishes, Flo said, "This would be a perfect time for some music, Sarah. We can digest while we listen."

The dishes were scraped and piled in the sink and on the counter. Everyone drifted into the living room. Rebecca sat on the sofa between her mother and her sister.

Natalka set her music down on the piano then arranged herself carefully on the bench. For a moment she sat still, watching Sarah, who stood nearby, her back straight, taking in deep breaths.

"We picked the Song of Songs from the Bible," Sarah said, "because tonight we're celebrating a religious holiday, the beginning of a new year. And people have interpreted this poetry as a love song to God, but it is also clearly just a love song. So we wanted to sing our praises to God, and to each other."

The two women exchanged intimate looks that surprised and warmed Rebecca. Natalka played a note. Sarah aimed at it, held it. Then she nodded at Natalka.

The younger woman stroked the keys softly while Sarah began to sing. Her throaty mezzo voice thrilled and soothed at the same time. Rebecca heard something she hardly recognized in it: joy.

> My beloved spake, and said unto me,
> Rise up, my love, my fair one, and come away.
> For, lo, the winter is past, the rain is over
> and gone;

Rebecca watched her new sister-in-law with awe, searched for David there. Her white hair had been orange once. Like David's. Rebecca had to make an effort now, to picture his hair orange, the fine hair on his arms impossibly orange. If he had lived longer it would have turned white, like his sister's. It was extraordinary — for the first time she could see a resemblance between mother and daughter, the delicate nose, the line of the chin. If she were Sarah, she would grasp Natalka with all her might and never let her go. Now that she had found her again.

So that you can always find me again. That was what Rebecca needed: a compass to show her the way. But a compass wouldn't help her find David again. Or Michael. Nothing could do that. But a compass might help her find something else. What was it she was looking for? A compass could only point north. And where was that? Was it someplace knowable?

> The flowers appear on the earth; the time of
> the singing of birds is come,
> and the voice of the turtle is heard in our land;
> The fig tree putteth forth her green figs,
> and the vines with the tender grape give a
> good smell.
> Arise, my love, my fair one, and come away.